Praise for *The Raven*

"I love Mike Nappa's style! With intrigue, action, and a main character snarky enough to cheer for, *The Raven* is a thrill ride into the stark territory between grace and the letter of the law."

Tosca Lee, *New York Times* bestselling author

"This is a superb series for those who love a great story filled with redemption and a gripping, quickly moving plot."

RT Book Reviews

"As part of his regular street performance, a deception specialist who goes by the name The Raven picks his audience's pockets while they watch. It's harmless fun—until he decides to keep the spare wallet a city councilman doesn't seem to miss, hoping for a few extra bucks. When he finds not money but compromising photos of the councilman and his 'personal assistants,' The Raven hatches a plan to blackmail the man. However, he quickly finds himself in over his head with the Ukrainian Mafia and mired in a life-threatening plot code-name[illegible]rmore.'"

[illegible]dreads

Praise [illegible]

"Mike Nappa's *Annabel Le*[illegible]iller, filled with unexpected twists and peopl[illegible] and memorable characters. From the first chapter [illegible], I found it impossible to put down."

Lois Duncan, *New York Times* bestselling author,
I Know What You Did Last Summer
and *Killing Mr. Griffin*

"*Annabel Lee* is compelling, fast-paced, and filled with fascinating characters. One hopes that Mike Nappa's eleven-year-old wunderkind from the title will reappear in future novels of this promising new suspense series!"

M. K. Preston, Mary Higgins Clark Award–winning novelist, *Song of the Bones* and *Perhaps She'll Die*

"A relentless surge of suspense and mounting tension coupled with an engaging mix of characters. With *Annabel Lee*, Mike Nappa skillfully sets the stage for a compelling series of Coffey & Hill Investigation thrillers."

Jack Cavanaugh, award-winning author of twenty-six novels

A DREAM WITHIN A DREAM

Other Books in the Coffey & Hill Series

Annabel Lee

The Raven

COFFEY & HILL • 3

A DREAM WITHIN A DREAM

A COFFEY & HILL NOVEL

MIKE NAPPA

AND

MELISSA KOSCI

Revell

a division of Baker Publishing Group

Grand Rapids, Michigan

Published by Revell
a division of Baker Publishing Group
PO Box 6287, Grand Rapids, MI 49516-6287
www.revellbooks.com

Printed in the United States of America

Library of Congress Cataloging-in-Publication Data
Names: Nappa, Mike, 1963– author. | Kosci, Melissa, author.
Title: A dream within a dream / Mike Nappa and Melissa Kosci.
Description: Grand Rapids, Michigan : Revell, a division of Baker Publishing Group, [2020] | Series: A Coffey & Hill novel
Identifiers: LCCN 2019037165 | ISBN 9780800726461 (paperback)
Subjects: GSAFD: Mystery fiction.
Classification: LCC PS3564.A624 D74 2020 | DDC 813/.54—dc23
LC record available at https://lccn.loc.gov/2019037165

ISBN 978-0-8007-3857-0 (casebound)

This book is published in association with Nappaland Literary Agency, an independent agency dedicated to publishing works that are: Authentic. Relevant. Eternal. Visit us on the web at: NappalandLiterary.com.

20 21 22 23 24 25 26 7 6 5 4 3 2 1

For Michele Misiak,
Karen Steele,
and Vicki Crumpton,
friends indeed.
M. N.

For my dad.
M. K.

Is all that we see or seem
But a dream within a dream?

Edgar Allan Poe,
"A Dream within a Dream"

Take this kiss upon the brow!
And, in parting from you now,
Thus much let me avow—
You are not wrong, who deem
That my days have been a dream;
Yet if Hope has flown away
In a night, or in a day,
In a vision, or in none,
Is it therefore the less gone?
All that we see or seem
Is but a dream within a dream.

I stand amid the roar
Of a surf-tormented shore,
And I hold within my hand
Grains of the golden sand—
How few! yet how they creep
Through my fingers to the deep,
While I weep—while I weep!
O God! can I not grasp
Them with a tighter clasp?
O God! can I not save
One from the pitiless wave?
Is all that we see or seem
But a dream within a dream?

SEVEN YEARS AGO

SOMEWHERE IN NEW ENGLAND

1

DREAM

"Get. Down."

He's driving too fast, looking too often at his rearview mirror. The world outside us is a strange, pale kind of twilight. There's no sun in the sky that I can see, yet there's still some kind of half-light, as if day is resisting night, refusing to go to bed like an ill-tempered child.

The gun resting on the console between us is still warm.

I could take it, I think. *I could grab that pistol while he's distracted.* But the steel in his voice makes me think twice. He did just kill a man, after all. I can still smell the wet, hot copper spray that blew from the dead man's body when the bullets hit.

The driver glances at me now, scowling.

It's a tight fit, even for someone with my bit of pudge, but I slide off the passenger seat anyway and try to squeeze into the leg space below. Apparently, I'm not good at this.

"Farther," he snaps. "All the way down. So no one can see you, even if we stop at a red light."

If we stop at a red light?

The sedan lurches left, hard, but the tires don't squeal. He guns the engine and, briefly, I feel dizzy, like I might have a concussion, like I might throw up if I'm given half a chance. Instead, I press myself deeper into the floorboards until he glances at me and nods. Then he does a double take.

"Don't you spew in my car. You understand?"

I nod and close my eyes. Seems a lot to ask of me at this point, not to throw up. But I don't want to argue.

"You spew, and I'll put you in the trunk with everything else."

His accent is strong, harsh, and hard to follow. I'm not from New England. Didn't grow up here and never quite mastered the nuances of the brash northeastern accent. For instance, to me that last threat sounded like, "Yah s'puh an ahl pudya in tha trunk wid everthin' else." It takes me a second to process what he's saying, and that seems to make him angry. He taps the brakes and leans down toward me while making another left turn. "Yah unnerstan?"

I nod again. *I understand.* There's nothing to do about it now except pay attention and make sure my mind translates his words—fast.

"W-what do you want with me?" I ask. My voice sounds thin, like the pale light fading around us. I try to concentrate so I can translate his accent in my mind.

"You was in the wrong place at the right time," he says. With my eyes closed, I can almost hear a grin in his voice. I have no idea what he's talking about. I'm afraid to ask.

Afraid.

The car screeches to a sudden halt, and the back of my head smacks lightly against the glove box behind me. I risk opening my eyes, and I see him tapping the steering wheel impatiently. I can't see the traffic, but I assume a car is stopped in front of us, maybe at a red light.

Now's my chance, I think. *Shove open the door and roll out into the street while the car is idling.*

My legs feel deadened from this cramped space, but that doesn't matter. I'll just fall out of the car and crawl away on my hands and knees. Hopefully somebody out there will see me, someone will wonder what's going on, and that'll be enough for him just to let me go.

"What is that? Is that blood?"

His eyes flick in my direction, and I feel my chest tighten like thickening cement. Callused fingers flash toward me and grip my wrist. He yanks at my arm, and I suffer the slow agonies of opportunity pulling away. "Di'ya geh bluhd in mah cah?" *Did you get blood in my car?*

"No, no!" I say. "It's cadmium red. Oil-based. It's what I was using when you, when you . . ."

He throws my hand back at me and hits the gas again, swerving to pass something in the street. I reflexively wipe at the drying paint on my fingers and tell myself again and again, *Don't throw up, Javie, don't throw up.*

The man barely looks at me, intent on speeding through the twilight streets of what I'm guessing is East Middlebury or Ripton by now. He's found a deserted route and is all business. I think we're heading out to the forestlands, because I can see tall sugar maple and beech trees shadowing the sky above us.

I sneak a look in his direction while he's occupied with the road. His cheeks are Pilgrim-pale, flecked with pockmarks that suggest he had a problem with teenage acne. His nose looks like a partially inflated balloon, bulbous and angry. He's got thinning brown hair, a chin shaved clean, and clear blue eyes that seem out of place in that face. He's wearing dark brown pants, a white button-up shirt, but no tie. And now his right hand is resting on that silver gun in the console between us.

"That's how you do it where I come from," he mutters to nobody. "That's how we do it Southie style. Whitey B., you see that? Yeah, you saw that, wherever you are."

"You're from Boston?" I say, and even I'm surprised to hear my voice ask the obvious question.

His face relaxes into a proud grin. "Born and raised," he says. Then he glances over at me and frowns. "Now stay down and shut up while I try and figure out these crazy-stupid roads out here in this crazy-stupid place."

I nod. Outside, night has finally pushed aside the last complaints of daytime and taken its rightful place of supremacy. The Southie flicks on the car's headlights, but the vehicle doesn't slow.

"Head down," he barks at me. "I got no time to deal with a skiddah like you right now."

Skidder. Boston slang for a worthless bum. *Is that what I am now?* I fold my arms onto the seat and bury my face into them.

I'm going to die.

There's silence as we continue into what I can only assume is more countryside.

But if he wanted to kill me, why didn't he do it back at the workshop? Why come in with guns blazing at Henri and then stop when he sees me?

In my mind's eye, I see a slow-motion explosion of bullets and flesh, a gruesome reminder of my recent past and the vivid memory-making mechanism that works in my brain. I force Henri from my thoughts, training myself to forget—at least for the moment. I can't relive that awful killing. Not another one, not yet. Another day, another time I'll say my respects, bid poor Henri a thoughtful goodbye. Right now I have to think of other things or maybe I'll go insane.

Don't throw up, Javie. Don't throw up.

It feels like at least an hour, maybe more, until he finally sighs and tells me I can raise my head.

"Almost there, skiddah," he says. "You still beatin' in that heart of yours?"

I nod, and then I realize he's looking at the road and not at me. "Yes," I say. "Where are you taking me?"

"Taking you home, skiddah. Taking you to your new home."

I want to ask what he means about a "new home," if he'll ever let me go. But all I can do is grieve. *I had a chance*, I think. *Back there, when he stopped at the red light, or whatever that was. I missed it. Lord, help my poor soul!*

It seems fitting to me, at this moment, that I'm praying the last words of Edgar Allan Poe. *Lord, help my poor soul.* I've wondered often if God answered that poet's prayer, or if it was just a cry into emptiness by a man lost in the blinding night.

"We're here."

It takes a few moments to make my legs work, to uncramp them and get the blood flowing again. It's dark, and we've parked at the end of a dirt road, surrounded by many trees. To our left is a small cottage—a literal "little house in the woods." Under different circumstances, I'd probably like it, windows warm with yellow light, the scent of smoke puffing through a fireplace chimney. But right now it's only a prison scene to me.

Southie stops unpacking the trunk long enough to look at me, hard. "Don't do it," he says, like he's reading my mind. He waves his hand and I see he's got the gun in it. "I don't feel like killing another bazo tonight."

My legs couldn't run right now anyway, I think. *But maybe tomorrow. Or the next day. He can't watch me forever, can he?*

My captor loads me with a long leather tube and a small wooden crate, then turns me toward the door. He's got a similar tube and a large stiff envelope, and I see he's carrying my art portfolio, too, still wrapped up in my portfolio case, almost ready to send. *So close*, I tell myself. *So close to being done. Should've finished that Poe project before I took the new job, before I got mixed up in . . . this.*

A broad man with a sour expression opens the door to the cottage.

"What took you so long?" he growls, and I hear an Irish brogue that's almost musical in its sound.

"Skiddah here needed a little handholding." The Southie grins. "But we got it all, no problem."

"Who's he?"

"Your new assistant."

The burly Irishman glowers at me in the dim porch light. I see now that ink is crawling up out of his collar and onto the left side of his neck. A mermaid maybe? Or a serpent? It's hard to tell in the light. "Can he draw?" he says.

"He's a forger," Southie says. "Caught him making a wicked-good copy of this one." He waves one of the leather tubes toward the Irishman. Rolled up inside the tube is an oil painting I've come to know very well.

"Don't need a painter," the Irishman snaps. "Not yet at least, not for a few more weeks. Maybe even a month. Need a penciller right now. A sketch artist."

"I can draw," I say suddenly. *Maybe if I make myself useful*, I think, *they'll keep me alive long enough for me to find a way to escape.*

"See for yourself." Southie shoves my portfolio into the Irishman's hands, then pushes past him to enter the cottage.

The stocky man looks hard at me for another moment, then unzips my work. He flips through a few comic book pages, nodding once or twice, making unintelligible grunts at the images he sees. Then he slaps the case shut again. He wraps his arms in front of him, pressing my artwork to his chest almost like he's giving it a hug.

His stare is hard to hold, but I try not to wilt under his gaze. He's looking at me as though he's trying to gauge whether it's easier to kill and bury me here in the woods or to invite me inside for dinner. Finally he nods, decision made.

"Clocks," he says to me brusquely. "I need lots of clocks."

PRESENT DAY

FRIDAY, NOVEMBER 10

2

TRUDI

Boston, MA

"Seats aren't bad."

Trudi Sara Coffey checked both of her tickets once more, then scanned the wide, stair-stepped aisle of Boston's TD Garden arena and nodded to herself. "Not bad at all."

In five minutes or so, at seven thirty, her beloved Atlanta Hawks would face the hated Celtics on their home court. Trudi was happy to see that row 13 in section Loge 12 was going to be close enough for a clear view of all the action on the parquet floor below. Surrounded by eighteen thousand milling Celtics fans, though, Trudi thanked her wiser self for choosing not to wear Hawks gear. Team loyalty only went so far, and when you were all alone in someone else's house, prudence suggested neutral colors and subdued cheering.

Too bad Samuel's not here, she thought absently. *He would've gotten a perverse thrill out of being a rebel Hawks fan in the arena tonight.*

She frowned at the thought, not because she cared whether Samuel got into trash-talking matches with drunk Celtics fans—he was ex-CIA, he could certainly take care of himself. But the thought of Samuel reminded her that she hadn't seen or heard from her ex-husband in several weeks, maybe even a month.

In times past that wouldn't have been so unusual. In fact, that was the norm in the first few years after their divorce. But after the Annabel Lee affair and the Nevermore incident with The Raven and Mama Bliss, she and Samuel had learned to coexist again. They'd even had a "frenaissance" of sorts. Not a romantic rekindling—no, definitely not that. But they had become comfortable again. No longer enemies. Almost friends. Trudi found herself feeling wistful. She would've enjoyed Samuel's company at this game.

Wonder where Samuel is tonight, she thought. She allowed herself a wicked grin before adding, *The pig.*

She stopped at row 13 and slid in, stepping past a dad and his school-aged son decked in green. Trudi took her place in seat 16, three chairs from the end of the row. She left empty seat 17 to her left, a little buffer space between her and the tween talking excitedly to his father. To her right, in seat 15, a dark-haired woman seemed to be watching her entrance with more interest than expected. When Trudi caught her staring, the woman quickly turned her attention back to the arena floor, where the game was about to begin.

Trudi instinctively began studying the woman for threats. She, too, was wearing neutral colors—a gray sweater over black pants—and had a long wool coat draped over the back of her seat. Maybe another out-of-towner? The woman had no drinks or snacks, which was suspicious. And was that a metallic bulge under the right arm of her sweater? Just the right size for a small handgun.

Trudi hesitated, cut off her train of thought, and then gave herself a lecture. *You don't have to be a detective all the time, Tru-Bear. Lady was just checking to see who's going to sit next to her for the following three hours. Doesn't mean she's a criminal or out to get you or carrying weapons of mass destruction. Loosen up and enjoy the game.*

She couldn't resist one last furtive glance to her right and was glad to see that the woman was now occupied with the imminent tip-off instead of with her. Trudi felt herself physically relax in the chair.

Hope she's not the chatty type, she thought, finally dismissing the woman. *Tonight I just want to watch a good game.* "Good" meaning that the Hawks beat the daylights out of the Celtics, of course.

She took a moment to breathe in the smells of popcorn and beer, to listen to the warm buzzing sounds of thousands of conversations, to take in the colors and lights and banners decorating TD Garden arena. Trudi sighed contentedly. *I could get used to this whole "consulting detective expert" thing*, she said to herself.

She'd done only two weeks' worth of work here on location in Boston and easy work at that. Mostly she just sat around on the movie set, eating treats from the craft table, reading books, waiting for the director or screenwriter to present her with some random question about detective techniques or organized crime practices. Once or twice an actor had bought her lunch and grilled her for "motivation" behind dialogue or for background information about famous, real-life heists like the story they were filming. Then, just about the time Trudi was beginning to feel restless, they announced they were done, moving on to the next location, which didn't require her services. Perfect. She couldn't have planned a better vacation if she'd tried.

Here's hoping more Hollywood moviemakers come calling, she said to herself in an imaginary toast. *If only for perks like free basketball tickets.*

Tomorrow she'd fly back to Atlanta, back to her Coffey & Hill Investigations office, where her assistant, Eulalie, waited with more mundane, real-life detective work. Trudi was actually looking forward to that. Tonight, though, she was going to enjoy the game. And hope her Hawks could play well enough to win in this decidedly hostile environment.

"Let's go, Hawks," she whispered at the tip-off. She noticed a scowl flash across the face of the woman beside her and then disappear just as quickly as it had appeared. Trudi reminded herself that maybe it was best to keep her fan affiliations quiet for the time being.

She stretched her legs into the extra space to her left and smiled despite herself.

When the director of *Heist Company* had gifted her with two passes to this game, she'd been tempted to give away one of the tickets. After all, she didn't know anyone here in Boston to bring along. But she took both tickets anyway and, in the end, decided she'd rather sit next to an empty seat than try to make awkward conversation with an almost-stranger on her left. *Good decision*, she told herself now.

Let's go, Hawks! she cheered inwardly. She glanced at the furrowed brow of the woman to her right and was glad she'd kept the sentiment to herself this time.

By halftime, Trudi was really enjoying life.

She walked the crowded hallway outside the arena floor and felt like she couldn't stop grinning. The Hawks were up by five. She'd treated herself to a Big Bad Burger (which she didn't finish) and an oversized soda (which she did). She'd even managed to beat the rush to the bathroom, so now with an empty bladder and a full stomach, she was ready for the second half. She thought of Samuel again, worried briefly about his recent absence, then shrugged. *Who needs him?* she thought. *Go, Hawks!*

Weaving through the crowd and treading down the now-sticky stairs of the arena, she stopped short.

"Who is that in my seat?" she said out loud.

Another step down and she realized the squatter wasn't in her seat exactly. He'd taken up residence in the seat to her left, seat 17, the place she'd deliberately kept empty. Trudi felt blood throbbing in her temples. She suppressed a vindictive fantasy of unleashing a round kick to the back of the man's head, took a deep breath instead, and then closed the gap between them.

"Excuse me," she said from the end of the row, "but I think you're sitting in my seat."

The man glanced up at her from underneath the brim of a kelly-green cap ornamented by a mischievous-looking leprechaun. He shook his head, then turned his attention to center court, where the Celtics Dancers were performing a sultry routine.

Trudi took a step closer, glad the end of the row was empty at the moment.

"Sorry," she said, tapping the stranger on the shoulder. "I don't mean to be a jerk, but that really is my seat." She fished in her pocket and pulled out her tickets. "See?" she said, showing him the unused seat number. "I need to ask you to move, please."

He looked annoyed, but he stood up, so Trudi stepped past him and took her seat in number 16 again. His eyes narrowed.

"Thought you said this was your seat," he said.

"It is," she said firmly, but she felt her face flush anyway. "Both these seats are mine."

"Well, since you're not using this one," he said, and he sat back down next to her. Trudi felt her jaw muscles tightening. This was rapidly turning into an unwanted confrontation.

She took a moment to study her opposition. He was bigger than average, probably six-foot-two or so. Flat belly, thick arms and legs. A shaved pate topped a square-jawed face. She noticed his skin held a bit of a tan, more color than most Boston folk she'd seen. This made her think maybe he didn't belong in this city—but at the same time he was also draped in a large, presumably expensive Celtics jersey that many of the locals were also wearing. Jeans and sneakers finished his ensemble.

"Listen," Trudi said after a moment, "you're going to have to move. That seat is taken."

"Relax," the man said without looking at her, "it's been empty all game. My ticket's way back in the nosebleeds. Why should I sit back there when this one's not being used?"

"Because it's not your seat. It's mine."

Now he rolled his eyes and turned toward her. He gave her an exaggerated "elevator" scan, sweeping Trudi head to toe in his gaze. Then he said, "Look, I'm sorry you got stood up tonight. You're a pretty girl and all. You deserve better. But don't take it out on me. If your boyfriend does happen to show up, I'll move. But until then, can we just watch the second half in peace?"

Now Trudi really was ready to kick this guy in the head. She stood to face him, fuming. *I haven't studied martial arts for twelve years just so some sexist Celtics bully can—*

She felt someone tugging on her sleeve.

"It's okay," a voice said behind her. Trudi snapped around and saw the woman in seat 15 smirking. "He's with me."

Trudi turned back to the squatter, but he was already ignoring her again.

"Please," the woman behind her said. "Charlie's a jerk sometimes, but he's mostly harmless. And he's with me. Everything's okay, really, and the game's about to begin again anyway. Ms. Coffey, Trudi, won't you have a seat?"

Alarm bells began sounding in Trudi's head.

3

DREAM

Boston, MA

Here's what I know: *I'm not crazy.*

I mean, I'm pretty sure I'm not. I guess nobody knows that kind of thing with absolute certainty, but still, if I had the courage to be a betting man, I'd bet I'm not out of my mind. At least I don't think so. Not today.

"What do you think, Kevin? Any bright ideas on the subject?"

I'm talking to a lamp in the corner of my motel room. I named the lamp Kevin when I was feeling unsure one day last week, when I wanted to test myself to see if I was still in my right mind. I'd just watched that old Tom Hanks movie on cable TV, the one where he's lost on a desert island. When Tom started talking to that volleyball like it was a real person, we all knew he was crazy. So, I figured, hey, if I can talk to a lamp as though it's a person while simultaneously understanding that it is, in fact, just an inanimate object, then my rational reasoning ability is unhindered, even in here, even in this claustrophobic room. And that means I'm not crazy.

Right, Kev?

It's 8:45 p.m. Five more minutes and I'll walk out into the parking lot and never look back. I should be glad no one figured out I was here. I should be grateful for that, for staying hidden.

Mr. Hayes kept his promise, kept me safe. At least for now.

Mr. Hayes says he's going to help me, if I help him. He says we can help each other. I think I believe him . . . unless I really am crazy and there's no Mr. Hayes except in my imagination.

But I remember . . . I had walked out into the fresh air. I hadn't understood why they let me go, but I didn't question it; I just started walking. Away from that place. Admittedly, there were a few people I'd miss, but being free was worth missing a few people, most of whom weren't in their right minds anyway. But was I in my right mind? Maybe this was all in my imagination. But I was pretty sure I didn't imagine things very often. It was more that my memories stopped my ability to function. But maybe my illness was getting worse . . .

Either way, I was simply happy to be free. That'd been my dream for so long, I almost didn't care if it was real or imagined.

Away from the fence surrounding the facility, I headed through a parking lot and then by another complex surrounded by a chain-link fence. I didn't know where I was going, but it seemed to be a main road, so I kept following it. When I walked past another fenced complex, I started to worry it would never end. *Maybe I'm stuck in a compound within a compound.*

Finally, the road ended at another road. To the right, I would have had to walk past more fence, but to the left, all I could see were trees hovering over the road.

I turned left.

I walked for what felt like miles and miles. The trees reminded me of the cabin and Paddy, of the last time I saw Paddy . . .

"France and Italy produce over forty percent of all wine consumed in the world."

I had focused on the sound of my footsteps on the pavement.

Finally, that road had stopped at what looked like a rural highway. I'd turned left last time, so this time I turned right, which also took me farther away from all that chain-link fencing. Every so often cars flew by me and blew dust and dirt around. I closed my eyes and tried not to breathe it in.

When I came to a sign in front of an ugly building with brick on the lower half and vertical siding on top, housing a real estate office and a contracting business, I started thinking about what to do. I couldn't walk this road forever. But I had no money, no friends, no family. Maybe I could find shelter, but was I even headed toward a town?

A black SUV tore into the drive, and I stopped so fast I stumbled. Or maybe that was because of all the medication in my system.

The door closest to me flung open. "There you ah." A tall man stepped out of the car and glanced between me and a small photo in his hand. Then he tucked the photo back into his inside coat pocket. "Hello, Dream. Glad to be outta that place finally?"

"Who are you?" I backed up a few steps.

He lurched forward and grabbed me by the arm, and another man quickly exited the car and held me from behind. "I got him, William."

I tried to wrestle free, but I was weak from all the walking and medication.

"Hello, there."

It was a different voice, thick. I struggled to look around and find the owner of the voice. William's friend had me too tightly around the shoulders.

And then I was free. I looked around. The man who'd been

holding me was on the ground, and a man I'd never seen before was aiming a gun at William. He was older than William, probably late forties, but there was something about him, besides the gun in his hand, that told me he was more than simply a passing Good Samaritan.

William started to reach toward his hip.

"Tsk, tsk," the new man said. "Why don't we just leave that Colt Combat Elite in its holster."

William stopped moving.

"Now," the new man said, "I'm going to take our friend here and be on my way."

"He stays."

"Not today." He motioned with his other hand. "Lie down on the ground."

William sneered.

"Maybe it would be easier simply to shoot. Cleaner, I think." The new man shifted forward.

William lay down on the ground.

"Cross your ankles and fold your hands behind your back."

William obeyed.

The new man grabbed my jacket sleeve in his free hand and pushed me toward a car parked in front of the ugly building. I inched in that direction but wasn't yet sure what the right thing to do was. The new man moved closer to William, and I thought maybe he was going to pull the trigger after all. But instead, he lifted William's head off the ground and hit him across the jaw with his gun hand. William's head flopped back to the pavement.

The new man came back to me and continued guiding me toward the green Toyota.

I pulled out of his grip and realized he hadn't been holding my sleeve all that tightly. "Who are you?"

"I won't hurt you. That's all you need at this precise moment. I'll tell you more, but we need to move."

I had hesitated.

He had shifted closer and spoken in a low voice. "I will not hurt you, Dream. You have my word. I'm here to help you."

Now I'm in the hotel room and remind myself, no, Dream. Mr. Hayes is real. You saw him. You spoke to him. He cared.

"Great. Now even I'm calling myself Dream."

Remember when your name was Javier? When Mom used to call you by your full name only when you were in trouble? Gregory Javier Union!

And remember how she'd just whisper, "Javie" when she needed a hug, when it was close to the—

Stop.

I can't . . . I can't take time to remember this, not right now. Mr. Hayes says I've got work to do tonight.

"Scotch bonnet and habanero are two of the hottest peppers on the Scoville scale. At forty-two years old when he took office, Teddy Roosevelt is the youngest American president in history."

In the hospital they taught me to do this. When I start to feel overwhelmed, when I start to remember things I don't want to remember, I can push those thoughts away by recalling simple, emotionless facts. It's that easy. And it works, most of the time. They even gave me a book of facts to help me. I read it twice, then I didn't need to read it again.

"Michigan joined the United States on January 26, 1837. Winston Churchill's last words were, 'Oh, I am so bored with it all.'"

I've always had a pretty good memory. Well, I used to have a pretty good memory. Now I don't know what I have. A Swiss-cheese memory? Some moments I see with perfect clarity. Others are just holes in my head. Blank spots I don't know how to fill. After I woke up in the hospital, well, it got harder to remember things.

I remember riding in a car, scrunched down, out of sight on the floorboard of the passenger seat. I remember a smell of wet, hot copper and thinking I was going to die. I remember . . .

"The noble gases are helium, argon."

Help me, Jesus!

"Neon, xenon."

Help me, Jesus. "Radon and krypton."

Okay. My hands aren't cramping anymore.

"Krypton is Superman's home planet."

Breathe in. Breathe out. Say, "Amen."

Good. Well, better at least.

I'm not proud of my past, of doing some of the things I know I did. But I was a different person then. And I didn't actually know what was going on, not really. Yeah, I could've guessed at some of it. I probably should've guessed it. But like I say, I was different. I was young. Mom was painfully gone. I was alone. All I cared about was myself. When they offered me all that money just to paint stuff, I didn't even think about it. I just said, "Yes, sir. I'll be there Monday."

Stop staring at me like that, Kevin. You weren't there. You don't know how it was.

Doesn't matter anyway, because the last thing I remember before the hospital was seeing a big Irishman pawing through my portfolio, looking at the work I'd done for my first legitimate freelance job. Work I never got to turn in.

But I've got a new job to do tonight, and it's time to go. *Coat on, Dream. Warm knit cap too. It's cold out there, kids. Gloves? No, not tonight.*

The right side of my coat sags heavily from the weight of the Smith & Wesson 686 revolver in my pocket. It's a pretty, little gun, I guess. Short barrel and a wood grip that fits okay in my hand, which is saying something. But I don't like it anyway. I feel nervous and sweaty just having it near.

I smell hot copper, Kevin.

Help me, Jesus.

Mr. Hayes says I need the gun. He says I should keep it with me at all times so I'll be safe. But if I'm the crazy one, will a Smith & Wesson protect me from myself?

No. I'm not crazy. If I were crazy, I'd still be in the hospital, right? They never would've let me go, right? Right, Kevin? Say something, you obstinate—

"It's time to go, Dream. Leave the motel key card on the bed. Leave everything. You don't need any of it anymore. Just take your coat, your hat. And your gun."

It's a five-mile walk from the Super 88 motel to the TD Garden arena. There's no snow or ice tonight, just low temperatures near freezing. That's to be expected in Boston this time of year. I think jogging occasionally will keep me warm enough for five miles. Besides, the cold will be extra motivation for me to keep moving forward.

For now, though, while I'm walking, I think I'll put the revolver in my left coat pocket.

Just to be safe.

4

TRUDI

Boston, MA

"Ms. Coffey, Trudi, won't you have a seat?"

Trudi snatched a look at the clock on the huge scoreboard above center court. Nine o'clock exactly. She'd been sitting next to this woman for an hour and a half, unaware that this lady knew her name—and who knew what else about her. The man in the leprechaun cap studiously ignored her now, and Trudi had to admit he'd won this round. She turned slowly and let her gaze drop onto the woman lounging in the seat next to her.

"Please." The woman gave a shark-like smile. "I won't bite. Not hard, at least." She laughed at her own joke, a practiced guffaw that must have sounded flat even to her own ears.

Trudi didn't say anything in response, but she did sink slowly back into her stadium seat. She let her eyes drift toward the woman, finally seeing her for the first time.

She was compact, lean, and muscular, with a confidence that Trudi guessed was often interpreted as arrogance. Her skin was tinted with the caramel of Central American sunshine, her face only lightly touched by makeup. Her hair, thick and coarse, was the color of unused charcoal briquettes and had a slight finger wave rippling through it. The woman's ashy-black eyebrows matched the texture and color of her hair and were perched quizzically above two amber orbs that seemed to take in everything around them.

A worthy adversary, Trudi thought. *Am I ready for this?*

The woman put out a hand. "My name is Tama Uribe," she said. She waited a beat or two, then withdrew her hand without complaint when Trudi didn't respond. "I've been hoping to have a few minutes to talk with you, but I was waiting for the right moment."

Trudi finally broke her silence. "Which alphabet do you work for?"

Tama Uribe flashed a quick grin, the first authentic expression Trudi had seen so far from the woman. She reached inside a pocket of her wool pants and produced a badge that read "FBI."

"Art crimes team," the federal agent said. "And no, you're not in any trouble. Like I said, I just want to talk a little bit."

Trudi nodded toward the man sitting to her left. "And Chucky the Leprechaun is here to make sure I stay around for the conversation?"

The FBI agent's grin grew wider, and she leaned in close. "Trudi," she said in a low voice, "if I wanted to make you stay, I wouldn't need Charlie's help for that."

There was silence between the two women while Trudi processed that comment.

On the parquet floor below, the Celtics won the second-half tip-off and raced toward a quick score. Apparently, the coach's halftime rant had given the players new motivation. Trudi did her best not to be distracted by the game, even though that was really what she wanted to do.

"So, what do you want to talk about?"

"Like I said, you're not in any trouble."

"I know that."

Tama nodded. "We're trying to get in touch with your husband—"

"Ex-husband."

"Right, ex-husband. Samuel Hill. And, no, he's not in trouble either."

"That's good to know," Trudi said. "Why do you want him?"

There was an awkward pause, during which Trudi watched Tama Uribe's mind sift through what she could and couldn't—or wouldn't—say. It registered with Trudi that the woman's eyes had narrowed just slightly and turned their focus inward, briefly, even though she was still staring at Trudi's face.

So this is what you look like when you're lying, Trudi thought. It was a trick her friend Tyson had taught her—how to look for physical clues to dishonest words. *Need to remember that. I should probably thank The Raven for the lying lessons as well.*

"Samuel Hill is a friend. We go way back to our college days. I need to deliver a message to him."

"Oh? You and Samuel went to the same college?" Trudi said. Tama nodded serenely. "Who was your favorite professor at Georgia Tech?"

"Uh." The FBI agent stumbled a bit but recovered quickly. "Professor Dawson, political science."

Chucky the Leprechaun snorted. Trudi leaned her head back so the man on her left could hear.

"You want to tell her, Chucky? Or should I?"

"Agent Uribe," the man said without taking his eyes off the basketball game in progress, "as was clearly indicated in your briefing report, both Samuel Hill and Trudi Coffey attended the University of Georgia."

Tama Uribe looked like she was going to curse, then shrugged in a "can't win 'em all" kind of gesture and charged forward anyway. "Where's your husband, Trudi?" she said. "It's very important that I talk to him. Soon."

"Haven't seen him," Trudi said.

"When did you speak with him last?"

"No idea."

The FBI agent let out an exaggerated sigh. "I can see that I've upset you, that you distrust me, but your first impression of me is not what matters right now. Please, maybe we can start this conversation over? Your husband—"

"Ex-husband."

"Ex-husband may be in danger. Perhaps you know where I could find him or leave a message for him."

Trudi didn't let her face betray the twisting that knotted her insides when Agent Uribe said the word *danger. Where are you, Samuel? Are you in some kind of trouble?*

"He's a cop now. Quit the CIA. He works out of the Zone 6 Police Department in Atlanta," Trudi said. "If I were looking for him, that's where I'd start."

"Hmm." It was Chucky the Leprechaun this time. Trudi glanced back toward the man on her left. He didn't say anything more, just shook his head.

"Well," Agent Uribe said, "he's been away from the office lately. But I'm guessing you knew that already."

Actually, I had no idea, Trudi worried. *If he's not checking in at the Zone 6 Police Department, then where is he?*

None of them spoke for a moment as all eyes absently focused on the game playing out below. One of the Hawks reserves tossed up an ill-advised three-pointer, which the Celtics turned into a fast break and two quick points. Trudi almost groaned out loud. Her team was losing now and definitely feeling out of sync.

"All right," Agent Uribe said. She leaned back in her seat and pretended to watch the game for a moment longer, then she spoke without bothering to make eye contact. "We'll be on our way, but, Trudi, you must know we're not stupid. I mean, first your ex-husband shows up unannounced in Boston three weeks ago, asking questions, poking around in FBI business. Next thing you know, The Dream is released with no advance warning, almost as if someone with CIA connections wanted it that way. Then they both just disappear into the mist while you show up in their shadows, maybe cleaning up their tracks, maybe acting as a diversion. Either way, it strains credulity just a bit, don't you think?"

Trudi didn't know what to say, so she blurted the first thing on her mind. "Who's The Dream?"

She felt the eyes of both FBI agents suddenly boring into her and wished she hadn't said anything. Tama Uribe studied her intently for a moment, then she stood. Her partner followed.

"You're a funny lady, Trudi Coffey," she said. She produced a business card and dropped it into Trudi's lap. "Let's stay in touch."

Trudi watched the FBI agents push their way out of the row and saunter up the stairs toward the exit. A dozen thoughts flashed through her mind after they'd left. What was that about, really? Where was Samuel, and why had he come to Boston? And what did the FBI have to do with this?

By the start of the fourth quarter, Trudi was both disgusted and agitated. Disgusted because it seemed as though someone had replaced her beloved Atlanta Hawks with a group of uncoordinated imbeciles dressed in Hawks jerseys. Boston, however, had come out after halftime firing on all pistons, and now the Celtics led 88–71. Trudi was also agitated because she couldn't get her mind off the mysterious Agent Uribe and her ominous warning that Samuel might be in danger.

Trudi grabbed her purse and headed toward the bathroom.

At this point during the game, the restrooms had been well-used and were a filthy mess—but at least they were mostly empty and quiet. Trudi found what she hoped was the least cholera-infected stall and locked herself inside. She was dialing her cell phone before the latch had fully clicked into place.

The phone on the other end cycled through four rings before dumping into voicemail. She heard her ex-husband's voice say, "You know what to do," and then the ubiquitous answering-machine beep signaled it was her turn to talk. She hung up. Just to appease her obsessive-compulsive tendencies, she dialed the number again.

"You know what to do."

Trudi hung up again, her foot tapping nervously on the sticky floor. She wished she could sit down, but there was no way she was doing that—not in here, not now. She tried to remember exactly the last time she'd seen or talked to her ex-husband.

It was before October 29. She knew that because she'd called to ask him to give her a ride to the airport, but he'd never even returned her call. She traced the days backward in her head. October 20 was when she saw him last, she decided. She remembered because she'd planned to work only a half day that Friday and had already sent her assistant home with time off. Samuel had shown up right around lunchtime, asking to borrow a book.

"So that was, what, three weeks ago?" she muttered to herself. "Usually Samuel and I connect at least once or twice a week.

Hmm." She glanced around at the walls of the bathroom stall and reminded herself, "Of course, I have been out of town lately."

She dialed another number.

"Hello?" The voice this time was young and feminine. Trudi heard music in the background and the buzz of conversation.

"Hey, Eula," she said, hating the way her voice suddenly echoed in the bathroom. "You on a date?"

"Um—"

"Of course you're on a date." Trudi laughed awkwardly. "Eulalie Marie Jefferson always has a date on a Friday night, right?"

"Actually, tonight was study group for my forensic psychology class, but somebody in the group found out it was, ah, my birthday, so they all insisted on taking me out to celebrate instead."

Trudi shot a grimace toward the stall door. *Forgot my assistant's birthday again! Bad Trudi, bad girl.* "Right, of course," she said out loud. "Happy birthday. I got you a present here in Boston. I'm bringing it to you Monday." It was a lie, but she intended to make it true by picking up some earrings or something at the airport gift shop tomorrow. That would have to do.

"Thanks, Trudi. You shouldn't have."

Well, I didn't yet, but I will.

"Is everything okay? Or were you just calling to wish me happy birthday?"

Trudi hesitated. "Just checking in, you know, to see how everything's going down there in Atlanta."

She heard a smile creep into her assistant's voice. "Trudi, it's almost ten on a Friday night, and you're a thousand miles away from here. Why don't you tell me what's going on?" She heard a shuffle on the other end of the phone. "Hold on, let me get to a quieter spot."

Somebody in the background groaned in concert with the sound of Eulalie's chair scraping away from the table. Trudi faintly heard a guy's voice say, "Come on, Eula, it's your birthday party! Just tell your boss you're busy for once." She tapped the toe of her boot against the corner of the stall and resisted the urge to say anything.

It is her birthday, and it is pretty late, she thought. *Maybe I should give this girl some kind of private life.* She squeezed her eyes shut and tried not to feel like the biggest jerk on the planet. Then she thought of Samuel and that was enough.

The restaurant's ambient noises faded with the sound of a door closing, and she heard Eulalie say, "Okay, I'm outside now. What's up, Boss?"

"Eula, when was the last time you saw Samuel?"

"Um, let's see." There was silence while Eulalie sent her brain backward in time. "Gosh, Trudi, I think it's been a while. When did we all go to CozyFloyd's BBQ in Douglasville?"

"September. Remember? It was right after Labor Day weekend."

"So, two months ago. That's the last time I saw him."

"How about phone or email? Heard anything from Samuel lately?"

"No, come to think of it, I haven't. Trudi, is something wrong with Mr. Hill? Should I be worried?" There was new tension in her assistant's voice.

"No, of course not," Trudi said. "I'm just trying to track him down, and you know how difficult he can be when he doesn't want to be found."

"Right. Sure."

She's not buying it, Trudi thought. *Knows me too well.* "Well, you go enjoy your birthday party. If you hear from Samuel, tell him to give me a call, okay?"

"You want me to go by his condo and knock on his door?"

"No, thanks anyway. It's not that important. Seriously, just go enjoy your party."

"What're you going to do?"

"Well, right now I'm at a basketball game, but the Celtics are winning big, so I'll probably just whine and go back to my hotel grumpy." *At least that is the truth this time.*

"Okaaay, well, if you need me, you know how to get me."

"Okay. Happy birthday."

"Go, Hawks."

She heard Eulalie step back into the noisy restaurant and then the line went dead.

Trudi stood in the silence for a moment longer before deciding to do exactly what she'd told Eulalie she was going to do: head back to the hotel and feel grumpy. She kicked open the stall door, headed out of the bathroom, and turned toward the underground parking garage.

She was going to have to exit through the North Station train depot to get to the garage, so she toyed with the idea of grabbing an ice cream or smoothie at Emack & Bolio's to take with her on the ride home. By the time she reached the bottom of the escalator, though, that thought was long gone. She found herself instead fixating on the one question she thought everything else hinged on: Who or what is The Dream?

5

DREAM

Boston, MA

Mr. Hayes said I should look for a woman with thick brown hair. Someone in her early thirties, about five-and-a-half-feet tall.

She's got a trim figure, he told me, but she's athletic looking. Strong. Not flabby or frail at all. She'll probably be wearing a look on her face that perpetually seems to say, "Don't mess with me." But if I'm lucky, he said, if I play my cards right, I might also see a smile that says maybe it's worth the risk anyway.

Mr. Hayes said Trudi Coffey would stand out in a crowd, that if I didn't recognize her when I first saw her, then I didn't deserve to recognize her. As usual, Mr. Hayes was right.

She is unmistakable once you know what you're looking for.

I didn't expect to see her yet. The basketball game is still going on upstairs, up in the TD Garden arena, and I figured she'd be the kind to stay until the end. I have been here on this bench, almost dozing, in North Station, eyeballing the escalator and waiting for the rush of people to start pouring through when the Celtics are done with the Atlanta Hawks. But there she is, suddenly appearing, all by herself, stepping off the escalator and heading toward the west elevator that goes down to the underground parking garage.

It was a freezing cold walk to get here, but I've been inside North Station for a while now and all my extremities have blood tingling happily through them again. In my left coat pocket, I can still feel the revolver hanging limply beside me. I'm watching Trudi Coffey, but I can only think about one thing.

Will I have to use the gun?

Trudi Coffey breezes past the oversized bench where I'm sitting. It's shaped like a giant wooden boulder, all one piece, carved and sanded into an oblong sculpture with a tapered top that flares down to form a little ledge-like bench encircling the whole structure. I almost feel like I'm sitting on the brim of a partially flattened top hat made for an enormous stick-figure man.

My thick, suede coat is nearly the same color of tan as the bench, and when Trudi walks by, I freeze like a cottontail trying to hide in plain sight. It's just a reflex, I guess. After all, I'm supposed to be hunting her, not vice versa.

She doesn't even see me.

After she's passed, it registers with me that she has beautiful eyes.

"Hazel," I whisper to myself. "Just like Mamá."

I'm tempted to keep that moment, to savor it, but I realize quickly that if I keep holed up on this bench, I will lose her. All my waiting, all Mr. Hayes's planning, will amount to nothing. My heart jumps into overdrive even before I start running to catch up. *Like a little rabbit*, I think, and the irony makes me almost smile.

She walks fast, like she knows where she wants to go and

nothing or no one is going to stop her from getting there. I close the gap between us just before we get to the west elevator and am careful to slow down early so she doesn't think I'm chasing her down, even though that's exactly what I'm doing. Then our world goes still, like North Station is holding its breath, waiting to see what'll happen next. I'm standing almost next to her, to the left and just a step behind her, as we both wait for the elevator to arrive.

It strikes me that Trudi and I are going to be the only ones riding the elevator down to the garage.

Now? I ask myself. *Do I do it now? Or stick with the plan and wait until she's beside her rental car?*

I get that rabbit feeling again, almost as an instinct. She's looking at me, studying me. Her eyes linger for a second on my coat pocket.

Am I standing too close? Have I crossed the invisible line into her personal space? Mr. Hayes is right. Even though her mouth never opens, her face says very clearly, "Don't mess with me." I mumble and take a step backward. "Excuse me," I say. She lets one more second pass before returning her attention to the elevator. I feel myself sigh in relief.

The doors open. We both step inside, and she selects the parking garage level from the button panel. She looks at me and asks, "That where you're going?" I nod, wishing that my top lip wasn't sweating, already betraying the fear growing inside me. I smell a hint of leftover perfume, I think, something that once might have been jasmine and orange blossom. And the doors close.

I'm still worrying about whether I should make my move now or wait until we're in the garage, when I realize my left hand has made the decision for me. Even so, my head won't let my hand point the revolver at her. I think I should say something, but no words come. She's staring at me now, waiting, but I've obviously missed my cue and now she's just watching a five-foot-two man wave his little gun at the elevator's button panel in silent mystery. *This might be funny*, I tell myself, *if I wasn't so scared.*

"Smith & Wesson, huh?" she says at last. "I prefer Beretta myself."

I nod. Now I'm sweating behind my ears too. She's very patient while I try to tell myself what to do next. The elevator slips into place on the garage level and the doors open again. Neither of us moves.

"What do you think?" she says. I think she might be grinning. "You want to take this outside or stay here in the elevator?"

I nod and motion for her to lead the way out of the elevator, and she does. The garage is cavernous, filled with cars but empty of people. Still, I know we can't stand here for long before somebody takes that same elevator down to where we are.

Follow the plan, I tell myself. *Mr. Hayes gave you a plan!* And now, at just the wrong moment, it happens again. My mind goes completely blank. I can barely remember my own name, let alone Mr. Hayes's plan. *Think, Dream, think!*

I've found Trudi Coffey, and I have a gun.

"I have a gun," I say, my voice thin and soft.

"I noticed," she says.

What was supposed to come next?

"Don't be afraid," I say.

"I'm not." Now she's definitely grinning.

Bits of the plan are leaking back into my memory, but it's taking too long and she's getting impatient.

"All right," she says. "You have a gun, and I'm not afraid. Is there anything else? Or should we just call it a night and head our separate ways?"

"No." It's coming back to me now. I can't let Trudi Coffey

leave Boston, not without me. "I need your help, Trudi." The grin on her face disappears so suddenly that I take a step backward. Her expression says, "Don't mess with me."

"Now you've got my attention, Little Man. How do you know my name?"

"Mr. Hayes said, he said . . ."

"Who's Mr. Hayes? Is that who you work for?"

"No, he's, I mean . . ." I'm losing what little control I had up to this point. "It doesn't matter. What matters is that I need your help. Will you help me?"

"No, of course not," she says. "You're holding a gun on me. Why would I help anyone who threatens me with a gun?"

"I, but, I mean—"

"Besides, I'm leaving Boston in the morning. If you need a detective, you're going to have to hire somebody local. But leave the gun at home. We don't often feel helpful toward clients who hold us at gunpoint."

"No, I—"

"Now, tell me who Mr. Hayes is and why he sent you to find me. That could be important." Her right foot taps impatiently as a new idea seems to appear in her mind. "Wait a minute. Does this have anything to do with The Dream?"

Now I'm the one who's stunned. How does she know my name? How does she know that and not know who I am? I see her thinking. She thinks faster than I do, maybe even faster than I did before the, before . . . well, she thinks faster than me.

"Mr. Hayes," she says, and her eyes narrow. "Are you talking about Darrent Hayes? From Atlanta?"

"Yes."

What else am I supposed to say? Mr. Hayes never told me what to do if she asked me that question. She rolls her eyes and starts walking slowly in a circle around me, still thinking.

"How'd you get mixed up with that guy, Little Man? You know he's a terrorist, right? Tried to blow up half a hotel when I was in it. Not a nice guy."

Now she's staring hard at me, and I'm surprised by the intensity in her eyes. The color seems to shift from soft brown to light green and back to brown again. The pigment is pure and gemlike, like tiger's eye infused with emerald slivers, or quality diamonds that sparkle in bright light. I can see why Samuel Hill fell for her.

"How about you?" she says to me. "Are you a terrorist too?"

"No, no!"

She nods, and I'm wondering where I lost control of this encounter. Even though I'm holding the gun, she's interrogating me.

"I believe you," she says, and that seems to settle it for her. "Look, I— What's your name? No, never mind. It's better if I don't know. I don't want to know, because I'm never going to see you again anyway. So listen to me. You need to get away from Darrent Hayes. Run as fast as you can and never look back. Trust me on this. Once you're safely away, call the police and tell them where he's hiding. There's probably a reward waiting for the guy who turns him in, so be sure to claim that after he's locked up in prison. Got it?"

I nod. I don't know what else to do.

"Good. Now, I've got to go. I've got problems of my own to deal with back in Atlanta, so put that gun back into your left jacket pocket and run away and hide. And call the police." She claps me on the shoulder. "I wish you the best."

She turns and starts to walk away. In a mild panic, I grab her arm. Then my left hand finally gets its nerve and before I know it, the barrel of the Smith & Wesson 686 is pointed at her ribs.

"Trudi, I can't let you go. I need your help."

I feel her muscles cord beneath my fingers.

"You don't know this about me yet," she advises through a tight jaw, "but I *really* don't like it when people touch me without permission."

I quickly drop her arm and step backward again. Part of me wants to wet myself, but I know I've got to retake control of this situation—and fast. I muster my nerve and try a bluff.

"Look," I say, waving the gun in what I hope is a threatening way, "no more talk. You're coming with me. Now. You're going to help me. And that's just the way it is, got it?"

Silence swells the air between us. She looks at the gun, then stares at my face. *She can see I mean business*, I think. *She knows I'm serious about this.*

"I see," she says, nodding at last. "I get it. But let me just ask you one question."

"What is it?"

"What's the hardest you've ever been kicked?"

6

TRUDI

Boston, MA

The small Hispanic man had seemed a little out of place when he stood next to Trudi outside the west elevator in North Station. He was shorter than she was by a good three inches, which was atypical anyway, and then he'd stood so close that she could hear him breathing in short puffs.

Situational awareness. That's one of the first things Samuel taught her way back when. Back when it mattered what Samuel thought about things. Be constantly aware of who and what is around you. "Be alert to everything," he'd say, "or you're vulnerable to anything."

She did a quick scan of her new companion. He was around five feet tall, she figured, maybe five-two, round in the middle, with shoulders that sloped down into short arms he held nervously at his sides. His face was full but not fat—what her mother would call "adorably plump," though she likened it more to a human caricature of a squirrel with a few nuts in tow.

She guessed he was close to her age, thirty-two or so, maybe a little younger. She settled on twenty-nine and decided that would be close enough.

His hair was dark, cropped short and nondescript. A thin mustache decorated his lip, but judging by the sparse tufts of growth on the rest of his chin and face, she guessed he didn't need to shave often and had probably never been able to grow a full beard. Deep brown eyes and a tan suede jacket were the most attention-grabbing aspects of the little man's appearance.

Especially the jacket.

Trudi noticed the man's coat was a little long for his height and the left side dipped farther than it should, weighted down by something heavy in the pocket. Her practiced eye could make out the silhouette of a gun handle and short barrel stored inside that pocket. Her senses went on sudden alert, but her mind questioned her instinctive response.

He seems harmless, she thought. *Maybe a little nervous. Is this accountant actually going to threaten me with a gun? Or does he just carry it for his own personal protection?*

Trudi entertained the idea that maybe he'd been mugged before—a smaller guy like him, walking alone, could be a target for just about any big-city street thugs. Maybe that was why he carried a gun. She wished for a moment that she'd brought her own Beretta 3032 Tomcat, but she didn't have a Massachusetts permit, so she couldn't carry it anyway. And besides, she was just a "consulting detective" on this trip. Why would she need a gun?

Trudi's eyes snapped back to the man when the elevator doors opened. Something seemed incongruous, and she couldn't put her finger on it. Inside she tapped the button for the parking garage and used that as an excuse to secretly study him a little further. "That where you're going?" she said.

The hands, she thought. *It's his hands.*

She saw old, flat calluses decorating the spot inside the thumb and at the base of the forefinger on his right hand, the kind of calluses that took years to form and become near-permanent fixtures. His left hand was soft, unblemished except for normal wear and tear.

You're right-handed, Little Man, she thought. *And judging by those calluses, you're an artist, not an accountant. A painter maybe. Or a penciller. Maybe both.*

He nodded at Trudi's question, and they both turned to face the front, watching the doors close as they began their journey down to the garage.

So, she wondered, *if you're right-handed, why is the gun in your left pocket?* In this proximity, she noticed dampness glittering on his thin mustache and glistening on the back of his neck. *Maybe he's not simply nervous*, she told herself, *maybe he's scared. Of what?*

From the corner of her eye, she saw his left hand dip into the coat pocket and come out trembling, gun filling his palm. His eyes were wide and busy, but he kept his gaze from addressing her directly. He seemed at odds within himself, and though Trudi respected the danger of the gun, she was more curious at this point than anything else.

She waited.

He's afraid of the gun, she realized.

She tried breaking the ice with a crack about Beretta handguns, but that didn't accomplish much. The elevator doors opened, and Trudi felt a little awkward, like she was watching a stand-up comedian who'd somehow forgotten the punch line to his first joke.

Part of her wanted to get it over with, to get on with solving her biggest problem—finding Samuel—but the fact that a small, seemingly innocuous man had appeared from nowhere and pulled a Smith & Wesson revolver on her made her want to be patient. *Every gun can kill*, she told herself. *Better to keep alert, see what's going on in this guy's mind.*

"Don't be afraid," he said at last, and Trudi had to choke back a laugh. Of the two of them, he was the one who was obviously scared. And then he said her name. A stranger, the second one tonight, knew her name—and both were carrying guns.

This was getting annoying.

"How do you know my name?" she said.

"Mr. Hayes said, he said . . ."

Hayes, she thought. *He works for somebody named Hayes. Hmm.*

There are a lot of Mr. Hayeses in this world. Did a Hayes work in the Boston mob? She would have to ask Samuel to check on that for her. She felt her frustration level rising. She had to find Samuel. Agent Uribe thought he was connected to someone named The Dream.

Maybe if I find The Dream, I'll find Samuel?

Her right foot started tapping involuntarily, and she decided she didn't care about that now. "Does this have anything to do with The Dream?" she asked, thinking out loud, mostly. The small man didn't answer. *He's got no idea who that is*, she told herself, *just like me*. She forced her mind to process and suddenly made a connection.

"Mr. Hayes," she said. She felt anger and worry flare up like twin flames in her chest. "Are you talking about Darrent Hayes? From Atlanta?"

The answer was not what she wanted to hear, but at least she now knew what she was up against. *Darrent Hayes*, she mulled. *I would've thought you'd want to stay as far away from me as possible.*

She heard herself talking, giving commands, but paid no attention to that. She had bigger issues to work through, and besides, it was time to end this little game and go back to the hotel, where she could think in the freedom of cookie-cutter corporate hospitality.

Six or seven months ago, Darrent Hayes had been Mama Bliss's right-hand man in the whole Nevermore plot. They'd planned to blow up the Ritz-Carlton Atlanta hotel—planned to kill a few hundred people just to accomplish the assassination of one politician. They'd almost pulled it off. If not for The Raven, they would have. In the end, Mama Bliss, the mastermind, had died and most of her cohorts had been captured. Only two of the key players remained at large—a Ukrainian mafia figure, Viktor Kostiuk, and the seemingly invisible Mr. Darrent Hayes.

The going theory about Kostiuk was that he'd made it back into hiding in Ukraine, but Darrent Hayes was another story. There were too many conflicting reports about his whereabouts and what had happened to him. He was dead, said some. He was with Kostiuk in the Ukraine. He'd retired in luxury and was living in the Bahamas under an assumed name. He was hiding in plain sight, living in California, working a blue-collar job until the time was right for him to reemerge. He'd given up all his earthly possessions and was traveling by foot across Asia, helping the poor and hungry as penance for his misdeeds.

"He's being protected," Samuel had finally said back in July, when he'd decided to give up because the trail for Hayes had gone completely cold. "Somebody in some government agency, either ours or a European alphabet, wants to keep him out of view."

"What makes you think that, O Wise Detective Man?" Trudi had asked.

"Look at the evidence," he said. "All those so-called 'leads' as to his whereabouts, all these new theories, all of them different, all coming out around the same time? It's misinformation and disinformation, classic CIA tactics. When you can't hide the truth, you flood the communication channels with half-truths until the real story is indistinguishable from the lies. Wars have been won using the same tactics."

"So, what do we do?"

Samuel shrugged. "Not much we can do, except be vigilant and hope that sooner or later somebody makes a mistake."

Maybe this little man in front of me is Darrent Hayes's first mistake, Trudi told herself. *Now that I know he's out there—and that he's watching—I'll tell Samuel. When I find Samuel, maybe he can use that information in his investigation. For now, I can't waste time getting caught up in the hunt for Darrent Hayes or in this man's troubles. Samuel needs me to find him, and that means it's time to go.*

She felt a hand grip her arm, just above the elbow. She resisted the urge to break the wrist of the hand that held her, but she also knew she'd had a stressful night, it was getting late, and her patience with this guy was wearing thin.

"You don't know this about me yet," she said evenly, "but I *really* don't like it when people touch me without permission."

He let go of her arm and took a step backward. The man's eyes fluttered, but he held his ground.

"Look," he said, fingers squeezing and re-squeezing the revolver in his left hand, "no more talk. You're coming with me. Now. You're going to help me. And that's just the way it is, got it?"

Trudi eyed the safety on the gun and saw it was still on. She measured the distance between them and judged there was room for a roundhouse kick. With her height advantage and leg strength, she'd be able to leap high enough to bring a kick crashing down from above his head, adding the force of gravity to her raw power and technique. Depending on where she hit him, she might break either his jaw or his nose, but at this point she was willing to let that happen.

The real hassle would be having to call the authorities to

report an "attempted mugging, with injuries" and then spending half her night filing a report at the police station. Still, maybe it'd be for the best. If this guy did know where Darrent Hayes was hiding, maybe it was better to get him into police custody, get him talking sooner rather than later.

I'll just have to sleep on the plane tomorrow, she told herself. To the man, she said, "I see. I get it. But let me just ask you one question."

"What is it?"

"What's the hardest you've ever been kicked?"

She watched a shudder slide through the man's entire body and worried just a bit when his breathing began to sound like he was hiccupping syrup. His left arm stiffened, and the Smith & Wesson started nodding up and down. She saw both his hands begin to twitch involuntarily. He took another step backward and gasped for air.

Don't have a heart attack on me, Little Man. Trudi wasn't sure what to do. She wanted to help him, but then again, he was aiming a gun at her rib cage. Sort of.

"Theoretically," he blurted suddenly, "ice that's only nine inches thick can support the full weight of a three-and-a-half-ton pickup truck."

"What?"

Trudi was mystified. Was this guy having a mental breakdown? A panic attack? She considered taking the gun from him by force, just to be safe. A mentally unstable person could do anything without being fully aware of what he was doing. *Better for him to do that without a gun in his hand*, she thought.

"Thrice the age of a dog is that of a horse; thrice the age of a horse is that of a man," he said.

Ancient Celtic wisdom literature? she said to herself. *Guess that's appropriate considering where we are right now.*

He took another step backward. The Smith & Wesson slipped from his hand and clattered noisily on the concrete surface below them. Trudi swept down and retrieved the gun.

"Elizabeth Taylor's fourth husband was Eddie Fisher," he said, looking first at the gun and then at her, then back at the gun again. "They were married from 1959 to 1964."

He turned and ran.

He looks like a round little hamster, she thought, *but he runs like a flabby penguin.*

She watched him loping down the parking garage aisle until he reached a distance of about fifty yards. Then he darted between a Ford Escape and a Toyota Corolla, but he misjudged his location and found a concrete wall facing him instead of another open parking aisle. He stopped, turned, turned again, then sank to the ground and out of sight.

Trudi felt like cursing. She wanted to leave, to go back to her hotel and then Atlanta, to find Samuel and get on with life. But this little man was obviously having some sort of emotional breakdown. She felt kind of sorry for him. Unbidden, Jesus's parable of the Good Samaritan leaped to her mind. A man is felled by robbers. Two religious folks pass by and do nothing. The third man, a Samaritan, stops, helps, heals. "Which of these three do you think was a neighbor?" Jesus asked. "The one who had mercy on him," a religious expert answered. And Jesus said, "Go and do likewise."

Go and do likewise, Trudi repeated to the heavens. *But this guy tried to shoot me!*

Despite her prayerful protests, she knew that wasn't exactly true. Now that she held the gun, it was obvious that this man had no intention of harming her. She wasn't sure he even knew how to operate a Smith & Wesson 686.

You've chosen a career that sometimes requires violence, she told herself deliberately. *But when violence isn't necessary, doesn't your faith require compassion?*

"And let's not forget," she said aloud, "it was your threat to kick him senseless that triggered this little episode."

She took a step in his direction.

"Little Man!" she called out. "Hello? Are you okay?"

There was no answer.

7

DREAM

Boston, MA

He told me to get down. The gun was still warm.

He killed Henri.

He just came into the gallery and started shooting. Didn't even ask Henri's name or what he was doing. Just aimed that silver handgun in his direction and fired three times.

I want to close my eyes, but I know if I do that, I'll see it all happen again. I'll watch Henri turn, see his eyes register shock, then pain. I'll see red mist spray from Henri's chest, watch him slump to the floor, see his eyes go blank as his soul separates from his body.

"Oh God." It's a prayer, a familiar one for me. "Oh God, oh God." It's what I say when I don't have words. "Oh God, please . . ."

How can someone just pull a trigger? Just feel a bullet fly from his hand, knowing death waits at the other end?

I curse my brain, this Swiss-cheese memory of mine that

remembers some moments so clearly, in such detail, and then blocks out entire months or years of my life without a second thought. Why do I keep seeing Henri die and keep forgetting the moment my mother passed? I know I was there when it happened. Why can't I remember?

"Jesus." I hear my voice say His name. It's not trembling anymore. I'm not choking anymore. "Help me, Jesus." It's a whisper, and God hears my prayer. I can tell because my eyes are open now. I'm done drowning. I'm aware of my surroundings again. I'm curled into a ball, knees to my chin, a Ford to my left and a Toyota on my right. I'm down here, in the parking garage underneath the TD Garden arena. It's cold.

The words of Edgar Allan Poe pop into my head. *You are not wrong who deem / That my days have been a dream . . .*

Am I dreaming?

And then another memory.

"Clocks," the Irishman had said to me at the door of the cabin, *"I need lots of clocks."*

"Patrick."

The Irishman's name was Patrick. We called him Paddy. He liked that.

I used to know this. I've tried for years to bring this name back to my mind but couldn't do it. Why does it make itself known to me now? Why here?

"Paddy," I say, and the Irishman's face doesn't strike fear into me the way the face of his partner once did. I can almost see him standing in front of me now, staring down at me between these parked cars, a mixture of curiosity and worry painting his expression. "Were we friends?"

"Were we?" he says, but his voice sounds different. Wrong somehow. Its pitch is higher than it should be, almost like a woman's voice.

"Are you okay, Little Man?"

"Patrick," I say, and suddenly I feel a great loss, a deep, unrelenting sorrow. "I'm sorry. I don't know why, but I'm so, so sorry." I'm sobbing and I can't stop. It feels somehow good to weep for Patrick. Or am I crying for me?

"Maybe you're sorry because you threatened to shoot me with this."

The Irishman is gone now—was he ever here? It is so real sometimes, this power of dreaming. In his place is Trudi Coffey, kneeling close beside me, holding out the Smith & Wesson 686 revolver. She sets the gun on the concrete by my feet.

"Do you know it's not loaded?" she says.

Yes, I know. It frightens me anyway.

"No matter," she continues. "Water under the bridge, right?"

I don't know what to say, so I don't say anything.

"All right," she says, and she settles down next to me, leaning her back against the side of the Toyota so she can stretch her legs and keep her eyes on me. "Why don't we start this over again. You know my name already. Want to tell me yours?"

From what seems like far away, I hear the elevator doors open and cheerful people walking out. *More will be coming*, I think. *The basketball game must be over, or almost over. Pretty soon this garage will be full of people.* I shake my head in disgust.

"Okay," she says, "no names. Want to tell me what this was all about? I'm headed back to Atlanta in the morning, but I'm here now, and I'm willing to listen."

The elevator dings again. More people exit. She ignores them, but I can't. I need to hide now. I need to disappear. But how will I do that without Mr. Hayes telling me what to do next? He's long gone by now, and Trudi Coffey was supposed to be the one to take his place. How can she help me if she's in Atlanta and I'm in Boston?

"I need a place to hide," I say. "People are looking for me. I need to get away from them."

"What kind of people?"

I shrug. I'm not sure exactly. I think everyone might be looking for me. How do I say that without sounding like a paranoid schizophrenic?

"You need to go to the police," she says. "Have you gone to the police?"

I shake my head. I don't know the exact reasons, but I don't think going to the police is a good idea.

"Mr. Hayes said not to trust police."

"Darrent Hayes is a terrorist. Of course he's going to say that. But you are not a terrorist. The police will help you."

"Why can't you help me?"

She sighs. "For starters, as I mentioned, I'm leaving tomorrow morning. Then there's that whole bit where you held me at gunpoint."

More people are coming into the garage. And now a few cars are lining up to leave as well. The smell of engine exhaust begins to mix with the cold air around us.

I'm out of time.

"So, for obvious reasons, I don't trust you," she continues. "I'm not about to take the risk of helping anyone I don't trust. Plus, you know, I've got a big problem of my own right now. I need to focus on that or someone I love could get hurt. May already be hurt."

"I can pay you. Mr. Hayes gave me money. I hid it, but I can get it and use that to pay you. How much do private detectives charge?"

She stands now, and I see disgust in her eyes and at the corners of her lips. "I don't want anything from Darrent Hayes except to see him behind bars. And as for you, go to the police. That's your best play in this situation, and it's my best professional advice as a private detective. Free of charge, so there's a bargain for you too. Go to the police. They'll help you."

I stand with her and nod. She hesitates, then sticks out her hand. "Until we're both in better circumstances," she says as a goodbye. I shake her hand and nod again. She turns to go, pausing just long enough to say, "Better get that gun out of sight. Don't want to scare any Celtics fans tonight."

I pocket the gun, left side of my coat again, and watch her walk away. She's out of sight quickly, gone, swallowed by groups of basketball fans who are jangling their keys and filling up the parking garage. More cars line up to exit, their exhaust burning the back of my throat and making me cough.

They go out in their warm cars, driving off to their warm homes. Tonight they'll sleep in their warm beds and never think twice about the lost man they left behind down here in the cold.

MONDAY

NOVEMBER 13

8

TRUDI

Atlanta, GA

Trudi Coffey was already tired when she arrived at the West Midtown office of Coffey & Hill Investigations. It was just a few minutes before eight o'clock in the morning, and she was wishing for the good old days back in college when she could down a strong cup of Red Eye coffee with a shot of espresso and not pay for it with headaches and insomnia later. She felt disappointingly middle-aged as she sipped on orange juice instead and turned the key to unlock her office door.

Coffey & Hill Investigations had been in this location for all seven years of its existence, something for which Trudi felt grateful. She liked spending her days as part of the strip mall community on this corner of Howell Mill Road and Ridgeway Avenue Northwest. She liked chatting with Annie the florist over in suite B1 and appreciated the convenience of the Kroger shopping center across the street—complete with Arby's and Taco Bell in the parking lot there. At least once a week she'd drop in on Tommy Ray over at the E. L. Pawn Shop, just to see what new treasures he'd brought in. She'd eaten her share of meals at FLIP Burger Boutique just down the road, had her hair done at Ambrosia Salon behind her building, and kept her business checking account nearby at the Bank of America branch office.

This spot on Howell Mill Road was a good place; it belonged to her, and she belonged to it. Being here made her feel at peace, reminded her that God plants little blessings in life if we take time to notice them.

She stepped through the small reception area of her office, walked down the short hallway, and passed the workroom/break room without a glance before stopping for a second to gaze into the empty office where Samuel Hill had once worked. She shook her head and headed back to her own sanctuary, the office where her desk, her books, her Beretta Tomcat, and her work waited patiently for her. She set down her orange juice, dropped a copy of the *Atlanta Journal-Constitution* onto her desk, and eased into her old, comfy chair.

She smiled despite the fatigue she felt. "Honey, I'm home," she said to no one.

It had been a long weekend, with little to show for it. Saturday had been taken up with getting from Boston's Logan International Airport to Atlanta's Hartfield-Jackson Airport. The problem was the pilot who'd figured it was okay to do a little morning drinking before coming to work. The delay in Boston while the airline called in a new pilot had caused Trudi to miss her connecting flight in Philly, which in turn bumped her to standby for later flights. In the end, she hadn't gotten home until late in the night.

She'd spent Sunday morning recovering from Saturday, and then she'd spent most of the afternoon and evening worrying about Samuel, trying to come up with a realistic plan for tracking him down. She couldn't dismiss the notion that he'd gone off the grid on his own, pursuing some random lead or working on some independent, clandestine effort. If that were the case, he'd be hard to find because he wouldn't want to be found. His years in the CIA had taught him well in that regard. Plus, Trudi had reasoned, it'd be a colossal waste of her time to search for a man who didn't need her to come looking for him.

At one point, late Sunday evening, she'd even convinced herself that her ex-husband was probably doing undercover work with the Atlanta Police. He was good at that, and he'd done it before. Maybe that was why the Zone 6 police staff had turned away FBI Agent Uribe with some cock-and-bull story about him having gone missing. They were just providing cover for their undercover op.

That had to be it.

She'd felt relieved at last and had gone to bed for some much-needed sleep, only to be awakened near midnight with the sinking realization that the whole "undercover operation" theory was just her own wishful thinking.

"Samuel would have told me," she said to the ceiling in the darkness. "Not that he was going undercover, just that he was going to be away for a while. That's what he's done every time since the Annabel Lee case, anytime he's going to be gone for a week or more. He knows I would worry."

And so she'd gotten up, gone to the attic office inside her cozy little home, skimmed the internet, wrote notes to herself, and tried to figure out where she should even start in order to find clues that would show where Samuel might have gone. It was close to 3:00 a.m. when the physics of exhaustion had finally sent her downstairs and back to bed. When the alarm went off at seven, she'd been tempted to exercise "self-employed prerogative" and roll over and go back to sleep. But nagging worry had pulled her out from under her covers and into her office anyway.

Now in her own chair, at her own desk, back where she belonged, she felt a mild surge of new energy run through her tired bones. She flipped open the *Journal-Constitution* and, at the same time, noticed a little pink carnation carefully placed in a paper cup and positioned cheerfully beside her desk phone. The note read, "Welcome back, Boss! Saved you some birthday cake—in the break room fridge."

She gulped down the rest of her orange juice and decided that stale cake for breakfast sounded just right. A few minutes later, she was licking chocolate icing off the corners of her mouth and, as was her custom, reading the classified ads section of the *Journal-Constitution*.

It had been more than two weeks since Trudi had been able to do this morning ritual, and she realized again today how much she depended on it. She had to do it, she knew, the way an obsessive-compulsive person had to arrange food on their plate according to color. But she also knew she wanted to do it, even though others were doing the same thing.

Trudi scanned the personal ads until a familiar advertisement came into view. It was only one line, one word actually, easy to miss, but it was there nonetheless:

Safe.

She let out a sigh and said a little prayer of thanks.

With that taken care of, Trudi's next order of business was to call Captain Stepp over at the Zone 6 Police Department. She checked her watch and remembered that, according to Samuel, the captain usually didn't roll into the station house until around ten o'clock, preferring to work into the evenings rather than come in earlier. "Not a morning person," Samuel had said with a smile. "Trust me, we're all happier this way."

Since she couldn't call the captain for a few more hours, she decided to dive into the work that had piled up in her absence. She started by checking the stack of phone messages Eulalie had left on her desk, then she opened her email client, and before she knew it, Trudi was lost in the familiar comfort of mundane office work. When she looked up again, it was eleven thirty and her stomach was growling.

She peered at the calendar and did a little calculation. Mondays this semester, Eulalie's class schedule at Georgia State ran until noon, which meant she wouldn't arrive at Coffey & Hill Investigations until one o'clock. "Too long to wait for lunch," she told herself. "And besides, FLIP Burger is on the way to the Zone 6 Police Department. Easier to talk to Captain Stepp in person anyway."

She was already mentally composing her to-go order as she locked the front door of Coffey & Hill Investigations.

At twelve fifteen, Trudi walked through the front doors of the Zone 6 Police Department headquarters, still savoring the aftertaste of a turkey burger with crushed avocado and pomegranate ketchup.

The first thing she always noticed inside the Zone 6 building was the smell, something like a mixture of stale air freshener, light body odor, and millions of Freon-soaked dust mites. She loved it. Like her office, it felt like someplace she could belong.

She stepped up to the reception counter and found the officer on duty speaking into a telephone. He nodded at her in recognition, but for the life of her, Trudi couldn't remember the young man's name. She tried to find a nameplate but couldn't see one. She gave up and just nodded back, pretending she recognized him too.

"Mm-hmm, yes, sir," he said into the phone. "Yes, well,

actually—yes, sir." He looked up at Trudi and smiled. "Actually, sir, she just walked in the door."

Trudi wasn't expecting that.

"I don't know, sir. Yes, I'm sure." He covered the receiver and mouthed to Trudi, "One second, Ms. Coffey." Then back into the phone he said, "Right. Yes, sir, I'll tell her."

He hung up the phone and stood, extending his palm for a handshake. "Thanks for coming, Ms. Coffey. Wow, you got here fast! Captain Stepp said to tell you he'll be right down and that you should wait for him over there." He motioned to a row of seats along the west wall.

"He's expecting me?" Trudi was still a little thrown by the reception she was receiving.

"Well, he was expecting you to call, but he sounded glad that you came by instead. He'll be out right away."

"Okay," Trudi said. *What's that all about?* she wondered. *How did he know I was going to call him?*

She heard her cell phone buzz in her purse, checked it, and saw a call had been forwarded to her voicemail from her office telephone. She listened to the message and the Captain Stepp mystery was solved. Not five minutes ago, he had called her, said it was important, and asked that she get in touch with him as soon as possible. The fact that she'd shown up in person only minutes later was just a convenient coincidence for everyone.

Trudi sat down to wait and then felt an uncomfortable tickle in her stomach. Why did meeting with Samuel's boss always make her feel nervous? And why was Captain Stepp suddenly trying to get in touch with her? She tamped down her worries and decided to let this situation play out in its own time instead of trying to predict what was going to happen.

It was only about five minutes before Captain Rexallen A. Stepp sauntered into the waiting area. He was an Atlanta native, a descendant of plantation slaves, proud of his heritage and his hometown. Like most of his plainclothes detectives, he wore a basic blue suit, a white shirt, and a matching blue tie. He was in his fifties but still thick and bullish in appearance. He'd managed to avoid the donut shop, so while his stomach wasn't exactly flat, it didn't pooch out like a spare tire either. The top of his round head was bald and ringed by a fringe that horseshoed his scalp with thin, graying hair. He looked both distinguished and formidable at the same time. He gave a tight smile when he saw Trudi stand to greet him.

"Thanks for coming on such short notice, Trudi. Were you already in the neighborhood?" he said, shaking her hand. He didn't wait for her to respond. "I probably should have called you sooner, but I heard you were out of town being a movie star or something."

"No problem, Rex," she said. "I wasn't exactly a movie star, but yeah, I did go up to Boston for a consulting gig on a movie set. Best vacation I've had in a while."

He tilted his head quizzically. "You were in Boston? Did Detective Hill go with you?"

"No. Was he supposed to?"

Captain Stepp furrowed his brow but didn't say anything.

"What's this about, Rex? Is it Samuel? I was just going to reach out to you when you called me. I think—"

"Not here," he said.

He took a step away and motioned for her to follow. He didn't look back when he passed through a side door and disappeared.

"Right," Trudi muttered to nobody. "No idea what's going on, so I guess I'll just follow the bald man into the dark room. What could go wrong?"

She hesitated just a second, then grabbed her purse and followed the captain.

9

TRUDI

Atlanta, GA

A moment later, Trudi and Captain Stepp were both settling into a small interview room off the main lobby. Trudi knew everything said in this room was videotaped and recorded for security reasons.

"All right," she said after they sat down. "Why don't you tell me what you know."

Captain Stepp favored her with that tight smile again. "Actually," he said, "it'd be better if you told me what you know first. I can't tell you everything I know, but it may be that you already know some of what I know, and then we can talk freely about the things that both you know and I know."

"Did you have to say 'I know and you know' so much, Rex? That sounds like pretty convoluted thinking."

"I know." He gave a small chuckle. "How do you think I've managed to stick around so long as a law enforcement bureaucrat in this city?"

"Where's Samuel?" She decided to get to the point.

"I was hoping you'd know the answer to that question," he said.

"What's that supposed to mean?"

"It means I don't know where your ex-husband is, Trudi, and I'm very interested in changing that fact. When was your last contact with him?"

"Been about a month," she said. "He came by my office in October, wanted to borrow a book."

"Which one?"

"*Complete Tales and Poems of Edgar Allan Poe.*"

"'A Dream within a Dream'? That poem?"

Trudi felt a little confused, but she pressed forward. "Well, sure, I guess. I mean, yes, that poem is in there. But I think he wanted 'The Raven.' I'd guess he was just doing some follow-up on that case since Max Roman's trial is set to begin soon."

"No," Captain Stepp said while nodding slightly, something Trudi saw as a strange juxtaposition of words and actions. *Disguising his true emotions. Doesn't want to communicate too much to me. He's always been hard to read.* "He would've wanted 'A Dream within a Dream.' Why not just get it at the library? Or find it online?"

She shrugged. "Sentimentality? He gave me the book as a present once."

"Probably he just wanted an excuse to drop by and see you," Stepp said matter-of-factly. "A pretty woman can have that kind of effect on a man."

Trudi didn't know whether to blush or say thank you for the offhanded compliment. She opted to ignore it. "All right, then. So why would he want that particular poem?"

The captain squinted in her direction. "You don't know?"

"No."

"Then I can't tell you what I know."

"Not that again. Can we stop with the you-know-I-know-you-know rhetoric?"

He smiled again, an authentic one this time. Trudi remembered why she liked this man, despite his guarded manner and occasional gruffness. The smile. When he smiled a real smile, she felt like she knew him, and he trusted her knowing of him. That kept her coming back, and she suspected that was why Samuel kept working for him.

"All right," he said, "I'll try."

He sat impassively, waiting for her to continue the conversation. Trudi decided to take a chance.

"How about if we do this, then," she said. "I'll start saying names, and you tell me whatever you can about the names I say."

"Shoot."

"Okay. Tama Uribe."

"FBI," he said, and she couldn't help noticing that his nose wrinkled slightly at the mention of her name. "Art crimes team, last I heard. Spent the early part of her career working under Bob Wittman out of the Philadelphia office. I think they were thick as thieves working together on the investigation into the art heist at the Isabella Stewart Gardner Museum. I know Bob really wanted to solve that one, but he retired in 2008, and I haven't really kept up on Agent Uribe since then."

"Gardner Museum heist? Believe it or not, that was part of the plot for the movie that just hired me as a consulting detective."

"That's interesting, but I don't see that your side job as a movie consultant is relevant to Detective Hill's disappearance at this point. Now, why are you asking about Agent Uribe?"

"You don't know?" He shook his head, and Trudi couldn't help grinning. "Then I can't tell you what I know since you don't know what I know."

Captain Stepp let out a legitimate laugh—a short, staccato burst that came and went quickly but had been there nonetheless. Trudi felt a childlike sense of accomplishment.

"No, but seriously," she said, "I don't know exactly what Tama Uribe has to do with anything. I met her under, um, unique circumstances when I was in Boston—"

"Why was she in Boston? I thought she was based in Philadelphia."

"I . . . well, she said she was looking for Samuel."

Captain Stepp leaned back in his chair, thoughtful. "And did she find Samuel? Had she seen him?"

"Okay, listen, Rex, obviously everybody thinks Samuel went to Boston for some reason. Agent Uribe thought so, you think so." She leaned forward in her chair. She couldn't tell if she was pleading now, or demanding, but either way she said, "Why don't you just tell me what Samuel was doing up there. Why he didn't tell me he was going. He knew I was headed to Boston for two weeks."

The detective studied her face for a moment before replying.

"All right, Trudi," he said. He settled back in his chair, folded his hands across his lap, and spoke. "Samuel said he was going to Boston. I don't know why. He didn't tell me that. He just came into my office on October 26, told me he needed a few days off, that it was a family emergency and he was going whether I gave him the time off or not. So I gave him three days off. As I understand it, he left the next morning, October 27. He said three days was all the time he'd need, but it's been over two weeks now and I can't locate my third-best detective despite all my best efforts. That can't be a good thing."

Trudi let that information sink in.

Her first thought was that her ex-husband would be galled to hear his captain call him "third-best." Samuel always insisted on being number one, no matter what the situation. That competitive fire was great if you were, say, playing doubles tennis with him, but it could also be really irritating if you were just trying to enjoy a relaxing double-date game night at a friend's house.

Still, Captain Stepp was right about one thing. If Samuel had said he only needed three days and then dropped out of sight for two weeks, there was no way that was a good thing.

Family emergency? she thought.

Inside, she felt a stone sink from her heart down to the bottom of her gut. If he wasn't talking about her, then there was one other woman he was thinking about. The *other* woman.

Part of Trudi, the part that remembered fresh pain from past sins, wanted to get up, walk away, and forget the whole mess. If Samuel had gone back to Saudi Arabia to see his wife, why should she care?

In her mind's eye, she saw a picture of a beautiful little boy. His face was cherubic, with tinted skin that reminded her of a freshly baked pumpkin loaf. His eyes were a light chestnut color, with slivers of dark pigment flaked within. He had long lashes, a chubby little jowl, and a delighted smile. She'd only seen this picture once, the face of Samuel's Arabic son, the fruit of his affair with that woman he'd met while on assignment in the Middle East some years ago. In the photo, the child wore a square headcloth, red and white pattern, with a double circle of black cord. He was looking up at someone, arms reaching out as if to receive a gift, or like he was asking to be lifted into his mother's arms. His mother, who was not Trudi Sara Coffey.

He would've turned seven in October, she remembered. She still didn't know his name and wasn't sure she ever would. She didn't know if she wanted to.

The boy's mother was a Saudi woman. Samuel had married his Arabic lover to protect her from archaic, brutal punishments prescribed for adulterers under Sharia law. She and her son were the reason Trudi's marriage had crumbled like overcooked wafers five years ago.

Well, in all fairness, she told herself, *the pig's lusty failure killed our marriage. He could have said no, but he made that choice anyway. Apparently, she didn't know he was married, though who knows if that would've made a difference? Samuel can be very charming in the right circumstances.* Still, it was hard not to blame the Saudi temptress, hard not to resent the fact that Samuel's beautiful little boy was that woman's child, not Trudi's.

To his credit, Captain Stepp didn't press while Trudi processed his information. He just sat in his chair, arms perpetually folded across his lap, waiting.

It made sense, Trudi reasoned, that if Samuel thought his wife and son were in danger, he'd go running back to Saudi Arabia to protect them. That was who he was, always the knight in shining armor, always the hero who saved the day, no matter the cost.

"Wait a minute," she said out loud, both to herself and to Captain Stepp. "You said Samuel went to Boston, right?"

"Yes. That can be verified."

"Agent Uribe also said he'd been seen up there," she said. *So if he was going back to Saudi Arabia, why make a pit stop in Boston?*

"That's good to know. Helpful."

"What about the no-fly order?" she said. "Didn't the CIA put him on a no-fly list?"

Captain Stepp nodded slowly, not really following Trudi's line of thinking. "Yes," he said, "an international no-fly order. He can't leave the country, but he is free to fly within the continental United States. Why?"

Is Boston a gateway to the Middle East? she thought. *Hardly.*

She felt her mind racing through possibilities. If he can't fly out of the country, would he try to sneak out? Maybe, but that kind of operation would take time to set up, and Samuel hadn't had that kind of time.

"Family emergency, he said?"

Captain Stepp nodded.

"Rex, here in the United States, I'm the only family Samuel Hill has. Did he think I was going to be in danger up there in Boston?"

"Trudi, your name never came up once."

She nodded. "All right, then. I have one more name to ask you about."

"Let's hear it."

"Dream."

10

TRUDI

Atlanta, GA

Trudi heard a car horn blare behind her and had to admit she hated it when distracted drivers paid more attention to their cell phones than they did to the road right in front of them. That didn't stop her from dialing, though she did take her foot off the brake and ease into the intersection before the green light changed back to red.

It was nearly one thirty in the afternoon, and Trudi needed to be two places at once right now. "That's why I have an assistant," she'd told herself just before calling the office.

"Coffey & Hill Investigations," Eulalie chirped brightly. "How may I help you?"

The sound of Eulalie's voice made Trudi cringe, briefly, with guilt. *Stuck for hours in the Boston airport*, she chastised herself, *and I still forget to bring home a birthday gift for my assistant? I am the worst boss ever.*

"Eulalie," she said, "how was class this morning?"

"Oh, hey, Boss. Class was the same as usual. Lots of boring lectures about psychoanalytical theories and psychotic acting out in a therapeutic setting. But by this time next May, all those boring lectures will add up to a master's degree in cognitive sciences and psychology for Terrence Jefferson's baby girl, so there is that."

"Then it's on to the PhD program, right?"

She heard her assistant groan. "You had to remind me of that, didn't you? I'm never going to finish school, am I, Boss?"

Trudi laughed despite herself. "Well, here's something to take your mind off psychology homework. I need to know all there is to know about the Gardner Museum art theft of 1990."

"Working some more on that movie?"

"No, this is just for me. Pull up what you can on the internet—I think the museum itself has a dedicated section on its website. I need a one-page, just-the-facts info sheet on my desk before I get back to the office."

She tapped her car's turn signal and rolled into a parking lot at 2900 Peachtree Road.

"Will do. When are you coming back here?"

Trudi found a parking spot near the front doors, then checked the clock on her dashboard. "I should be there by two fifteen. Give or take."

"Wait, you want me to compile all there is to know about the Gardner heist, organize it into bullet-point format, and have it waiting on your desk in"—there was a pause while Eulalie did a calculation in her head—"forty-two minutes?"

"Yep. Why do you ask?"

"No reason. Listen, Trudi, been great talking to you, but I really need to get off the phone now. My boss doesn't like me taking personal calls at the office."

"You're the best, Eula. Remind me to do something nice for you soon."

"No worries, Boss. I'm sure my birthday present from Boston will more than make up for it. Did you like the cake?"

"Cake was great," Trudi said, cringing again at the thought of the nonexistent birthday present. "Now get to work, you loafer."

"Already on it, Boss."

She hung up to the sound of Eulalie's fingers tapping on a keyboard. "I really should give that girl a raise," she muttered. "Or at least a birthday present."

Trudi breezed through the broad entrance to the bookstore and stopped just long enough to ask a clerk, "Edgar Allan Poe?" The worker walked her all the way back to a case in the literature section where two rows of Poe editions and other poetry filled the shelves.

When she'd left the Zone 6 Police Department fifteen minutes ago, Trudi was wishing she hadn't loaned Samuel her collectible copy of the *Complete Tales and Poems of Edgar Allan Poe*. She could have just gone back to her office and found what she needed. But now that she was in the bookstore, pulling a thick paperback copy of the same book off the shelf, she was glad she'd stopped here.

Been too long since I sat inside a bookstore, reading, she thought. Despite everything going on—or maybe because of everything going on—it felt nice, like a calm before a storm.

She found an inviting leather chair situated in a back corner and claimed it as her own. After checking the contents, she flipped to page 967, where she read:

> Take this kiss upon the brow!
> And, in parting from you now,
> Thus much let me avow—
> You are not wrong, who deem
> That my days have been a dream;

Yet if Hope has flown away
In a night, or in a day,
In a vision, or in none,
Is it therefore the less gone?
All that we see or seem
Is but a dream within a dream.

I stand amid the roar
Of a surf-tormented shore,
And I hold within my hand
Grains of the golden sand—
How few! yet how they creep
Through my fingers to the deep,
While I weep—while I weep!
O God! can I not grasp
Them with a tighter clasp?
O God! can I not save
One from the pitiless wave?
Is all that we see or seem
But a dream within a dream?

"'But a dream within a dream,'" Trudi whispered the last line of the poem to herself. "Is this poem why they call him The Dream? And if so, what makes it so important to him that he would take it as his name?"

She'd hoped to find some new clue, some hint to lead her forward in the search for Samuel, but Poe's poetry seemed to be just that—poetry. Pretty words written long ago. Still, she wasn't ready to give up completely on this lead. She ran through a mental rerun of the last part of her interview with Rexallen Stepp at the Zone 6 Police Department.

"I have one more name to ask you about," she'd said.

"Let's hear it."

"Dream."

When she'd said that name, Captain Stepp had reacted physically.

"Where did you hear that name?" he asked, leaning forward, elbows on the table across from her.

"Agent Uribe," she said. "In Boston."

"That makes sense," he said. "She would be interested in him."

So, The Dream is a man. That was a start at least.

"Why?" she pressed.

Captain Stepp shook his head. "Classified. Can't tell you. Sorry."

"You can't tell me anything? Come on, Rex. I know his name. Just tell me who he is."

He shook his head again but asked, "Did she think Dream was still in Boston? That would be surprising, but it would explain why she was there."

Trudi was tempted to say, "I can't tell you. It's classified." But instead, she said, "Uribe didn't know. She thought Samuel would know. Or that I would know." A pause. "Hey, Rex, why does the FBI think I would know the whereabouts of a man I've never heard of, a man who calls himself, of all things, The Dream?"

"They probably know you're an Edgar Allan Poe expert, as well as a detective. Would make sense."

"Why? What does Poe have to do with anything?"

He started to say something, then stopped himself. He stood up, signaling that the time for their meeting had come to an end.

"Trudi," he said, "you've been very helpful. I'm sorry I haven't reciprocated as much as you want me to. But you keep looking for Samuel, and I'll keep looking for Samuel. I promise to keep you in the loop if I find anything relevant. You promise me the same?"

She promised.

"Okay, then." They shook hands, then by way of parting,

he said, "I will tell you this. Agent Tama Uribe has spent the bulk of her career following leads related to the 1990 Gardner Museum art heist. She's relentless about it."

"And?" Trudi said.

"I'm just saying, she's very interested in the Gardner Museum heist. Some say she's obsessed with it. You understand my meaning?"

"No."

Captain Stepp just grinned at that point. "You're a detective, Trudi. You'll figure it out."

Now Trudi closed the paperback copy of *The Complete Tales and Poems of Edgar Allan Poe* and carried the book to the register. She paid cash for it, knowing she was buying a duplicate of a book she already owned. She justified it by saying this would be her reader's copy while the other would be what it was supposed to be—a protected collector's copy. Plus, she figured as long as Samuel had the collector's edition, she was going to need something to refer to whenever she felt the need. Sure, the internet contained the complete works of Edgar Allan Poe—accessible twenty-four hours a day.

Sometimes a girl just needs a good book in her hands, she told herself. She was okay with that.

11
TRUDI

Atlanta, GA

Eulalie was waiting at the reception desk when Trudi got back to the office. It was two nineteen in the afternoon.

"Hi, Boss," Eulalie said. She was young and effortlessly pretty, with creamy brown skin, milk chocolate–colored eyes, and a head full of thick, dark, bouncy ringlets, about shoulder-length. Trudi had felt young and pretty like that once, though not so much anymore. She wished she'd appreciated it more when she'd had it.

Eulalie spotted the Barnes & Noble bag in Trudi's hand and pointed to it with a smile. "Is that my birthday present? Ooh, I love good books, and you always pick out the best in literature."

Trudi tried not to blush in embarrassment. "No, I, uh, forgot and left your present at home. Sorry! I'll bring it tomorrow." *Must remember to buy a birthday present for Eula tonight.* "This is just . . ." She pulled out the paperback and showed it to her assistant.

Eulalie's head tilted to the side, a question on her lips. "Don't you already have that one?"

"Yes, of course," Trudi said.

"Of course," Eulalie echoed, as if that settled it, but her eyes still held the question.

"I mean, yes, I have a collector's copy. This is a reader's copy."

"Of course," Eulalie said again.

"And besides, Samuel has my original. He borrowed it a few weeks ago and never brought it back."

"Mm-hmm."

"Anyway. Did you get what I asked for? The Gardner Museum info?"

"On your desk."

"You are good, Eulalie Jefferson. I'm going to be sad when you grow up, get your PhD, and move on to a real life."

The assistant dimpled. "Ah, you're just saying that because you forgot my birthday present."

What? Trudi felt mild panic. *Did she figure me out already? I have been training her to be a detective . . .*

"At your house," she continued. "You said you left it at your house, right?"

"Right. Yes. It's at my house. Nothing big, just a little something to let you know I think you're an important part of this agency."

"I'm sure I'll love it." She dimpled again.

"Okay." Trudi figured it was time to change the subject. "Do I have any appointments this afternoon?"

"Nope. You said to keep today clear in case you needed a little extra time to catch up after your trip."

"Okay."

"And I want to hear all about life on a movie set sooner or later. Did you have a good time?"

"Yeah, it was great. I'll tell you all about it, but for now I've got some work to do. I'll be in my office if anybody needs me."

"Got it."

Trudi went back to her sanctuary and found, just as Eulalie had said, a one-sheet summary of the basic facts of the Gardner Museum art heist of 1990. She skimmed the sheet. She'd looked up a lot of this information before heading out to be a movie consultant, but now one item on the list suddenly looked conspicuous.

"Five million–dollar reward," she said out loud, "for the return of the stolen Gardner Museum paintings."

She set down the info sheet and tapped her fingernail on the desk.

"There are a lot of people who would do almost anything for five million dollars."

She opened the Poe paperback again and reread page 967.

"But what does Edgar Allan Poe's poem have to do with a five million–dollar art theft reward? Unless . . ."

She stood up, grabbed a pencil, and paced around her desk for a moment. She felt frustrated, like she should be seeing something obvious, but she'd left her glasses at home. Thinking out loud often helped her work through a problem, so she started talking to herself.

"A dream," she said. "No, The Dream." She began unconsciously tapping the pencil on her thumb. "And the Gardner Museum. And Samuel gone missing. And five million dollars."

Don't forget Darrent Hayes, she told herself. *Could he have something to do with this? He knows Samuel's been hunting for him. Maybe he decided to make a preemptive strike?*

She heard a buzz on the intercom, followed by Eulalie's voice.

"Ms. Coffey," her assistant said, "there's a cavalier gentleman here, asking if you might have time to squeeze him into your schedule today."

Trudi threw the pencil to the ground and jumped across her desk. She slid open the top drawer on the right side and yanked out her Beretta Tomcat. She tried to sound calm as she spoke into the intercom.

"Certainly," she said. "Tell him I'll be right out."

Trudi knew she only had a moment or so to assess the situation. She leaned down to view the small video monitor situated under her desk, hidden on the left side. She was grateful for Eulalie's composure under pressure—and that her assistant had remembered the warning code.

"If there's a threat in the waiting area," Trudi had taught her, "tell me that someone 'cavalier' is asking for me. You know, a 'cavalier young lady' or a 'cavalier gentleman.' Something like that. I'll answer using the word *certainly*. For instance, 'That's certainly interesting, I'll be there in a minute.' When I say *certainly*, that's how you know I've gotten your message. Then just wait for me. Don't do anything until I get there. Got it?"

Trudi had instituted this code warning after the Annabel Lee case, when a maniacal goon had managed to take both her and her ex-husband hostage for a short time. Now she was glad she'd been careful to plan for this kind of contingency.

On the video monitor, the one-room reception area of Coffey & Hill Investigations was in full view. Eulalie was sitting calmly, both hands lying flat on the surface of her desk. The Cavalier Gentleman was pacing a bit but seemed comfortable with the situation, as if he'd done this kind of thing more than once.

He was pale white, definitely a minority here in the racially diverse city of Atlanta. "Pilgrim stock," she whispered to herself. "Out-of-towner maybe?" She checked the clip on her Beretta, just in case. The visitor wasn't young—she guessed somewhere in his forties—but he was solid, with a body shape that was reminiscent of a block of ice. He wore tan pants and a gray suede jacket, zipped all the way up to his chin.

Judging by the stainless-steel barrel and rosewood grip, Trudi pegged his gun as a Colt Combat Unit series handgun. "Magazine capacity of eight bullets. More than enough to do serious damage in here."

The Cavalier Gentleman seemed like he was starting to get impatient, so Trudi tapped the intercom. "On my way out." She tried to sound bright and unaware. She reached over to the button on the underside of her desk, on the right side, and pressed it hard. She checked the clock. *Three-oh-three exactly*, she noted.

She stuffed her Beretta into the back waistband of her jeans, took a deep breath, and walked down the short hall toward the reception area.

12

TRUDI

Atlanta, GA

Trudi hesitated in the hallway long enough to sneak into the little break room just outside her office. A moment later she appeared in the doorway to the reception area holding two cups of coffee and wearing a friendly smile. The phone rang, but no one seemed to notice.

"Thanks for stopping by," she said casually. Then she pretended to see the Colt Combat handgun for the first time. She nodded toward the gun as it swung in her direction. "Oh, I guess this isn't a social visit?"

"Trudi Coffey?" The Cavalier Gentleman said her name like it was an insult. The phone stopped ringing.

Trudi took a step into the reception room, deliberately avoiding eye contact with Eulalie. She sipped out of one of the paper coffee cups.

"You're from Boston, right? I can tell by the accent." She took another casual step forward. "I doubt that gun is necessary. I just came back from Boston. Lovely city."

The man shoved a fist into his left jacket pocket and came out with a small photograph. He glared at the photo, then back at Trudi.

"Trudi Coffey." He said her name as identification this time, apparently confirmed by what he saw in the picture. The phone rang again.

"You know," she said, "when a strange man from Boston points a gun at your heart and says a name, you usually have two choices. You can deny everything, tell him you don't know nothin' 'bout no Trudi Coffey, and hope he leaves it at that. Or you can say, 'Yeah, I'm Trudi Coffey. Why don't you put that gun down and come back to my office so we can talk about whatever it is that's bothering you?'" She sighed theatrically. "I think I'll try option two this time. So, yeah, I'm Trudi Coffey."

"You talk too much," he grunted. The phone rolled into voicemail.

You're an ugly troll, she wanted to say. Instead, she held out a cup and said, "Coffee?"

He waved the gun toward her. "You're coming with me," he said.

"Sure," Trudi said, shuffling still closer to the gunman, "just let me grab my coat."

She motioned toward an empty rack near the entrance to Coffey & Hill Investigations but never turned her gaze away from the Cavalier Gentleman's eyes. When she saw them flick in the direction where she'd pointed, she didn't hesitate.

The first cup of coffee she sprayed directly up his flared nostrils, knowing that the hot liquid would burn his breath away and splash angrily into both his eyes. Before he could even scream, she'd smashed the second cup squarely into the man's throat, causing hot coffee to pour down inside his coat while he choked for air from the blow. His arms flew inward, instinctively clutching toward his pain.

Trudi ignored the burning splash of coffee on her hands and instead pressed forward, slipping inside his flailing arms and ramming her right shoulder into his chest. His gun hand came right to her, loose and trembling. She used both hands to snap his right wrist back until his fingers fully released the Colt. When the back of his head cracked against the wall, she thought he might already be unconscious, but just to be sure, she delivered a hook across his jaw. His weight sagged, and then his body fell to the floor.

There was no blood, but the carpet, the wall, and her clothes were now a mess of coffee stains. *Should've known better than to wear my third-favorite blouse today*, she thought. Then she noticed her left hand was red and swollen. She glanced over at Eulalie and saw her wide-eyed assistant staring.

"Eula?" she said, holding up her left hand.

"Right. Sorry. Just, wow, you move so fast. I knew what was coming, and I still couldn't see it all happening, even when it was happening right in front of my face."

"Don't know if you're aware of this, Assistant, but hot coffee stings like acid on bare skin."

"No, yeah, I'm on it. Sorry!" She jumped to her feet and headed to the break room.

"Bring me some handcuffs too!" Trudi shouted after her.

She heard a snort and a groan and saw that the stranger was regaining consciousness. She reached out and scooped up his gun, then yanked on the man's ankles to pull him toward the middle of the room until he lay flat on the floor. When he started to roll to his side, she kicked him, hard, in the ribs.

"Don't move, and I might let you breathe a little longer." He started to curse at her, so she kicked him again, with her heel this time, hard enough to knock the wind out of him. “See, this is why I always wear boots,” she said. “Now, I dare you to move again.”

He coughed for breath, then let his head and shoulders drop back to the floor. His lips were already blistering, and his face and neck were bright with red, splotchy spots forming on his skin. Trudi almost felt sorry for him. Almost.

Eulalie returned with an ice pack and a pair of handcuffs. Trudi gripped the ice in her left hand and felt instantly better.

“Name,” she said to the man.

He called her a bad word.

“Eula,” she said, “looks like our guest needs another cup of coffee.”

“No.” He coughed. “No. My name is William O’Shaughnessy.”

“Fine. Roll over, Billy Boy. It’s time for my assistant to apply your handcuffs.”

The man complied, still working at recapturing his breath and grimacing at the burns on his neck and cheeks. After Eulalie had the cuffs on, Trudi allowed the stranger to slump into a chair in the waiting area. She unzipped his jacket and slapped the ice pack onto his neck, motioning for him to keep it in place with his chin.

“How much time do I have left, Eula?” Trudi said, never taking her eyes off O’Shaughnessy.

“It was three-oh-six when the security company called the second time,” she said.

“What?” The stranger’s voice sounded a bit strangled still.

“Please,” Trudi said. She exaggerated an eye roll for his benefit. “Did you think you were the first goon with a gun to storm into my office? Or that we didn’t have a silent alarm that alerted our security company that something was wrong?”

William O’Shaughnessy looked like he was going to curse again, this time at himself instead of Trudi.

"Security company procedure is to call twice to assess the situation. No answer on our end? That means they called the police at what, three-oh-seven or three-oh-eight?"

"Sounds right," Eulalie said. "Figure anywhere from eight to fifteen minutes for the blues to get here, depending on where the nearest squad car was at the time of the call."

Trudi checked the clock. It was three sixteen. "All right, Billy," she said, "you're going to jail anytime between now and three twenty-three this afternoon. I'm guessing it won't be your first visit. So, you want to tell me what this was all about? Or should I just wait until the cops sweat it out of you?"

O'Shaughnessy said nothing. Trudi took a chance.

"Does this have anything to do with The Dream?"

The man's eyes lit up with interest.

"Okay," he said, his Boston accent warming with a co-conspiratorial tint. Trudi let the syllables wash through her mind and found she didn't have much trouble understanding what he had to say, even with his swollen tongue doing the talking. "Look. I came in all wrong. I see that now. Should've just come in talking. With respect. I get it. My profuse apologies to you and your pretty assistant there."

Inside, Trudi rolled her eyes again, but outside, she just tapped the Colt Combat handgun against her thigh and said, "Time's running out, Billy Boy."

"Just tell me where he is. That's all I came for anyway. I can make it worth your while."

"Well," Trudi said, "I'm already keeping your gun. Don't have a Colt. It'll be a nice addition to my collection."

"Keep the gun. I've got a dozen just like it. What I don't have is the location of The Dream. Tell me that, and nobody bothers you ever again."

A dozen questions formed in Trudi's mind, but the one that

came out of her mouth was, "Why would I know where The Dream is?"

"That's you in the picture with him, right?" He nodded toward the photograph, now slightly crumpled, stained with brown liquid, and lying on the carpet. Eulalie walked over and picked it up. "We have friends inside the TD Garden arena, and they don't mind sharing surveillance video from time to time."

Eulalie handed Trudi the picture. She saw herself in the image, all right, standing inside an elevator next to a short, nervous-looking Hispanic man. She wanted to strangle somebody, mostly herself. *So you're The Dream*, she thought, studying the image. *Everybody's looking for you, and you come directly to me. Why are you so important?*

"Don't know The Dream," she said, "let alone where he is."

"Right." O'Shaughnessy snorted. "And you two just happened to meet at a Celtics game last week, purely by accident."

"I stand in lots of elevators with lots of strangers. Everybody does. Doesn't mean I know those strangers or their secret hideouts."

Trudi heard the faint whine of sirens in the distance. She passed the picture back to her assistant and decided to try a new topic.

"What do you know about Samuel Hill?" she said.

"Couldn't find him neither. That's why we came looking for you."

"Who is 'we'? Who're you working for? And what does Samuel Hill have to do with The Dream?"

O'Shaughnessy ignored her questions and instead shot furtive glances at the front entrance. She could see him getting antsy now that the sirens were getting closer. She positioned herself between the visitor and the door and brought the Colt into clear view between them. *Don't want him entertaining ideas of running*, she thought.

The Bostonian let the ice pack drop into his lap.

"Tell you what," he said breathlessly. "Let me go before the cops get here. You got a back door, right? You can leave the cuffs on me, just let me go. I'll meet you in an hour, anyplace you like. I'll bring ten thousand dollars for you, and you bring the address of The Dream for me. Everybody wins, right?"

"No."

"Twenty thousand."

"Tempting. But no."

"Fifty grand. Cash. Clear and tax free."

"Eulalie, open the front door," she said. "I believe our friends are here."

William O'Shaughnessy closed his eyes and sighed.

13

TRUDI

Atlanta, GA

"I miss Daylight Savings Time," Trudi grumbled to the front porch of her home.

Her cell phone told her it was only six twenty-eight in the evening, yet darkness was already in full bloom in her neighborhood. Two weeks ago she still would've had almost half an hour until sunset, and she missed that little half hour. Instead, porch lights dotted Center Street Northwest like giant amber fireflies arranged in neat rows, telling her body it was late when it wasn't even quite time for dinner.

"How is it the middle of the night already, when it's only six twenty-eight?"

She slid a key into the dead-bolt lock and pushed her way inside. After locking the door behind her, she paused to exhale, drop her things on the floor, and then let herself flop onto the couch. *Police reports always give me a headache*, she thought. *But Tylenol is all the way in the kitchen, and right now I just want to lie here and not think about anything.*

Her brain refused to cooperate, though. She tapped a button on her cell phone and spoke into the microphone. "Copy surveillance video from the office and email it to Officer Hummel by noon," she reminded herself. She ended the voice memo, then hesitated and started it again. "And find Samuel."

That last memo wasn't a necessity, she knew, but it gave her an outlet for the growing frustration that continued to gnaw, unseen, inside her.

The past few hours had been both busy and boring at the same time. In her observation, the thing that happened most at a police station was waiting. If someone could find a way to tax the time spent waiting on police personnel to gather the right forms, take down the relevant information, arrange witnesses in the right rooms, and so on, well, that would probably wipe out the federal deficit in record time.

Still, she wanted William O'Shaughnessy safely behind bars, and it was generally a wise idea for a private detective to stay on good terms with the local police department, so she bit her tongue and let the staff at Atlanta's Zone 5 Police Station do their jobs without complaint. Now, three hours or so later, she stared at the walls of her comfy little West Midtown home.

Ten years, she thought. It had been just over ten years ago when she and Samuel had bought this place. "Our 'first' home," she told herself ruefully. Who knew it would also be their last?

Trudi pushed herself up and went into the kitchen. She found the Tylenol in the junk drawer and then opened the refrigerator to find something to wash it down with. Orange juice would do just fine. She unscrewed the cap and then hesitated. She always hesitated—even though Samuel wasn't around to chide her about drinking straight from the container. Just to spite him, she downed a swig from the OJ bottle. Then she put it back in the refrigerator and closed the door.

Days like this, she hated coming home. Work was easier. It kept her busy, and there was less quiet.

The old pine floors creaked as she walked back over to the couch and sat down. She thought about watching TV or reading or turning on some music. But that felt like too much effort. The white couch seemed to suck her into it.

She looked over at the kitchen doorway clad in old white-painted trim and thought about food. Maybe cook something? Or maybe just a salad or a can of soup? Then she noticed the built-in niche of shelves in the dining area next to the kitchen and remembered the weekend she and Samuel had built it. It'd turned out much better than Trudi had thought it would, especially since Samuel had tickled her side while she'd tried to brush on the final coat of glossy white paint.

With a sigh, she rested back against the arm of the couch.

Why don't I just sell this house? she thought. But she knew she wouldn't. She'd never say it out loud, but she still loved the place.

A knock at the front door brought Trudi to full alert.

She grabbed her phone off the ottoman and tapped the application for the camera on the front porch.

It was the woman from the basketball game. Tama Uribe, FBI art crimes team. Why was this woman here, now?

Trudi brought up the camera at the side of the house to make sure Chucky the Leprechaun wasn't snooping around while Agent Uribe distracted her. Nothing on the right side of the house, and nothing on the left. Triggered by a motion sensor, the light on the back porch flashed on. Trudi switched to the backyard camera. "Ah, there you are, Chucky," she whispered to herself, "lurking in my backyard." She watched as he rattled the door to the shed. It was locked with a padlock, but he was able to pull the door open just a bit and used the light from his phone to peek inside.

Did he think Samuel was hiding in the shed?

Another knock, much louder, pulled Trudi's attention back to the front of the house. "Come on, Ms. Coffey," Uribe spoke through the door. "You know we saw you go in."

Trudi considered just not answering, but she knew Agent Uribe wouldn't be so easily put off. After all, she'd followed her all the way down to Atlanta from Boston.

Trudi grunted. She pushed herself up to her feet and walked over to the entryway.

She unbolted the door and opened it. "What a pleasure to see you again." She smiled. "What was it, Agent Udell? Udeh?"

Uribe smiled that same shark-like smile.

Trudi stepped back to allow her inside. Then she closed and bolted the door, keeping the FBI agent and her partner separated. Uribe walked into the little living room.

Trudi stood in front of her. "What can I do for you?"

"Just figured I'd stop by to see if you've heard from your husband yet." Trudi followed the woman's eyes as they cataloged everything in the living room.

"Ex-husband," Trudi corrected. "I'm not sure why you think I'd hear from him, or care to hear from him."

"I know you do keep in touch."

"You're FBI, so I can guess how you'd know that. But why would you want to know that?"

Agent Uribe shifted a couple of steps to the side, looking around the living room until her eyes rested on the black spiral staircase in the corner. She craned her neck, trying to see up to the finished attic space. "I told you why it's so urgent I get in touch with him."

Trudi stepped in front of her and cut her off. "No, you didn't. You just said you need to talk to him."

"I said he may be in trouble."

That made Trudi's heart tighten. "If he's in trouble, why isn't his 'alphabet' helping him? Why would the FBI be involved?"

"You want to discuss jurisdictional issues?" Uribe looked to her right, past the entry, toward the guest bedroom.

"He's not here," Trudi said. "You can stop nosing around. Oh, and Chucky won't find him in the backyard either."

Uribe raised an eyebrow and nodded. "Samuel is involved in something in which I specialize."

"Something to do with art? Why in the world would that be so dangerous?"

"Classified."

Trudi smirked. "I hate to burst your bubble, but the kinds of things Samuel is usually involved in are not related to art."

"I hate to be rude, but you are just a private detective. There are many things you don't know."

"Enlighten me."

"I'd love to, but like I said, classified." Uribe glanced over Trudi's shoulder toward the doorway to the kitchen and dining area beyond.

"And yet you keep looking around as if you think I've got Gustav Klimt's *Woman in Gold* decorating my kitchen." She watched Uribe carefully, trying to decipher her.

Uribe smiled but said nothing.

Yeah, Trudi thought, *she definitely thinks I'm hiding Samuel.* Whatever was going on, Samuel was in deep for Uribe to be this desperate to find him.

"Samuel has more connections overseas than here," Trudi said. "He may not be as helpful as you think."

"He has plenty of connections in the US."

So, whatever's going on is in the States. "He's a police officer now. Art theft isn't a big problem for the Atlanta PD."

"Obviously, your husband is much more connected than a hometown PI like you is allowed to know."

Is she trying to make me feel inferior? Nice try. It sounded like whatever Uribe was interested in was related to CIA, not Atlanta PD. "Like I said, he's my *ex*-husband. I don't much care what he's involved in."

"Yes, of course." Agent Uribe went on, "Nevertheless, you need to provide me whatever information you have."

"And why is that?"

"Have you ever been arrested for hindering an official FBI investigation?"

She didn't actually say it was an official investigation. Slick choice of words. Now it was Trudi's turn to smile. "Tell me, Tama"—she emphasized the woman's first name—"why exactly is the FBI so desperately in need of help from a 'hometown PI' like me?"

Uribe's jaw tightened. "Just checking up on every possible lead."

"You followed me all the way down from Boston. Obviously, the FBI is pretty desperate. Or is it just you who is so desperate?"

Agent Uribe started to say something but was interrupted by a knock at the back door. She looked over Trudi's shoulder toward the back of the house.

"Chucky's getting impatient," Trudi said. Then she added, "You're pretty fast to flash the badge, but he isn't. Perhaps he doesn't have one?"

Uribe didn't answer.

"What a shame. I hope he doesn't feel like a lowly, hometown PI without that shiny little piece of jewelry."

Uribe took a step toward the back door.

Trudi cut her off. "Where do you think you're going?"

14
TRUDI

Atlanta, GA

Trudi parked outside the Inman Station Townhomes. It was only about an hour after she'd walked up to her own front door, but now it was even darker outside. The townhome she approached had no lights on inside, though she was sure motion-sensor cameras were hidden in the shrubbery and the tree hovering around the second-floor wooden balcony.

No one was in sight. She sat on the wooden bench on the tiny front patio, mostly hidden from view behind the tree and shrubbery.

A few minutes later, a little Kia pulled up next to Trudi's car, and Eulalie got out. "What's with all the spy stuff?"

"Long story," Trudi said. "You made sure no blue Impalas followed you here?"

"No creepy, fashion-challenged blue cars followed me here."

"Good. Thanks for coming. I owe you an extra day off."

"Just the birthday present will do."

Guilt rattled inside Trudi. She took out a nylon wallet from her back jeans pocket. "Keep an eye out for me." She knelt in front of the door.

Eula leaned against the post, where she could watch the parking lot and also partially block Trudi from view. "Whose house is this, anyway?"

Trudi took two small metal tools from the wallet and rattled them in the lock. "Samuel's."

Eula looked over with a raised eyebrow.

"No psycho ex-wife stuff, I promise." Trudi went back to picking the lock.

Eula laughed.

She had the door open in less than a minute.

Trudi walked in, flipped on a light switch, and closed the door behind Eula. Trudi had never been inside Samuel's new place. He'd invited her over once after the Annabel Lee case, promising handcrafted artisan pizza from a recipe he'd picked up in Tuscany. But she'd made some lame excuse, and he'd gotten the hint.

Trudi took in a deep breath of stale air and scanned the room. She replayed the last hour in her head.

The knocking on the back door of Trudi's little house had become even more aggressive, like pounding. Agent Uribe had shifted, trying to get around Trudi.

Trudi had stayed firmly planted between the FBI agent and the back door. She'd pointed toward the front of the house. "You can leave the way you came."

Uribe smiled. "And leave poor Charlie outside?"

The back door rattled then. *No way is Chucky getting in through that door*, she thought. Samuel had had it reinforced with steel. Trudi had wondered about all the extra security at the time—but that was before she'd found out he was CIA.

The two women were now almost nose-to-nose.

"Are you really sure you want to get in my way?" Uribe said. Her breath was hot and short, her eyes beginning a slow burn.

"Definitely."

There was a pause. And then . . .

Uribe slowly backed up. "It's not wise to make enemies of the FBI." She turned, unbolted the front door, and walked out.

Trudi let her muscles relax, then bolted the door behind the agent. Through the peephole she saw Uribe and Chucky get into an unmarked, dark-blue Chevy Impala and drive away.

"All right, Tru-Bear," she said to herself, "it's time to find your missing husband." She rolled her eyes as she corrected herself. "Ex-husband."

She called Eulalie on the way to her car.

Now Trudi turned a circle in Samuel's living room, taking in the furnishings, trying to think like the man she'd once loved. Samuel's place was very different from the home they'd shared together. She walked through the kitchen to a large open living space with twenty-foot ceilings and exposed ductwork. To the left were two staircases, each starting from the center of the left wall and going up in opposite directions. One went to what looked like a loft above the pool table room in the back of the house, and she assumed the other staircase led to the master bedroom, the only fully enclosed room in the place. On the wall opposite the staircases sat a comfortable-looking sectional couch that would have fit nicely in a La-Z-Boy gallery in the eighties. She imagined Samuel falling asleep there while watching a football game on the TV awkwardly positioned by the stairs.

The thing that most struck her was the scent of the place, that naturally lingering perfume of a person. She hadn't realized how much she missed that.

"So, whatcha want help with, Boss?" Eula was still standing in the kitchen.

"I'm hoping to find anything Samuel might be hiding here, something that might give a clue as to where he disappeared to. I need some of that profiling skill of yours."

"I didn't think you were worried about him."

"I'm starting to be," Trudi admitted. "He doesn't usually disappear without telling me first."

"But this isn't the first time he's disappeared?"

Trudi hesitated.

"It's not uncommon for CIA operatives to go on long assignments," Eula said.

Trudi raised an eyebrow. She'd never told Eula about his being CIA, and she was sure Samuel never had either. He'd only told her—his wife—because she'd about beaten it out of him.

"He's working PD right now," Eula said, "but I'd assumed that was just in between assignments, or maybe he's laying low for a while."

Trudi didn't deny it. She needed Eula's help, and the more she knew, the better she could profile. "He's supposed to stay in the country."

Eula turned and stood at the front door, surveying the kitchen like an artist who sees more in a painting than the brushstrokes. "Okay, tell me about him."

"You wrote a paper about him, 'Law Enforcement Personalities,' or something. Don't you already know all about him?"

"Most of what he told me was straight out of a textbook. I've seen enough to know it wasn't really him. He doesn't show who he is on the surface."

"Is that how you figured out he's not just PD?"

"Part of it. I figured he was a government agent of some kind. CIA was an educated guess."

"And I just confirmed it for you."

Eula grinned.

Trudi smiled and shook her head. "I'm glad you're on my side."

Eula gave a mini bow.

"Well, he's always been a risk-taker," Trudi said. "He seems to think he's impervious to harm."

"Type T personality. Kinda figured that one."

"He seems careless on the surface," Trudi said. "But he's actually intelligent and calculating. I think he lets people think he's careless, and maybe even a little dumb, so he can hide behind it."

"And mask his actual plans and motivations."

"Exactly." He reminded Trudi of Percy from one of her favorite books, *The Scarlet Pimpernel.*

Eula nodded slowly and looked around the kitchen. "Mmm . . ."

"Not the freezer or the oven," Trudi said. "Samuel isn't that amateur." She climbed up onto the granite counter and flashed the light on her phone into the vent above the peninsula. Clean.

Eula got down on the floor and checked under the stove and refrigerator. "Nothing but dust bunnies."

A soffit was above the cabinets, so nothing was up there. As Trudi looked through his cabinets, it started to bother her that she was going through his things. The generic peanut butter he liked to put on toast—it had to be melty. The All Season he liked to put on steak, burgers, pretty much any kind of meat. She didn't like feeling as though she was invading his privacy. She would be mad if he did this to her. But if he didn't like it, he shouldn't have disappeared on her like this.

They didn't find anything in the kitchen, so they moved on to the living room. Trudi paused to consider. There was a shelf under the nearest staircase, but she didn't think he'd put anything of interest there. It would be too easy to find—simply tip the shelf to dump everything across the floor. Next to the other staircase was stereo equipment and the TV. She ejected the Blu-ray disc slot but found nothing.

Eula sat in the middle of the sectional. "He's a 'sit in the middle of the couch and take up the whole thing' kind of guy, isn't he?"

"Definitely."

Eula slipped her right hand between the cushions and pulled out a black, metal handle. She pressed the button on the side, and a spear point blade shot out of the handle.

"Very handy, Samuel," Trudi muttered.

A knock at the front door made them both pause.

Trudi walked back through the kitchen to the front door. There was no peephole, and if she peeked out the blinds, whoever was at the door would know someone was in here. If she had access to Samuel's cameras, she could bring up the feed from the front patio.

Another knock.

She decided to risk it and peeked out the blinds. A woman in slippers and a flowered housecoat was standing on the front porch, half-leaned over a cane. Her skin was such a deep color that Trudi could barely see her features in the dark. Then the woman looked at the window and smiled.

Eula came back to the kitchen and stood by the refrigerator, behind the front door.

Trudi took a good look around the parking lot. All the cars were the same ones that had been there when she arrived. No dark-blue Impalas.

After turning the dead bolt, Trudi opened the door. "Good evening."

Still smiling, the woman glanced past Trudi and into the townhouse. "Is Samuel home?"

"Do you live next door?"

"Two doors down. Samuel is always nice enough to help me carry my groceries inside. I haven't seen him for a while. I was hoping he was home so I could give him his payment—fresh-made ambrosia salad."

"When's the last time you saw him?" Trudi asked.

Though she continued smiling, the woman hesitated to answer.

"I'm sorry, I forgot to introduce myself," Trudi said. "I'm Trudi, a really old friend of Samuel's."

"Oh! You're Trudi. It's nice to meet you." She extended her left hand, the hand not holding her cane.

Trudi shook her hand, surprised at how strong her grip was. "Nice to meet you too, ma'am." Then she added, "Do you mind telling me when you last saw Samuel?"

The woman hesitated again.

"I haven't heard from him," Trudi said, "and I'm starting to worry."

"Ex-wives generally don't mind when they don't hear from their ex-husbands."

"You have an excellent point." Trudi sighed. "But he doesn't usually just disappear without warning. He's probably fine, but he is still my friend and I worry."

"Worry enough to break into his house?"

Trudi suspected the woman had seen her pick the lock, though Trudi had thought they'd been hidden pretty well by the tree and shrubbery. This woman was sharp. "Yes, ma'am."

The woman smiled. "An honest answer. Samuel was right about you."

The corner of Trudi's mouth pulled up. "And now you believe I'm who I say I am."

"Can't be too careful."

"I agree." Trudi added, "Now, will you tell me when you saw him last?"

"I don't remember the date, but a good couple of weeks."

"Did he say anything that sticks out to you, or did he seem stressed?"

"No. He was his normal ornery self."

"Ornery is a nice way to put it."

"I always taught my babies to be nice." The woman shifted back a step. "Well, I'll leave you to your snooping. I do hope you find something useful."

"Thank you, ma'am."

The woman turned and slowly hobbled out with her cane.

Trudi closed the door, and they continued their searching.

Trudi walked back through the living space to the room with a pool table and back wall covered in raw corrugated metal. She looked through the built-in shelves to the right. Then she turned toward the pool table, suddenly interested. *Samuel isn't much of a pool player*, she told herself. Maybe he was renting the place furnished? She walked around the table and noticed a glint somewhere among the triangle of balls set up at one end. She lifted the nine ball out of the middle and found a small, silver key underneath. It was beat up and a little rusty at the top.

Eula stood quickly from her investigation of the area under the pool table. "What's that?"

Trudi smirked.

"Maybe there's a lockbox somewhere." Eula glanced over at the shelves.

"He's had this little trinket forever, since I've known him. He used to keep it in his nightstand drawer. He'd tell me it was from his childhood—one time it was to the lock for his old bike chain. Next time, it was to his cash box for his lawn-mowing money."

"Do you think maybe it's nothing but a distraction?"

"Like he hid it someplace that appeared like he was trying to hide it, but he was really taunting someone to find it?"

"Then the burglar or enemy spy or whoever would waste a bunch of time trying to figure out what the key unlocked."

"Yeah, that sounds like him." *Very nice, Samuel.*

"Wow," Eula said.

Carefully, Trudi set the key back down and dropped the nine ball into place.

Upstairs, Eula checked the guest bedroom.

Trudi took the other set of stairs, toward the front of the house. It was another bedroom, larger. There was a king-size bed to the right and a closet and bathroom to the left. The dark gray walls made the room feel intimate.

She paused in the doorway to consider.

Finally, she glanced up at the ceiling, at the metal rafters. She tilted her head. *That's it, Samuel,* she thought, *isn't it?*

Next to Samuel's bed, she slipped off her boots and stepped up onto the mattress. The rafters were still a couple of feet above her head. Tae kwon do had helped her to be pretty good at jumping . . . for a chick. She bent her knees, sprang, and grabbed the rafter on her first try. Holding her weight with her right hand, she felt the flat surface of the metal with her left. Nothing. She shifted a couple of feet, now directly over Samuel's pillow. That's when she felt it.

She grabbed the stack with her left hand and dropped down onto the bed. It was a handful of pictures.

"All right, Samuel," she said out loud. "What's so important about a few photos that made you think they should be hidden?"

She sat cross-legged in the middle of the mattress and flipped through the pictures. The first was a shot of a little boy with golden skin and a bright smile—the kind of smile a child saves for the daddy he doesn't get to see very often.

Trudi sighed.

There were so many reasons for the sadness saturating her that she couldn't quite identify them all.

She set that picture down next to her and looked at the next one. A smile curved her lips, and then it fell like a little girl stumbling.

The picture showed Samuel in a traditional black tuxedo and Trudi in a long, white lace dress. He was placing the wedding ring on her finger, and they gazed at each other with the most perfect trust and happiness. It was the happiest Trudi could remember having ever felt.

She put that picture to the side. Facedown.

She did that with three more pictures, all from their wedding. The next one was a little different, but it hurt just as much. It was of Trudi smiling at the camera, on the verge of laughing. From the trees in the background, it looked like the shot was from one of the times Samuel had stolen her away for a picnic. Her hand started to curve into a fist, but before she crumpled the picture, she set it facedown with the others.

Eula stood in the doorway. "There's nothing in the other bedroom. I don't think he uses it." Then she added, "I'll let you do this room by yourself."

Trudi looked over. "Thanks for all your help."

"I'm sorry we didn't find anything more useful."

Trudi shrugged. "It was a long shot." Samuel had always been careful when it came to the secrecy of his work. After all, how many years had he been able to hide his profession from her? All while living under the same roof.

Eula went back down the stairs and left.

That was all the pictures—nothing that could help her find Samuel. And she was confident there was nothing else to find in this place. *Thanks for making this as difficult as possible, Samuel,* she thought. *Pig.*

She had no more ideas and no energy to think.

Exhaustion seemed to overwhelm her. She lay back on the bed, on Samuel's pillow, intending to rest for just a few minutes. But she was out before she realized she was starting to doze.

What felt like a short time later, maybe an hour, she bolted upright, still on Samuel's bed. She'd woken from the feeling of knowing she wasn't alone.

"It's been a while since I had a woman in my bed." Samuel was seated in the chair in the corner, elbows on the armrests. "I almost forgot how peaceful you look when you're asleep."

TUESDAY

NOVEMBER 14

15

DREAM

Jacksonville, FL

I try to focus on cleaning the breakfast dishes, but I can't help but hear them in the next room. I almost wish my mother hadn't taught me Spanish—if I spoke only English, I wouldn't understand.

"How he talks," one of the men grumbles. "He thinks he's better than us."

My Spanish is not a Mexican accent, but an accent of someone from Spain. My mother and I didn't know the difference when we were learning the language.

"He doesn't have any pride in his heritage. What was that he made for breakfast?" The same voice adds, "He can't even make guacamole."

I stop washing the dishes and look out the window at the cars flying by on Interstate 95. If I let my vision blur, I can almost see the water under Monet's *Floating Studio*, just smudges of color.

"How long do we have to keep him?" one of my roommates asks.

"Until his friend stops paying the rent."

I hope to hear from Mr. Hill soon. He said he'd be back for me, but he didn't say how long that would be. And what will happen then? I'm not sure what to think of Mr. Hill. He seems personable, but there's something not totally serious about him and yet a little too serious. He reminds me of someone I met before—completely different but a little similar . . .

"Electricity does not move through a wire," I mumble, "but through a field around a wire."

"What're you talking about?" One of my roommates has come into the kitchen.

I stay turned away, focused on the blurry cars.

"*Te crees muy muy*," one of them says. "Let's go. We'll pick up some decent breakfast on the way to work."

I try to ignore their insults. Part of me wishes to be in that parking garage in Boston still. I think back, trying to remember everything Mr. Hill had told me.

Trudi Coffey had walked away from me, and I had sat there on the freezing concrete. The cold had seeped into me until I started shivering. Or maybe I'd been shivering the whole time. People wearing lots of bright green walked by and stared at me. I didn't want to think of how I'd failed, of what Mr. Hayes had said could happen to me if I failed.

"The dot over the letter *i* is called a tittle."

"Hey, buddy, get outta here."

"Didaskaleinophobia is the fear of going to school."

"What? I said get outta here. This is my car."

"Just leave him alone, Brad." It was a female voice now. "Give me the keys. I can scoot over to the wheel from the passenger seat." A rattling sound.

I flinched. The sound—it was like the keys the guards at the hospital carried.

I squeezed my eyes closed. I didn't want to remember that. "An ostrich's eye is bigger than its brain."

And then I looked around and everyone was gone—no cars, no people. I wasn't sure if I'd fallen asleep or if I'd just lost the time somewhere. I felt like the Salvador Dali painting *The Persistence of Memory*. My time and my mind warped and wrapped around ledges and tree branches.

I couldn't feel my fingers or my toes or my butt. There was no place else for me to go. I didn't know anyone. Mr. Hayes had told me to get Trudi Coffey to help me, but I'd failed. There was no other plan. And so I sat there.

The garage was quiet, so quiet.

I had no place to go. Maybe I should have started walking. Maybe that could have been safer. But maybe if I had stayed there, Mr. Hayes would have come.

My stomach had finally stopped grumbling at me. It must've given up hope.

"Excuse me, sir."

I didn't look up.

Footsteps moved closer, and black boots came into my field of vision. "Hey." The voice was sterner. "You need to leave. There's no loitering here."

"I don't know where to go."

"Well, you can't stay here."

I wish I had Kevin to talk to.

No, I'm not crazy.

I watched the boot kick my shoe, but I didn't feel it.

I tried to get up, to run away, but I stumbled back down onto my numb butt. I tried to grab the concrete column to pull myself up. My feet wouldn't work. I fell onto my knees, and pain shot through me like a fish being speared.

"Are you drunk?" the man asked. A security guard maybe?

"I don't drink." I kept trying to get up, but my feet wouldn't work.

"Drug addict, then."

Anger flushed through me. "No." Feeling started to return to my feet, the splintering pain of body parts awakening.

"Stop wasting my time," the man said. "Get going."

Hugging the column, I managed to get to my feet. I couldn't get steady enough to walk.

He pushed at my arm. "Move!"

"Hey!" Another male voice echoed through the garage. A tall man with a strong build walked up. His stern demeanor relaxed, and he smiled at me. "How's it going?"

"Who're you?" the security guard asked.

I finally managed to get steady enough that I could look at the guard properly. He was thick like the other man, but not in a muscular way. *Security* was printed in yellow letters across his cheap nylon jacket. The uniform looked familiar. I remembered wearing something like that before.

The new man flashed a gold, shiny badge. He slipped it back into his breast pocket before I could read the print on it. "I'll take it from here," he said to the security guard.

The guard hesitated.

"This man is a witness in a major crime," the new man said. "You can either be that guy who helped with the front-page bust, or you can lose your license for hindering an investigation."

I kept my mouth shut and let the new man talk. But part of me worried he could be more trouble for me than the security guard.

"You just need to get him outta here," the guard said.

"That's the plan." The new man smiled at the guard. "I need to get him to a safe house."

"All right. Just move quick."

The new man kept smiling while he watched the guard turn and walk away. "Rent-a-cop," he muttered. Then he turned to me. "And what're we going to do with you?"

"Who're you?" My feet were reasonably steady under me now, as good as they were likely to get.

"Hill," he said. "Samuel Hill." His eyes twinkled as if he was laughing at a private joke.

Mr. Hayes had told me his name. *Maybe he can help me?*

He reached to shake my hand. "And I hear your name is Dream?"

"That's what people call me."

"How'd you get a name like that?"

That answer would make me think of my mother, so I didn't answer.

"Well," Mr. Hill said, "the question remains—what're we going to do with you?"

"How do you know who I am?"

"Got a call."

"From who?"

"Don't know." He shrugged. "But I think you might be useful."

"How?"

"Don't know that yet either."

Talking to Mr. Hill made my head hurt.

"Tell you what," Mr. Hill said. "Let's go get something to eat, and we can figure out how useful you are."

I hesitated. It wasn't as if I had any better options, so I followed him toward a car. He opened the passenger door and let me sit.

"Where're we going?" I asked when he took the driver's seat next to me.

"Let's see who's open for breakfast around here." He took his phone out of his breast pocket.

"No place public."

"Food is usually served in public places. And I need some coffee." Then he looked at me more closely. "You're afraid. Of someone in particular?"

"I'm not sure." More accurately, *I don't know if I can trust you yet.*

He smiled a little. "Look, you've seen I can deal with people pretty darn well. Plus, I know how to use a gun . . . and hold on to it." He took my revolver out of his waistband.

I felt my eyes go a little wider. I was both agitated at having lost my one weapon and relieved.

He kept smiling as he slipped the gun back into his waistband and then put the car in gear. I didn't object any further.

On Canal Street, he led me into a coffee shop in a brick building. He ordered, and we sat at a table in the back.

He sipped his coffee. "So, is Dream your real name?"

"No." After carefully inspecting it, I took a bite of my feta and spinach croissant. My stomach pain returned. I kept eating to try to appease it.

"When's the last time you ate?" Mr. Hill asked.

I finished my food and wiped my mouth. "I ate a candy bar from the motel vending machine yesterday."

He raised an eyebrow. Then he leaned closer, elbows on the table. "So, why would someone think you could be valuable to me? Are you connected to someone? What kind of work do you do?"

"I paint."

"That's what you do for a living?"

"No."

"Can you help me out a little here?"

"Who are you? What're you trying to do?"

He nodded. "Fair question. To be honest, I can't tell you a whole lot. I guess it all comes down to that I want to make sure my family is taken care of."

I was pretty sure I knew what he was getting at, but I wasn't sure if I should trust him. *He has a badge*, I reminded myself. But he'd also lied to that security guard, with an impressive amount of ease.

"Do you know anything about the Irish mob?" I asked.

"Not a ton, but I can get information. Is that who's after you, why you don't want to be seen in public?"

I nodded.

"I can protect you."

"How?"

He leaned closer and spoke more quietly. "Let's just say I have connections." He cocked his chin. "If I can be persuaded to use them."

I paused as I looked at him, at how serious he was for once. Finally, I said, "I need help remembering."

16

TRUDI

Atlanta, GA

"Samuel!" Trudi jumped up from the bed. "Where have you been?"

"Oh, here and there."

She crossed her arms and scowled at him. Then she glanced at the spot on the bed where she'd laid the pictures. They were gone.

"Everything is fine, Tru-Bear. It's nice to see you, but you can go home now."

"Have you bumped your pretty little head?" she asked. "Concussion make you lose your memory, or your hearing? Where have you been? People have been asking." She slipped on her boots.

"I'm asking you nicely. Please go home and let it go."

"I don't even know what I'm supposed to let go." She threw her hands up. "What's going on?"

"It has nothing to do with you."

"Well, I seem to be getting dragged into it." She sighed. Then she moved closer and felt her expression soften. "You're still my friend, Samuel."

He paused, barely noticeable. "I just need to watch my back right now. It's nothing new. But I don't want you getting involved."

"Why do you need to watch your back? You haven't been working any nasty cases lately." Then she thought about her conversation with Uribe. "You're back working for the CIA."

"Go home, Trudi."

She set her hands on her hips.

He stood from the chair and was now just in front of her. She had to look up.

"Maybe you can intimidate perps or terrorists or the occasional used car salesman," she said, "but it doesn't work on me, cowboy."

He rested his hands on her upper arms. She shook him off. He walked around her and toward the bedroom door. He was halfway down the steps before she followed.

"Where're you going?" she demanded.

He kept walking.

"Samuel."

He made it to the landing, and she grabbed his hand to put him in a hammer lock, his arm wrenched behind his back.

Looking at her over his shoulder, he said, "I'm impressed." Then he shifted his weight and muscled out of the lock, though she still had a hold of his hand.

Close to his side, she pulled his arm into a gooseneck lock, with his elbow pressed to her chest, his arm tightly bent, and both her hands clamped down on his wrist, making it almost touch his forearm.

With his free hand, he pushed up hard on his palm. As he pulled out of the grip, he twisted his hand to wrap around her wrist to put her in an arm bar.

But she rotated her hand and pulled up for a simple wrist release. "Are you having fun, Samuel?"

"Little bit," he admitted, and she saw the amusement in his eyes.

She pushed at his chest, and he stepped back, against the wall. "You're playing with me," she said. "You were going to tell me the whole time, weren't you?" That was why he'd sat in the chair and waited for her to wake up rather than getting what he came for and leaving her there.

"I didn't expect to find you here in my bed. But who am I to pass up a convenient opportunity?"

She pushed at his chest again, and he laughed.

"Okay, fun's over," she said. "Tell me what's going on."

"I'll tell you as much as I can."

"No, you'll tell me everything."

"You don't have clearance."

"You've kept a lot of secrets from me over the years. You owe me this one small thing."

"Wow, I'm impressed. That's high-level manipulation right there."

"No, it's the truth."

He took a resolved breath, and the amusement seeped out of his eyes. "I've made an enemy of the wrong Arabic family. It was bound to happen sooner or later."

"You haven't been working the Middle East for a while." Then she raised her eyebrows. "You're talking about Samir Sadeq Hamza al-Sadr. The lowlife who helped Dr. Smith try to kidnap Annabel."

"In my line of work, I have enemies. It's not surprising."

"His family is trying to kill you, aren't they? That's why you disappeared."

"I just need to watch my back until we figure out a way to neutralize them."

"You know darn well there's no neutralizing them. They're incredibly powerful and connected, and they don't forget a grudge." After they'd gotten back from Alabama, she'd researched the family, just in case. Then she added, "They blame you for killing Samir, don't they? You didn't kill him. I did."

"The circumstances killed him. Truck trusted me to ensure Annabel's safety, and that's what I did, while utilizing whatever connections I needed to. It lays on my head."

"That's not how it went, Samuel. I'm not your lackey. I acted on my own, not on your orders."

"Do you really think that family is going to lay the blame on a woman? They don't think women have the ability, or the right, to act on their own. You did the right thing—merciful, even—in finishing him off. He would've tortured and killed you if he could, and he would've handed Annabel over to Smith and she would've died too."

"I know it was the right thing, but it still remains that you didn't kill him."

His eyes deadened. "I would've killed him. For hurting you. And I wouldn't have been as merciful."

There were a few seconds of silence between them.

Then her forehead furrowed in confusion. "If it's Samir's family who's coming after you, why did a man named O'Shaughnessy come to my office looking for you?"

A deep grumbling sounded outside, a large truck on the main road.

Samuel glanced toward the front door. "We should get out of here. I took a chance coming back here at all."

"Go to the office?"

"There's a safe house in Atlanta. I'd like you to stay there for a while."

So, that was why he'd stuck around and waited for her to wake.

He'd *wanted* her to push him hard to tell her what was going on just to make her more nervous—and more likely to go to a safe house. "Yeah, that's not gonna happen."

He sighed. "I don't want to draw any more attention to you. We're fairly certain the al-Sadr clan doesn't have anyone in the country yet, but I don't want to take any chances. There's a restaurant down the street that should still be open, corner of Edgewood and Hurt."

"Okay. I'll meet you there." Trudi turned and headed toward the door.

Samuel peered out the kitchen blinds.

Trudi reached for the door handle but then stopped and turned to face Samuel. "Don't try ditching me."

"You don't trust me?"

"Depends on the day."

"Is it an every-other-day kind of schedule?"

"Leap year and the thirty-first of November." She walked outside.

Samuel followed.

She noticed his car was different—a Honda Accord, not his silver Ford GT. A rental car maybe?

A few minutes later, they parked along the road. The place was an old, one-story, white-brick storefront. The Edgewood side of the building was tree-lined and pleasant; the Hurt Street side had no trees, and the band of grass along the road was patchy, mostly dirt. Inside at the bar, Samuel positioned himself at the end, where he could watch the exits.

The bartender—a tall, big-boned woman—walked over. "What can I get you to drink, sweetie?"

"Just a Sprite, please," Trudi said.

"Me too," Samuel said.

She was sure he wanted something harder but was too concerned with keeping his wits about him.

"Who's O'Shaughnessy?" Trudi asked as soon as the bartender walked away. The place wasn't crowded, and the music was a little on the loud side. She was confident no one would overhear anything important.

"Will you please at least consider the safe house?"

"I thought I was just a stupid female and not of any concern."

"That doesn't mean they wouldn't use you against me. I haven't exactly concealed how I feel about you."

"We're divorced."

"And yet I chose to live in the same city as you, and my home isn't far from yours."

There were a few seconds of silence. The bartender delivered the drinks.

"I'll be careful," Trudi said. "But I'm not going to a safe house."

Samuel sighed. "Will you at least consider it, Tru-Bear?"

Trudi paused. "If I'm hidden away, I can't help you. No, I will not consider it." Then she asked again, "Who is O'Shaughnessy?"

"O'Shaughnessy isn't connected to the al-Sadr clan. He's involved in something else I'm working on."

"Why in the world are you working on something else when you have your own butt to cover right now? That's ridiculous. Someone else needs to handle whatever else it is you're working on."

"It's not something I'm going to pass off."

"It's something to do with a friend of yours, or at least someone you feel responsible for. Isn't it?"

"It's someone I feel responsible for." He kept his voice low. "It's a long story, but he's in trouble with the Irish mob. I have him stashed in Jacksonville, but only for a few days. It's not safe."

She kept her voice low as well and barely moved her lips. "You can't possibly deal with al-Sadr *and* the Irish mob. You're going to get yourself killed."

"What do you want me to do? I don't trust anyone else."

She paused, carefully reading him. "Do you trust me?"

17

TRUDI

Atlanta, GA

Trudi knew Samuel was manipulating her. Even as she drove her car down Moreland Avenue with him in the passenger seat. Whatever his reason for protecting this person from the Irish mob, it had to be important, and perhaps she could help get this one thing off his plate. The likelihood of his getting himself killed would drop from nearly 100 percent to maybe 50.

"You should sleep," Samuel said. "I'll drive."

She merged onto I-675 South. "Who's Agent Uribe?"

"Who?"

She looked over to see if she could decipher if he was being honest. "FBI. She's asked me twice now where you are."

"What've you told her?"

"I didn't know anything to tell her."

"Are you sure she didn't follow you to my place?"

She smirked. "Do you know who she is?"

"All I can say is I doubt she's doing anything officially."

"She said she's from the art crimes team."

"Who in the world would think I'm involved with art crimes? Not exactly my repertoire."

"That's what I said. But she seems pretty sure of herself."

"I don't know." He shook his head. "Maybe al-Sadr has someone on the inside. We don't really know."

She wasn't done talking about Uribe, but she was even more concerned about al-Sadr. "You're with the CIA. How can they not know?"

"You've researched the family. You've probably started to see how deeply embedded they are."

"Embedded in what?" She glanced behind her and changed lanes.

"Most major organizations."

She glanced at him. "You think they have ties in the US, don't you?"

"We're not entirely sure." Then he went on. "Are you sure you don't want me to drive for a while? It's a long haul."

"What about this guy who's in trouble with the Irish mob? How'd he get in trouble with them?"

"That's actually something I'm hoping you can help with."

She glanced over at him. Headlights from a passing car flashed across his face.

"I think he has PTSD. Large chunks of his memory are gone, chunks that I need."

"What exactly do you need from him?"

"Wish I knew. All I know is he has information I need. I think he's willing to help, but he can't in his current state."

"Wait a second . . . What does this guy look like?"

"Mexican, short, splotchy facial hair, kind of a meek way about him, like he's scared of his own shadow."

"Little Man," she murmured. *The Dream.*

"What?"

She sighed. "I think I may have already met him."

"Are you having delusions now too?"

"Shut up. Did he have a Smith & Wesson revolver in his left coat pocket? Did he blurt out random facts for no apparent reason?"

"Yeah. How'd you know all that?"

"I met him in the parking garage at TD Garden."

"What were you doing at TD Garden?"

"Keep on topic here. The guy I met seemed kind of crazy."

"PTSD."

"Can it get that bad?"

"I've seen worse."

"Do you really think you can get him fully, you know, with it?"

"I think you can."

"Are you serious? Last time I saw him, I threatened to kick him."

"Am I correct to assume he flashed the Smith & Wesson at you? Your threat was warranted."

Do other divorced couples talk about guns and threats not *in reference to each other?* Trudi wondered. "Still, that wasn't a great introduction. There's no way he's going to feel comfortable with me."

"Sure he will." Samuel settled back into the passenger seat, as if ready to take a nap. "Just pull out that sweet charm of yours."

"This is me we're talking about, Samuel, your *ex-wife*."

He grinned. "Exactly."

She rolled her eyes. "No better options, huh?"

"You remember that time we were investigating that cheating husband, Barley or Barclay?"

"Barkley."

"Right. Remember the guy pulled a gun on me, and you

took him down from behind, a kick to the knee, I think. Then I pinned him to the ground and disarmed him, and you started talking to him like my ninth-grade algebra teacher. You gave him a rundown of everything he'd messed up and why he should be thankful his wife hired us instead of cutting off appendages."

Trudi laughed.

"The guy shut up and listened to you. He even apologized when you were done."

Trudi remembered that. She'd been shocked that the guy seemed earnest.

Samuel smiled that cocky grin of his. She'd always pretended to hate that grin, but she thought it was cute. "So, how do you know about this guy?"

"Anonymous phone call that I'd find him in the TD Garden garage."

"How do you know this isn't some kind of trap?"

"The guy used a CIA code word."

"If he's CIA, why didn't he tell you who he is?"

Samuel shrugged.

Trudi guessed it wasn't uncommon for spies to keep their identity concealed even from each other. Espionage was not an environment that nurtured trust.

"The PTSD guy is called Dream, right?" she asked.

"Dream or *The* Dream, not totally sure. Why?"

"I think I have an idea why Agent Uribe is asking about you."

"The art crimes chick? Why?"

"She said something about The Dream. She said he was released with no advance warning, as if someone with CIA connections wanted it that way. Released from where?"

Samuel frowned. "Prison?"

"Maybe that experience is why he has PTSD?"

"I don't know. The way he recites random facts when he's

stressed makes me think someone taught him that, like some kind of mental health professional."

"There are therapists in some prisons, right?"

"I think we're still missing something."

"A lot of somethings. What about Agent Uribe? How does she know about The Dream, why does she care, and how did she know you'd get involved with him?"

Samuel sighed. "We need The Dream to get his memory back."

A few minutes later, Trudi pulled off onto an exit in Macon and found a gas station. She walked inside to the register and paid the attendant cash before heading back out to the car. Samuel got out as well and scanned the station as she pumped the gas. He didn't get back in the car until after she did.

"Want me to drive for a while?" he asked.

"No, I'm good."

"Come on, you have to be dragging."

She pulled to a stop before exiting the gas station. "Do I need to remind you who scored higher in that offensive driving course we took?"

"I just thought you might be tired. You work hard."

"You really think I don't know why you want to drive, cowboy?"

"Now I'm in trouble for being a nice guy?"

"One more thing to add to my list of annoying Samuel traits: control freak." She turned out of the lot.

"Pot calling the kettle black, princess."

She took the ramp to merge onto Interstate 16. "At least I own up to it." Then she added, "You haven't told me where in Jacksonville."

"Nope, I sure haven't."

She rolled her eyes. "I'll trade with you in Savannah. Good enough for you?"

The drive across 16 was long—and boring. It was a good thing she'd gotten gas when she did. All the exits looked like the kinds of places where you'd hear "Dueling Banjos." As promised, she let Samuel drive once they hit Savannah, and a couple of hours later, they entered Jacksonville. They didn't make it far past the city limits, not into downtown yet, when he exited. Just off the freeway, he parked outside a dumpy apartment building.

"Stay here," Samuel said. "I'll go get him."

"I'm not waiting here."

"Do you think seeing the woman who threatened to kick him is going to help put him at ease?"

"I only threatened to kick him one time." She sighed. "All right, all right. Hurry up."

She sat and waited. A good ten minutes passed. She was just about to call him to see what was taking so long when he emerged from the stairs, followed by the same man she'd met the other day. The Dream stopped when he saw her.

Samuel turned and talked to him. Trudi cracked her window so she could hear. ". . . not like you have any better options," Samuel said.

The Dream looked at Trudi again. She smiled and waved.

"See," Samuel said, "she's not going to hit you. I promise."

The Dream followed him to the car and sat in the back seat as directed by Samuel.

While Samuel backed out of the parking space, Trudi turned in her seat to talk to The Dream and try to put him at ease. "Sorry to wake you so early."

"I was awake."

She wanted to ask what had taken so long, then. "Early riser?"

"I was awake."

Making great progress already, Trudi thought sarcastically.

Samuel merged onto I-95 North, and The Dream watched

the freeway flash by out the side window. She decided to allow him some quiet time to acclimate. Samuel stopped at a tiny gas station not long after making the turn onto the long, boring stretch of 16. Trudi insisted on taking the wheel and letting him get some sleep. The Dream continued to sit quietly in the back seat. She wondered what was going through his head and worried he might try making a run for it at the gas station.

After they passed Forsyth, Trudi nudged Samuel. He blinked hard and sat up straight. "How close are we?"

"Not into Atlanta yet. Where're we going?"

"Head toward Buckhead."

"Are you kidding?" One of the most upscale areas in the city?

"Let's just say we acquired a condo from an unwilling benefactor."

That didn't make her feel any better. "You're positive it's completely safe?"

"Completely. The benefactor had good reason to make sure no one knew about this place."

"I'm gonna need a little more detail than that if you want me to make sure my friend Dream here is safe."

In the rearview mirror, she noticed Dream perk up a bit. "You're going to leave me with her?" Dream asked Samuel.

Samuel turned and looked at Dream. "You're going to have to trust me on this. I know you didn't get off on a good foot with her, but she's the best person to help you right now, a whole lot better than me even." Samuel turned back to Trudi. "It was a condo the leader of a recently deposed drug cartel kept for his mistress. Both were recently killed, and they were the only ones who knew about it. Everything's in the name of a clean alias."

"What about the neighbors? Yuppies aren't known for minding their own business."

"Let's just say you look a lot like the mistress—"

"Great. Thanks for the compliment, Samuel."

"Okay, she wasn't Mother Teresa, but it's still a good way for you to blend in, and Dream is the right ethnicity to fit in as one of the cartel's henchmen."

"What do you want me to do?" Dream's voice shook slightly.

"Nothing," Samuel said. "Once we get you inside, you won't be leaving the condo. And on the way in, just don't talk." Then he added, "Stand straight and don't fidget."

Trudi glanced at Dream in the rearview mirror. "Don't worry. I'll draw the attention to me. And I'm sure Samuel knows a back way in."

North of downtown, Samuel told Trudi to exit onto Lenox Road, and then they made a left. Next to a two-level shopping center with a Saks Fifth Avenue and a Nordstrom Rack was a high-rise. Samuel directed her to park in an underground parking garage at the shopping center. Trudi took a minute to put on some heavy eyeliner and shiny lip gloss. Then they made their way toward the high-rise.

"Keep your hands in your pockets to keep yourself from fidgeting," Trudi told Dream.

He did as she said.

Trudi let her hair down and shook it out.

It was late enough in the morning now that people had already left for work, so the building was quiet. They took the stairs and made it up to the fifth floor without seeing anyone.

In the hall, a middle-aged man was exiting a condo. Trudi walked in front and arched her back as she walked. She smiled at the man as they passed, and he didn't seem to notice anyone other than Trudi.

"Nicely done, Tru-Bear." Samuel took a key out of his pocket and opened a condo door.

As soon as she was inside, Trudi relaxed her posture back to normal and wiped the vapid smile off her face. "Don't expect to see that again anytime soon."

Samuel grinned. "It's planted in my memory now."

Trudi started walking through the condo to get a feel for the layout. She didn't like being so high up—it made good alternate escape routes harder. Though she had to admit that the mahogany-clad living room was gorgeous.

A few minutes later, Samuel was still in the entry hall with Dream.

"I don't think I can do it," Dream said.

Samuel's voice was low. "You're just going to have to get used to handling a gun."

WEDNESDAY

NOVEMBER 15

18

SAMUEL

Boston, MA

"Yeah, yeah," Samuel said into the phone.

"Out of all my agents, you're by far the biggest pain."

"I do appreciate the compliment." Samuel glanced behind him through the darkness and changed lanes on Interstate 84. He had a lot of hours of driving ahead of him until he neared Boston. Now if he could convince his handler to get off his case.

"You need to learn what constitutes a compliment."

"I think I'm pretty clear on that."

"Just be careful. We have reason to believe al-Sadr will have people in the country within a week. I did you a favor and got you released—don't make me regret it."

Samuel had been picked up by the CIA. They'd been concerned about his falling into the hands of al-Sadr because he knew too much. "Hey, you're the one who gave me the idea for this project." He poorly imitated his handler's voice. "Surely, a PI/CIA operative/detective could figure this out."

"Yeah, I'm starting to wonder if that was wise."

Then Samuel caught the timing his handler had said. "Where're you getting your information? I haven't heard anything for about a week."

"If you checked in like you're supposed to, you might know things like this."

"Okay, okay. Lecture over." Samuel blew by an eighteen-wheeler. "Tell me what you know."

"We have an asset inserted in a major oil family in Saudi Arabia with some kind of tie to US immigration. We're not sure what kind of tie—we just know they've been able to get people into the country under the radar. And the asset has gotten us word that the family has been in discussions with al-Sadr. There's talk of a November twentieth deadline."

"If they're sourcing it out, they probably plan on sending more than one person." Getting one person into the country wasn't such a large task—send several people to the border in different areas until one gets through. This sounded a lot more strategic.

"That's what we think. Now, are you going to start doing what I tell you to do?"

"We have such a good thing going. Why ruin it?"

His handler started griping again. He was pushing all the right buttons to keep the phone call going longer to help him stay awake. His mind started to wander.

"You're just going to have to get used to handling a gun," Samuel had told Dream.

Finally, Dream had admitted, "They frighten me."

"Why does he need to handle a gun?" Trudi had come back to the entryway.

"He won't as long as you're around." Samuel smiled at Trudi, while hoping Dream kept his mouth shut. Though Samuel was pretty confident his threats that Dream keep quiet about Samuel's plans had thoroughly penetrated the fear center of his brain.

Trudi hesitated for half a second. Samuel kept eye contact.

"I'll keep him safe." Trudi smiled at Dream.

Dodged a bullet there, Samuel thought. Then he said to Trudi, "Can I talk to you privately for a second?"

She walked back the way she'd come, and he followed her to a room covered in mahogany paneling.

"We shouldn't leave him alone too long," Trudi said. "I think he might bolt at any second."

"He doesn't have any place else to go. He won't run."

"Sometimes I miss that psychic ability of yours," she said sarcastically.

"I'm sure you do."

She smirked. "So, what did you want to talk about that we didn't already cover in the almost six-hour car ride down to Jacksonville?"

"I'm leaving your car in the garage. I have another stashed down there."

"And you needed me alone to tell me that?"

"I just wanted to tell you thank you. For not destroying the pictures."

Trudi paused, and her voice was quieter. "You're welcome."

"I'm headed back up to Boston, so I won't see you for a while."

"I'll call you if he remembers anything interesting." He'd given her the number of his burner cell.

He took a step closer. She leaned back. He moved closer, and she looked at him with that warning in her eyes. He kissed her cheek, the first time he'd touched her like that in a very long time. And certainly the last time he would ever touch her.

"Thanks, Tru-Bear." He turned and walked away, out of the condo.

Samuel came back to himself and sat straighter in the driver's seat.

"Are you even listening?" his handler asked.

"November twentieth. Everything has to be done by November twentieth."

"Let me say this again, though I'm sure it'll fall on deaf ears. You need to go underground now. Right now. Get out of the country, disappear."

"You're absolutely right," Samuel said. "Deaf ears."

"You're too valuable an asset to be playing around like this."

"You mean I know too much to be allowed to fall into terrorist hands."

"That too."

"I feel the love," Samuel said. "We've already been through this. I'll disappear—once my plan is finished."

"You don't even have a plan."

"I have the start of one. I'll figure the rest out."

He passed a sign for an upcoming rest stop and changed lanes. He'd needed to use the restroom for the last ten miles. "Question for you: Have you heard of an FBI agent named Tama Uribe?"

"FBI?"

"Yeah. At least that's what she says."

"Why would you be asking about an FBI agent? Has she approached you?"

"She's been trying to get in contact with me. Harassing Trudi. I'd like to figure out what she's after and make her back off." He parked and got out of the car.

"Why does she want to talk to you?"

"Don't know." He passed a few people while walking up the sidewalk toward the men's room. He kept his expression open, maybe even a little smile in his eyes, all while watching each person carefully.

A man in jeans and an overcoat stood to the side, lit a cigarette, and looked over at Samuel.

"Evening," Samuel said. The man looked away.

Into the phone, Samuel said, "Look into her, all right?"

"Why don't you just reach out to her yourself?"

Samuel paused for a second. Several thoughts skittered through his mind. "You want me lying low, remember?"

"If she's FBI, I wouldn't worry."

"Hang on a second." Samuel muted the phone while he used the restroom and washed his hands. "All right, I'm back." He walked out of the restroom and into the cold.

"What is that shouting?" his handler asked.

"Couple of guys about to get into a fight. Ignore what I say for about ten seconds."

"What?"

Two men were arguing on the sidewalk, with a young girl, maybe twelve, standing to the side, looking scared. Phone still to his ear, Samuel kept walking down the sidewalk.

"You cut me off!" one of the men yelled at the other.

"There are thousands of beige Toyotas on the road," the other man said. "You're confused."

"Don't try denying it!"

Samuel talked into his phone. "Yeah, I got it. I said I got it." He bumped shoulders with the larger man. "Whoa, sorry about that."

"Watch it, buddy."

Samuel talked into the phone again. "Yes, I got it. Generic peanut butter from Walmart. Nothing else." He rolled his eyes and covered the mouthpiece. "Women. Can't live with them, can't have any fun without them."

"Just get outta here."

"Man, I'm getting yelled at from all sides. Not my day." Samuel walked past them. And then he turned quickly. "Say, can you tell me how to get to"—with his elbow up, still holding his phone, he slammed into the other man—"wow, I'm sorry. You all right?"

That man huffed and walked away.

Samuel turned to the larger man. "Maybe you can tell me how to get to—"

That man walked away as well. The girl, apparently his daughter, followed. She glanced back at Samuel. He smiled and winked, and she grinned.

Samuel continued to his rental car and got in. "Okay, fun's over."

"You need to be more careful."

Samuel started the engine. "Let me ask you something. Someone dropped something that I suspect is going to be very useful in my lap. Anonymously. How do you think that someone could have found out about what I'm trying to get done?"

"If this person, or thing, is useful, use them and get it done."

"Hey, got another call coming in. Talk to you soon." He ended the call and tossed the phone onto the passenger seat. *That seals it*, he thought, *trust no one but Trudi from now on.*

19

DREAM

Atlanta, GA

I finally wake. I look out the window, at the afternoon sun. I sit up in the bed, and it takes me a few seconds to remember where I am, what'd happened. This is the condo in Atlanta. And I'm not alone—that Trudi is here somewhere. My need to use the restroom is the only thing that gets me out of the room.

I keep my coat on and walk down the hall. Trudi is sitting in a chair close to the foyer.

"Hey," Trudi says with a smile. "Sleep well?"

I'm shocked at how well. She probably didn't expect me to sleep so long. Neither did I.

When I don't answer, Trudi says, "So, I understand you've lost some memories."

"Yes." I stay several feet away from her.

"Samuel asked me to help you remember."

"He believes something in my memory might be useful."

"Okay, what do you say we get started, then?"

"I'm not sure what to do."

"Let's just talk." She moves closer to me.

I step back, against the front door.

She stops. "Hey, don't worry. I know we got off on a bad foot, but you can't really blame me for being aggressive when you pulled a gun on me."

"I know." I do get that rationally, but I feel too off-balance and out of my element to be completely rational.

"Okay." She smiles. "You're trusting Samuel, right? And he trusts me. So, that means you can trust me too." She adds, "And didn't Darrent Hayes tell you to find me so I could help?"

I stay put.

"Here, I'll go into the living room, and you can follow. I'll sit on the other end of the couch, and we can talk. That work?"

I nod.

She turns, trusting I won't bolt out the door, and walks into the next room. *That wins you some points*, I think. I follow and sit on the end of the couch. The wood paneling and furniture make the room feel dark, except for the light coming in from the windows.

"So," she says, "is your name Dream or The Dream?"

"Either."

"I assume that's not your real name."

"No." I expect her to jump to the next logical question, the same question everyone asks—*what's your real name?* I don't like to give it. It feels too personal.

"Okay, I'll go with just Dream, then. Make it simpler."

I nod.

"So, what do you do for a living?" she asks.

"I haven't worked in a while."

"What did you do when you did work?"

"Ar— Security guard."

She grins. "I heard that. You were going to say something else."

"I made a living as a security guard." Then I add, "I know that probably sounds funny."

"I don't think you're weak. I think you've been through a traumatic experience and haven't dealt with it properly. What were you going to say before you said security guard?"

"Artist."

"What kind of art?"

"Anything."

She raises an eyebrow, waiting for a better response.

"Realism, Impressionism, and some graphic novels. A lot of literature-based themes."

Her eyes light up. "What kind of literature?"

"Steinbeck, Melville, Poe . . ."

"Impressive." I feel she wants to keep talking about the literature, but she moves on. "Do you have any theories about what you're blocking out?"

"I try not to think about it."

"Let's go at it slowly. All right?"

I nod.

"What's the last thing you remember before your memory gets fuzzy?"

"I . . ." I squeeze my eyes shut. "The letters *VVSOP* on a cognac bottle stand for Very Very Superior Old Pale."

"I'm sorry," Trudi says. "What?"

I keep my eyes closed, and she's quiet.

Her voice is muted, like she's talking more to herself. "An anxiety-control exercise." Then her voice is louder but still gentle. "Let's go even slower, all right?"

I nod, eyes still closed.

"I'm going to see if I can find us some food. Take some time and relax. You're safe here." Her quiet footsteps sound and then disappear down the hall.

I take a deep breath and open my eyes.

This room is way too fancy for me, but it's better than the apartment in Jacksonville. Quieter. I look out the window for a few minutes. It's still so green outside, even in November. It looks odd.

"Jackpot," Trudi calls from another room. "Samuel must have had some food brought in. I'm going to cook us something. You just relax for a while." Then I hear pots and pans clanking.

Finally, I decide I need to try harder. Be braver. Dr. Brone told me that so many times, but now I feel ready. Maybe.

Okay, she said to start with the last thing I remember before my memory starts going fuzzy. But time itself seems fuzzy. I'm not sure of the order of things. An image of a man with a bulbous nose comes to me . . . Southie . . .

"He's a forger," Southie had said. "Caught him making a wicked-good copy of this one." He had waved one of the leather tubes toward the Irishman. Rolled up inside the tube was an oil painting I'd come to know very well.

"Don't need a painter," the Irishman snapped. "Not yet at least, not for a few more weeks. Maybe even a month. Need a penciller right now. A sketch artist."

"I can draw," I said suddenly. *Maybe if I make myself useful*, I thought, *they'll keep me alive long enough for me to find a way to escape.*

"See for yourself." Southie shoved my portfolio into the Irishman's hands, then pushed past him to enter the cottage.

The stocky man looked hard at me for another moment, then unzipped my work. He flipped through a few comic book pages, nodding once or twice, making unintelligible grunts at the images he saw. Then he slapped the case shut again. He wrapped his arms in front of him, pressing my artwork to his chest almost like he was giving it a hug.

His stare was hard to hold, but I tried not to wilt under his gaze. He looked at me as though he was trying to gauge whether it was easier to kill and bury me here in the woods or invite me inside for dinner. Finally, he nodded. Decision made.

"Clocks," he said to me brusquely. "I need lots of clocks."

I wasn't sure how to respond to that.

"Well, get in here," the Irishman growled. "You waiting for an engraved invitation?"

I glanced around at the thick woods.

"We're miles away from another human being. You'll get lost, starve, and be eaten by a bobcat. Be my guest if you'd prefer that fate." He started to close the door.

I hurried toward him and slipped into the cottage.

"Maybe you're not as stupid as you seem," the Irishman said. "Come here. I need clocks."

I walked in a little farther, and the worn wood floors creaked. I couldn't see where Southie had gone to. I felt like I needed to keep close track of him or else he might show up behind me and press that silver gun of his to the nape of my neck. Drawings covered the white walls of the main living space and a small dining space to the left. Maybe he'd gone into what looked like the kitchen off the dining space.

"I said come here," the Irishman bellowed from a drawing desk on the far right wall.

I did as he said.

"Sit."

I sat.

"Clocks. Draw me clocks." He handed me a pencil and pointed at a large drawing book in front of me.

"What kind of clocks?"

"All kinds." He pointed at the paper and then walked away.

I focused on the task and drew the old mantel clock we'd had when I was growing up, the kind with a wide base that curved over the clock face like a wave. Then I drew a grandfather clock.

"No. Clock faces." The Irishman had returned to look over my shoulder.

I made one with Roman numerals and another with a simple serif font. Then I started on one with digital numbers.

"I said clock *faces*."

I abandoned the digital clock and started on one with calligraphic-style letters and ornate filigree hands.

"Keep going," the Irishman said.

Finally, I asked, "What are these for?"

"A map."

"A map for what?"

"Keep drawing." He walked away.

I hear footsteps. "Did you remember something?" Trudi has returned.

"The start of something," I say.

She smiles. "Good."

I expect her to drill me for more. *You'll never get your memories back if you don't push hard*, Dr. Brone had said so many times. But I hadn't wanted to remember then. I remind myself that now it's all different.

20

TRUDI

Atlanta, GA

"What's in this?" Dream asked.

"Lots of things. It's a casserole." Trudi saw that her answer was not going to be enough for Dream. "Mostly chicken, plus potatoes, cheese, peas, a little onion, and some spices." At least she was pretty sure that was all she'd put in there.

Dream poked his fork at a piece of chicken and took a bite. Then he took another, so she figured the casserole had passed the test.

They ate quietly for a few minutes. She was fairly certain he'd remembered something, but she decided not to push him to tell her. *Just let him relax and get comfortable with me.*

"You like books?" Dream asked.

She was thinking of offering a little information about herself to make it easier for him to open up. "That's what I studied in college."

"You like Poe?"

"I *love* Poe. He does dark with such artistry. It's not just about being shocking and different. It's about saying something. Something deep and difficult."

He nodded. "I agree." He took another small bite.

"So, let's try this," she said. "I'm going to be an open book and blurt out a bunch of stuff about me. Even if it doesn't help you feel comfortable with me, it'll be entertaining."

His eyes smiled, and the corner of his mouth twitched.

Here it goes. "My name is Trudi Sara Coffey. Samuel is my ex-husband. I'm a private detective by profession. My favorite color is pink, though I don't admit that to very many people. My favorite car is a 1990 Mercedes-Benz 420 Class sedan, but not in pink."

Dream smiled a little.

"My secret indulgence is peanut butter spread on warm toast. I don't have a ton of close friends, but the ones I have are special. I mean that as a positive *and* with quotations."

"Huh?"

She made air quotes. "*Special,* as in Willy Wonka or the Addams Family or Weird Al Yankovic. Interesting, never boring."

He grinned.

"My friend Tyler was a sneak thief but the most talented magician I've ever seen, and he's proposed to me more than once, though I think he's over that now. Eula is my assistant and my employee, but she's also a dear friend and an amazing resource. She's a lot more talented than she knows. She's also into roller derby—I still can't get over that one. And though I would *never* admit it to him, Samuel is still my best friend." *The pig.*

"Then why are you divorced?"

"He did something unforgivable." Then she decided if she was going to be blunt, she had to do it properly. "He has a child with a woman in another country. I do believe he's learned from his mistake, but—"

"There's no coming back from that."

"Sometimes, I really wish there was, but there just isn't. You can't get trust back after that. Or at least I can't."

"I understand."

"Let's see," she said as she pursed her lips. "What else?"

"What's your biggest fear?"

"Bringing out the big guns now, huh? Hmm . . ." She took a breath, and her smile faded. "That Samuel will fall in love with someone else, that he loves the mother of his son." *I can't believe I just admitted that, and out loud to another person.*

Dream nodded slowly. "I get that." He paused. "What does a private detective do, exactly? It's not like those old noir movies, is it?"

"Nope. Nowadays, it's a lot of online research."

"But you know how to fight?"

"I do. I train in tae kwon do, and I regularly go to the gun range."

"You have a gun?" He sat straighter and leaned away from her slightly.

"Of course. I know they scare you, but in the right hands—someone with proper training and a level head—they're perfectly safe. Having a gun means I can better defend myself. And my friends." She tilted her head and smiled a little.

He let his posture relax. Then he poked around at his food.

"Do you not like it?" she asked.

"No. I mean, no, it's good."

"But . . . you have a hard time trusting other people. Especially with food?"

He looked down at the plate and pushed the food around more. Then he took a small bite. It was like he had to see every angle of each piece of food to make sure there was nothing wrong with it, or maybe hidden under it.

"Have you been drugged before?" she asked.

Finally, he looked up. He nodded. "At least I'm pretty sure that's what happened."

"I'm really sorry. I don't expect blind trust from you, but I hope I'm being transparent enough to help set you at ease so that you don't think I'll hurt you." She wondered, though, if what he thought was being drugged, and surely truly felt like it to him, was actually medication administered in a mental facility.

She ate very slowly the rest of the meal, and he continued to talk a little with her, though she still dominated the conversation. Eventually, he made it through his plate of food, which she took as a good sign.

They went into the living room.

"Do you want to take off your coat?" she asked. It was the same coat he'd worn in Boston. It looked heavy for a Southern November.

He shook his head.

She sat on the couch closer to the windows, and he fished something out of his pocket. She almost jumped up, but then she reminded herself Samuel never would have allowed Dream in the car with them with that gun still in his pocket. He took out what looked like a small flashlight. *But the room is well lit*, she thought, *especially with all these windows.*

He clicked it on and pointed it at the couch, and she realized it was a black light. He checked the area where he'd already sat very closely. *To make sure he hadn't sat on anything nasty?* Then he checked the rest of the couch and moved on to the armchair.

She didn't see anything on the furniture. But then as he turned, she thought she noticed something.

"Hey," she said, "can I see that for a second?"

"Okay." He handed her the little light.

She took his hand. He started to pull away but stopped when she said, "Trust me for just a second."

She flashed the light at the back of his left hand.

He stared at his hand and drew his eyebrows together.

"Do you know where you got this?" She looked closely at the tattoo, visible only in black light.

"I don't know." He pulled his hand back and started wringing his hands, almost as if he could smear the tattoo off.

"You've never been tattooed?"

"The Irishman."

"The Irishman? Is that someone you know?"

"He liked clocks."

"What happened to him? Is he the one who tattooed your hand?"

He walked around the armchair, still wringing his hands. "Grapes explode when you put them in the microwave."

He's on the edge. Be careful with him. She kept her voice soft. "Hey."

He kept walking around the room. "Charlie Chaplin once won third place in a Charlie Chaplin look-alike contest."

She cut him off as he walked between the windows and the couch. He stopped, and she took his hands.

She made her voice even softer. "Tae kwon do literally translates 'foot hand way.'"

He took a breath but kept his gaze diverted. "Uranus is the only planet that rotates on its side. Charlotte Brontë first published her works under the name Currer Bell. Dunkin' Donuts serves about 112,500 donuts each day."

Trudi smiled. "Now I'm hungry for dessert."

He finally looked at her.

"Come on. Let's find something sweet in the kitchen."

He didn't respond, but he didn't pull away when she held his hand to lead him. In the kitchen, he stood next to the small, round table.

She started opening cabinets. Canned soups, measuring cups, boxed meals . . . "Here we go." She turned, holding a box of Little Debbie snack cakes. "Do you like Swiss Rolls?"

He hesitated but then sat in the chair.

"Here, we'll split a package." She set a couple of small plates on the table, opened the package, and put one roll on his plate and one on hers. She sat and took a bite. He did as well.

"Feeling better?" she asked.

He nodded.

"Chocolate cures all."

"Including Dementor attacks."

She laughed out loud. "You've read *Harry Potter*?"

"The books were in the library at the . . ."

"Hospital?"

He hesitated.

"Something traumatic happened to you," she said in a sympathetic voice. "Maybe a lot of somethings. I'm guessing a doctor taught you to recite factoids to keep certain memories back."

"A nurse. Clara."

"She was kind."

"She didn't treat us like . . . crazy people."

Trudi had the feeling he had been about to say something other than crazy people.

"She gave me the book," he said. "Until Dr. Brone took it away."

"Wait, you memorized a whole book?"

He nodded.

"Wow. I wish I could do that." *This guy is a lot smarter than anyone gives him credit for*, she thought. *Including me*. "So, would you mind if I looked at your hand with the light again?"

He sat a little straighter. "Okay."

She took the small light out of her pocket.

He set his left hand on the table, palm flat.

She gently laid her fingers on his to try to soothe him, and she clicked on the light. "It looks like an eagle," she said. It kind of looked like the eagles often found on the tops of flagpoles, except that it sat on a square base with a "1" on it. Its wings were outstretched away from its body but partially bent, and it looked like it was holding something in one claw.

"What's that underneath?" Dream asked.

She moved the light below the eagle. Scroll-like text spelled out "the dream within Dream."

"As in the Poe poem? 'A Dream within a Dream'? But it's not quite right. Do you have any idea what that means?" she asked.

"I don't know."

"You don't remember getting this done?"

He shook his head. Then he said, "I have some on my back, but they're normal. Black ink, not like this."

"What's it a picture of?"

"It's not a picture. It's the poem. 'A Dream within a Dream.'"

Is this why Samuel borrowed my Poe book? He somehow knew this poem was going to be related. Maybe he'd gotten a tip, like how someone had called and told him where to find Dream. But who would do that and why? To help Dream? "Is that why people call you Dream?"

"No. That's what my mother called me."

Interesting to note that he was able to talk about his mother without getting upset. She guessed his trauma was more recent, not related to childhood. "Is that why you chose that poem?"

"I didn't choose it."

She assumed the Irishman had chosen it. She worded her question carefully to help Dream avoid thinking of him. "Do you think it was chosen because of your name or for some other reason? Maybe some meaning in the poem?"

His gaze shifted away from her, and she worried she was losing him again. But then he said, "It was a tribute. To me. He didn't explain more than that."

"I get the feeling you didn't feel like you *could* ask for more explanation."

"He wasn't really so bad. But Southie scared me." Dream started wringing his hands again.

Trudi rested her hand on his, and he stopped. "Change the subject whenever you want to, okay?"

He swallowed. "I want to help you."

She didn't correct him that he was really helping Samuel, not her.

"Why did he want to make a tribute to you?" she asked.

"Because I'm talented. I can draw and paint. That was important to them."

"Why?"

"I made copies of paintings for them."

Forgeries. But of what? "Would you mind showing me the writing on your back?"

He tucked his coat more tightly around himself.

"I have a thought," she said. "I need just a little more of your trust. For only a few minutes."

There was a long pause.

"Okay," he said.

She stood, and so did he. She helped him remove his coat. He turned and lifted the back of his shirt. She pushed it farther up, to his shoulders, and he reached up and held it in place. The pretty gold of his skin provided a nice backdrop for the simple but scroll-like letters spelling out the poem down the middle of his back. Something about the calligraphy seemed to bring the cant of the poem to life, like the words themselves were singing.

Then she shined the black light at his skin.

"It's just the poem," he said. "I wasn't sure I wanted it, not something covering so much, but he insisted. He said I'd be thankful someday."

Trudi stared at his back.

"I'm not sure if I'll ever be thankful for it, but some nights, there's a certain comfort for me knowing the words are there, and no one can take them away."

"It's not just the poem."

He looked at her over his shoulder. "What?"

"There's more tattooed than just the poem. A lot more."

THURSDAY

NOVEMBER 16

21

SAMUEL

Boston, MA

"Lady trouble?" the bartender asked.

Samuel just smiled a little and took another drink of his Sam Adams. He'd made it to Boston and driven around for a while until he found an open bar at 8:00 a.m. It was the kind of place that seemed clean until you started looking in the corners and crevices.

"Thought so." The bartender, a bear of a man wearing a dingy apron around his gut, set a basket of pretzels in front of Samuel. It felt like an offering to the weary-hearted.

The bones of it, Samuel supposed, was a woman problem, but not like the bartender thought. Best to let him think it was something standard and not as complicated as reality.

He kept going over his options of who was trustworthy. His handler wasn't being upfront with him about something, and Samuel couldn't seem to find the angle. If Truck were still alive, things would be easier. He could trust Truck, and Truck would be able to scrape away the sludge and find the truth. It all came down to the fact that there was only one person he could trust. But he needed to keep her as far away from al-Sadr as he could, which was why he'd come back to Boston and not stayed with her.

Someone sat down on the stool next to him. "Crown and Coke, please."

Samuel stood. He was furious at himself for not noticing who'd come in the door. "You're under arrest," he told Darrent Hayes.

Darrent looked at him and raised his eyebrows.

"You have the right to remain silent," Samuel said. "Anything you say can and will be used against you." He reached for his handcuffs and remembered he didn't have them. He hadn't anticipated coming across the traitor he'd been hunting, not in a random bar on the outskirts of Boston.

"You're gonna want to hear what I have to say first." Hayes remained seated on the stool.

The bartender stood there looking back and forth between them.

"Aren't you curious," Hayes asked, "why I show up all of a sudden like this? I've evaded you since Nevermore, and now here I am."

Samuel took his badge from inside his jacket and flashed it to the bartender, just to let him know who was in charge. Then he put his badge away and nodded to tell him to pour the Crown and Coke. The burly man set the drink in front of Hayes and moved away, down to the other end of the bar.

Samuel took his stool but shifted his jacket so his gun was within easy reach. "So, what does the terrorist want to talk to me about?"

"Ouch." Then Darrent added, "Says the man who has a second wife in another country."

Samuel's right fist clenched. Then he calmed himself and asked, "What made you decide to become a terrorist?"

"Terrorist?"

"Yes. I believe studying the minds of the unbalanced will help me to better anticipate their behaviors."

"You don't even know me."

Samuel glanced around to be sure the bartender was out of earshot, and he lowered his voice. "I know you're a CIA agent—former agent—who turned against his country and helped commit murder."

Darrent raised his eyebrows.

"You were in place at Mama Bliss's to oversee the shipment of weapons. And then you turned your back on your country by helping set up Nevermore."

"I'm impressed. No one was supposed to know an agent was planted there. How'd you figure it out?"

"Awareness."

Hayes rolled his eyes. "Yes, we all know you're Super Agent, aware of everything."

"No, I meant your awareness. You notice more than your average store manager. Too bad you couldn't use that awareness to find a moral compass."

"Loyalty doesn't mean anything to you, does it? I'm starting to regret everything I've done for you. All for a brother-in-arms."

Samuel snatched Darrent by the coat lapels. "I'm no brother of yours." He pushed him as he let go. "What's this nonsense about everything you've done for me?"

"We should talk someplace more private."

"Or I could just take you to the nearest police station, and we could talk there."

"Have you figured out if it's The Dream or just Dream?"

"Sleep exploits? Stay away from Freudian theories."

"I respect the loyalty," Darrent said. "You refuse to move on until a certain person is taken care of. Even though that person wants nothing to do with you."

"Delusional now as well?" *Play him off as the idiot he is or push for whatever information he has and risk allowing him to extrapolate more?*

"Just well connected."

"I'm not interested in your connections."

Darrent snapped, "I dropped Dream in your lap. Just make sure you get the job done before al-Sadr finds you."

The phone call telling me where to find Dream and that he'd be useful, Samuel thought, *it was Darrent.* He snapped back, "I'm a long way from having what I need. Next time, try being *actually* useful."

"I saved your son. Is that not useful enough to you?"

"*I* take care of my son. He's safe."

"Now that I moved him, he is."

"Are you psychic now? He's been faded. No one knows where I hid him and his mother but me."

"And the agency."

Samuel's unsettling conversation with his handler ran through his head. He couldn't trust the agency anymore. But he certainly couldn't trust Darrent Hayes either. This could simply be a ploy to learn the location of his son and the boy's mother. He wouldn't put it past Hayes to work with al-Sadr. And what about Dream—was that simply a ploy to get to Trudi?

Hayes lifted his chin. "Some things are starting to come together for you, am I right?"

Samuel glanced around to be sure the place was still empty. The bartender had escaped to the back room. "All right, I'll bite. Tell me what you know about my handler."

"I don't know anything about your handler."

"But you know who it is."

"Yes."

"How?" No one was supposed to know that. Samuel had been given assurance that his handler would not be known by anyone but him and three top-level people in the agency. Samuel wanted to be sure his identity and the details of his life were safe.

"Let's just say I have a special kind of clearance level."

"Meaning you operate outside directives."

Hayes shrugged.

Samuel grabbed Hayes's arm and started to lead him toward a green vinyl-covered booth on the other side of the bar, farther from the door.

Hayes pulled his arm away. "Back off, man."

Samuel got in his face. "What do you expect? A hug and slap on the back? You're a terrorist. I'm willing to hear you out, but I also need to watch my own back. I can't risk someone overhearing something they shouldn't."

Hayes paused, obviously considering. Then he headed toward the booth in the corner. They sat across from each other. Samuel kept an eye on the door and the rest of the room, while sitting toward the edge of the bench.

"How'd you find me here? How'd you even know I was in Boston?"

"You want to keep Trudi safe by keeping your distance, and you suspect that once Dream remembers what you need him to remember, being in Boston will be helpful to secure things until Trudi can get here."

Impressive. Samuel didn't know how Hayes knew about Dream and what he wanted Dream to remember, but he'd leave that alone for now. "How'd you know I was here? I've never been to this bar before."

"Exactly. Someplace you've never been, where you could blend in casually, close to the freeway. To be honest, it was a crapshoot. I've been to at least ten bars and coffee shops."

"Why did you want to find me?"

"If I'm going to help someone, I do it properly. Nothing halfway. I don't have all the information you need, but I might have some key details."

"Why on earth would you want to help me? I've been tracking you for the sole purpose of arresting you."

"Mama Bliss said she owed you."

As simple as that, huh? Samuel thought. "What do you know about Dream?"

"About as much as you, I suspect. I assume you've figured out his real name and researched his past."

"I can't find anything much beyond several years ago." Samuel had put a call in to a contact in the prison system and had gotten a call back just after arriving back in Boston. He hadn't told Trudi because he feared his throwaway cell wasn't secure—his handler had the number. Plus, Trudi would gripe at him for leaving her with a convicted felon without having researched his past first.

"But you know where he worked before disappearing."

"The Gardner Museum. But you don't know for sure if he knows anything about the heist. He worked there long after the theft. Why would you assume he knows anything?"

"You also know the circumstances of his arrest when he resurfaced."

Samuel nodded. So, it was a guess, but a very good, educated one. And this Uribe and O'Shaughnessy both also seemed to think Dream knew important details. Samuel's gut told him to pursue it, so he would.

Finally, he came to the question that made him the most

edgy, though he rationally knew he had nothing to worry about. "What do you know about my son?"

"You faded him and his mother, and very well, I might add. I'm impressed."

"A terrorist is impressed with my work. I'm not sure whether to be flattered or concerned."

"Do you want to know or not?"

Samuel waved his hand palm up, as if to say, "Go on."

"They were in a residential compound in Saudi Arabia, about to be moved to a dense Indian community in Florida. No one should've ever guessed you'd put them close to you and yet not right with you. With their particular features, very similar to the people in the Kerala region in southern India, they would've fit in well, especially since you'd taught them English with an American accent."

Samuel kept his expression carefully impassive. *He nailed it exactly. I need to move them. Now. But who can I trust?* The agency was out—if he couldn't trust his handler, he couldn't trust anyone. Truck was gone, and there was no one else he trusted other than Trudi. Maybe The Mute? But he didn't know where to find him.

"But they never made it to Florida," Hayes said.

Samuel clenched his jaw and waited for Hayes to continue.

"It was the residential compound they were in until everything could get put in order for their flight to Miami. Daesh claimed the attack was retaliation for crimes against Islam committed by the 'apostate' Saudi government. From what I was able to find, Dalal shielded Atif. She covered him with her own body. He wouldn't have survived any other way."

Samuel only stared at Hayes. *He's lying. He has to be lying.*

"I am truly sorry to have to tell you she's dead. She didn't deserve to die, but she died honorably."

Samuel tried to absorb the news. He'd never been in love with Dalal, but she was a good woman. He respected how she survived in a society that viewed her as more of a thing than a person and how well she took care of Atif. But then he narrowed his eyes as he carefully watched Hayes. "How can I trust anything you say?"

Darrent reached into his jacket pocket and pulled out a square cloth with a red-and-white pattern and held it out to Samuel.

Samuel took the fabric and felt the familiar material. He brought it to his nose. It smelled like the oil Dalal put in her hair. It was Atif's headcloth.

And then Hayes laid a picture on the table. It was Atif sitting in a window seat of a small airplane. He could see the thick clouds outside the window. Atif had been crying. It was one of the very few times Samuel had seen his son not smiling. Atif had never been on an airplane before. The only way this picture could have been taken was on the flight to Miami or if Hayes had taken the boy on a different flight. The trip to Miami was to be on a commercial plane, and Hayes would have had no way of getting his hands on a picture like this. Not unless he had taken the boy out of the country himself.

"Where is he?" Samuel demanded.

22
DREAM

Atlanta, GA

"You all righ'?" Paddy, the Irishman, asked.

I nodded, my face against the floor. The pine was scratched and dinged like the pockmarks on the Southie's face. I heard that little noise Paddy made when he smirked, and then the needle started buzzing again.

The needle hurt, but I was beyond caring. Paddy had asked me if it was all right that he did this project. I took that as progress. Exactly what kind of progress, I wasn't sure. The Irishman was an odd one, kind of erratic, but I'd discovered that was born from extreme intelligence, the kind of intelligence that walks the crazy line.

"I thought about gettin' you fluthered first," Paddy said. "But I decided you're a sound kind of bloke."

I assumed fluthered meant drunk.

"You have this one memorized?" he asked.

I nodded.

He paused the needle, and I figured that was my cue to recite, so I did. "'Take this kiss upon the brow! And, in parting from you now . . .'"

He resumed the needle when I started the fourth line of the poem.

"Darn fine memory you have there," he said when I finished reciting. "That's why I picked this one. As a tribute."

Before I was able to ask what he meant by that, the Southie walked in the front door. "What's this nonsense?" I'd gotten a lot better at understanding his heavy accent and didn't need to translate in my head anymore. "Skiddah needs to be finishing that Rembrandt."

"He got done this mornin'," Paddy said. "This is somethin' else."

The Southie walked closer, his boot an inch from my face. I didn't dare move with the needle still stuck in my back. "Don't look like nothing but some funny writing."

"It's a poem by Edgar Allan Poe," Paddy said.

"How's that gonna—"

"It's goin' to be beautiful." Paddy continued to puncture my skin with the needle. "Clocks. Dream, where're the clocks?"

My speech was a little tight as I withstood the pain of the needle. "The ones you had me draw when I first got here?"

"Yeah. Where're the clocks?"

I come out of the memory and return to the present. I'm sitting at the table while Trudi finds something for us to have for breakfast. "It's clocks," I say. "The rest of the tattoo, it's clocks, right? Clock faces."

"Yeah . . ." Trudi says. "I thought you didn't know there was anything else."

"I remember now. Paddy tattooed the clock faces I drew."

"Who's Paddy?"

"Can you take a picture of them?" I stand and lift my shirt to show her my back.

"Um, sure. I can try." She takes her phone out of her pocket. She holds her phone in one hand and the black light in the other. "I don't know if I can— Here, let me try with less fluorescent light." She flips the switch on the wall.

Then it flips back on. "It's no good. I can't get a good shot of all of it. The black light just can't cover the whole area."

"Can you draw it?" I ask.

"There's no way I can copy this. It's waaay beyond my skill level."

"I just need a basic representation."

"Do you think it's important somehow?"

"Yes." I offer no further explanation.

To my surprise, she says, "Okay, I'll give it a shot. Let me find some paper." She rummages through a few drawers until she finds an old, beat-up notebook and a pencil. She sits at the table, and I stand there holding up my shirt.

"What do you think of the poem?" I ask.

"The calligraphy is amazing."

"No, the poem. I'm curious what you think it means."

"The most common thoughts are that the narrator is leaving someone, and he feels like his time with them was like a dream."

"Why is it dream within a dream?"

"I think he's emphasizing. The experience wasn't just a dream, not just once removed from reality, but twice removed."

Her description reminds me of my time with my mother. I can barely remember her sometimes, and yet she's always there, always a force in my life.

"What do you think it means?" Trudi asks.

"I used to think it meant insanity."

"I could see that." The sound of her pencil continues. "But you don't think that anymore?"

I hesitate. "I think maybe it's freedom."

The sound stops. "Like there's a certain amount of freedom in being insane?"

I nod. "But I don't want to be insane."

"But you do want freedom."

I don't respond. Freedom is my most powerful desire. Freedom from whoever is after me, freedom from my memories, freedom from incarceration.

Some time passes. The sounds of the pencil on the paper continue—I miss that sound. I wasn't allowed to draw at the hospital, other than in my sessions with Dr. Brone. They considered pencils a possible weapon. There is also the sound of the eraser several times.

"Make sure you get the minute and hour hands right," I say.

She continues to draw, and the feathery sound of her drawing helps keep me calm.

"You think all this means something?" Trudi asks.

"I think it's a map."

"A map to what?"

"I'm not sure yet." I have some thoughts, but I want to work them out in my head first.

"Does it have to do with what Samuel wants you to remember?"

"I think so." I know Samuel isn't totally sure why I'll be useful. I suspect Mr. Hayes told him about me but very little about my past. It's still sketchy to me, but I think I know what Samuel wants.

The sound of the pencil stops. "Wait," Trudi says. "This is about the Gardner Museum heist, isn't it?"

I look at her over my shoulder.

"I'm right, aren't I?"

"I need to think some things through before I give you an answer." There are still a lot of things I don't remember, and a lot that Paddy never told me.

23

SAMUEL

Boston, MA

"Why would you help my son?" Samuel asked Darrent. "What's in it for you?"

"You mean, do I have ulterior motives?" Darrent raised his black eyebrows. "You worry I'll hold Atif ransom to get you to back off."

"Seems the most logical explanation for your behavior."

"I can't argue with your logic, but I assure you that's not my motivation. I'm not really worried about getting arrested."

Samuel smirked.

"Not by you, anyway," Darrent said.

"And why is that? You committed an act of terror in Atlanta, and I'm an Atlanta police detective."

"Because you're too focused on much more important things than me right now."

Samuel couldn't argue that. "So, the question remains—why are you getting involved?"

"Like I said, Mama Bliss said she owes you."

Samuel only glared at him.

"That doesn't seem like enough motivation for most people," Hayes admitted. "But for me, nothing is more important than loyalty. I worked for Mama Bliss for more than half my life. I owe her loyalty."

"What about loyalty to your country? You worked for the CIA just as long—they don't deserve your loyalty?"

"We can debate whether my motivations are right or wrong all day. The fact remains, I can help you."

Samuel leaned closer and growled, "Where is my son?"

"He's in England. I used your idea and integrated him into an Indian community."

"Who's with him? Who's protecting him?"

"I have a friend who's ex-MI6. His family lives in an Indian community not far from London. Atif is with him, his mother, and his aunt. They're telling people he's a distant cousin who's staying with them for a while."

"Why is he *ex*-MI6?"

"He followed his conscience, but not everyone agreed with his determination of right and wrong."

"I'm going to need a little more detail than that."

"It's a little complicated, but the high points are that his wife was kidnapped, and he did what he had to do to save her. Unfortunately, she'd been badly beaten, and she died in the end. But at least he had a couple of more days with her."

"Someone came after her because of his position in MI6?"

"They held her ransom and demanded he deliver a weapons shipment. But he didn't think they'd let her go even if he did deliver, and he wasn't about to arm them further."

Samuel nodded. "Where exactly is Atif? The address."

"I'll happily give it to you, but you should leave him there.

He's safe, and you have too many plates spinning. Plus, al-Sadr is tracking you."

"*Trying* to track me," Samuel corrected. "I'm the best person to protect Atif. He's *my son*."

"That's exactly the attitude that could get him killed."

Samuel shifted in his seat but then managed to stop himself from reaching across the table for Hayes's neck.

"Why're you here and not with Trudi and Dream?" Hayes asked. "Anyone who's close to you is in the line of fire."

Samuel felt his entire body tighten, perhaps because he was angry and trying to control it, or perhaps because he knew Hayes was right. Having Atif with him was not a good idea. But he didn't trust Hayes. If Atif couldn't be with Dalal or with him, he wanted his son with Trudi, but that was impossible in the present circumstances. As he worked the situation through in his mind, he realized he had only one option: leave Atif where Hayes had hidden him.

"All right," Samuel said. "He can stay, but he doesn't get moved without my okay, and you don't tell anyone in the agency where he is or about anything I'm doing."

"If I'm a traitor, why would I still have agency connections?"

"Didn't you say you have a special kind of clearance level?"

Hayes smirked.

"And there's one more thing I need." Samuel took out of his breast pocket the small notebook he'd started carrying when he'd become a detective for Atlanta PD, flipped it open, and started writing. Then he paused and added, "Well, I need a couple of things."

Samuel walked through South Station toward the MBTA Commuter Rail lost and found. The place was packed as always, and he kept his stride casual and his expression friendly.

He hadn't arrested Hayes. He'd left him there at the bar. He still questioned that decision.

When he passed Barbara's Bookstore, he thought of Trudi. But then he pushed the distracting thoughts out of his mind and stopped at the lost and found.

"May I help you?" the clerk—a young, freckled girl—asked.

"I lost my wallet," Samuel said. "It's been a while. I've been retracing my steps, and this is the last place on my list. I'm really hoping you have it." The Agency wasn't aware of this ID—that unsettled feeling wouldn't go away, and he wanted to drop off the radar.

"What's it look like?"

"It's one of those long travel wallets. You know, has everything, including my passport. Man, I really hope you have it. I've been freaking out."

She smiled. "I can imagine. Passport and everything. Let me take a look." After going through some items, she looked up.

Samuel smiled his most charming smile, the same one he knew was in the picture on the license in the plain, black wallet she was holding.

"What's your name?" she asked.

"Michael Casey."

She asked him several more questions, including his address and birthday.

He answered each one. He'd gone over all of it in his head on his way to the station.

He lifted his chin, trying to peek at the wallet.

She pulled it away.

He let his smile start to fade.

Then she grinned. "Yeah, it's yours."

He set his hands flat on the counter. "Holy cow. You had me so disappointed."

"Female prerogative." She handed him the wallet.

"To disappoint men?"

"If we so choose."

"My wife must've taken the same class as you."

She giggled.

He tapped the wallet on the counter. "Thank you so much for your help."

"Anytime."

He walked away, back through the station.

When he headed outside to the overcast skies, he noticed a Latina woman standing by the Dukakis plaque on the gray block of the exterior of the building. He walked in the opposite direction.

Footsteps sounded behind him, matching his pace. He carefully monitored the distance from him to the sound of the footsteps. About ten feet back.

More people joined them on the sidewalk, and he couldn't track the footsteps anymore. Instead, he watched reflections in storefronts and the windows of a passing bus.

He turned onto Kneeland Street and then South Street. The woman continued to follow. He decided he was hungry anyway, crossed the street, went back to the corner, and stopped in at the South Street Diner. It had to be one of the last true diners in the country. It had corrugated metal siding on the façade and a huge sign shaped like a coffee mug on the roof. Inside, it was mostly empty. It smelled like potatoes and beef and grease. His stomach rumbled.

A few seconds after he took a stool at the counter, he heard the door open and close.

"What can I get ya, honey?" the waitress asked from the other side of the counter.

The woman's Boston twang made him smile a little. Samuel

had almost expected to hear a Southern accent coming out of the waitress's mouth, maybe because he'd grown so accustomed to the waitress at the little restaurant he liked down in Atlanta.

"Let's start with coffee," Samuel said as he picked up the menu she'd set in front of him.

"Coming right up."

She walked away, and Samuel browsed the menu. Right on cue, the Latina woman sat down next to him.

The woman ordered a water, and the waitress brought that and Samuel's coffee. Then the waitress headed back into the kitchen.

While still browsing the menu, Samuel asked, "So, where's your friend?"

No response.

He set the menu down and looked at the woman. "Are you going to ignore me now, Agent Uribe? And after you've gone through so much trouble to follow me."

Uribe set her menu down as well and smiled at him. There was still a shrewdness in her eyes.

"You've been knocking on every door to find me, and now you have nothing to say?"

She continued to smile. "I'm sure your wife told you about our conversation."

He didn't correct the lack of *ex-* in front of *wife*. "She said you're chomping at the bit to talk to me. Well, here I am."

"Just as easy as that, huh?"

"I'm an easy kind of guy, Agent Uribe."

"There are those who would say otherwise."

"And there are those who say the *Mona Lisa* wasn't painted by da Vinci. Doesn't mean they're right."

She reached into her breast pocket and set her credentials on the counter.

"Are we playing show-and-tell? I have a badge as well—want to see it?"

"Mine is a bit higher on the totem pole."

"I think we both know that's not entirely accurate."

She tucked her credentials back into her pocket. "What do you know about The Dream?"

"Didn't take psych in college."

"Don't play with me, Samuel. You know who I'm talking about."

"The Dream is a person? Unusual name."

"Okay, we can do this roundabout if you prefer. What're you doing in Boston?"

"Picking up the wallet I lost. As I'm sure you know." He was willing to bet she'd somehow found him on the South Station security camera footage and guessed he would come back for the wallet. Maybe she had paid off someone in the security staff to watch for him, since South Station was a major transportation hub.

"And why were you here in the first place?"

"Mini-vacation. Sightseeing. Boston is a beautiful city, and I'm a sucker for American history."

She smirked. "Very cute."

He grinned. "That's what I keep telling Trudi, but she says I'm not as cute as I think I am."

She gritted her teeth, and her eyes narrowed slightly, her focus seeming to turn inward. "Look, I know you know who The Dream is. I'm willing to bet you stashed him somewhere. He's important to an investigation I'm handling. Obviously, you don't know this, but he's dangerous. Extremely. I need to locate him, now."

"If he's dangerous, what's he doing free?"

"He was released without notice, as I'm sure you're plainly aware. I suspect you had a hand in it."

"I assume he was being held in this area. How would an Atlanta PD detective get someone released from a facility in Massachusetts?"

"As you've said, your credentials and connections don't stop at the Atlanta PD."

"I would still have no idea how to get something like that done." And that was honest. He had a lot more connections overseas than in the States.

"Where is The Dream now?" she demanded.

He widened his eyes innocently. "Got me." Then he asked the question he really wanted an answer to. "Why are you so sure I have any idea what you're talking about? How do you even know who I am?"

24

TRUDI

Atlanta, GA

Trudi let Dream walk down the hall and into one of the bedrooms. He hadn't answered her, but she was certain she was right: his tattoo was a map to the stolen artwork from the Gardner Museum heist.

Her first question: Was he purposefully keeping things from her?

Then she reminded herself he didn't owe her anything. He barely knew who she was, and their initial introduction had been traumatic for him. She just hoped he'd let her help him.

Then she wondered about Samuel. *Is this what he wants Dream to remember? But why does he need this information?* Samuel had never been a treasure hunter. What typically motivated him was love of country, love of family, and of course, the adrenaline rush. Could all this somehow be tied to national security? But how?

Then she suddenly remembered—she hadn't told Eulalie she wouldn't be in to the office today. Her assistant was probably worried. Trudi took her phone from her pocket and dialed the office.

"Coffey & Hill Investigations. How may I help you?"

"Hey, Eula, it's me."

"Where are you? I was really starting to worry."

"Got pulled into a little side project with Samuel."

"You found him?"

"Yeah. He's all right."

"A little side project, huh? That's a tauntingly vague answer. Does it involve your friend Billy Boy?"

"I think it might, actually."

"Should I know anything else?"

"That wouldn't be a good idea. What I would like is for you to take the next couple of days off."

"Why?"

"I can't be sure another Billy Boy won't show up at the office."

"But there are things that need to be done. Emails, appointments."

"Take my laptop home with you so you can answer any urgent emails. Forward the office phone to your cell. Cancel all the appointments."

Eula hesitated. "All right, Boss. But promise you'll call me if you need anything."

"Deal. Now, pack up your stuff."

There were shuffling sounds in the background. "Oh, by the way, Captain Stepp called for you."

"I'll call him next."

Trudi stayed on the phone with Eulalie until she was in her car and driving home. Then she dialed the number for the Zone 6 Police Department and asked for Captain Stepp.

"Trudi," Captain Stepp greeted. "Have you found Samuel?"

"Yes. He's fine."

"Good. He was starting to have me worried." Then he said, "But that's not why you called, is it?"

"Not really," she admitted. "You knew about The Dream and his tattoo."

"I have connections in the FBI." Obviously, he was still being careful about what he would say.

"Tama wants Dream so she can use his tattoo to solve the Gardner heist. She either wants the accolades or the reward. But can she claim the reward if she solves it in the course of her duties?"

"There are plenty of ways around such inconveniences."

Trudi supposed that was true. She took his response as confirmation she was likely right about Tama's interest in Dream.

"The one question I still have," Trudi said, "is how did she know Samuel would get involved with Dream before he even knew himself?"

Captain Stepp sounded concerned. "Are you sure about that?"

"He got a tip and found Dream in the TD Garden garage after Tama had already come to me looking for Samuel. What do you think that means?"

"I think we have more painters on the canvas than we thought."

"Do you—" Trudi stopped talking when she heard a sound in the common hallway.

"Is something wrong?" Captain Stepp asked.

Trudi kept her voice low. "Hang on." She walked quietly over to the door and looked out the peephole. She stepped back and murmured, "Oh no."

"What's wrong?" Captain Stepp asked. "Where are you, anyway? Is Samuel with you?"

"We're in Buckhead," she whispered. "The Meridian Buckhead condos on Peachtree Road. Please send some backup."

"What's going on? Another armed man like the other day?"

"Several. I don't know how they found us." Then she realized what must have happened. "They must be tracking my phone somehow." That was her best guess, anyway. They must've decided to track her since they couldn't catch up with Samuel.

"I'm sending some cars." There was a muffled sound, like him putting his hand over the receiver. Then she heard his voice. "Meridian Buckhead condos on Peachtree Road. I want three cars there. Now!"

"That's not in Zone 6," someone responded in the background.

"Go!"

His voice was back, no longer muffled. "Just hang tight." There were sounds in the background, rushed footsteps.

Someone pounded on the door to the condo. "Just send out The Dream. We'll leave." It was a heavily Boston-accented male voice.

"We don't have that much time," Trudi said to Stepp. "If your guys get to a small, nervous Middle-American man, help him."

Additional pounding on the door, more like someone kicking it.

Then the door flung open and smashed against the wall, revealing three men in the hall.

Nine minutes, she told herself. *That's the average police response time.* Stepp's men were farther out, but surely, all that noise would cause neighbors to call the local zone, and surely, Stepp would too. *I just need to keep them away from Dream for nine minutes.* She hoped Dream kept his head on straight enough to stay in that bedroom and hide.

"Where's our friend Dream?" a very large, middle-aged man asked. His dark hair was receding, and his voice sounded thick, like his vocal chords were crowded by fatty tissue.

She raised her voice, as if surprised and confused. "Who?"

Then she added, "Who are you? What do you want?" She kept her phone tucked in her palm.

"Doan mess around, lady. Just give him up." This man was much younger and was wearing a flat-brimmed baseball cap with the Red Sox logo on it.

"Give up who? I'm the only one here."

The third man brushed by the other two and marched into the condo. He seemed more serious, more calculating. She'd been watching him carefully as soon as the door flung open. He was middle-aged but in good shape, and he had a large, dark mole on his right cheek. He made no facial expression, absolutely nothing. Impossible to read.

He stood very close to her. The only reason she allowed it was to let him think he had her scared and to keep him thinking she wasn't a threat. Obviously, they hadn't talked to Billy Boy about her yet. "Doan play with me, little girl."

Eight minutes.

She met his gaze. "Watch who you're calling little girl."

An expression flitted across his face for the first time, a smirk. Then it was gone like dust in the wind.

She continued to meet his gaze and stand her ground. She chose not to pull out her Beretta Tomcat that was holstered inside the back of her waistband. She didn't have hollow points loaded that would be stopped by drywall, and she was afraid a standard round might go through a neighboring wall and hurt someone.

He shifted slightly, his movement telegraphing his intention. Before he could grab her throat, she shoved his hand to the side and forced him off-balance enough to turn him. Then she wrapped her right arm around his neck, his throat tucked into her elbow, and held her left bicep to lock the choke. Then she tightened her right arm to put pressure on the arteries on the sides of his neck that supplied blood to his brain.

The other two men drew their weapons.

Seven minutes.

"Want to shoot your boss?" Trudi asked.

The man with the mole and no expression grabbed at her hands. She pulled him backward, throwing him off-balance.

The other two looked back and forth between her and the man she was holding. They looked like bobblehead dolls.

"Well," Trudi finally said, "we can just stand here all day, or you two can go back down the way you came, and after five minutes, I'll release your boss here back to you." *And that will give bossman two minutes to get down to the lobby and meet my uniformed friends.*

"Stupid—"

"Hey," she said, cutting off the guy in the Red Sox ball cap. "Didn't your mother teach you to be respectful toward ladies?"

"You ain't no lady," the guy with the thick voice sneered.

"Well, aren't I just heartbroken."

The guy in her grip struggled. She squeezed tighter, and she felt him weaken. But he was still conscious.

Six minutes.

"We ain't goin' nowhere," Ball Cap said.

"You don't have a lot of options right now," Trudi said. "Here's the reality: I don't know who this 'The Dream' is. He's not here." *Please stay hidden, Dream!* "You can stand here and push me to tell you something I don't know, or you can get out of here before the police arrive."

"You didn't have time to call no police," Thick Voice said.

"That's who I was on the phone with when you showed up." She nodded toward her phone she'd dropped on the floor when she'd grabbed the guy with the mole on his cheek. "A captain, actually. He may still be on the line."

"You're full of it."

"You can come pick up the phone and find out for sure, or you can be smart, err on the side of caution, and get out of here to regroup. Up to you."

"I think we'll just take you with us," Thick Voice said.

"I really don't think you're in the position to make that kind of threat."

Five minutes.

He wiggled his gun like a schoolgirl with a fairy wand.

With her eyes, she pointedly indicated the man she was holding.

Thick Voice sneered.

She grinned.

Thick Voice took a step forward.

He stopped when she tightened her arm. She could see the man she was holding was turning red. She couldn't squeeze anymore or he'd pass out and be dead weight.

The standoff continued. Trudi decided to be quiet and not antagonize any further.

Four minutes.

Then she noticed movement out of the corner of her eye, in the hallway to her right.

Dream, just stay back. Hide.

She didn't give any indication he was there but watched peripherally. He'd stepped out of the bedroom door and was just standing there.

Get out of sight. Hide.

Dream remained still. Maybe he was petrified with fright and couldn't get himself to move?

The guy with the ball cap lunged.

Trudi pulled the man in her arms back, more off-balance and shielding her better, and tightened her bicep to put more pressure on the sides of his neck.

Then he lost consciousness.

Three minutes.

The man was nothing but dead weight, too heavy for her to hold on to. She shoved him toward Ball Cap, and they clattered to the floor. Before Thick Voice could get a shot off, Trudi jumped over the two men on the floor and landed a sidekick in his chest. He was so well protected with all his girth that he didn't fall, but he did stumble back into the common hallway. She threw a hook across his chin, and he turned.

"Dream!" she yelled. "Run. Now!"

25

DREAM

Atlanta, GA

The same men, I think. *Two of them are the same men who tried to grab me after I left the hospital.*

"The dark meat on roast turkey has more fat than the white meat."

I squeeze my eyes shut.

"Dream! Run. Now!"

"No two zebras have the same pattern of stripes."

But the images keep coming. I can't stop them . . .

The door closest to me flung open. "There you ah." A tall man had stepped out of the car and glanced between me and a small photo in his hand. Then he had tucked the photo back into his inside coat pocket. "Hello, Dream. Glad to be outta that place, finally?"

"Who are you?" I backed up a few steps.

He lurched forward and grabbed me by the arm, and another

man quickly exited the car and held me from behind. "I got him, William."

I tried to wrestle free, but I was weak from all the walking and the medication still draining from my system.

And other images came . . .

He shot Henri. That was all I could think. Some man with a pockmarked face walked in and shot Henri, a man I'd worked with side by side, someone I'd talked to about everything. He was dead. I'd never seen someone die before.

The canvas Henri had been working on was all red, not with paint but with his own blood.

Henri was on the ground. Not moving. Not breathing. Just nothing.

The man walked over to me. All I could do was stare at Henri. His skinny limbs lay awkwardly in the most uncomfortable way. And then I remembered comfort didn't exist for him anymore. He didn't feel anything anymore.

"You paint that?"

I looked at the man with the pockmarked face.

"I said, you paint that, skiddah?"

His accent was so thick, I almost couldn't understand. I looked at his face and then down at his hand, at the gun.

Then I realized I still had something in my hand, my paintbrush.

He took the paintbrush out of my hand and tossed it. My favorite fan brush. It hit the wall somewhere in the corner and clattered to the floor with a tiny *clink*, *clink* sound.

I stumbled backward. He'd pushed me. "Get with it."

Henri was dead.

He grabbed me by the shirt and pulled me close to him. He set the barrel of his gun on my cheek, almost in a gentle way—gentle like how my mother had touched me when I was a child.

"Javie," she called. Finally, my mother walked around the side of the house. "There you are. I've been calling."

"Sorry," I said. "Almost done. I promise."

She stood next to me and surveyed my progress. The garden in our backyard was splashed across the canvas—the huge maple leaves, the Jack Frost Ligustrums, and bursts of color from marigolds and peonies and sunflowers in the corner, and pink roses. Mom loved the pink roses the best. Dad had planted them for her.

"It's like a dream," she whispered.

I looked over at her.

"You make everything beautiful," she said.

"I'm just trying to do your garden justice."

"You made it better." She rested her gentle hand on my cheek. "Having you has made my whole life feel like a dream. Having a child was my dream, and now I get to watch you create your own. A dream within a dream."

And the pink roses changed to red. But it was wrong. It was smooth but liquid, not like softness of petals.

It was a knife. Covered in blood.

It was in my hand. *How did that get in my hand?* It didn't make sense.

Someone's shaking me. "Dream!"

I open my eyes. Trudi is in front of me, holding both my arms. "Please," she says. "Snap out of it. I need you to focus. We have to get out of here."

I nod.

She holds my hand and pulls me out the condo door. We have to step over the men on the floor, two of them inside the condo and one large man out in the hall. She runs, dragging me along, and I try to keep up.

I feel numb. I try to hold on to that. It helps me not to think. I decide to blindly trust Trudi to lead me. I have no other option. Either that or have another breakdown.

"I'm guessing they have someone in the lobby," she says. "Police should be here any second, but I don't want to risk going down in the elevator where they'll expect us." She hits a push bar on a metal door, and we enter a concrete space, a stairwell.

We run down the stairs. She's fast. I try to keep up.

We head down a couple of flights.

Then she stops on a landing.

"What're you—" I start to say.

She holds up her hand, a command for me to be quiet.

I'm quiet.

A metal clang from somewhere below us reverberates up the stairwell.

She turns and shoves me from behind toward a door. She quietly opens the door and continues shoving me, pushing me through. I turn and catch the door before it clangs shut and allow it to close slowly, quietly.

She smiles at me and then takes my hand. Down a hall, we slip around a corner and stop. Everywhere I look is a dead end, just halls of closed doors.

Trudi presses herself close to the wall and draws her gun from a holster hidden in the back of her jeans. "Don't get nervous," she whispers over her shoulder. "I plan on using it as a deterrent. I don't want to fire with so many innocent bystanders."

I feel myself slipping into another panic attack and close my eyes. *Keep quiet, Javie. You have to be quiet and calm.*

But what if they're not deterred by the sight of the gun? What if they have their own guns?

The sound of the metal stairway door pauses my mental panic like a sudden freeze.

We're perfectly still while we wait, watching the corner, waiting for an enemy face to appear.

26

SAMUEL

Boston, MA

"I said, how do you even know who I am?" Samuel asked Agent Uribe.

"Honey." The waitress had returned. "Are you all right?" she asked Uribe.

Samuel looked at Uribe. If she played any kind of game, he'd walk out and disappear.

Uribe smiled at the waitress. "Aren't you sweet. Yes, ma'am, I'm fine."

The waitress eyed Samuel but walked away.

"Are you going to cooperate?" Agent Uribe asked Samuel.

"Are you going to answer my question?"

"I should think it's pretty obvious."

"Let's pretend I'm as stupid as you think I am."

"I know a lot of people, Samuel."

"And why would anyone you know care that I'm taking a vacation in Boston? Forgive me, but I'm a little lost on this one."

"I think you're about as lost as a bloodhound."

"I appreciate the confidence. Unfortunately, it's a bit misplaced." His theory was that she'd caught wind of the questions he'd started asking around Boston about the Gardner Museum heist a couple of weeks ago, but he'd been careful to stay under the radar.

"Let's try this," she said. "Tell me what you know about The Dream, and I'll be on my way."

"If I knew something, I'd tell you. Why is this Dream person dangerous? What did he do?"

She leaned closer. "He murdered two men in cold blood."

"I never have gotten that saying. *In cold blood.* What does that even mean?"

Agent Uribe gritted her teeth. "It means he showed no remorse. He feels no empathy."

The waitress walked back over. "Do you want to ordah somethin' to eat?"

"No, tha—"

"Absolutely. I'm famished." Samuel smiled and picked up the menu. "Hmm . . . are the jalapeño poppers good?"

"If you like hot."

Samuel pursed his lips. "Maybe the burger, beer, and fries. What's a Narragansett? Wait, isn't that the name of a town?"

Uribe was glaring at him.

"They make lagahs," the waitress said.

"Eh, maybe I shouldn't have a beer. What about . . . kabobs? You serve kabobs? That's interesting."

"Is that what you'd like?" The waitress sounded slightly annoyed.

"No, I don't think so. Just give me a cheeseburger and fries." He folded the menu.

The waitress wrote down the order and went back into the kitchen.

Samuel turned back to Uribe and probably enjoyed the frustration on her face a little too much. "So," he said, "who was it that this Dream person killed, anyway?"

"Does that matter? Killing is killing."

"I think it matters quite a lot. Killing isn't necessarily the same thing as murder."

"How could they possibly be different?"

"Well, if some madman with a gun walked into this diner right now and you had to shoot him with your side arm in order to defend innocent civilians, that wouldn't be murder."

"That would be in the line of duty. The Dream is not law enforcement."

"What if that waitress had a gun behind the counter and did the same exact thing? That wouldn't be murder."

"Do you have a point with all this?"

"Just wondering about this Dream person you're so interested in."

"He killed two people. He was found with a bloody knife in his hand. He had no defensive injuries. He's a murderer."

"What's his side of the story?"

"He says he doesn't remember. Conveniently."

"Witnessing something like that could be awfully traumatic. I've seen memory loss from something like that."

"Are we going to get back to the point anytime soon?"

He grinned. "What was the point of your visit again? Oh, right, you think I know where this Dream person is. Sorry, Agent Uribe. I'm just a tourist here in Boston. If you asked me about something that went down in Atlanta, or perhaps some other key locations in certain countries, I could help you, but all I know about Boston is what I learned on my tour down the Freedom Trail. Man, that was some good stuff. You ever been on that tour? Boston Common is beautiful, though I'm sure it's even lovelier during spring. And seeing the Old North Church, where Robert Newman and Captain John Pulling climbed the steeple to signal to Paul Revere and William Dawes that the British were coming, was amazing."

"Okay," she said. "Obviously, you're not going to tell me where he is."

"Would if I could."

She smirked, then opened her mouth but stopped when the waitress came over with Samuel's burger.

"This looks delicious," Samuel said. "Thank you."

The waitress walked away to help an elderly woman and a little girl who'd come in and sat at a booth in the other end of the diner.

Samuel took a big bite of the burger and chewed slowly, partially because he was hungry and partially just to annoy Uribe. In his experience, people got messy when impatient and frustrated, and if he was good at one thing, it was frustrating people.

He squeezed some ketchup onto his plate and dipped a few fries in it. The food tasted better than it should have. He'd barely been eating.

"All right," Uribe said. "You're not going to tell me where The Dream is. Just tell me what you've found out so far, and I'll leave."

Samuel finished chewing and swallowed. "Found out about what? You mean the Freedom Trail?"

"Don't play with me, Samuel."

He popped a fry into his mouth and chewed while looking at her.

"The Gardner Museum heist," she said.

"You think this Dream person knows something about that?"

"He was an art forger."

"You're saying he forged some of the missing artwork?"

"So exquisitely that he had to have had access to the originals."

He smiled. "Now it makes sense. You're from the art crimes team, right?"

"Exactly."

"I read something about that heist once. Those guys were pretty brazen. They were never caught, right? Does the bureau have any theories about where they disappeared to? I mean, the guards saw their faces. That should've helped, right?"

"I need to find that missing artwork, Samuel."

And there it was. He knew what was going on with Uribe, why something about her hadn't sat right from the very beginning.

27

TRUDI

Atlanta, GA

Dream stood quietly behind Trudi while she watched the corner and listened intently to every sound. Several strategies went through her mind. They could head down the elevator and hope the police had arrived, but was that too much of a risk? Would any officers stay in the lobby, or would they all head up to check out the condo and sweep the rest of the floor? They could try the stairs again, but that risk was almost as unknown. The one benefit was that they could easily stop and hide on any floor much more quickly.

Trudi focused on her breathing.

The footsteps moved slowly closer.

A man turned the corner and stopped.

Not one of the men who'd attacked them. He was older, probably late sixties. "Who're you?"

Trudi smiled, thankful she had her Beretta concealed behind her leg. "Just waiting for a friend to get home. Hope no one minds if we wait in the hall."

He eyed her suspiciously.

"We can go back downstairs," Trudi said. "We were just hoping to surprise her." *Please don't ask me who.* She needed to get this man to go into his condo and stay out of the way. And she couldn't risk his calling security—that would complicate things in ways she couldn't anticipate. She smiled sweetly.

The man glanced at Dream. Trudi risked looking at him as well. The pleasant smile on his face made him look like a different person, someone not dealing with so much pain.

The old man turned back to Trudi and smiled. "Have a nice evening." He continued down the hall.

"Nice job, Dream."

He nodded, smile now gone.

"That was hard for you, wasn't it?"

"Yes."

She squeezed his shoulder. Then she turned back toward the corner.

"What should we do?" Dream asked.

"I think the only choice we have is to try the stairs again. I don't think the elevator is a good idea."

"Okay."

"Thank you for trusting me."

He nodded.

She holstered her gun in the back of her jeans but kept her right hand on the handle. With her left hand, she took Dream's. Slowly, they walked out from around the corner. Obviously, whoever they'd heard in the stairwell before had either passed this floor or wasn't one of the men looking for Dream.

They headed back into the stairwell and started down the stairs, stepping as quietly as possible so they could hear any noises in the stairwell shaft. They made it down to the bottom floor. There were no police officers. She took her hand off the handle of her gun and made sure it was properly concealed.

"Can you look not scared for a few minutes?" she asked Dream.

"Why don't we just ask someone for help?"

"Because I can't be sure who those guys have with them or who in the building they've gotten to. They could've paid someone off or threatened them. Plus, I won't get some innocent person involved in this." Then she asked again, "Can you look not scared for a few minutes?"

He took a breath. She rubbed her thumb across the back of his shaking hand. He managed to get his expression to a reasonable state. His forehead was still furrowed, but he looked more worried than terrified.

She led him through the main-floor common area and out to the parking lot for the shopping center next door. They had to walk through the open expanse of parking spaces to get to the little building with stairs down to the underground parking. She kept ahold of Dream's hand, partially to soothe him and partially to make sure he didn't bolt away from her in fear.

Sunlight was fading. Dream jumped when a pole light overhead popped on. She held his hand tighter and kept moving. For once, she was thankful for the fading light. It made it more difficult for someone to see them walking across this blank expanse.

Down in the underground parking, they stayed close to the concrete columns as they made their way to Trudi's car. Shadows lurked in the corners and seemed to tiptoe farther out while they walked.

"Where do you think those men are?" Dream asked.

"Hopefully still knocked out."

"But you think they left another in the lobby, right?" He glanced over at a particularly deep shadow between two large SUVs.

"Maybe. That's what I would've done, but it doesn't mean that's what they did."

"I don't hear any sirens. Were you telling the truth that the police had been called?"

"Yes. They might be in the building arresting those men right now. Let's just hope that's the case." She kept his hand and watched him. He didn't break into random facts like she'd thought he would. Maybe this experience was different enough that it didn't make him remember things he didn't want to remember, or maybe he was managing to focus better with someone helping him.

About ten yards from her car, Trudi took the keys from her pocket. Thankfully, she'd taken to keeping her keys, as well as a small wallet, in her jeans pocket. She liked handbags, but they got in the way sometimes.

A loud, deep voice reverberated off the concrete walls. "There he is!"

"Run!" Trudi ordered Dream. She kept his hand, and he ran with her toward her car. She was faster, but he mostly kept up.

"Hey!" Heavy running footsteps sounded behind them.

"Stop!" the same deep, commanding voice yelled.

"Get in," Trudi told Dream. She unlocked her car with the remote, jumped into the driver's seat, and shoved the key into the ignition.

"Will they shoot at us?" Dream asked.

"They want you alive."

"They might shoot at you."

"They won't hit me." She put the car in reverse and slammed her foot down on the gas. Tires squealed as she backed up and cut the wheel. She shifted into drive and punched the gas again.

At the end of the row, she turned the corner.

Tires squealed from somewhere behind them.

She glanced in the rearview mirror. A second later, a car turned the corner, following them.

She muttered under her breath.

Dream wrung his hands.

"Hang in there," she said. "I know this area a lot better than they do."

He kept wringing his hands, but he was quiet.

She flew up the ramp and turned onto Peachtree Road, then Tower Place Drive. When she pulled up to the intersection for the main road, Lenox, the left signal was green, so she turned.

Horns blared.

The car that was following them, a black Escalade, blasted through the intersection. The light had turned. Cars on Lenox skidded to a stop.

She swerved through traffic, trying to lose the Escalade.

At the light for Piedmont Road, there was a slight break in the traffic, and she cut through and made a left turn.

The Escalade was a couple of cars back and got stopped at the light.

She shifted into the right lane and made the turn into the Kroger shopping center. Past a line of small shops, she turned into the parking area in the corner between two buildings and pulled into a space on the other side of a jut out on the side of the Kroger store.

"Why'd you stop?" Dream asked.

"We'll be easier to find if we keep careening through traffic. They're a lot more likely to assume we're still in flee mode and blow by."

Dream sat very still, staring at the wall and wringing his hands. She could almost hear his internal struggle to stay calm. A mural on the side of the Kroger building paid homage to the history of the site, a disco in the seventies. Dream's gaze traced each line of the paint, a dancing man in a white leisure suit, a woman with colorful makeup and Farrah Fawcett hair, and a disco ball in the middle.

"It's pretty," Trudi said.

Dream didn't respond.

She glanced behind them, watching the lot. There was no way they'd seen them pull in here. They'd been stuck behind too much traffic. But just in case . . . she stood from the car. She didn't unholster her weapon for fear some random shopper would walk by and freak out at seeing a gun. That could draw a bunch of attention they didn't need. She wished she had her phone.

Dream stayed in the car. She was proud of him for managing to stay calm and even be useful.

Several minutes passed.

How long do I wait until I get Dream out of here?

A car turned the corner.

She reached for her weapon, but the driver, the very large man from the condo, already had a Glock with a silencer aimed at her. "Uh-uh, little girl."

How'd they guess where we went? Maybe they knew the area better than she'd assumed.

"Just give us The Dream."

"No."

"You don't have much choice."

"That's what you thought last time, isn't it?"

The back door of the Escalade opened, and the man with a mole on his cheek stepped out.

"Wake up from your little nap?" she asked.

He smirked, but no emotion entered his eyes.

The passenger door opened, and a large man stepped out, not one of the others she'd seen. This man was much taller and large from muscle rather than fat. "You think you can handle all of us?" he asked in a deep, sonorous voice.

"If I have to." *Dream, get out of the car and run.*

Dream did stand from the car. But he didn't run.

He walked to the end of the car and spoke to the tall man. "I'll come if you leave her alone."

The tall man looked over at the man with the mole. "We can't have her following us."

"I won't tell you anything if you hurt her."

The man continued as if Dream hadn't said anything. "But we can't leave a mess behind either." He looked at the man in the driver's seat. "The tires."

He fired and blew out both of her back tires.

Dream walked over to Trudi.

"Don't," she said. "We can get out of this together."

"You've been kinder to me than you should already." He took both her hands and squeezed. There was fear in his eyes, overwhelming fear, but also determination. Then he let go and walked toward the Escalade. He muttered under his breath, surely more random facts.

"Dream, don't," Trudi said.

"Thank you for everything." His hands shook as he pulled himself up into the car.

The other men joined him.

The man with a mole lowered his window and tapped the end of a .45 pistol on the edge of the door. "Keep that attitude in check, missy."

The Escalade drove away.

Trudi looked down at her hand, at the paper Dream had folded into it.

28
DREAM

Atlanta, GA

". . . needs them fah collateral fah that arms shipment. He's gonna kill us."

"We'll get him to talk."

They're talking about me in the next room. With my arms and legs strapped to a chair, I can't fidget. That usually helps me expend some of my nervous energy. I feel it building up inside me. "Any month that starts with a Sunday will have a Friday the thirteenth in it," I mumble.

I try to distract myself by looking around the house. From what I gathered while they were talking in the car, this place is a vacation rental. It's nice, all wood floors and molding. It's also on a huge lot buried in trees. No one can hear anything that comes from this house.

"He ain't said nothin' but gibberish."

"Let me rephrase. *I'll* get him to talk." Footsteps sound from around the corner.

I look over as the man with a mole on his cheek turns the corner, closely followed by the younger man with a baseball cap on. The younger man takes a drag from a cigarette pinched between his index finger and thumb.

"Ready to give us what we need?" the first man asks.

I turn my head away, facing forward.

"Asking nicely isn't working. We'll just have to move on to phase two."

This man, especially with his accent, reminds me of Southie. "Richard the Lionheart only visited England twice during his reign and could only speak French."

"Give me that," the man with the mole says.

"Watchu gonna do, Johnny?" the younger man asks.

Johnny takes the burning cigarette and pushes it into the skin of my arm.

I yell out in pain.

The younger man laughs.

"That enough for you?" Johnny asks me. "Or do we need to get moah creative?"

I keep my mouth shut by literally biting the insides of my lips. I don't want to tell them about the tattoo, about how it's a map. I want Trudi and Samuel to find the artwork. Mr. Hayes said if I help Samuel, he'll hide me, "fade" was what he called it. And I want to help Samuel and, especially, Trudi.

"Creative, it is. Good. I was always an inventive child. Drove my mothah nuts sometimes." Johnny stands in front of me and leans down. A couple of inches from my face, he clicks a lighter and relights the cigarette. "Like the smell of Marlboros?" he asks.

All I can do is stare at the red embers at the end of the cigarette.

He grabs me by the chin and slowly moves the embers closer. I try to struggle, try to shake my head free.

The younger man stands behind me and forces my head still.

The cigarette moves closer. The smell makes me feel sick.

It's so close I can barely see it. He holds it under my nose, and it's so hot I can smell my nose hairs burning. And then the inside of my nose is burning.

I yell out. I scream.

I keep screaming.

He keeps pushing the cigarette farther up until I feel like my brain is catching on fire.

I feel tears running down my cheeks.

I can't move other than gripping the chair so hard my fingers feel like they'll break.

My mind jumps away from me again . . .

I waited and listened. I couldn't move, and my knees were so tight to me that I thought they might break off. I'd managed to shimmy myself under the sink. Thankfully, I'd lost weight since coming here. Somehow, miraculously, I fit myself inside the cabinet and closed the door.

The alarm kept blaring. Southie had had an alarm system set up so that if anyone approached—or left—the cabin, he'd know. I stayed there in the bathroom cabinet, waiting for the alarm to stop. But it didn't stop.

And then there were voices—loud, aggressive. Not Southie's voice and definitely not Paddy's.

"Where are they?" someone roared.

"Where're what?" It was Southie.

"The paintings."

I'd made the mistake once of pointing out to Southie that they weren't all paintings. Some of them were drawings and a Chinese vase and one finial. That'd gotten me punched in the face and knocked out.

The first voice continued to demand the paintings with lots of obscenities mixed in.

Then there were bangs all over the cabin, probably from furniture being knocked over and doors being kicked in.

I stayed in the dark cabinet, waiting to be discovered and wondering who was there and who would cross Southie like that. Then I realized who it had to be—the one who had originally hired me to forge the paintings. When I'd first started working for him, I hadn't known who he was, but I'd eventually come to understand he was Irish mob. A lot more dangerous than Southie.

Then the bathroom door opened and banged against the wall.

Sweat dripped from the side of my face to the bottom of the cabinet.

There was the sound of the shower curtain rings gnashing across the metal rod.

I barely breathed.

Heavy, booted steps stopped. I couldn't tell if they were in the middle of the room or right outside my hiding place.

"Find anything?" someone called from another room.

"Ain't nothing in heah." The booted footsteps walked away.

There was a loud thud, like someone being slammed against a wall, and then lots of yelling and arguing.

It wouldn't seem to stop. I got lost as to whose voices were whose. I tried to find Paddy's voice but couldn't. *Maybe he got out.* I told myself that over and over.

But I didn't really believe it.

Should I go try to help him, make sure he's safe? But how would I be able to make anyone safe?

And then the voices stopped.

It was a long silence.

Maybe they left. Maybe Paddy will come find me any second.

But then I heard the same booted steps, probably passing by the open bathroom door. There were voices again, but they were calm, conversational.

Then there was nothing.

For a long time, I stayed in that cabinet, feeling like a piece of a jigsaw puzzle. My legs were numb. My shoulders burned with pain. But I stayed put.

What felt like hours later, I finally pushed the cabinet door open just a crack so I could peek out. I could see out to the hall, but no one walked by. Slowly, I unwedged myself and spilled out onto the bathroom floor. The hexagon tile was cold against my sweaty skin.

I pulled myself up to standing by holding on to the counter. My legs burned like embers as they tried to wake. I hobbled out to the hallway and dragged my hand along the wall to keep myself steady.

I saw something on the floor, something that hadn't been there before. Paddy and I always kept our supplies tidy and would never leave something on the floor. There was liquid around it. Before I realized what it was, I picked it up.

It was a bloody knife.

My hand was wet and sticky from touching it.

I didn't understand what was going on. It felt like my brain was stopping me from figuring it out as a protection mechanism.

And then, on my right, against the wall by my work station, I saw Southie. He'd been stabbed so many times, his midsection looked like a showerhead.

Tears ran down my cheeks.

"Paddy!" I ran to him from across the room. He was lying on the floor near the kitchen, half on his side. I rolled him onto his back, expecting him to look at me with that dry expression of his. But his eyes looked straight up at the ceiling, no life.

I sobbed.

My mind felt like a blur, like trying to understand an impressionist painting with your face an inch from it.

"Where's the rest?" Dr. Brone asked.

"The rest of what?" I asked.

"You're not telling me everything. I know when a patient is holding back."

"I don't know what you want."

"I want the full truth. You can't heal until you get everything out. Every detail. Every single thing."

I shook my head. I didn't want to think about it. I didn't want to remember any more.

He stood and walked slowly behind his chair. He was tall and thick and looked more like a Marine than a doctor, especially with his buzz cut. The room was one open space, with nothing but plastic chairs. It was where we had group sessions, as well as where I met Dr. Brone for my private sessions. I wasn't sure if he had private sessions with anyone else.

He picked up a chair and slammed it against the floor.

I jumped.

A few minutes later, I walked out of the room, legs shaky. I made it to the common room but lost the little strength I'd had and plopped down on the floor behind a sofa. Someone on the other side of the room was screaming, and someone else was yelling at him to shut up.

"Just breathe." A man was sitting next to me. I was sure he hadn't been there a second ago.

I looked at him, trying to figure out who he was. He wasn't a doctor, and he didn't seem like a patient.

He smiled at me.

I started to feel calmer.

"There you go." His voice was gentle yet held my attention. "Feeling better?" he asked.

I nodded.

He smiled again. "Good."

"Who are you?" I asked.

"Not important right now. Just remember, I'm here for you."

I closed my eyes for a few seconds and just breathed. When I opened them, the man was gone. I looked around, but he wasn't anywhere.

"Did you hear me?" It's Johnny, the man with the mole on his cheek.

There's so much pain. So many places.

But then I remember the man and how he helped me feel calm when I was certain I could never feel calm again.

"Where ah the paintings?" Johnny demands.

I look up at him. "I don't know where they are."

He pauses. "Well, then you're dead weight."

29

SAMUEL

Boston, MA

Trudi wasn't answering. He'd called over and over and over. He'd even tried calling Eula, but she hadn't heard from Trudi other than when she'd told her to stay away from the office. Eula had said Trudi hadn't seemed particularly stressed, just cautious.

The only reason she wouldn't answer was if something was wrong. *But she would find a way to let me know what was going on. Has something gone that wrong?*

He'd managed to ditch Uribe by using the men's room and then slipping out when she was talking to the waitress. He made it back to his rental car and headed toward the airport.

He was worried about Trudi, and more than ever, he needed to hear her voice. Atif kept popping into his mind—how scared he must be, how terrified he was without his mother to soothe him. Samuel couldn't stand the idea of his sweet, innocent boy crying himself to sleep every night. He gripped the steering wheel so hard, he thought he might break it.

He'd used up a lot of his calm dealing with Agent Uribe.

And knowing what Uribe's agenda was, though helpful, set him on edge even more. An FBI agent couldn't collect a reward for doing her job. *She's out to find the art and get the reward, or rather, sell it on the black market.* Which meant the artwork wouldn't get back to its rightful owner. And if she was dishonest enough to do that, she might be capable of a lot worse.

Samuel parked at the curbside check-in at Logan International Airport and walked inside.

"Sir, you can't leave your car there. Sir!"

Samuel continued walking. The flags of many nations hung high above his head as he wound his way through a maze of blue rope toward a counter.

"Sir! Your car will be towed if you leave it there."

Samuel waved his hand toward the man who'd followed him inside. "Tow it." Then he looked at the woman at the counter. "I need the next available flight to Atlanta."

After paying a hefty sum, Samuel walked away with a ticket in the name of Michael Casey. He had to wait almost three hours for the flight. He headed toward the terminal, not sure how he was going to pass the time without going insane. His mind kept spinning, always returning to one of two thoughts: *I shouldn't have left Atif* or *I shouldn't have gotten Trudi involved.* And mixed with those thoughts was his grief for Dalal's death. While he hadn't loved her, not like he loved Trudi, she'd been a dear friend and the center of his little boy's world. One more way he'd failed his son. Then he worried about his handler, if his instincts were right. And Agent Uribe, her obvious desperation. And the Irish mob that was after Dream and had possibly found him. And al-Sadr, who could topple everything if they caught up with Samuel too quickly.

He stopped walking and took a breath. *Get your head straight, Samuel. You're better than this.* He usually was, but this time things had gotten personal.

Before continuing, he glanced behind him, casually watching his surroundings, and noticed a man about ten yards back. He'd noticed the man before. The man had stopped as well, apparently to read a sign.

Samuel started forward but glanced back again a few seconds later. The man had also resumed walking, still about ten yards back. Though he was dressed in American clothing, the man was the right ethnicity to be al-Sadr. *Could they have gotten into the country faster than anticipated?* Then he remembered from where he'd gotten that November 20 time frame: his handler.

Samuel got in line to go through security. If the man was al-Sadr, maybe he'd back off and not risk getting flagged by TSA.

But the man got in line several people behind Samuel. He noticed a woman glance back at the man with that cautious expression that usually angered Samuel. He'd known so many good people from the Middle East who did not deserve to be treated like terrorists just because they had similar skin color and features.

The line moved slowly. Samuel put his shoes, phone, belt, badge, jacket, and wallet into one of the plastic bins. He'd had to leave his sidearm in the rental car.

"How's it going?" Samuel asked the TSA officer watching the bag scanner.

The officer nodded.

"So, what's the oddest thing you've ever seen in a bag?" Samuel asked.

The officer didn't look up, but the corner of his mouth twitched.

"That good, huh?" Samuel said.

"I should write a book."

Samuel laughed. "I'd read that."

"But it shouldn't be sold in the airport bookstores."

"Freak people out too much?"

"Not in a safety way but a who-are-these-people-I'm-sitting-next-to way." He continued to watch the monitor even while he talked.

"Oh, that's just too good not to ask."

The officer smiled. "We take the privacy of the passengers very seriously, sir."

Samuel laughed.

Then it was his turn to be scanned.

While he took his things from the plastic bin, he chatted with the female TSA officer at that end of the line. This kind of open friendliness tended to set people at ease and make them think he wasn't paying close attention, and all the while, he saw every detail. He saw every item in every bin—the book of fairy tales and silver martial arts kicker necklace a young mother had, as well as the ratty wallet and $2,500 Brooks Brothers trench coat a middle-aged man had. He saw the amount of care each TSA officer put into their work, and where the weak links were.

The man he'd been watching, who he'd determined was probably of Saudi-Arabian descent, tied his rubber-soled dress shoes and slipped a slim wallet into his front pants pocket. He carried nothing else with him, not even a jacket. Even with so little to retrieve from the bin, he seemed to take longer than most people.

Samuel put his jacket on and headed toward the terminal. So did the other man, maybe two seconds after Samuel.

Instead of following the majority of passengers straight toward Gate B15 and beyond, Samuel turned right down a hallway toward Gates B4 through B14. It would've made more sense to have gone through the larger security area closer to those gates.

After reading the signs, the man turned and followed Samuel.

Samuel passed a few shops on his left and continued past the other security area toward several restaurants.

So did the man.

Samuel paused to consider: Starbucks, Asian Too, McDonald's, Au Bon Pain, or Sbarro.

The man passed him and walked up to the long line of people waiting at Starbucks.

Samuel walked up to the shortest line, which happened to be McDonald's at the moment, and ordered a small soft drink.

He sipped the sugary drink while walking away. He felt like he did need the sugar and caffeine. He hadn't gotten to finish his meal at the South Street Diner.

Before ordering a coffee, the man walked away in the same direction as Samuel, down the hall toward the gates.

On the right, Samuel passed the American Airlines Admirals Club and then veered to the other side of the hall and into the men's room. He went into one of the stalls and waited, watching through the crack in the stall door.

Several seconds passed.

He heard the restroom door open, and then someone came into view—the same Saudi man wearing a plaid dress shirt and no jacket.

Another man was at the sinks washing his hands. Samuel waited for him to finish and leave. By the time he was gone, the Saudi man had finished at the urinal and was washing his hands.

Samuel walked out of the stall and spoke in Arabic. "May I ask who you are and why you're following me?"

30

DREAM

Facility for the Criminally Insane
Massachusetts

My cell. I tried not to think of it like that, but that's what it was. The heavy metal door had windows with wire mesh running through them and thick mullions that were essentially bars. I squirmed on my thin mattress, turning away from the door and facing the wall instead. The paint had been partially peeled off by some previous resident. I vaguely wondered where that resident was now. Likely not released. I'd never seen anyone released from here.

There was a loud bang on the metal door. "Hey, time for group."

I rolled out of bed and stood. After handcuffing me, the officer led me down the hall.

Then I sat and waited in the large room filled only with plastic chairs.

I heard Boot's shuffle before I saw him enter the room. He refused to wear anything other than his old military boots, but we weren't allowed shoelaces, so his heavy boots scuffed along the floor while he walked.

He flopped down in a chair a couple down from me. "How ya doin', Dream?" We'd discussed once in therapy that my mother had called me Dream as a nickname, and now it'd pretty much replaced my real name here.

I shrugged.

"What's gotcha down?" Boot never seemed to realize he was in a state prison. Sometimes it was nice that he acted like we were in normal society, but sometimes it was frustrating.

I didn't answer.

"Still can't remember everything the doc wants, huh?"

"Don't want to remember," I corrected.

"I hear ya, man. That last mission in Fallujah, I try my darnedest to forget. I wish I had your problems remembering."

"You do, dippy." Wavelength sat in one of the chairs between me and Boot. She turned her blonde head toward me. "Remember last time? He couldn't even remember his kids' names."

"I can absolutely remember my kids' names."

"Yeah?" she said. "What are they?"

"Marsha, Jan, and Cindy. They're adorable girls. Growing up too quickly." Then he smiled a little. "Marsha looks a little like you, actually."

I figured he had a couple of girls, and they probably were actually blonde. Those were the details that were pretty consistent. I wondered why he blocked the actual facts, though.

Wavelength spoke to me again. "Looking a little tired, Dream."

"Couldn't sleep."

"Couldn't or didn't want to?"

I shrugged.

"Don't worry about it," she said. "You just get through however you can."

Sometimes I wondered what she'd done to get in here. Maybe nothing, like me. Or I was pretty sure I hadn't done anything. But maybe that was part of the memories I was always blocking. Maybe I was a psycho and just didn't know it. Maybe I was a ruthless killer trapped in this weak mind.

"Quiet, please." Dr. Brone had come in. He sat in a chair directly across from me, and most of the room sat down and quieted.

For a while, Dr. Brone talked about all the usual things. I sat quietly, looking at him, but not hearing much of what he said.

Then it was time for our break. Well, Dr. Brone called it a break. It was really a pause while the orderlies made us take our meds.

"How are you, Javie?" Instead of an orderly today, a middle-aged woman with a softness about her face and figure and emerald green eyes handed me my pills.

I smiled. "Hi, Clara."

She handed me a little paper cup of water. "Are you doing okay?"

I downed the pills with the water and shrugged.

She took the cup from me and then held my hand. "You remember the book?"

"All of it."

"Did I mention how impressed I am?"

I smiled a little. "Thanks."

"Your mind is yours. You can control it if you really want." She squeezed my hand and moved on to the next patient.

I waited while the other patients took their pills.

"No, no, no!" It was Wavelength.

"You can use your telekinesis, right?" Clara asked. She leaned closer to Wavelength and spoke more quietly. "It's a lot easier if you let everyone think you took your meds, but you use your telekinesis to stop the pills halfway down."

Wavelength paused. Then she took the cup of pills and the water. She downed the pills and then winked.

"Impressive." Clara smiled.

Wavelength was always better—calmer and happier—when she took her pills. I was glad Clara could get her to take them. That made me wonder why my pills always made me feel horrible. Did Dr. Brone not have my dosages right?

Screaming. I looked over as Clara backed away from a patient, a man with a long beard who never talked, other than obscenities. I'd always stayed away from him. He swung a fist toward Clara's face.

I stepped out of line and so did Boot. We stood in front of Clara. I knew I couldn't defend her. I didn't have the skills, nor did I want to be put in solitary for fighting, but I could be a shield.

A guard ran across the room and grabbed the screaming, flailing man. Then Dr. Brone injected him with something. He fell limp. Two orderlies dragged him away.

"Well, that was exciting," Dr. Brone said. "Back to your seats."

I asked Clara, "Are you okay?"

She smiled, but her hands were shaking. "Yes, I'm fine. Thank you both."

"Dream," Dr. Brone called, "take your seat."

I headed quickly across the room to my chair, closely followed by Boot.

"So, Dream," Dr. Brone said, "dream anything interesting last night?"

Several of the others snickered. He made the same joke every day.

"No," I said.

"It's healthy to discuss your dreams."

"I don't usually remember them."

"Usually?" He raised an eyebrow and took a pen from the front pocket of his lab coat.

I resisted the urge to sigh. "Once in a while, I dream about my childhood."

"Nothing else?" He never seemed interested in my childhood for some reason. Perhaps he'd read my file and determined my childhood had been comparatively uneventful, other than having been adopted from Mexico and losing my father and later my mother.

"No," I said.

He scooted forward to the edge of his chair. "Do you know what makes a good doctor, Dream?"

I shrugged.

"The ability to see when someone isn't being fully honest. I am a very good doctor, Dream."

"I don't remember anything else. Just lingering feelings when I wake."

"What kinds of feelings?"

"Fear. A lot of fear. And a feeling that nothing's ever going to be right again."

"There is one way to make everything feel right. Get it out in the open. Stop suppressing."

"I just don't think I'm ready."

Anger flashed across his eyes. "I'm telling you that you are ready, Dream."

How can he be so sure about that? A part of me wanted to believe him, that I could feel okay again, that I didn't have to be afraid every second of every day. Then I remembered there were a few times I hadn't felt afraid. Those moments were what gave me the little strength I had.

"Dream," Dr. Brone demanded.

I looked at him.

"What aren't you telling me?"

"I don't remember what happened before I was arrested."

"Because you're not trying."

"I can't."

"Why?"

"It's bad. It's really, really bad. I can't handle it."

"You have to handle it, Dream."

I shook my head.

"All right. Start with what happened before the arrest, several months before. You were in that cottage for a year and a half."

I didn't remember having ever told him that. "I can't remember anything."

"Because you're not trying. You're being lazy."

My shoulders sagged.

"Who was at the cottage with you?" Dr. Brone asked.

"Paddy, I think." That was his name, wasn't it? I could almost picture him. And then I saw blood and felt myself cringe. "Aircraft are forbidden to fly over the Taj Mahal."

"What?" Then he went on. "Who was Paddy? What did he do at the cottage? Was he another painter or a captor?"

I shook my head. "If the sun stopped shining, it would take us eight minutes to be aware of it."

"What are you doing?"

Boot spoke up. "It's what he does when something's too hard to remember. He recites facts from a book. It helps."

Dr. Brone looked at Boot and then back to me. "Who taught you that?"

I didn't answer.

The doctor turned to Boot. "Who?"

"I don't know." I knew he did know. I was happy he kept his mouth shut.

Dr. Brone stared at me. I looked at the cheap tile floor.

"Nurse Clara," he said. "I've seen her talking with you more than needed." He stood and said to the room, "Stay in your seats. The guards are watching." He walked out of the room.

"He's going to fire her!" Wavelength said.

"He doesn't have that kind of authority," Boot said.

"He's a doctor. She's a nurse. He's in charge. He's going to fire her."

I fidgeted with my hands. "Swing singer and crooner Harry Connick Jr. started playing the piano at the age of three."

Whispers circulated. Most of the group stayed pretty quiet with the two guards in the room, but I could hear how agitated they all were. Everyone, at least in their lucid moments, liked Clara. She treated everyone like a human being, even the inmates who seemed barely human.

Dr. Brone returned about ten minutes later. He picked up his clipboard and continued the session. Thankfully, he decided to move on to someone other than me, but he didn't tell us anything about what he'd done. Had he fired her?

Finally, group was over. Since I hadn't shown any violence since coming here, I was allowed a little time in the common area. There was a TV and several couches, along with a couple of patients in wheelchairs, drooling down their fronts.

The first orderly I saw I asked about Clara.

"Are you supposed to be in here?" the huge man asked.

"I'm allowed. As long as I behave." I walked away and waited for him to leave. I understood why they had to be so stern, especially after seeing that man try to attack Clara earlier, but it was hard to be treated like that.

A nurse rolled another drooling patient into the room.

"Excuse me?" I said.

"Are you ready to go back to your room?" I liked when they called it a room, not a cell.

"No, thank you. I just wanted to see if you know where Nurse Clara is."

She paused, and there was a barely noticeable sadness behind her eyes.

"She's gone," I said. "Isn't she?"

"I think she's being moved to a different facility."

I nodded. "I'm ready to go back to my room now."

She got a guard to escort me. The metal door to my cell clanged shut, and I slumped down in the corner of the concrete room. "I'm sorry, Clara," I whispered.

I fidgeted with my hands. And then started rocking. And then banged myself against the wall. Tears fell down my cheeks. Anger filled me like it never had before. It was my fault. I'd hurt one of the only people who'd been nice to me. *It's my fault. It's my fault.*

My head bounced back on the wall, and I kept doing it. I closed my eyes and tried to focus on the pain.

"Javie."

I opened my eyes. The gentle man was back.

"Stop, Javie."

I stopped.

"It's not your fault."

"It is." Tears slowly rolled down my cheeks.

"You tried to protect her."

"I failed."

"God does not leave us."

I hesitated. "Will He stay with Clara?"

The man smiled that calm, kind smile of his. "Of course. She asks for His help often. He is with her." He reached over and rested his hand on mine. Calm flooded me, the way fear usually did. "He helps those who are in trouble and lifts those who have fallen."

I breathed and then leaned my head against the cold wall.

There was a bang on the metal door. "Who're you talking to in there?" The guard looked in through the window.

The kind man was gone.

"Dr. Brone wants a private session with you," the guard said.

31

SAMUEL

Boston, MA

The Saudi man stopped washing his hands. "Excuse me?" he said in Arabic, definitely with a Saudi accent.

"I said, why are you following me?"

"I'm not following you. Who are you?"

"Let's not play games."

"I don't know who you are." He shook the water off his hands and bypassed the hand dryer.

Samuel stood in his way, blocking the door. "Do you even know why they sent you?"

"Who? No one sent me. I'm on my way home to Atlanta."

Samuel stared him down.

"I don't know who you are," the man said. "Move out of my way."

Samuel grabbed his wrist, put him in a lock, and pushed him against the wall.

"What are you doing? Let me go!"

Samuel held the lock with one hand and patted the man's

pockets with the other. He'd expected some kind of weapon, but perhaps getting something past security had proved too difficult. Samuel took the man's wallet out of his pocket and flipped it open: an American driver's license with an Atlanta address, cash, Mastercard, debit card with Wells Fargo, and several pictures of him with a smiling woman in a hijab and a couple of kids, one taken in front of the ATL sign in Woodruff Park in Atlanta.

Samuel let go and backed up. "I'm sorry. I thought you were following me."

"Are you insane?" The man took his wallet and rushed out of the restroom.

Samuel stayed in there for a few minutes to get his head straight.

His throwaway cell rang. He took it out of his pocket and looked at the screen—a 678 number, Atlanta.

"Hello?" he answered.

"Samuel?"

"Trudi. Thank goodness. I've been trying to call you. What's going on?"

"I'm sorry, Samuel. They took Dream."

"Are you all right?"

"I'm fine. But they took Dream, Boston mob. He went with them to make sure they left me alone."

Samuel rested his hand on the counter and leaned his weight on it. *Thank goodness she's all right.* "How long ago did they take him?"

"About twenty minutes. I'd lost my phone before we got out of the condo, so I had to go buy a throwaway. I tried your cell, but it was dead. I called Eula out of desperation. She had your new number. What happened? Why'd you ditch your old phone?"

"I don't think it's secure anymore. You said you got out of the condo. Where'd they catch up with you?"

"The disco Kroger. I'm hoping you can call Stepp and get him to pull traffic camera footage and see if you can figure out where they took Dream. They were in a black Escalade with tinted windows, Massachusetts plates, 267BRP."

Samuel set all that to memory.

"Can you call Stepp now?" she asked. "I'm worried what they're going to do to Dream."

"You got out of there, right? You're someplace safe?"

"Stop wasting time. I'm fine. Just call Stepp."

"All right, all right. I'll call you back within half an hour."

She ended the call.

He sighed and then dialed the number for the precinct mainline. He was transferred to Stepp's office.

"Samuel. Where are you? What's going on?"

"Do you remember when you first agreed to take me on? I told you there may come a time when I couldn't give you the full story."

"Yes."

"That time has come. Though I'm sure you've put together a fair amount."

"A fair amount," he agreed. "Where's Trudi? Do you know if she's all right? She asked me to send officers to a condo building in Buckhead, but she wasn't there when they arrived."

"I'm sure she left a trail of destruction."

"Someone took a beating. Found blood on the floor. But everyone was gone."

"She must've just knocked out her attackers. She wouldn't seriously injure someone unless she had no choice. But I just talked to her. She said she's safe."

"I'm relieved to hear that, but I'm sure you didn't call just to tell me that."

"I need a favor. I can't give you details, but I need to track a vehicle on traffic cameras. Black Escalade with tinted windows, Massachusetts plates, 267BRP. It left the Piedmont Peachtree Crossing shopping center about twenty minutes ago."

"That's the Kroger center, right?"

"Yes."

"Let me ask you, do you need to find the vehicle because it was involved in a crime? I need some kind of narrative."

"It was a kidnapping. I have strong reason to believe the assailants plan to harm the victim and may kill him."

"All right. I'll get it done. I'll put it under the category of cooperating with a federal agency."

"Thank you."

"Call you back." Stepp ended the call.

Samuel put his phone in his breast pocket and ran his hands through his hair. Then, sure the Saudi man was long gone, Samuel walked out of the men's room and turned toward his gate.

He was halfway through the terminal when an authoritative voice from behind him said, "Stop right there, sir."

Samuel stopped and turned around. "Is there something wrong, officer?"

The officer looked back at the person behind him, the Saudi man. "Is this the man who attacked you?"

"Yes, sir."

Several people had stopped to stare.

"I think you must be mistaken," Samuel said. "I have a very familiar look about me."

"I'm positive, officer," the Saudi man said.

"I need you to come with me for questioning," the officer said to Samuel.

"I'll miss my flight." Samuel pulled his eyebrows together and furrowed his forehead a bit.

"You can reschedule."

"I really need to get home. My wife is pregnant and due to deliver any day."

The officer put his hand on his handcuffs.

Still with the furrowed forehead, Samuel shuffled reluctantly forward. Thank goodness he'd heard from Trudi. If he hadn't known she was all right, he wouldn't have been able to handle this so calmly. He followed the officer back through the terminal, and eventually, they made it to a security office.

The officer patted Samuel down, then took his wallet, phone, and badge out of his pockets and handcuffed him to a table. He set the items on the table, out of Samuel's reach. Interestingly, he didn't seem to take any notice of the badge.

"This isn't necessary," Samuel said.

"We'll just chat a bit, sir, and then we'll decide what's necessary." He looked like the captain of the football team—young, blond, and thick.

"Look, please bring me whoever's in charge."

"Do you have a story to tell?"

"An interesting one, actually."

He smirked. "The man you attacked has an interesting story as well. So, why'd you attack him? Because of his skin color, nationality, or just because you're crazy?"

"Please bring me whoever's in charge. You'll be glad you did."

"Is that a threat?"

Yeah, someone sounds like he's on the 'roids. "Certainly not." Samuel smiled.

The officer left the room.

Samuel sat there for at least ten minutes. Although he didn't feel patient, he maintained the illusion of it on the outside. Trudi had sounded pretty concerned about Dream, which meant she would go to extremes to help him. He knew she was smart enough not to be reckless, but she was also the kind of person to put herself in harm's way to help someone else.

Finally, the door opened and a man, probably in his midsixties, walked in. He had wrinkles and white hair, but his gray eyes were sharp as a switchblade. He sat across from Samuel. "I hear you have a story for me."

"First, I apologize for confronting that man. I honestly thought he was following me. I can't tell you every detail, but I do have good reason to be cautious."

"Not every Muslim is a terrorist."

"That I know better than most."

"And how is that?"

"Again, I can't tell you everything, but I will tell you that I'm a government agent."

The man picked up Samuel's badge. "Atlanta PD isn't usually referred to as a government agency. If this is even real." He tossed the badge back down on the table.

"I'm currently working as a homicide detective while on stand-down."

The man raised an eyebrow. "Stand-down?"

"For my and my family's safety. There's a particular family in the Middle East that's not especially happy with me right now."

"You told my officer you had to get home to your pregnant wife."

"Yes, I did. In my line of work, sometimes twisting the truth, when it doesn't hurt anyone and to make circumstances work in my favor, is necessary. I know that sounds kind of horrible, but if you'd been in the situations I've been in, you'd understand."

"Lying is wrong, especially to law enforcement. That's pretty simple."

"I wish the world were that simple," Samuel said. "Let me explain a bit about what's happening, and perhaps you'll understand.

The mother of my son was recently killed, my son is being protected by someone I don't trust, and the person I care about most in this world, besides my son, is in danger. I need to get back to her. That's why I'm trying to catch a flight."

"And yet you found time to attack an innocent stranger in a restroom. Do you have any idea who he is?"

"Like I said, I thought he was following me."

"I'm still waiting for some kind of evidence for anything you've said."

"Unfortunately, I don't have evidence, and even if I did, I couldn't share it with you."

"Convenient."

"In my line of work, you don't keep evidence of anything on you. You commit all intel to memory. That's the only place I can guarantee is safe." When his phone started ringing, Samuel looked over at it. He recognized the Atlanta PD number. "That's my captain in Atlanta."

"I'm sure it is."

"It's very important that I talk to him. Please."

"We're not done here."

"You can put it on speaker if you want."

The officer picked up the phone, looked at the screen, and then clicked the button to send the call to voicemail. "That man you attacked, he's from Saudi Arabia."

"I realize that."

The officer raised his chin. "I'm surprised you admit it."

"Why wouldn't I? I've worked in that area of the world for years. I speak Arabic. I recognize the different accents."

The officer smirked. "You really must think I'm stupid."

"What?"

"To admit all that to me."

And then Samuel realized what was going on.

32

TRUDI

Atlanta, GA

While she waited for Samuel to call her back, Trudi searched for transportation. She had a spare tire in the trunk, but only one. She tried searching for a nearby mechanic who would come make repairs, but they all required the car to be towed to them. She didn't have time to wait for that. Taking a cab or an Uber to find Dream would possibly put that driver in harm's way. Not an option. That left one possibility.

Eulalie answered after the second ring. "Hi, Boss."

"Hey, I have a huge favor."

"Of course. What do you need?"

"A car."

"What's wrong with yours? Is everything all right?"

"I'm fine, but someone I'm trying to protect isn't."

Keys jangled in the background and then she heard Eula's light footsteps. "I'm on my way. Where are you?"

"Do you know where the disco Kroger is?"

"Yeah, I think so."

Trudi gave her proper directions.

Eula's car engine came to life in the background.

"Make sure you're not followed," Trudi said.

"I was taught by the best. I got this."

While she waited for Eula to arrive, Trudi watched the time, willing Samuel to call back soon.

Finally, her phone rang. But it wasn't Samuel's number.

"Hello?"

"Trudi, it's Stepp."

"How'd you get this number?"

"When I couldn't get ahold of Samuel, I called your office. Your assistant gave me your number."

Right, Eula forwarded the office calls to her cell. "What do you mean you can't get ahold of Samuel? He called a little while ago, right? And gave you his new cell number."

"Yes, but he's not answering. He asked me to use traffic cameras to follow a black Escalade out of the Piedmont Peachtree Crossing shopping center."

"Yes. He did that for me. Someone we're protecting was kidnapped, and I think he's in serious danger. Can you please tell me where that Escalade went?"

"I have people gearing up."

"They could be too late."

"I'm not throwing officers into danger without proper preparation."

"I'm not asking you to. Just tell me where the Escalade went."

"Sending a civilian into danger is worse, Trudi."

"I'm hardly your average civilian. You know that."

He sighed. "I do know that. But you are still a civilian."

"They left from here, so I'm probably closer than you and your people are. I have a better chance of getting to him before they seriously hurt him. Or even kill him. He's an innocent—"

Eula zoomed into the lot and stopped behind Trudi's defunct car. She jumped out. "Have the location yet?"

"Not yet." Then she held her phone closer to her mouth and told Stepp, "Eula's here. Can I call you back?"

"It'll be the same answer," he said.

"I understand where you're coming from." She ended the call and sighed.

"What's going on?" Eula asked.

Trudi gave her a quick rundown. She didn't go into detail about Dream's past and importance, just that she was helping Samuel and desperate to find a kidnapping victim.

"How're you going to find him?"

"I'm not sure yet, but do you mind if I take your car? I don't have a lot of other options."

"Are you crazy? You think I'm going to let you go off and find those guys all alone?"

"I don't need—"

"Nope." Eula held her hand up. "I'm sorry, Boss, I'm not doing as ordered this time. Just get in the car, and let's go."

Trudi searched her mind for a way to keep Eula out of this. By the determined look on Eula's delicate features, she saw she wasn't winning this one. She walked around the back of the car and climbed into the passenger seat.

Eula got behind the wheel. "Where to?"

"The office."

Eula raised an eyebrow.

"We're picking up the .22. If you're so determined to come along, you will carry something to defend yourself with. You got your conceal-carry permit, right?"

Eula nodded and then put the car in gear and drove back through the shopping center toward the road.

The .22 wasn't powerful, but that was what Trudi had used

to teach Eula how to shoot. She was already accustomed to it. And Trudi would use the short drive to think of a way to get Stepp to cooperate.

She had to keep pushing thoughts of Dream, her fear of what those men could be doing to him, out of her head. *Maybe Stepp's men will help him.*

"Park around back," Trudi said.

"Feeling cautious after that William guy showed up at the office? Did you ever figure out who that guy was?"

"He's with the same organization as the men who took my kidnapping victim."

Eula's forehead furrowed. "I'm missing a lot to the story, aren't I?" Eula parked at the back door to Coffey & Hill Investigations.

"Tons. I'll tell you as much as I can. Wait here while I get that .22. Then we'll need to figure out what in the world we're going to do next." Trudi stood from the car and took her keys out of her pocket. She wasn't entirely sure why she'd had Eula park out back. The Irish mob wouldn't show up here again—they already had what they wanted.

She slipped inside and moved toward her office without bothering with any lights. She grabbed the .22 from the safe in the cabinet below her bookshelves and tucked it into her waistband. It fit perfectly. That was why she'd bought such a small gun. Then she headed back toward the door. When she walked outside, she noticed a car that hadn't been there a few minutes ago, a car she'd never seen parked back there.

Two men stepped out—one with darker skin and a beard and the other with auburn hair and freckles. They paused to talk, and then the bearded man glanced at her.

Something's wrong.

Eula stood from the car. "What's wrong?" Then she looked over at the men, and her back straightened.

"Eula," Trudi murmured. "Get in your car and get out of here."

Eula stayed put.

The men approached from around both sides of Eula's car. "Trudi Sara Coffey," the bearded man said. It wasn't a question.

Eula backed up to stand next to Trudi but kept her keys concealed in her fist. "Who are they?" she whispered.

"We're just here to ask some questions," the bearded man said. "About Samuel Hill."

"No need to be concerned," the freckled man chimed in. He held up a badge.

Trudi raised her eyebrows. "Homeland Security." Though she wasn't going to blindly buy that they were in fact Homeland Security, not with everything Samuel had going on. Trudi stared at the bearded man. "Samuel has gotten himself into trouble."

"That's an understatement," Freckles said.

Eula faced the freckled man, who was probably about her age. "What does that have to do with Trudi?"

"We need to see how deep this goes."

"How deep what goes?" Eula asked.

The bearded man addressed Trudi. "We need to speak privately."

Trudi glanced around at the empty back drive lane. "We are speaking privately."

"He means me," Eula said.

"You can head out. I can handle this." Trudi hoped Eula listened.

The bearded man interrupted. "My associate will take the young lady home."

So he can interrogate her and perhaps take her into custody anyway? Trudi thought. She shifted forward, in front of Eula. "That's not happening. First," Trudi said, "Samuel Hill may be a pig, but he is not a terrorist. He's spent his entire adult life defending the country and its citizens. I don't even want to know how many times he's risked his life." The thought kept her up at night sometimes.

"It looks like he's switched sides. It's not that uncommon."

"What's your evidence that he's switched sides?"

"Classified."

Trudi rolled her eyes.

"When was your last contact with Samuel Hill?" the bearded man asked.

She considered lying and saying over a month, but they might already know that was a lie. "A little while ago. We're working a kidnapping case together."

"Kidnapping of whom?"

"Some guy who got involved with the Boston mob. They have him now, and we need to go get him."

"Two pretty little things like you are gonna go up against the Boston mob?" Freckles asked.

The bearded man gave him a warning look, and Freckles shut up.

"Yes, we are," Trudi said to Freckles. "Please excuse us."

The bearded man stepped closer and got in Trudi's way to the car door. "I'm afraid our discussion about Samuel Hill isn't quite over."

"He can be a pig sometimes, and he's not a terrorist. That's about all I got."

"You were married to him, and that's all you know?" Freckles asked.

"Apparently, I'm not that great an investigator when it comes to my personal life." *Which isn't altogether untrue*, she realized.

"I was hoping not to have to do this," the bearded man said. "We're going to have to detain you until you become more cooperative. As well as Miss Jefferson."

"Eula is just an employee."

"A very trusted and highly intelligent employee who's studying human behavior. She may have noticed things that you haven't."

Trudi clenched her fists.

Eula murmured, "Don't."

Trudi took a breath and aborted her thoughts of fighting their way out of this. "Okay," she said to the bearded man. "Let's do this in my office."

"I'm afraid—"

"I may have information in my files that might help you. My memory isn't great, but I keep files on everything."

The bearded man paused to consider. Then he nodded.

Freckles led the way in the back door, followed by Eula, Trudi, and the bearded man. Before Trudi made it a few steps, the bearded man took her Beretta Tomcat and the .22 from her waistband. "Let's ensure we have a civil conversation," he said.

A phone rang. The freckled man took a cell phone out of his breast pocket and answered.

The bearded man directed Trudi and Eula toward the sitting area in the front of the space.

"How did that happen?" the freckled man said into his phone.

33

DREAM

Facility for the Criminally Insane
Massachusetts

"Have a seat, Dream," Dr. Brone said.

The guard released my arm.

Dr. Brone looked at the guard. "Why was he not handcuffed during escort?"

"He's never shown signs of violence."

"Except those two people he murdered." Dr. Brone stood from his desk chair. "He will always be cuffed during transit, even just a stroll down the hall. Do you understand?"

The guard's upper lip tightened. "Yes." He walked out and closed the door.

I hid my clenched fist behind my back.

"Angry, Dream?" Dr. Brone asked.

I said nothing.

Dr. Brone reclaimed his chair. "Why would you be angry with me?"

"I'm not violent."

"And yet you slaughtered those two men. Not just killed but slaughtered."

"I don't remember any of that. I don't hurt people." Then I added, "Not like you."

Dr. Brone leaned back in his chair. "Not like me?"

I kept my fist hidden behind my back. If he thought I was dangerous, why would he be alone in this room with me—no guard, no handcuffs?

"Come now, Dream. You can't make a statement like that and just leave it lingering in the air."

"Why did you fire Clara? She's the only one who makes a difference around here."

"You mean she's the only one who coddled you. I hate to remind you, but you are not simply a mental patient, Dream. You are a prisoner and will be treated as such."

I clenched my fist tighter until it shook.

"Now." Dr. Brone smiled. "Have a seat so we can have our session."

I hesitated.

With his eyes, Dr. Brone pointedly indicated the chair across from him.

I relented and sat in the plastic chair.

"Let's see if you've learned to be more cooperative," Dr. Brone said. "You'll never get well unless you submit to therapy. You need to tell me everything you remember about the last few years."

Snips of images flashed through my mind . . .

"I said, what do you remember?" someone roars. It sounds like they're yelling in my ear, but I don't see anyone.

"My neighbor installed a second front door. He's always wanted a Tudor house," Paddy said.

I paused in my drawing of an ornate clock face and looked over at him. He'd never made a joke before.

He was grinning. "No response?"

I turned back to my drawing. "My brother was always a little dull. His name was Matte."

Paddy snickered. "My friend learned about mixed-media art in collage."

I rolled my eyes. "What is an artist's favorite sushi? Tempera."

We went back and forth a few times until we were both howling with laughter.

Pain. I try to open my eyes. But aren't they already open? I can't tell. I see blurs, but I'm not totally sure it's not simply light through my eyelids. Something smears across my vision, and pain sears through my head.

"What do you know? Where are the paintings?"

"What do you remember, Dream?" Dr. Brone asked yet again.

"I don't remember anything."

"Stop lying to me."

"I'm not."

"I know you're not this stupid, Dream."

"I'm not stupid." At least I liked to think I wasn't. Sometimes I really wasn't sure.

I fall and come to a jolting stop. I can't tell if I'm on the floor or if I've hit a wall. One second, I'm sure it's Dr. Brone yelling at me to tell him where the paintings are, and the next second, I think it's Southie. But why would Southie ask me that?

Something hits me. A fist or maybe even a brick.

I taste blood.

I squeeze my eyes shut and then force them open.

Finally, I remember where I am. Atlanta. The man yelling at me sounds a lot like Southie. The yelling stops, and I think maybe he's talking to someone else. I try to focus my eyes. They don't want to work properly. Then I realize it's because the right one is mostly swollen shut.

"He's coming out of it," a different voice says.

"Hit him again."

"He's had an awful lot."

"Hit. Him. Again."

A shadow kneels next to me, and then there's a prick of my arm.

A shot.

They're drugging me.

34

SAMUEL

Boston, MA

"You think I'm a terrorist," Samuel said.

"Do you admit it?" the officer said.

"I'm simply clarifying what you think. Am I correct?"

"How would you define *terrorist*?"

"Well, if you ask my wife, she'd say anyone who eats the last of the peanut butter is a terrorist."

"You are not amusing, Mr. Casey."

"That's what my wife says."

"Answer the question, please. Are you a terrorist?"

"Do you really think an actual terrorist would admit to it? And do you really think they see themselves as terrorists? They see themselves as righteous." When he saw no response from the security officer, Samuel added, "No, I'm not a terrorist. I'm a loyal American and will be to the end."

"A righteous American who feels all Muslims should be expelled from the country?"

Samuel laughed.

"This is not a laughing matter, Mr. Casey!" The officer rested his hand on the table and leaned closer to Samuel. "Do you have any idea who the man is that you assaulted? He's here in asylum status. Extremists in Saudi Arabia made attempts on the lives of him and his family, all simply because he supported his wife's efforts to improve rights for women. All they want is for every person to be treated like a human being. Then they come here and have to deal with people like you."

"If that's accurate, then he has my deepest respect. I know what it can be like over there. The mother of my son went through countless trials, probably more than I even know about."

"Your story seems to morph the more you talk. First, you have a pregnant wife, and now you refer to her as the mother of your son. Do you have a child or not? Do you have a wife or not?"

"No matter what I say, you're going to filter it through your own preconceived assumptions about me, aren't you?"

The officer pulled up a chair to the table and sat. "I'm simply listening to what you have to say until Homeland Security gets here."

Samuel tilted his head. "You called them before questioning me."

"With what you said to my associate, I didn't have much choice."

"What I said to who?"

"On the way from the terminal to here."

"To the blond kid? I didn't say anything to him on the way back here." Nothing beyond needing to get back to Atlanta.

"You can save your story for Homeland Security. They're already researching your background."

"What did he say? Does he think I have a crush on him or something?"

"When someone tells one of my officers they should have brought a bomb, I tend to take notice."

Why would that kid lie so blatantly like that? Samuel played connect the dots in his head until he came up with a possible scenario. He had a major enemy at the moment, an enemy highly skilled at corrupting young minds. But he was fairly certain the kid didn't know he was doing al-Sadr's bidding. Maybe they'd convinced him he was being a good American and putting a terrorist behind bars. *How ironic.*

"You've gotten quiet all of a sudden," the officer said.

Samuel smiled. "I'll hold my peace until my lawyer arrives."

The officer smirked. "Terrorists don't get lawyers."

Samuel continued to smile and said nothing further.

A few minutes later, the officer got up, picked up all of Samuel's things, and left the room.

Samuel bent over his hands and nudged the cuff of his jacket with his nose until he could grasp the lock pick he kept tucked there with his lips. He pulled it out, carefully positioned it, and held it tightly with his teeth. He had to twist his hands around until he could get the cuffs laying just right so he could fit the pick into the lock. First, he twisted counterclockwise, torqueing his neck in the process, until he heard a click, the double lock bar releasing. Then he repositioned the pick in his mouth so he could twist it back the other way, releasing the single lock bar. He held that in place while he twisted and pulled his hand to push the handcuff open. Once he got one hand out, it was much easier to free his other hand.

He replaced the lock pick into his jacket cuff and stood with his ear to the door to try to hear where the officers were.

"How sure are you?" the older officer was saying. "Mr. Najjar says he didn't hear anything like that."

"He murmured it under his breath. I was closer. I heard clear as a bell."

Clear as a bell in the bustling terminal, huh?

Samuel stood there until he heard footsteps—two sets—walking away. He cracked the door and paused, listening. Nothing. He walked out, quietly closed the door, and headed out of the security area.

Just outside, he passed a female security officer. He smiled his most charming smile and said, "You have a nice day now. Thank you for everything you do."

"You too, sir."

You're very welcome, he thought.

He forced himself to keep at the same pace as the people around him. Luckily, a large flight had apparently just landed, and its passengers were all heading toward baggage claim. He stayed with the group, directly behind an abnormally tall man, which helped him hide his face from security cameras.

He made it outside without any alarms going off. He wasn't sure about the airport's security procedures or exactly how big a threat they considered him—if they would issue a lockdown once they found him missing or if they would handle it more quietly so as not to cause panic. All he knew was his first priority was finding transportation and getting out of there.

They'd taken his ID, which was no longer clean anyway, so he couldn't rent a car. They'd taken his wallet and cash, so he couldn't even take a bus, not that public transportation was the best idea right now. Maybe he could hail a cab, get out of there, and ditch them without paying. *But don't a lot of cabs have cameras in them?*

He had only one option: hitchhike. But he couldn't exactly stick out his thumb right here. He had to be more subtle.

He found a spot tucked in a group of people waiting for a shuttle to the long-term parking lots and watched for an opportunity. In front of him in the group was a young blonde woman. She spoke to no one. He could probably charm her into giving him a ride.

In the adjacent pickup zone, a parking guard told a man parked along the curb that he couldn't sit there. A middle-aged man with an airport employee badge walked out of the terminal and waved to the man. He waved back. "Hey." Then he turned back to the parking guard. "Do you know if the Delta flight from Paris landed? It was supposed to be in forty-five minutes ago."

"I don't know, sir, but you can't park here. This zone is for pickup only. You can loop the terminal until you see your passenger." Then the guard rushed off to stop someone from double-parking and stopping traffic.

Samuel casually walked over to the man who was waiting for the Delta Paris flight. He was young and bright-eyed, the kind of man who got stepped on a lot. "So, you work here?"

"No. Sorry. If you want information on flight arrivals, you can ask inside."

"Oh, I saw you wave to that guy."

"I do business here. That's all." The young man glanced at the doors leading to the terminal one more time, sighed, and took his keys from his pocket.

Samuel had a hunch and decided to go with it. "She stood you up, huh?"

"What?"

"The girl you were supposed to pick up. Let me guess, you had to take off work and make all kinds of arrangements because she didn't want to take a cab."

At first, the young man didn't answer, and then he sighed like a deflating balloon.

Samuel slapped him on the back. "Happens to the best of us, man." He kept a close eye on the parking guard and the door to the terminal. "So, how hot is she?"

"I'm here, aren't I?"

Samuel laughed. "Is she French or just visiting Paris?"

"Visiting her grandmother. She was raised in the city, close enough to the Eiffel Tower that they could see it from the roof of the building."

"And you're a sucker for a French accent, right?"

The young man sighed.

"Michael, by the way." Samuel held out his hand.

The young man took it, and they shook. "Jimmy."

"So, you gonna wait around any longer?"

"What's the point? She either decided not to take the flight or was just playing me from the start, trying to see how much a fool she could make out of me."

"Hey, maybe her grandmother got sick all of a sudden, and she's been too busy dealing with that."

Jimmy shrugged, but he did seem to hold his chin a little higher.

"You know what?" Samuel said. "Maybe your trip here wasn't a total waste. My ride bailed on me. My little sister. She said something about an emergency at school. Probably some whiny political rally, knowing her. Would it be crazy of me to ask you for a ride?"

"Which direction are you headed?"

"Where're you going?"

"Mansfield."

Good, south. "Bit of a hike for ya, huh?"

"Tell me about it."

"I'm going to Foxborough."

"That's not far from me at all."

Samuel raised his eyebrows and smiled with half his mouth. "So, is it crazy to ask you for a ride? I don't really have the extra scratch for a cab."

Jimmy shrugged. "Why not? Get in."

"Nice. Thanks, man."

"You got luggage?"

"Airline lost it. You believe that? It is *not* my day."

"I feel ya. Get in." Jimmy walked around to the driver's side, and Samuel sat in the passenger seat.

As Jimmy pulled away from the curb, Samuel watched the side mirror, making sure he got away clean.

"So, what's her name?" Samuel asked. "Wait, let me guess. Nicole." He said it with a French accent, more like *Nee-coal.*

Samuel kept the conversation going for a while. Jimmy was a good guy, not pathetic, just nice and a little too trusting, the kind of person who mistakenly assumed people were as nice as he was.

Jimmy turned on the radio at some point. Alternative music played in the background while they talked. Then the DJ came on. "I don't think anyone was surprised last night to see Miyasa Nichols win the finale of *America's Favorite Artist* . . ." Samuel stopped paying attention to the DJ and focused on Jimmy.

Jimmy asked about Samuel, and Samuel made himself out to be younger than he was to help the bonding process. He felt really bad for tricking Jimmy like this, but it was just as much for his protection as anything else.

The word *fugitive* on the radio caught Samuel's attention. He listened to both the news announcer and Jimmy's story about his mom's latest crazy diet.

". . . man identified as Michael Casey escaped custody at Logan International Airport about thirty minutes ago. He is about six-foot-one to six-foot-two, has short, dark hair, Caucasian, and is wearing jeans and a dark-blue jacket. He is said to be extremely dangerous, though authorities are not yet releasing the details surrounding his detainment."

Jimmy looked over at Samuel, at his jeans, his jacket, and finally his short, dark hair. "Didn't you say your name was Michael?"

35

TRUDI

Atlanta, GA

"So, he was using an alias," Trudi said.

Agent Anand, the darker-skinned man with a beard, said, "Michael Casey." He'd moved one of the chairs from the small waiting area by Eula's desk to face Trudi, and he'd also moved a chair next to him and had Eula sit. The freckled man, Agent Kelly, sat next to Trudi.

Trudi raised her eyebrows slightly, while trying not to eye the bulge in Agent Anand's jacket where both of her guns were tucked.

"The name means something to you."

"Those were the names I'd wanted to name our children. Michael for a boy and Casey for a girl." She'd assumed he'd forgotten all about those names. "And you figured out his actual identity through facial recognition?"

"You haven't yet answered my question," Agent Anand said. "Have you ever heard your ex-husband speak poorly of Middle Eastern people?"

"He doesn't talk about his work. Everything he does is classified."

"Every single person of Middle Eastern heritage is not related to his work. The more you avoid my questions, the longer this is going to take."

"He doesn't like terrorists," Trudi said. "But it has nothing to do with ethnicity. He'd feel the same if they were Irish or Indian." She sighed. "His current wife, the mother of his son, is Saudi Arabian."

"And why did you choose to hold back that little tidbit of information?" Agent Kelly asked. "We've been painfully grinding away at this for over two hours."

Trudi stared him in the eye. "Because I didn't yet trust that you are who you say you are."

The corner of Agent Anand's mouth twitched. "And you feel now that we are who we say?"

"I trust that you are with Homeland Security and that you're on the up-and-up."

"Showing you a *badge* wasn't enough?" Agent Kelly said.

Agent Anand held his hand up toward Agent Kelly. "She's being cautious. We can't fault her for that, especially not in her current circumstance."

"Speaking of cautious," Trudi said, "I would like to know what that phone call Agent Kelly received was about." They hadn't discussed it in front of her and Eula. Agent Kelly had apparently texted the pertinent info to Agent Anand. Agent Kelly had been on edge since. Agent Anand, however, was much harder to read.

Agent Anand leaned back in his chair, appraising Trudi. "I suppose it doesn't hurt anything to tell you. Samuel Hill escaped custody."

Trudi showed no emotion and only nodded. *Looks like I'm finding Dream on my own.* She figured Samuel had good reason to escape custody, maybe even something related to al-Sadr. The CIA would probably require him to disappear.

"I've been open with you," Agent Anand said. "How about that openness goes both ways? Has Samuel been acting differently lately?"

"Mr. Hill doesn't act differently," Eula said. "He never shows what's going on under the surface."

"I'm sure that's the case, for the most part," Agent Anand said. "But I suspect Ms. Coffey is different from most." He faced Trudi. "It's fairly obvious he still feels a strong connection to you."

"We're divorced. We occasionally collaborate on cases, but that's it."

"And yet he chose to use the names you'd chosen for your children as his alias."

Trudi didn't answer.

"This Saudi wife of his," Agent Anand said. "Do you know her name, anything about her?"

"You mean if she has ties to extremists?"

He nodded.

"As I understand it, she's a good woman. Samuel never would have gotten involved with her unless he trusted her. He didn't ever tell me much, as I'm sure you can understand."

Agent Anand turned to Eula.

"What?" Eula asked.

"You interviewed him for a college paper, and I've found in my experience that assistants often pick up on a lot more than people realize."

Eula glanced at Trudi, and Trudi gave the slightest nod.

"She came from a poor, simple family. What we might call salt of the earth. She's a good person and a good mother. Samuel trusted her with their son. That says a lot. I have my interview notes. I asked him tons of questions, things meant to dig into his psyche. You'd probably be interested."

"Perhaps," Agent Anand said.

"I can take her home to get them," Agent Kelly said.

"Actually," Trudi said, "I gave her the back office to use for her studies."

"I left the notes there." Eula shifted to the edge of her seat. "Shall I . . . ?"

Agent Anand nodded toward Agent Kelly. "Go with her."

Eula led Agent Kelly down the hall.

Agent Anand addressed Trudi. "You said something about keeping files."

Agent Kelly's raised voice sounded from the back office. "Hey, get down from there."

Agent Anand stood and motioned for Trudi to head down the hall. Trudi stood, pretended to trip over her chair leg, and then headed down the hall, and he followed.

They came into the room. "What's going on?" Agent Anand asked.

Eula's voice came from the large closet in the back corner. "I'm just getting my research. I had to climb the ladder to get it."

"It's not up there," Trudi said. "Remember, we put the holiday decorations up there so you wouldn't have to climb the ladder all the time." She walked into the closet and glanced up at Eula on the ladder.

Then Trudi closed and locked the door.

Eula jumped down from the ladder, and Trudi opened the hidden door covered in shelving, the door that led to the outside. Trudi was surprised the agents hadn't noticed this office was Trudi's, not Samuel's old, unused office, or that there was a second back door on the outside of the building. But then doors in shopping centers were moved all the time. Some unused doors were even left in place sometimes, presumably to save the expense of blocking them in.

Eula unlocked her car with her remote and jumped in the driver's seat. Trudi sat in the passenger seat. Eula punched the gas as Trudi closed her door. She stuffed her throwaway phone, which she'd swiped off the desk when she'd pretended to trip, into her jeans pocket.

"How long do you think it'll take them to figure out we're gone?" Eula asked.

"The lock on the closet door is pretty sturdy. It'll take them a little while to get it open. Hopefully, they think we've just locked ourselves in there."

"So . . . how big a crime did we just commit?"

"If we're lucky, we'll get off with a fine. But the max for escaping custody is two years in prison. It might be different, though, since they're federal agents."

Eula nodded. When she turned at the next corner, she added, "It's worth it if we can save that kidnapping victim from being killed."

"I still need to figure out where he is. Head toward the Zone 6 Police Department."

"Are you sure?"

"Stepp is the only one who has the information I need."

"Alrighty, then." Eula turned at the next light.

"Nice job, by the way."

"You caught on to what I was doing awful quickly."

Eula took as many back streets as possible to get to the station. Trudi was impressed she knew the area so well. She turned onto Hosea L. Williams Drive SE and found a spot to park along the road a little way down from the station.

"If they have an APB out for my plates already," Eula said, "we're out of luck."

"We're risking it going into the station. If our escape was called in already, Stepp will have to detain us. Why don't you leave? I'll call you when things calm down."

Eula lowered her chin and smirked.

Trudi sighed and stood from the car. She was disappointed she wasn't able to protect Eula but also thankful for her help.

They walked up the steps of the two-story, all-stone building. It reminded Trudi of old colonial architecture. Inside, she asked for Captain Stepp. No one gave them much notice—that was a good sign. *The trick is getting this done quickly but not looking rushed*, Trudi thought. *Oh, and pulling one over on Stepp. Not an easy thing to do.*

"Trudi," Captain Stepp greeted, and he motioned for them to follow him to his office.

Once they were in his office, he closed the door. "Are you all right?"

"We're fine."

"I've been trying to call Samuel, but he's not answering."

"I think he might be in trouble." Trudi noticed Eula surreptitiously looking over Stepp's desk and the papers covering it.

"What kind of trouble?"

"I'm not really sure. I'm hoping you can help. You seem to have some connections. Any strings you can pull to get more information?"

"Maybe . . ."

Trudi paused. "But you're not going to tell me."

"We've been through this. You're a civilian. I'm limited in what I can tell you."

"It doesn't matter that he's my family?"

"No matter what I think of your abilities and intelligence, I'm still limited to the rules governing me. Rules that I respect.

If I start breaking them, how can I be an effective law enforcement leader?"

"Yeah, I understand what you're saying. But you don't actually expect me to accept it, do you?"

"Not at all." Then he added, "What about your kidnapping victim?"

"I'm so worried about Samuel, I haven't really thought about it. Were you able to find him?"

"I sent a team. No one was there."

"Are you sure you got the right place?"

"We lost them on traffic cameras eventually, but there were only so many ways they could go from there. They didn't show up on any other cameras, so the vehicle had to have stopped in a particular pocket neighborhood. We canvassed the neighborhood but found nothing."

"Do you think they switched cars?" Trudi glanced at Eula, who continued to look at the papers on Stepp's desk without his noticing.

"It's the only reasonable assumption."

"Assumptions are one of your enemy's best weapons," Eula said.

Trudi and Stepp both looked over at her.

"Samuel said that once," Eula added.

"Samuel is an intelligent man," Stepp said. "But I'm stuck with assumptions for now."

Trudi sighed. "We'll get out of your hair, then."

"Actually," Stepp said, "I need you to stay here for some questioning. I need everything you have on Samuel so I can locate him."

Interesting that Homeland Security didn't contact Stepp right away when Samuel was detained, Trudi thought. Maybe he didn't have his Atlanta PD badge on him. Or maybe they didn't believe he was Atlanta PD and thought the badge was fake. Or they thought it was stolen—his ID didn't match his name in the Atlanta PD roster, after all.

"Let me take Eula home first. I'll come back."

Captain Stepp hesitated.

"I don't want her involved in this," Trudi said. She suspected Stepp didn't have any extra officers available to give Eula a ride home. He was stretching his department thin covering all their regular calls, plus helping Samuel and Trudi.

"I'll see you back here within half an hour."

Trudi nodded. Then she and Eula headed down the hall together and back outside.

"Got the location?" Trudi asked under her breath while they walked down the steps to the sidewalk.

"Yep."

They got into Eula's car and started down the street. They were passing East Lake Golf Club on Second Avenue when Trudi's phone rang . . . Captain Stepp.

"Hello?" she answered. "Did you think of something?"

"I just received a call from Homeland Security. Would you like to explain yourself?"

Trudi mouthed to Eula, "No major intersections."

Eula nodded and turned onto a side street.

"I have to do this," Trudi said to Stepp. "I'm sorry. I'm dropping Eula off, and then I'm finding Samuel." She ended the call.

"You're not getting rid of me," Eula said.

"Yeah, I'm getting that impression. But I want Stepp to think you're not involved, and I want him looking for us in all the wrong places."

"And we're going after Dream, not Samuel, right?"

"Samuel can take care of himself. He'll reach out if he needs help." *If he remembers this throwaway cell number.* "Plus, he has the CIA to back him up. Dream has no one."

"This guy made an impression on you, huh?"

"You know when you just have a gut feeling about someone? Dream is innocent, and he's terrified. And he sacrificed himself so they would leave me alone."

"What about weapons? They took your guns."

"We'll have to improvise." Trudi really didn't like not having her Beretta Tomcat. "Where're we headed?"

"Actually, it's near where I grew up. I know the area pretty well."

Eula had to take a zigzag route to avoid major intersections and those pesky cameras. It took over an hour to get to the neighborhood. They drove slowly down the streets, looking for the black Escalade or any sign of Dream.

36

DREAM

Atlanta, GA

I can almost feel the drugs in my veins, creeping through me like evil thoughts. It feels like that last session with Dr. Brone . . .

"Drink your tea," Dr. Brone said.

I did what he said. He'd somehow figured out that I liked chamomile. I hadn't had it in a very long time, not since Paddy had made it for me that last time.

"Do you feel relaxed?" Dr. Brone asked.

I sat back in my chair.

"There you go. Now, let's have a conversation, shall we?"

He started to look blurry. "What's going on?" I asked.

"You're safe. It's time to open up. You just needed some help letting go of your walls."

I blinked hard, trying to make the blurriness go away.

"Can you hear me?"

I blinked again.

"Dream, can you hear me?"

Some small voice in the back of my mind whispered to be quiet. I listened to the small voice. My mind often wasn't quiet enough to hear it, but when I could, when I followed it, it was always right.

His breath washed over my face. "Dream!"

"Listen to me!" It's the Southie-like voice again.

That little voice tells me to be quiet.

Something hits my cheek, and I tilt sideways. There's a loud bang and pain in my side. It takes several seconds for me to realize someone has hit me hard enough that my chair, with me still tied to it, has fallen over.

"Why isn't it working?"

"I've never seen it not work before. They're usually drooling and babbling by now."

"Maybe he's not, ya know, alert enough."

"I can make him alert."

Heavy footsteps approach me on the floor.

My mind jumps to more images, more memories. It's like my mind is trying to defend me by pulling me away . . .

"Where's Dr. Brone?" Wavelength asked.

"As I understand it, he's found a different position elsewhere." Our new group doctor looked at her clipboard, scanned the room, and focused on the chair next to me. "You must be Boot."

"Yes, ma'am."

"I like them. They give you style."

"That's what I keep tellin' people."

The door opened, and a guard walked inside. "I apologize for interrupting, Dr. Miles."

"We were just getting to know each other."

"Warden Fields would like to see someone in your group. Javier Union."

The others glanced around at each other in confusion.

I stood up.

"Come with me," the guard said.

I followed him out into the hallway. Instead of handcuffing me, he kept a strong grip on my arm and guided me. We walked awhile, to an area I'd never been before. Finally, we made it to some kind of office space.

Still holding my arm, tight enough that my hand was feeling tingly, he knocked on a door.

"Come in," a strong voice called.

The guard led me inside and waited while a man with straight posture and black hair typed something at a computer.

A few seconds later, he stopped typing and looked up. "Please wait outside," he said to the guard.

The guard reached for his handcuffs.

The black-haired man held up his hand. "That's not necessary. Just wait outside the door."

"Yes, sir." The guard walked out and closed the door. He remained close enough that I could hear his feet shuffle.

"Do you know who I am?" the man asked me.

"The warden?"

"Superintendent Fields." He stood, and his black hair shone in the fluorescent lights. His hair had a slight curl to it. It reminded me of pictures of Edgar Allan Poe, though Warden Fields's face was much squarer than Poe's. "You're wondering why I called for you."

I nodded.

"I've been reviewing your file. Considering your offense, you've been quite docile since you arrived here." He paused but hadn't asked a question, so I didn't respond. "Is that because you're saving up your violence or managing to suppress it?"

"I don't feel violent."

He raised his chin slightly. "I'm curious, Javier . . . Or do you prefer to be called Dream?"

I appreciated that he bothered to ask. "Javier."

"I'm curious, Javier. Why did Dr. Brone meet with you so much?"

"He said I needed help opening up. Is he gone?"

"He met more with you than any other patient. By far. I'm just curious as to why."

"Is he gone? Will Nurse Clara come back?"

"You have no idea why he focused so much on you?"

I shook my head.

Superintendent Fields paused, assessing me. Then he called out, "Guard!"

The guard walked back in.

"Please take Javier back to his group session."

"Yes, sir." The guard led me back.

"We never saw Dr. Brone again."

"Why not?" The voice sounds odd, not like the warden's. Then I realize it's the Southie-like voice. I must have said that last bit out loud.

I shake my head.

Someone smacks me across the temple.

"How can you tell the difference?" I asked.

Paddy pointed to the squirrel closest to the window. It was munching on a nut it'd found in the dirt. "See the tail. It's bushier than the others'. See?"

"Yeah, I think so. I guess I just never paid attention to the differences from one squirrel to the next."

Paddy smacked me on the back. I wasn't sure if it was a friendly thing or a disciplinary thing. "Great artists have to see everythin'. Every little detail. Every difference. Every uniqueness. That's where the beauty is. Do ya get that?"

I watched the squirrel as it chewed, holding its tiny paws up to its face. This one held its food a little differently than the others, with its paws more under its chin. I grinned. "It looks like it's shoving food in its face."

Paddy smacked me on the back again. "Bang on." Then he added, "Except, it's not an it. He's a he. His name's William, and that other one over there, his name's Paul."

"You name them?"

"Of course. Everyone deserves a name, now, don't he? In this country, everyone gets to be special. We have all these people mixed together, all different. If you can't find the uniqueness in all this, you should give up any aspirations of art right now."

"Darrent Hayes," the dark-skinned man said. "At your service. At least for the time being." Several miles away, and more turns than I could keep track of, from where he'd taken me away from those men in the black SUV, he'd pulled off the side of the road.

"I don't understand. Who are you? Who were those men?"

"The big question is, how did you get out of custody?" He raised an eyebrow.

"They just said I was released. I didn't ask why."

"Wise decision." He smiled a little. "I was wondering if you'd be able to help, if you were stable enough. Do you feel stable enough?"

"Stable enough for what?"

"Very good."

"What do you mean by that? 'Very good' what?"

"Anyone pretending to be something they really aren't always protests too much. If you'd have proclaimed your ability to function, without knowing the circumstances I'm proposing, I might have sent you back."

"Sent me back to prison?"

Mr. Darrent Hayes smiled again. "Let's have us a little chat." He put the green Toyota in gear and continued down the road.

"What do you want to *chat* about?" I asked.

"Do you like helping good people?"

"Of course."

"I believe you," he said. "Not everyone really means it when they say they like to help good people." He glanced over at me. "But I believe you."

"You don't know me."

"I know a fair amount, actually."

"How?" Then a thought hit me . . . "Do you know Dr. Brone?"

"Was that one of your doctors? No, I don't know any Dr. Brone. That's not who I want you to help."

"Who do you want me to help?"

"A dear friend of mine owes someone a debt. She died, unfortunately, so the debt is now mine."

"Who is it?"

"The only name you need to know right now is Trudi."

"Why do I need to know Trudi?"

"Why do you need to know Trudi?" It's the Southie-like voice again.

"Does Trudi know where the paintings are?" the voice demands.

I press my lips together hard.

Something stabs into my hand.

I scream.

"You can either talk or scream. Talking involves a lot less pain. Your choice."

"The king of hearts is the only king without a mustache in a standard pack of playing cards."

"You choose screaming, then. All right." He takes my pinky and twists it until it cracks.

I scream.

Then, somewhere deep in my mind, I remember that man's voice, that kind man from the hospital. "I'm with you, Javie."

I force my mind away from the present, to the past, anywhere but here . . .

I looked at Paddy's lifeless eyes for a long time. He was the closest thing I'd had to a friend since my mother had died.

Sirens.

I didn't fully register the sound at first.

"Freeze!" someone yelled.

I looked over at the open front door. Several police officers had come inside, and I could see red and blue flashing lights outside. The officer nearest me was aiming a gun.

I indicated Paddy on the floor with my hand but couldn't make any words.

"Drop the weapon and put your hands in the air!"

I realized he was aiming his gun at me. I looked down at my hand. A bloody knife.

"Drop the weapon. Now!"

I let it clatter to the floor.

Another officer wrenched my hands behind my back and put handcuffs on me. "You have the right to remain silent . . ."

"Let me make myself cleah," a calm voice says. "You don't have any rights. Especially not the right to remain silent." There's a metallic clicking sound as he pushes a black something into another black something . . . a magazine into a gun. He pulls back the slide and lets it snap into place. "Do you know what happens to people who aren't useful, Dream?" He presses the barrel of his gun to my head.

37

SAMUEL

Boston, MA

“Yeah,” Samuel said. “My name’s Michael. Common name.”

“That description on the news sounds just like you.”

“Kinda sounds just like half the guys at the airport. Dark hair and jeans. Wait, are you saying you think I’m that guy they’re looking for? Are you serious?”

“Should I be serious?”

You had to choose now to stop being trusting, didn’t you, Jimmy? “We’ve been talking for how long? Do I strike you as dangerous? Hey, if you’re worried, just drop me off on the side of the road. I’ll walk from here.”

“We’re nowhere near Foxborough.”

“I’m not about to ride with someone who’s upset by my presence. You’re a nice guy, Jimmy. I wouldn’t do that to you.” Samuel put his hand on the door handle, ready for Jimmy to stop.

Jimmy focused out the windshield and kept driving.

Finally, Samuel asked, "Do you believe me?"

Jimmy paused. "Did the airline really lose your luggage?"

"Yeah. Why else wouldn't I have any?"

"Which airline did you fly on?"

"Delta."

"Where's the lost baggage counter for Delta?"

Samuel tried to remember if he'd seen it and where.

"At least tell me what it looks like," Jimmy said.

"Has the Delta logo all over it. Lots of red and blue accents."

Jimmy smirked, obviously seeing right through Samuel.

Samuel couldn't help but smile a little. "You're a smart guy, Jimmy."

"Are you Michael Casey?"

"No."

Jimmy glanced over at him.

"Michael Casey is an alias."

"Why do you have an alias?"

"You don't seem freaked out."

"I don't tend to get freaked out until there's a reason." He rolled his eyes. "Unless the woman is about five-ten, with long, dark hair, figure like Jessica Rabbit, and has a French accent."

"Sounds like reason enough to freak out to me."

Jimmy laughed a little under his breath.

"I have several aliases," Samuel said. "Most of them are backstopped by the CIA, but Michael Casey was special—I put that one together myself and didn't share it with anyone."

"Are you an agent?"

"I really can't give you much information. It's for your safety. That's part of why I lied to you."

"You know how that answer sounds, right?"

"I get that, and you're right. Doesn't change the truth of

it." Samuel paid attention to where Jimmy drove to be sure he stayed on route.

"You want me to keep my mouth shut, you need to give me something."

Samuel sighed. "Fair enough." He paused to think. "I am an agent. I work primarily in the Middle East. I've made a nasty enemy over there, and it's followed me over here."

"If an extremist group is after you, why is airport security looking for you?"

"Complicated. My theory is that they got to one of the young security officers and convinced him I'm the terrorist and to do whatever was needed to get me detained."

"And you just happened to wander into his hands? Lots of security in an airport that big."

"I messed up and got myself noticed."

"That is pretty complicated."

"Welcome to my life."

"So, why were you in the airport in the first place?"

"Are you saying you believe me?"

"I'm listening is all I'm saying at the moment."

"I think I had you pegged wrong."

Jimmy turned off the radio, which meant he didn't care to hear any more updates about the fugitive at large. Interesting. "How'd you have me pegged?"

"Nice guy, too nice for his own good."

Jimmy shrugged. "Probably right. You think nice guys can't be perceptive?"

"Maybe not if *Nee-coal* is in the room."

"Guilty."

"Can I ask what you do for a living?" Samuel asked.

"Let's just keep the topic on you for now."

Samuel sighed. "Why was I in the airport in the first place?"

For some ridiculous reason, he decided to keep telling the truth. It was a gut thing, and he'd learned to listen to his gut. "My best friend is in trouble. Trouble that I got her into."

"Her? Is her name *Nee-coal* too?"

"My version of *Nee-coal.*"

"But only a friend."

"Because I royally messed up several years ago. But she's decided to be my friend again. I take what I can get."

"What kind of trouble is she in?"

"She's trying to save someone who's in deep with the Boston mob."

"Boston mob and Middle-Eastern extremists? Busy guy."

"Yeah, I kinda chose to stir the pot with the Boston mob. This guy has information that I need."

"All this ties together somehow, huh?"

"Crazily enough, it does."

"You know, you're really good at coming off as trustworthy."

"Kind of important in my line of work."

"And yet your *Nee-coal* saw through you."

"Yeah."

Quiet. Jimmy continued driving down I-95.

Finally, Jimmy asked, "Where are you actually trying to go? Did you land in Boston, or were you trying to catch a flight?"

"Trying to get down to Georgia."

"How're you planning on doing that now?"

"No idea. Hitchhike, I guess." Then Samuel added, "As long as you don't turn me in."

Jimmy paused. "I'm not going to turn you in."

Samuel cocked his head curiously. "You're an interesting person, Jimmy. You gonna tell me anything about you, other than your taste in women?"

"Trying to decide if I'm really not going to turn you in?"

"Something like that."

"I'm just your average twentysomething."

"In some respects, yes." His taste in music, his tendency to trust beautiful women too easily, how he dressed, how he complained about his nosy mother. "But there's something more."

"I've had to learn to be perceptive and also to be tough in certain situations. People try to take advantage of twenty-eight-year-old CEOs."

"Are we talking CEO of a video game store? Or something a bit more involved?" Samuel had had a hunch about Jimmy—now to see if following that hunch would pay off.

"My dad passed several years ago and left me a Beechcraft King Air. He'd made me get my pilot's license. I took the little money I had and started an air taxi service. We have ten planes now and two jets."

Samuel resisted the urge to grin. "Explains why you know your way around the airport."

"I prefer regional airports. It's easier on our customers, but we'll use Logan International if requested."

"So . . ." Samuel said. "Would it be crazy if I asked for a ride?"

Jimmy smiled. "Saw that one coming."

"I really hate to ask, but I'm in a major bind."

Jimmy fished a cell phone out of his jacket pocket and dialed. Samuel could faintly hear the phone ringing.

"Hey," Jimmy said. "My old Beechcraft King Air is still at Mansfield Municipal, right?"

Samuel could barely hear the voice on the other end of the line. "Yeah."

"Have it fueled up for me."

"Joy ride?"

"Something like that."

"Okay. On it. Gimme about half an hour."

"Thanks." Jimmy ended the call and glanced over at Samuel. "You've got yourself a ride."

Jimmy drove them to Mansfield Municipal Airport, which was nothing but a bunch of grass half-covered in melting snow, a single runway, a few buildings, and a tower. Jimmy's employee had everything ready for him. They boarded the plane. It had several round windows on each side and propellers attached to the fronts of the wings. Inside, Samuel had to duck so he didn't hit his head on the low ceiling.

Jimmy slid into the pilot's seat. "Sit wherever you like."

Samuel took the seat in the first row and across from Jimmy on the right side of the plane so he could see Jimmy. "How long will the flight take?"

Jimmy was checking gauges. "Once we're in the air, about three hours."

"So, did I ruin any of your plans with this last-second trip?"

Jimmy continued to check gauges and controls. "Actually, this is a pretty good distraction from being stood up."

"Maybe that's why you decided to believe me with very little evidence."

"Probably. But maybe it'll be a good story to tell my kids someday."

"Will those kids speak French?"

"Probably not."

"Good," Samuel said. "You deserve better than her."

Jimmy got clearance from the tower and started his taxi out to the runway.

The three hours passed slowly. Samuel had never been fond of waiting, and the closer he got to Atlanta, the more anxious he was to get to Trudi.

They landed at a regional airport up near Chamblee. It was

more substantial than Mansfield Municipal but nothing like the international airports. Samuel and Jimmy stepped out onto the tarmac in the darkness and shook hands.

"I cannot thank you enough," Samuel said.

Jimmy slipped Samuel some cash and his business card. "You gotta tell me the full story. You know, someday, when all this is declassified." He grinned.

Samuel flicked the card with his index finger. "Definitely."

Samuel headed toward the terminal and considered his next move. He needed a phone and transportation.

He found his way to what appeared to be the main drag, a four-lane road separated by a narrow, grassy median with trees popping out of it every so often. That road dead-ended into Flightway Drive. He heard traffic coming from straight ahead on the other side of a hill, so instead of turning onto Flightway Drive, he crossed it, found a spot where the brush on the hill wasn't too thick, climbed the hill and then a fence, and jumped down onto a guardrail. Then he recognized Chamblee Tucker Road, a four-lane highway. He didn't see much, except for a small, dumpy shopping center with several cars in the parking lot. It was brick with black box signs with white letters on what looked like an ugly gray stucco canopy. The tenants included a fish store, a family support center, a CrossFit place, and at the end . . . an electronics store. It was too late at night for anything to be open, but he walked up the steps to the door anyway. He looked through the glass door and saw light from somewhere in the back, and he could also see a display of cell phones.

He knocked loudly on the door.

No response or movement from inside.

He knocked again, louder. The glass quivered under his fist.

He kept knocking.

Finally, someone came walking out of the back: a middle-aged, balding man. He came up to the door and spoke through the glass. "We're closed."

"I know. I'm sorry," Samuel said. "My old lady kicked me out and didn't give me my cell. I gotta call my boy to come get me."

"We're closed."

"Come on, man. I got money." Samuel held up a few of the bills Jimmy had given him. "I just need a quick burner cell. Ain't no pay phones around anymore. It's either get a phone or spend the night sleeping in front of your door."

The man sighed with an annoyed expression.

Samuel waved the money.

"Whatever." The man turned the bolt and opened the door. "Make it quick."

"No problem. Just give me the cheapest prepaid cell you got, and I'll be outta your hair."

The man grabbed a packaged flip phone and rang it up.

"You install car stereos here?" Samuel asked. There was a set of keys sitting on top of an invoice on the glass countertop.

"Yeah."

"I've been thinking about changing mine out."

"If you have a car, why can't you drive to your friend's place?" The man took Samuel's money and opened the cash drawer.

"She took my keys. You believe that?"

"You must have done something pretty bad."

Samuel rolled his eyes, then grinned slyly.

The man laughed a little and handed Samuel back his change.

"Hey," Samuel said. "Can I take a look at those headphones? Do they work with this phone?"

The man's smile faded quickly, but he turned and grabbed a pair of packaged headphones off the back wall.

Samuel pocketed the keys on the counter.

The man took a closer look at the package. "No, these don't work with that phone. Bluetooth only."

"All right. No problem. Thanks, man."

"Yup." The man put the headphones back on the shelf.

"See ya." Samuel walked out of the store and waited around the side of the building for a few minutes for the man to head back to whatever he'd been busy with before Samuel had interrupted. Samuel surveyed the parking lot, trying to match the car key in his hand to a car in the lot. He spotted a silver 2008 Chrysler 300 with chrome wheels. *That's got to be it*, he thought.

He walked back around to the front of the building and glanced in the shop. There was no movement from inside. He headed toward the Chrysler, unlocked the door, got in, started it, and drove out of the lot and onto Chamblee Tucker Road.

He held the wheel steady with his knee and tore open the phone packaging. Luckily, the phone came with a partial charge. Because he couldn't remember Trudi's throwaway cell number, he dialed the office line so he could get the number from Eula.

After the rings stopped, it went to a generic voicemail. He called again, and this time a man answered the phone. "With whom am I speaking?"

Samuel knew that tone of voice, that sound of authority. He ended the call. *What happened?* Had Homeland Security picked up Eula—and surely Trudi too—because of their connection to him?

His next call was to the Zone 6 Police Department. With all that was going on, Stepp could very well still be at the precinct. Sure enough, he asked for Stepp and was connected immediately.

"Samuel?" Stepp answered.

"Do you know where Trudi is?"

"Where're you calling from?"

"Please tell me where Trudi is. Did Homeland Security pick her up?"

"They did, but she escaped from custody. I don't need to tell you what a serious infraction that is. Both of you have committed crimes today. I cannot support this, Samuel. You need to turn yourself in."

"I didn't do what they're accusing me of."

"Then they'll sort it out. You need to trust the system."

"Saving lives is more important." He let that sit for a moment. Stepp was famous for telling his officers that saving lives trumped everything else. He would say no matter what was in the way—a perp or policy—save the life.

Stepp didn't respond.

"Please tell me where that black Escalade went."

"Are you in Atlanta?"

"Please."

"How in the world did you get to Atlanta? There's no way you got on a flight after Homeland Security flagged you."

"Please help me. I need to know where that Escalade went."

"Answer the question."

"Sometimes things have a way of working out when your motivations are good. My motivations are good. I just want to protect Trudi and save an innocent life." He knew in his gut that Dream was innocent. "I need your help."

"Traffic cameras lost the Escalade. I've already sent a team to the last known location. They didn't find anything."

"I still need to try."

"You think you can do what a SWAT team couldn't?"

"SWAT is trained to go in and take care of it when things go sideways. I have a different skill set. I find the trouble and stop it before it turns sideways."

"Confident, aren't we?"

"Yes. And what could it hurt to tell me if you've already checked it out? And this way, you'll know where I am. If I'm not successful, you'll likely be able to find me and bring me in, right?"

There was a pause, surely while Stepp thought about that.

"They turned off Lower Roswell Road, toward the Chattahoochee River. But that's where we lost them. We scanned the neighborhoods. No sign of a black Escalade. There are a lot of houses back there. Unless you do a house-to-house search, good luck."

"Thank you. I'll call you when I find them." *If I find them.* Samuel ended the call.

Samuel headed west, avoiding main roads wherever possible. Thankfully, the Chrysler 300 had darkly tinted windows, making it difficult for anyone to recognize him.

Finally, he came to Lower Roswell Road. He glanced around at each side street and skipped anything that looked like standard, tightly packed subdivisions. He came to a road with larger houses spread farther apart and drove toward the river. More trees crowded the houses. He skipped by any houses with cars sitting out front. The kidnappers would've pulled any cars they had into a garage or hidden them somewhere on the property.

He continued circling the neighborhoods of large homes.

After about half an hour, he came across a home in the middle of a thick pocket of trees at the end of a winding drive. He couldn't even see the place from the road. He pulled slowly into the drive, watching for security cameras mounted in the trees. At a bend in the drive, he spotted something shiny under a huge pine tree. It was a very small glimmer. He'd have never seen it if he hadn't been looking so hard at his surroundings. He pulled the car into an area of low brush and got out. He tugged a low-hanging branch back. *Yup, this is the place.*

He crept through the dark woods toward the house he could

faintly see through the mostly bare branches. It was all brick with four closed garage bays. A wooden porch wrapped around the house like a hug.

Hidden by some brush, he crouched down and observed the house, analyzing entry points, planning his approach. The front door was too exposed. He couldn't see the back, but the trees looked thinner behind the house, which would make his approach easier to see. The garage possibly had a side door. That area was crowded by thick magnolias. He could creep through the woods around the house and get a better view—

The sound of a gunshot from within the house rang out through the trees.

38

TRUDI

Atlanta, GA

"I want to try this way," Eula said. "The houses back here are a lot farther apart and are separated by tons of trees."

"We're heading closer to the river, right?"

"Yeah."

"They're nicer homes, I assume. They'll have better security. Help me watch for cameras. The guys who took Dream could be using the security system to watch for people approaching."

Eula turned onto Conway Drive. The houses were definitely bigger. A couple were almost completely hidden by pines. They pulled to a stop at the curb of the first one.

"If anybody asks," Trudi said, "we're just taking an informal tour of beautiful Atlanta homes."

Eula nodded.

Trudi stepped from the car so she could peek through the trees a bit better. She jumped back in the car. "A couple of Mercedeses in the drive. I don't think that's it."

Eula pulled up to the next house, and Trudi did the same thing. "Too many lights on inside."

The next few houses were easier to see because they were surrounded mostly by deciduous trees rather than pines. It was late enough in the year that they'd shed most of their leaves.

Just before a cul-de-sac, Eula made a left.

"Isn't this a driveway?"

"There are a couple of houses back here that are super secluded, much closer to the river."

Eula paused when the drive split.

"I caught a glint up in that tree to the right. Possibly a camera. Try the left first."

Eula turned and crawled up the asphalt drive. "See any cameras?"

"No, but see that pine?" Trudi pointed to the left.

"Gotcha." Eula pulled off the drive and toward a huge pine with a low-hanging canopy. Eula's little car slipped under the branches. She shifted into park. "Now, let's just hope the ground isn't too soft and the car gets stuck."

"We haven't had any rain. I think we'll be all right."

"You think this is the place?"

"I don't know, but we should check it out. Or I should check it out. You can stay here and watch the car."

"Watch it do tricks? Right." Eula stood from the car, and so did Trudi. Eula looked at her over the roof. "I appreciate how you're trying to protect me, but I'm not leaving you."

"This isn't your fight. You don't have to."

"It's not your fight either. You're doing it to help someone in need. I'm watching your back."

"I am your boss, you know."

"Want me to quit?"

Trudi turned and slipped out from under the branches. Eula followed.

"No, I don't ever want you to quit," Trudi said.

Eula grinned. "Now I feel loved." She started quietly through the trees.

Trudi cut in front of her and took the lead.

"Yes, Mom," Eula whispered.

Trudi glanced back and stuck out her tongue.

Eula smiled.

About thirty feet through the dark woods, Trudi stopped behind a massive live oak. Eula crouched down behind a huge Ligustrum hedge. The house was all brick with a huge wraparound porch, the kind Samuel loved. All the garage doors were closed. No lights were on, unless you looked at the one window at the right angle, where you could see a faint light, probably from a back room.

"You think this might be it?" Eula whispered.

"I think someone's here but trying to make it look like no one's home."

"Worth checking out, then."

Trudi nodded.

"How do you want to go in?"

Trudi nodded toward the garage on the left. "I bet there's a side door."

They slowly made their way through the trees to the side of the garage. Trudi had been thankful for the dry ground for parking the car but not so much when it came to creeping through the woods. Every dry leaf and twig seemed to be a cannon of noise to her ears. Thankfully, they were far enough from the house that no one should be able to hear them.

As long as no one was watching from some dark corner around the side of the house.

They made it to the side of the garage, half-buried in overgrown magnolias. Peeling paint covered the old wooden door.

"Stay here for a second," Trudi said.

Eula opened her mouth.

"Just until I figure out how to get the door open. Watch my back."

Eula nodded.

Trudi walked across some patchy grass to the garage door. First, she tried the knob. Locked, of course. *A girl could hope*, she thought. She felt the top of the doorframe for a key. No such luck. *Okay, break it down or pick the lock.* But she didn't have her lock-picking set because Agent Anand had taken it. She looked around for anything she could use as a tool.

In the hedge along the edge of the garage, she spotted some kind of plastic. She pushed the dry branches to the side and found a Coke bottle that looked like it'd been there only a short while. *Perhaps from someone walking this area on patrol?*

She held the bottle against the corner of the brick wall and grated it back and forth until a hole formed. Then she used her hands to tear the bottle apart and make a small rectangle of plastic, about the size of a credit card but thinner.

She tossed the rest of the bottle back into the hedge, slipped the plastic rectangle between the door and frame above the latch, pushed down with the plastic, and ratcheted the door back and forth by holding on to the knob. The door rattled.

Pop. The door opened.

Eula stepped out and followed Trudi into the dark garage. The only light was moonlight coming in through the line of windows across the garage doors. They paused to let their eyes adjust to the almost complete darkness.

"Is that," Eula whispered, "an Escalade?"

"Yes."

"Looks like we're in the right place."

"I think so." Trudi carefully made her way around the front of the garage, crouching under the windows in the doors, past the backs of three other cars—a Mercedes GLA, a Lincoln Continental, and a Corvette. She examined the Escalade.

"Same one?" Eula asked.

"Same license plate."

"Let's look around for a weapon. There should be something useful in a garage."

"From what I can see, this place is more of a showroom." There were no tool shelves, no shelves at all, no pegboards with hooks—nothing but clean walls and shiny cars.

Eula raised her finger, as if flicking a light bulb over her head. "The Escalade. If they knew they were kidnapping someone, and who knows what else, they probably have something good in there." She pulled on the back hatch and just barely got it open in the cramped space.

There were no guns, of course, but there was a bag of tools, along with duct tape and rope.

"I knew there was a reason I keep giving you paychecks," Trudi whispered.

"Because of my dazzling personality." Eula stuck her hands out to the sides and wiggled her fingers.

"That too."

They looked through the bag of tools. Trudi took a Phillips screwdriver and stuffed medium-sized wire cutters into her waistband. Eula found a flathead screwdriver and a large wrench.

"I would prefer a longer-range weapon," Trudi said. "But this is a lot better than what we had a few minutes ago."

"You mean squat?"

"In your classes, have they taught you knife fighting?"

"Just knife defense."

"Okay. Try to think of all the scenarios they teach you to defend against."

"And basically try to turn my training around to the attacker side."

Trudi nodded. "And remember, these guys inside are armed."

"Do you know what kind of guns?"

"I saw a Glock 19."

"Okay."

"Are you ready? You sure you want to do this? You can wait in the car and be ready to get us out of here."

Eula held up her chin. "Lead the way, Boss."

Trudi walked over to the door leading to the house and listened for any sound from inside. She heard faint voices and the sound of a cabinet closing. She held a finger up to Eula.

A voice with a heavy Boston accent said, "Anything yet?"

"Nothing."

"How's Johnny?"

He expressed Johnny's displeasure with several curse words.

"I'm shocked the guy's still conscious."

"Not anymoah. At least not at the moment."

"Where is he?"

"Steer cleah of the front living room."

Footsteps sounded away from the garage.

Trudi gave it a few extra seconds to be sure they were out of earshot. Then she tried the knob, careful not to make any sound. It was unlocked. She slowly opened the door, which led into a hallway.

She walked in.

To the right was a dark laundry room, a coatrack, and a bench along the wall. Straight ahead was the brightly lit kitchen. She gave herself a few seconds to let her eyes adjust to the light reflecting off the white cabinets and white marble counters.

Eula walked into the hallway behind her and silently closed the door to the garage. Trudi continued to curse herself for not finding a way to keep Eula out of this.

Trudi headed into the kitchen and glanced around, trying to get a feel for the layout of the house. An old-school, sectioned-off kind of house or more of an open-concept? The kitchen did open to a family room with a fireplace but that was as open-concept as this corner of the house got. *Good*, Trudi thought.

To the right, between the kitchen and family room, was a doorway that led to a hall. Trudi peeked around the edge of the cabinets. White marble floors at the end of the hall made her think that was probably the entryway. She couldn't see much else other than that.

"I have your back," Eula whispered.

Trudi nodded and crept toward the hall. She didn't feel comfortable with Eula watching her back. Not that she didn't trust Eula to be diligent. Trudi just didn't usually feel comfortable with anyone else other than Samuel in a situation like this.

The next room on the right was a large formal dining room dominated by a massive wood table with a live edge. A little farther down was a coat closet on the left, and then the hall opened up to a large foyer with a white curved staircase. Trudi peeked around the corner and up to the second-floor railing. No one in sight. *Head upstairs or continue searching the downstairs?*

She paused to listen.

A few seconds passed. Eula quietly waited.

Trudi thought she picked up faint voices from the other side of the downstairs. They'd already been through many rooms, but she figured a house this size probably had additional living areas, maybe a library, an office . . .

Trudi looked back at Eula, pointed up, and mouthed, "Watch."

Eula nodded.

Trudi slipped out from around the corner and headed toward the other end of the foyer, past the stairs. She trusted Eula to watch the upstairs landing and kept her focus forward.

At the opening to a very wide hall, Trudi paused at the corner. This had to be the front living room, the one where Johnny was brooding. She didn't see a way to get past it without being seen.

She glanced at Eula and mouthed, "Watch my back."

Eula stood with her back to the hallway wall so she could watch all directions peripherally.

Trudi edged closer to the living room doorway. Then she rubbed her fingers over the drywall, making the slightest sound.

She heard the feathery sound of fabric as someone stood from a couch or chair. Then quiet footsteps.

She saw his boot before she saw his face, estimated his height based on their prior interactions, and swung a horizontal back elbow strike. She made contact with his cheek, turned to face him, landed a front elbow strike to the other side of his head, and caught him by his shirt before he stumbled into the glass coffee table and alerted the whole place with the sound of breaking glass. He was pretty heavy, but she managed to set him down on the floor without too much noise.

Eula rushed into the room and grabbed the tiebacks off the curtains. She tossed one at Trudi. "Tie one hand to the couch leg."

"That won't hold him."

"If I tie his foot to this cabinet, he'll be too stretched out to be able to muster any leverage. And let's hope you knocked him out for a good while."

Trudi did as Eula asked. Johnny lay on the floor, on his back, with his left hand and foot stretched as far as possible, tied to heavy, solid-wood furniture. No way could he sit up or even bend either left limb, and even if he managed to roll over, nothing was within reach of his right hand for him to grab. It would at least slow him down quite a bit.

Trudi patted him down. "No weapons." She'd expected him to be the type to be armed at all times.

"How many more?" Eula asked.

"Three." The young kid with the flat-brimmed baseball cap, the heavy guy with the thick voice, and the big guy she'd seen in the parking garage back in Buckhead.

Trudi headed down the hall, followed by Eula.

To the left, they found a guest bathroom and what Trudi guessed to be an office or guest bedroom. The door was closed. Trudi moved to the other side of the door, same side as the knob, and motioned for Eula to get behind her. Trudi had been lucky to catch Johnny off guard. It was possible the commotion of that altercation had been heard from this room and the inhabitants were lying in wait. With her back to the wall, she reached over and knocked on the door.

Something inside the room rustled. "What? I'm trying to get some sleep." The voice was thick. "What do you want?"

Trudi knocked again.

Heavy footsteps sounded on the wood floors.

The door opened, and Trudi waited for the thick man to emerge. Instead, she heard a gun being drawn from a leather holster.

She pivoted around the doorframe, into the room, and pummeled her fist toward the man's face. He managed to lean back enough that her fist glanced off. He tried to aim his 9mm at her, but he was off-balance.

She stabbed him with her Phillips screwdriver, hoping he was thick enough that the shank hit only fatty tissue, not major organs.

With a shaking hand, he aimed his gun at her. Eula pushed his hand up and to the side, directing the aim away from them, and raked the gun backward, out of his grasp. And then she had it in a strong two-handed grip, aimed at him.

He glanced back and forth between Eula and Trudi, with a hand clutching his gut where Trudi had stabbed him.

Then he opened his mouth wide, obviously about to yell.

Trudi threw a hook at his jaw, and his head snapped sideways. He fell to the floor with a loud thump.

"That was loud," Eula said.

"Too loud. Let's move."

Eula took point with the 9mm. They moved more quickly but still quietly. The last space they came to had double glass doors. As they approached, Trudi could see Dream tied to a chair. The chair was one of two on the other side of a huge wooden desk, surrounded on all walls by bookshelves reaching to the ceiling. Trudi opened the door, and Eula swept the large space.

Trudi ran over to Dream. His head was slumped against his chest. The fingers on his left hand looked broken, each in two places, as if each finger had five joints rather than three.

"Dream," Trudi said. "Dream, wake up." She tucked her screwdriver into her waistband and started untying his hands.

"What's that he's hooked up to?" Eula asked, still watching the door.

There was an IV in Dream's arm. "Probably some kind of drug to make him talk." Trudi unhooked it and tossed the tube away.

She reached her hand out to tap Dream to rouse him, but she hesitated for fear of causing more pain by touching one of his abrasions or broken bones. She patted his knee. "Dream, please wake up. We're here to take you away, but I need you to wake up. I don't think we can carry you." At least not while defending themselves from the other two men in the house.

Dream didn't move.

"Is he . . ." Eula asked.

"No. He's breathing. I can see his chest moving."

She rubbed his knee and talked to him, but he continued to be unresponsive. Figuring loud noises would bother him, Trudi clapped her hands in front of his face.

His head jerked upright. His eyes were swollen almost shut. "Please don't," he mumbled.

"It's Trudi."

"Clara?"

"No, Trudi. I'm here with a friend. We're taking you with us."

He tried to open his eyes better. "Trudi?"

"Yes. Can you stand?"

He looked around the room. It had to be nothing but a blur to him.

"Do you remember your book of factoids?" Trudi asked.

"Clara gave it to me. Dr. Brone took it away."

"But you showed him—you already had it memorized."

He nodded slightly.

"Give me some facts. It'll help you concentrate." She hoped it would be cathartic. He'd originally used it to stop memories he wasn't ready to deal with, but she hoped it'd become comforting in its familiarity.

He hesitated.

Very gently, Trudi rubbed his right fingertips.

He murmured, "Alexander the Great died of alcoholism at the age of 32.

"John Steinbeck wrote many short works, including *Of Mice and Men*, *The Pearl*, and *The Moon Is Down*.

"About 1.6 million British women have hair-loss problems."

Trudi continued rubbing his fingertips. "A little better? Can you stand?"

He nodded, a little more movement than last time. Then he shifted forward in his chair. Trudi was relieved to see him move his legs, that they hadn't been broken. He tried to hoist himself up but plopped back down.

"I'll help." Trudi moved so she could wrap an arm around him. "Tell me if I hurt you."

He hoisted himself upward again, and this time she was able to pull him the rest of the way up.

"Excellent," Trudi said.

A gunshot rang out, and Trudi snapped her attention to the door where Eula had been standing.

39

DREAM

Atlanta, GA

I don't fully understand what's going on. Trudi is here, that much I'm pretty sure of. I can't see her very clearly, but I recognize the kindness in her voice. Part of me wants to insist she leave, get to safety, but I'm too relieved that she's here to take me away.

A gunshot.

I try to open my swollen eyes wider to see what's going on.

"Eula!" Trudi exclaims.

"I'm okay," I say. "Help her." I can't see clearly enough to know what's going on, but I hear the concern in Trudi's voice.

She removes her arm from around me, and I manage to stay on my feet by holding on to the desk.

"Eula. Are you all right?" Trudi says.

Quiet.

I blink and get the haze to clear a bit from my eyes. My eyes are still just slits, but I can see. This Eula person, a young woman with skin a little darker than mine, is standing in the doorway not moving, even as Trudi shakes her arm.

"Eula," Trudi says again. "It's all right."

"He came at me so fast from around the corner." Eula's voice was just above a whisper. "He was aiming his gun at you."

"You did the right thing." Trudi rubs a hand over Eula's arm and shoulder.

"Is he . . . Will you check?"

"He's gone, sweetie. You did the right thing."

"Will you check? Maybe if we call an ambulance."

And then I notice the large man, the one who'd held me still while Johnny tortured me, lying on the floor, unmoving. Blood. It all reminds me of Paddy. I close my eyes. *The most popular pub name in Britain is the Red Lion.*

Keep it together, Javie. Keep yourself together.

Please, Jesus.

Medical experts have noticed that people who stutter rarely do so when alone or when talking to pets.

"He's gone," Trudi says again.

Eula nods.

"Are you all right?"

"I've never . . . I've never even aimed a gun at another person before."

"I know. And the fact that you're so upset just shows what a good person you are. You're grieving for someone who wanted to kill you."

Eula nods. Then she takes a deep breath. "Is Dream okay? We need to get out of here."

"There should still be one more in the house somewhere."

Eula nods.

"Here, let me take that, and you help Dream." Trudi takes the gun out of Eula's grip. Eula gives it up easily and walks over to me.

"Hi, Dream," Eula says. "Can I help you?"

"Thank you." I feel myself slipping, about to fall. She puts her arm around my back and helps me stay on my feet. I'm surprised at how strong she is, given her size.

I hear a metal sound and look over at Trudi checking the weapon in her hands.

"Can you walk?" Eula asks.

"I think so. Will you help?"

"You just put as much weight on me as you want."

I take a few steps with her help. But then Eula tightens her arm around me and pulls me to a stop. Trudi is holding her hand up. Then she waves to the side, and Eula helps me hobble quickly away from the double French doors. Trudi stands to the side of the left door and watches.

I think I hear quiet footsteps, but I don't fully trust my senses. Then a man appears at the edge of the doorframe.

"Samuel!" Trudi says. She holds her gun down at her side.

"Tru-Bear. Thank goodness."

"How'd you find us?"

"Long story. Let's get out of here." Then he looks past her. "Eula. What're you doing here?"

"Long story." Trudi points toward the door. "Let's get out of here. But be careful. I think there's one more in the house."

Samuel starts toward the door.

"You should help Dream," Trudi says.

"I've got point," Samuel says.

"I've got the only decent weapon in the group. I have point. You should help Dream."

Samuel pauses. I can see just well enough to comprehend the look Trudi gives him, the kind of look that's better not to argue with. My mother had a look like that.

Samuel walks over and wraps an arm around my other side.

He's strong and holds me up almost by himself. We slowly walk back through the house.

When we make it to the entryway, Samuel quietly says, "Out the front. I just came from there, and it was clear."

Trudi glances back. "It's too exposed. Why'd you do that?"

"I heard the gunshot."

She rolls her eyes, but she does head for the front door. Before she opens the door, she looks back.

"Eula and I will watch our six," Samuel says.

Trudi takes a good look out the tall window next to the door and then walks out.

I hear a door closing from upstairs.

"Take Dream," Samuel says to Eula. He lets go and runs up the stairs.

Trudi turns back, as if about to run after him. Then she looks at Eula and me. "Get Dream out."

I hobble as quickly as I can across the porch and down the brick steps. Trudi follows, while watching behind us.

I glance back through the open doorway and see the young man in the ball cap tumble down the stairs. He lands on his back and aims a gun toward the second-story landing.

"Get Dream to the car," Trudi says, and then she runs back toward the house.

"They might need help," I say.

But Eula keeps pulling me along. "They have it. I'm getting you to the car."

"But you can help them. Leave me."

"They risked themselves to get you out. I am *making sure you're safe.*" She is more commanding than I thought this pretty girl could be.

I let her lead me away from the house and into the trees. It's not as if I have enough strength to fight her. Once we make it to the tree line, it's slower moving. I can barely walk, and all the brush, twigs, and dry leaves on the ground keep tripping me. I don't want to fall and take her with me, so I move slowly and carefully.

"Just do your best," she says, and then she glances back at the house.

"I can sit down here and be out of sight. Leave me and go help them."

She pauses and glances back again.

"Please," I say.

"Okay." She helps me sit down on the ground. "I'll be right back." She runs back toward the house.

I sit there in the darkness and try not to feel the pain radiating through my body. Almost every part of me hurts, which in an odd way almost makes handling it easier. I can't fixate on one particular pain. Instead, I fixate on something else. *Please, Jesus, help them.* I remind myself that there are three of them and only one of him.

But maybe he shot Samuel before Trudi and Eula could get there.

But I would have heard the shot, right? Unless he had a silencer on his gun. I wasn't able to see nearly well enough to see that detail.

Maybe I hadn't seen clearly and he hadn't had a gun at all. It could've been something else, right?

If I start doubting my senses, though, I will start doubting everything about my reality.

Calm down, Javie.

I try to focus on being as silent as possible and listening.

All I can hear is the scuttling of tiny animals in the dry brush. I try to believe they're something pleasant like chipmunks, but I know they're probably lizards or insects.

I hear no other sounds.

Then there are footsteps, quick.

I want to look behind me toward the house and the sound of the steps, but I can't move that much. I can barely hold myself upright.

"We're back." Eula squats down next to me.

"Are they okay?"

"We're fine, Dream." It's Trudi. She squats down on my other side. "Are you ready to go?"

I nod and try at least to get up to my knees. I can't push myself up, and my legs are weak. I can't even remember everything they did to me. Things hurt, and I don't know what's causing the pain. *A bruise, a cut, a broken bone?*

"I have you." It's Samuel's voice from behind me. I feel his hands under my arms, and he lifts me to standing. Then Eula is there with an arm around me again, and Samuel comes over to my other side. We start moving forward.

"We parked under that pine." Trudi points off to the right.

"We should take mine," Samuel says. "It won't be noticed as missing until morning, maybe even Monday. We'll be long gone by then. I'm sure Stepp's put out a BOLO for Eula's plates."

Trudi says, "All right."

"You stole a car?" I ask.

Samuel answers with, "Long story."

Samuel and Eula help me into the back seat. Samuel takes the driver's seat, Eula sits next to me, and Trudi sits in the front passenger seat. Samuel backs the car out of its odd parking place in the brush and heads down the driveway at a normal pace.

"How are you?" Trudi asks me.

"I'm fine." I feel like I've been ripped apart and patched back together with a rusty needle.

The car starts dinging.

"Where's the nearest hospital?" Trudi asks.

"No hospital," I say.

"Are you crazy? You need a doctor."

"That's where they'll expect me to go. They'll find me, and you. No hospital."

"He's right," Samuel says. "Put on your seat belt."

That's what that dinging is from.

"He needs medical attention," Trudi says.

"What he needs is to get away from here. Once we get far enough away from Atlanta, then I'll set his broken bones and sew up any major abrasions. Until then, he should rest."

I lean my head back carefully against the seat.

"We should give him to Stepp, then," Trudi says. "He can protect him and get him medical attention."

The dinging continues.

"I'm not sure his release from custody was entirely on the up-and-up," Samuel says. "*Please* put on your seat belt."

"Custody?" Eula asks.

I sit back up. "I didn't do what they say I did. I remember now. I didn't hurt anyone."

Trudi reaches back and sets a hand on my knee. "I don't think you would hurt anyone. If you remember what happened now, I'm sure it can be proven. Stepp will make sure you get a fair shake."

"If the FBI jumps in, Stepp won't have any choice but to turn him over," Samuel says.

"Please don't," I say to Trudi. "I don't want to talk to anyone but you and Samuel."

"I don't think you have much of a choice."

The dinging seems to get louder, or am I just imagining it?

"He does have choices," Samuel says. "And he's right not to trust anyone. You think Agent Uribe would care about his well-being? Do you really want her to have custody of him? The people in this car are the only ones we can trust right now."

I try to nod in agreement, but it hurts.

"What exactly do you want to do?" Trudi asks Samuel.

"We're headed back up to Boston. If we're not all driven mad by the seat belt alarm."

"Why in the world would we go to Boston?"

"Because that's where the Gardner art is." Samuel looks at me in the rearview mirror. "At least I assume it's in that area?"

"Yes," I say.

"Do you remember, then?" he asks.

"I remember some things. I think I have an idea of where to start."

"Why are you both worried about the Gardner art right now?" Trudi demands. "Why does that even matter? We need to get him safe. Isn't going to Boston playing right into the hands of the people who are after him?"

"If he finds the art and turns it in to the authorities, he's of no further use to anyone. He won't be in danger anymore. His value, both to the Irish mob and to Agent Uribe, is his knowledge of the missing Gardner art. If it's found and given to the authorities, he has zero worth to them."

The dinging is starting to feel like drums being played on my head.

"They might still come after him out of spite."

Samuel makes a turn onto what looks like a main road. "And if he is a cooperating federal witness against the mob and also hands over millions of dollars in missing art, he's a lot more likely to get protective custody."

Trudi gently squeezes my knee. "Are you up for this?"

"I want to be faded. I want to disappear. Please."

Trudi focuses on Eula. "What about you? We can drop you off somewhere."

"I'm wanted now too, for escaping federal custody." Eula turns to look out the side window.

Trudi looks at her for a few seconds and then sits back and straps on her seat belt. The dinging stops.

"*Thank you*," Samuel says in an exasperated tone.

Trudi focuses on me. "If we're going to do this, let's figure out exactly how we're approaching it. And maybe talking will help you take your mind off things."

"Paddy never told me exactly where the artwork is," I say. "He never even told me about the clues he hid in my tattoo."

"So, you do think the clocks are clues to find the art?" Trudi asks.

"Yes. He didn't tell me much. Maybe because of Southie, maybe because he didn't really trust me. I don't know. But he told me something I think will help it all make sense."

40

TRUDI

Atlanta, GA

When Samuel jerked the wheel, Trudi looked from Dream over to Samuel. “What’s wrong?”

“Nothing I can’t handle.”

“Thanks for the crystal-clear answer.”

“Just keep working with Dream.” Samuel glanced in his side mirror, punched the gas, passed an Audi Q7, and slipped back into the right lane.

Trudi looked out the back window. “One of Stepp’s men spotted you.” She turned back to Samuel. “I’m right, aren’t I?”

“I think so.”

“Which car is he driving? Is it a uniform or a detective?”

“The black Dodge Charger three cars back.”

“Do you know who it is?”

“Can’t see well enough. Too dark out and the Charger has tinted windows.”

“How do you know he saw you?”

"I'm psychic, remember?" Samuel grinned.

Trudi rolled her eyes. "Seriously, how do you know?"

"He's tailing us. Hasn't been more than two cars back for a few miles, and he's made the same turns down two different streets."

Trudi looked out the window to see where exactly they were. "So, you're driving in circles."

"Until I can lose him." He smiled. "Or until I can draw him away." He took a phone from his pocket and dialed one-handed.

Trudi glanced at Eula, who was still staring out the side window.

"Samuel Hill to speak with Captain Stepp, please."

Trudi refocused on Samuel. *What in the world is he doing?*

"I found Dream," Samuel said into the phone. Then he gave the address to the house they just left. "Send paramedics. I don't know how long I can keep Dream alive, and I think there may be more men in the house." He paused to listen. "I don't know. I . . . I think someone's here. Send backup, quick." He ended the call. Then he glanced in the rearview mirror.

Trudi looked out the back window. About thirty seconds later, the Charger made a U-turn in the middle of the road and sped away.

"Now to hit I-85 and get out of Atlanta," Samuel said.

"Very impressive, Samuel," Trudi admitted. "But do you think we should take 85?"

"Right now, Stepp thinks I'm at the house. We need to use the opportunity to get out of the city. In a while, I'll find alternate routes, as many back roads as possible without losing too much time."

Dream slouched back in his seat and rested his head on the leather.

"Are you comfortable?" Trudi asked. "Other than your fingers, do you think you have any broken bones?"

He very slightly shook his head.

She noticed he seemed to be focused on keeping his gaze up. Then she realized . . . "I'm sure your fingers will heal," she said. "You'll still be able to paint."

"I'm right-handed," he said. "He didn't hurt my right hand just in case his boss decides he still wants to use me to copy artwork."

She tilted her head. "A part of you wishes he'd have hurt your right hand too."

"My art's done nothing but get me into trouble." He shifted uncomfortably in his seat.

Eula scooted closer. "Here, lean on me."

He rested his head on her shoulder.

"I want to see your art someday," Trudi said. "Not some copies you made, but your art, from your mind. I bet it's beautiful."

He didn't respond. She hoped he was sleeping.

Samuel drove I-85 for over an hour. Then he stopped at a gas station, filled the tank, and came back with a map—one of those big atlases. None of them had a phone with a navigation app on it, and the owner of the car apparently had not paid to renew the built-in navigation system.

"I can't believe anyone sells maps anymore," Trudi said quietly. Dream was still leaned on Eula's shoulder. She wasn't sure if he was actually sleeping, but at least he was resting.

"Me neither." Samuel opened the map. A few minutes later, he said he'd found a back road that should take them pretty far.

He drove for another half hour before pulling off onto what looked like a dirt access road for utility workers.

He put the car in park and turned in his seat to look at Dream. "How do you feel?"

Dream slowly sat up, and Trudi could see from how he moved that he was still in a lot of pain.

"I need to patch you up," Samuel said. "It looks like most of your cuts and burns have clotted, but they need to be cleaned out and sewn up or they could get infected, and I really need to set your broken bones."

Dream nodded.

"It's not going to be pleasant. I bought some first aid supplies at the convenience store, but they didn't have much for pain."

"I'll help," Eula said. It was the first time she'd spoken since well before they'd left Atlanta. She opened her door.

Samuel got out and opened Dream's door. He held out a bottle of water and four ibuprofens. "Let's start with this."

Dream took the pills. "Do you know what you're doing?"

"I have field training. Honestly, I don't have a lot of experience setting anyone else's broken bones or sewing stitches other than my own. I'm sorry in advance for the pain."

Trudi tried not to imagine Samuel setting his own broken fingers in some dirt-floor hut in the middle of the desert.

Dream slid to the edge of his seat and set his feet on the ground. Eula had gotten out and was holding the bag of first aid supplies. Trudi sat in the back seat behind Dream and slid closer, either to offer support or to hold him still while Samuel did what had to be done.

"I'm going to clean that cut on your hand first. It looks really deep."

"He stabbed me," Dream said.

"He stabbed your hand?" Eula said. "Can you still move it?"

"I haven't tried."

"It hurts too much," Eula surmised.

Samuel took some gauze and rubbing alcohol out of the bag. "I gotta open it up," he said. "It's going to hurt."

Trudi wrapped her arms around Dream. Eula held his wrist, pushing it against his thigh to help keep his hand still, and with her other hand, she held a flashlight so Samuel could see what he was doing.

Samuel spilled some alcohol on the wound and then rubbed at it with the gauze.

Dream tightened his body and grunted in pain.

Samuel worked for several minutes before he felt it was clean enough. Sweat poured down Dream's face, but he remained relatively still. That was the worst of the cuts. There were several other cuts and what looked like cigarette burns, but at least it took less time to clean them. Samuel bandaged everything with gauze and topical antibiotic/pain reliever.

Then Samuel started setting Dream's broken fingers. Trudi could hear the grating sound as the two ends of the bone ground against each other, and then Dream cried out in pain.

Trudi hugged him as tightly as she could. "It'll feel better once it's done. Hang in there."

Samuel set the next bone, and Dream cried out again. But he, amazingly, barely moved.

"Use your factoids," Trudi told him.

Samuel set the next bone.

"Please, Jesus," Dream said through a clenched jaw.

Trudi silently prayed with him.

It felt like it took forever for Samuel to finish getting them set. He made Dream try to move his fingers, at least from the base joint. Dream managed it, but with a lot of pain. Then Samuel sent Eula to find some strong but slender and straight twigs from the nearby trees. Samuel used white medical tape to splint all of Dream's fingers on his left hand.

"That's the best we can do for now," Samuel said to Dream. "I think the circulation is all right; you have good color. Now you should try to sleep."

Eula said to Trudi, "I'll stay in the back with him."

Trudi let her take the back seat. Helping Dream seemed to be good for her. Eula had Dream lie down on the seat and rest his head on her leg. He carefully laid his left hand on his stomach.

Samuel backed the car off the bumpy dirt road and turned onto the rural highway headed northeast. He flipped the headlights back on.

Trudi kept looking back at Dream, hoping to see him resting peacefully. It took a while for him to close his eyes. Eventually, he fell asleep.

Trudi looked back at Dream one more time. Then she looked at Eula, at how she was stroking Dream's damp hair.

Trudi whispered to Eula, "You're a good person."

A tear escaped Eula's lashes. "I'm trying to believe that."

"I know you're a good person. I'll believe it for the both of us."

More tears fell down Eula's cheeks.

Trudi smiled gently at her and then turned back around in her seat. She knew Eula well enough to know it was best to let her work it out herself in her own time. Pulling the trigger had been the right thing to do. Trudi knew Eula would eventually be able to believe that.

Trudi slouched back in her seat and tried to sleep. She fell into kind of a semi-conscious state. She wasn't fully alert but was aware of each bump in the road and every turn.

A couple of hours later, she sat up and blinked the sleepiness out of her eyes. She spoke quietly to Samuel. "I'll drive for a while."

"I'm all right."

"When's the last time you slept?"

"Eh, I don't need sleep."

"I'm reminded of that stakeout we did that time. What were we watching for? That thief our client suspected was casing their small business, I believe. How did that case turn out again?"

"We caught the guy. Served the max sentence, if I remember correctly."

"It took a little more work than we'd thought."

"A little more."

"And why is that?"

He raised his eyebrows. "I don't remember."

"It wasn't because someone fell asleep during his shift and the thief hit our client's business during that little snooze fest, was it?"

"Did you just say *snooze fest*?"

"Don't change the subject."

"Miss English Major uses the phrase *snooze fest*? What is that, a fiesta for sleepwalkers?"

Trudi laughed despite herself.

At the next drive—looked like a gravel road leading to some trailers—Samuel pulled off and parked. He took the map out from where he'd stuffed it between the seat and the center console and showed Trudi where they were and what his intended route was. They traded seats.

In the back seat, Dream was still asleep on Eula's leg. Eula had her head rested back against the headrest, but her eyes were open.

Trudi took over driving, and Samuel folded his arms and slept.

The drive was all bumpy asphalt and dark trees. Spanish moss swayed like shadows of monsters, yet something was beautiful about it all. Like one of Poe's poems.

Sometime after she made the turn onto the next rural highway, she heard a faint rustling from the back seat. She looked in the rearview mirror to see Dream sitting up.

"Want more ibuprofen?" she asked quietly.

"I think it's making my stomach upset."

"Are you hurting?"

"I'm getting used to it."

"You can rest more."

"I thought you could use some company."

She smiled. "I'm all right."

He spoke more quietly. "I need some company."

She looked at him in the mirror. "Nightmares?"

He didn't answer, but she sensed the turmoil within him.

"You've changed," she said.

He tilted his head curiously.

"I don't know if it's that you're stronger or if you've always been this strong and you're maintaining a façade better than you used to."

"I couldn't lose control there," he said. "Or else I might tell them one of your names."

She whispered, "Thank you, Dream."

"But I still use my fact book. I've been thinking it rather than saying it."

"Good. I think that was a great way for you to have control over your own thoughts."

"Do you still have that drawing?"

"The one of your tattoos?" She was thankful he'd been able to slip that to her before they'd taken him.

"Yeah."

"I put it in a, ah, more private place so Homeland Security wouldn't take it when they searched me."

"What?"

"Long story. Nothing for you to worry about." She leaned, lifted her right hip, and slipped her hand into the side of her jeans. She'd folded the paper and tucked it against her hip, held tight to her by her undergarment. She held it between two fingers so he could take it from her.

"I can't see well enough. Not yet."

She set the drawing in the cup holder. "Before, you said Paddy told you something that you think might make everything make sense."

"It was an odd comment. He was random sometimes, but I learned to get him, you know?"

She glanced at Samuel sleeping beside her and thought of how sometimes she knew everything he was about to say before he uttered one word. "I know what you mean."

"It was right after he was done with the tattoo on my back. He helped me sit up and took a swig of his drink. Then he said, 'The beginning of revolution is where to look.'"

Trudi drew her eyebrows together. "That's pretty cryptic."

"I thought he was just laughing at his own joke at the time. He did that a lot. Sometimes, I got what he was saying, especially anything to do with the work we were doing. But this time, I didn't understand him at all. I just got up and went to get some water."

"But you think you understand now?"

"He was really into the work. I don't think it was just the money for him. I think he liked the game. But there was one other thing he was really interested in. He hadn't been born here. He still had a heavy Irish accent. He'd only been here I think five years or so. He liked the Boston area and the history, specifically any history related to the birth of the country."

"There's a lot of history in Boston. We need to narrow it down."

"The Old North Church," Dream said. "That's where we need to go."

FRIDAY

NOVEMBER 17

41

TRUDI

Somewhere in North Carolina

"The beginning of revolution," Trudi said. "As in the beginning of the American Revolution?"

"I think so," Dream said.

"But wouldn't that be the battle at Lexington?" Trudi asked.

"I don't think that's what Paddy meant."

"Why?"

"Because he named the squirrels William and Paul."

"Huh?" Eula asked.

"He named them William and Paul. It was important to him."

Eula looked at Trudi with a confused expression.

Trudi started to wonder if Dream wasn't as stable as she'd thought. He was definitely still not your "normal," average man, and rightfully so, but now she started to wonder if he could help figure out the tattoo, or if any of it meant anything. But then she realized . . . "William Dawes and Paul Revere?"

"Yes."

"But they weren't at the church. They were the riders, warning everyone that the British were coming."

"And they knew to give the warning because of the lanterns."

"That's why you think it's the Old North Church."

He started to nod, and then he grimaced.

"You're still in a lot of pain," Eula said. "You need to sleep some more if you can. It'll help you heal."

"She's right," Trudi said. "We know where we're going now. We can figure out the rest when we get to Boston." She wished they could talk about it more and figure out the clues, but she kept that to herself.

Dream did manage to get back to sleep, and Eula drifted off as well.

The only sound was the tires on the asphalt.

After a few hours, Eula woke and took the wheel. Trudi napped in the back seat.

On the long stretches between big cities, they took I-95, which sped up the trip. They kept taking turns driving and sleeping, and by the time they crossed the Connecticut border, Samuel was back at the wheel and the sun had fully risen. He took them through Connecticut, then Rhode Island, and toward Boston.

"How exactly do we get to the Old North Church?" Samuel asked Trudi, who was in the passenger seat, holding the atlas.

"Not yet," Dream said.

"What do you mean 'not yet'?" Trudi asked.

"You need to eat."

"We're kind of in a hurry," Samuel said.

"Why? All those men in Atlanta were arrested by your Captain Stepp, right?"

"And we're headed to the hotbed of people looking for you."

"None of them know I'm here. We can afford to stop for fifteen minutes. You need to eat."

Trudi said to Samuel, "He should eat too. He probably hasn't had any food for a couple of days."

"Okay. I know this little hole-in-the-wall."

"You make it sound so enticing," Trudi said. Anything sounded pretty good right now.

"Best grits in all of Boston. Probably the only grits in Boston."

"Northern grits?" Trudi scoffed.

"Old Southern lady moved up to be closer to her daughter and grandbabies."

Trudi narrowed her eyes. "I'll give it a shot."

"You don't think it's possible to cook good grits north of the Mason-Dixon Line?"

"Something with the air."

"Grits need humidity?"

"Yup."

He laughed.

A little while later, Samuel exited I-95 and turned onto Highland Avenue. After crossing a river, he turned into a small shopping center, or as the sign put it, "Lifestyle Place." He backed the car into a parking space under a tree by a brick building with red and white vinyl awnings.

They all stood from the car.

Trudi remembered . . . "I don't have any money." Homeland Security had taken her wallet to check her ID.

Samuel looked at her from over the roof of the car. "I have some cash."

Dream tugged his jacket sleeves down and gingerly put his left hand in his pocket. The swelling of his face was better, but he still looked pretty bad. Trudi motioned for Eula to walk first. She was lovely enough, even while dealing with all this stress, to draw attention away from Dream.

While they walked across the parking lot, Trudi caught Samuel covertly watching every direction. She did the same.

It was well past the lunch rush, so the waitress sat them immediately. Samuel requested a table at the back. Trudi made sure to sit on the end closest to the window, and she motioned for Eula to sit opposite her, so both Samuel and Dream were a bit better hidden.

The place was small, with old wood floors—almost looked like barnwood—and it smelled like hot grease and chicken.

"How'd you find this place?" Trudi asked Samuel.

"When I first came up here, I stayed at the Sheraton down the street for a few nights."

A waitress walked up to the table. "What can I get you?"

"Is it too late for breakfast?" Trudi asked.

"Anything you want."

They ordered, and before the food came, Trudi made Dream take four more ibuprofen, hoping food in his stomach would help it not get too upset from the painkiller.

They ate quietly. Trudi kept thinking about the drawing of Dream's tattoo, trying to decipher it. Now that she had something to start with—Old North Church—she started to have some theories.

But then she noticed Eula's expression. Eula was trying hard not to show anything, and doing a good job, but Trudi knew her well enough to see her thoughts eating away at her. Trudi set down her fork and reached across the table to take Eula's hand.

Eula looked up.

"Thank you," Dream said.

Eula looked over at him.

"For saving my life," Dream added.

"You saved both of our lives," Trudi said. "He had a gun

drawn, aiming at Dream and me. He was outnumbered with no other options. He was going to shoot."

Eula took a breath. "I know he was."

Trudi squeezed Eula's hand.

Then they all went back to their meal.

When the waitress brought the check, Trudi took some cash from Samuel and walked up to the register at the front of the restaurant to pay.

"Everything taste all right?" the cashier asked.

"Tasted like home."

"You're from the South? How long you been away?"

"Not long."

The waitress took the cash and started counting out change.

Trudi glanced out the windows. She squinted her eyes as she focused on a man in a passing car. He looked like . . .

The car drove by, and a few seconds later it came back by. Through the driver's window, she could see him better.

The waitress handed her the change.

"Thanks." Trudi went back to the table.

She laid down a tip.

"Keep the rest," Samuel said.

Trudi pocketed the cash. "It's probably nothing, but . . . a man in a black Mercedes just drove by the restaurant."

"Okay . . ." Samuel said.

"He looks a lot like Samir. Neatly trimmed Americanized beard and what looked like a fancy suit. But it's really in the eyes—clear, alert, and busy."

Samuel stood and looked out the windows. "You said he drove by?"

"Twice. He pulled in, then turned around and drove back by."

"Did he leave or pull into a parking space?"

"I couldn't see, and I didn't want to get too close to the window and draw attention to myself. Do you think it could be someone from al-Sadr?"

Trudi could almost see his thoughts zooming through his eyes like ticker tape. "Wait here," he said and walked toward the front of the restaurant.

Trudi followed. "What're you doing? He might see you."

"I need to know if it's someone I need to be concerned about, don't I?" He continued forward and stopped next to a coat stand at the front door and looked out the window. He cursed under his breath.

Then he walked back over to the table.

"You think it's a relative of Samir's?" Trudi asked.

"It's his brother." Then he muttered, "Had to be early, didn't he?"

She figured he'd studied all known members of the clan and had their faces memorized. "What do you mean 'early'?"

"Intelligence has them getting across the border around the twentieth."

"I'm sure there's a back door out of here."

"I'll draw him away, and you get out with Eula and Dream. Go find the artwork."

"Samuel."

"No, Tru-Bear. I'm not negotiating this one."

"We need to stick together."

"Having three other people with me will just slow me down. I'm better off working alone."

Sums up our marriage, right there, she thought.

"Just trust me," he said. "I'll draw him away and lose him, and then I'll meet you in a couple of hours. Boston Common."

"Fine," Trudi said. "But at least take the weapon." She had the gun she'd taken from the house back in Boston tucked into her waistband and hidden under her shirt.

"Wow," Samuel said. "You're actually offering it? I thought I'd have to pry that from your cold, dead hands."

"As if you could even then."

"You keep it. You might need to defend Dream if certain people catch wind he's in town."

"I really think you should take it."

"I can handle myself. This is going to be cat and mouse, not combat." He took the Chrysler key fob and gave it to Trudi.

"Huh, I always think of you as a pig, not a cat or a mouse."

"Oink, oink." He walked around the table to where Dream stood, watching their conversation. "Come here for a second." Samuel drew Dream into the hallway and toward the restrooms.

Less than a minute later, they came back out. Dream had his splinted left hand out of his pocket now, and he was wearing a focused expression Trudi would expect him to wear while painting a masterpiece, not walking out of a restroom.

Samuel didn't stop as he walked by. "Boston Common, two hours." He headed past the waitress station and into the kitchen, as if he were a busboy late for his shift. Surely, he was headed for the back door.

"Stay here," Trudi said to Dream and Eula. She headed for the front of the restaurant. A couple of old men were seated at a booth in front of the windows. She slid in next to a man with wispy white hairs on top of his head.

"That's what I think the president—" The man with wispy hair looked over at Trudi. He did not have a wispy voice. "Is there something I can help you with?"

Trudi smiled. "Just wanted to see something out the window." She set her hand on his arm. "You don't mind, do you?"

He narrowed his eyes. Trudi kept smiling, and then he said, "I suppose it won't hurt."

His friend with a full head of gray hair and an old, brown bomber jacket looked outside. "Pretty normal day out there today."

"I have a hunch." She patted the table. "Don't let me interrupt. What were you saying about the president?"

Thankfully, the subject seemed to be a hot topic for these men. They continued their conversation as if she hadn't interrupted. She pretended to be interested, while watching outside, mostly hidden behind the man next to her.

A couple of minutes later, Samuel walked out from the left side of the building and up the sidewalk along the street. From this angle, she could better see the parking lot. The black Mercedes was parked two cars down from the Chrysler 300.

Samuel crossed the drive lane and continued down the sidewalk, only maybe fifteen feet from Samir's brother. *Stop being so reckless!* she mentally yelled at Samuel.

The driver's-side door of the Mercedes opened, and Samir's brother stepped out, keeping one foot still inside the car. He stared at Samuel, then glanced around at the people coming and going from the other shops in the little "Lifestyle Place."

Still walking casually, hands in his pockets, Samuel looked over at the Arab man and smiled his most dashing smile. It was kind of like Prince Charming, Peter Pan, and the Cheshire Cat all in one.

The Arab man reached under his jacket but then stopped.

A couple of women wearing yoga pants walked from the Massage Envy Spa across the way toward the parking lot.

Samuel waved and headed toward them. He called out something, but Trudi couldn't hear. The two women stopped and waited for him to approach. Trudi wanted to roll her eyes. *That man could charm his way into Wonderland.* If a strange man approached her like that, she was more likely to clench her fist than wave back.

Samuel stopped and talked with the women. Both he and the women maintained a casual posture, like old friends chatting.

The Arab man slowly approached.

Samuel, what are you doing? Trudi thought.

42

SAMUEL

Boston, MA

Samuel smiled at the two women. He could almost feel Trudi glaring at him through the restaurant window, though he couldn't see her. "I'm so sorry to bother you," he said to the two women in yoga pants. "Can you help me? I'm looking for Men's Wearhouse."

The blonde on the left laughed and pointed off to her right, over Samuel's shoulder.

Samuel glanced back across the street, which was really an excuse to keep an eye on his surroundings. "Duh. My mother always told me I was blind. Maybe I should ask you where to find Pearle Vision while I'm at it."

"Are you new to the area?" the brunette asked.

"Brand new. Starting a job on Monday. Thought I'd pick up a new suit."

Ahmad, Samir's younger brother, continued to walk slowly toward them.

"Exciting," the brunette said. "So, what kind of job?"

What's an impressive job title? "VP of marketing."

"Wow."

Ahmad walked up and smiled at the women and then at Samuel. "How fortuitous to meet you here, Samuel."

"Hello," Samuel said. "Do I know you?"

"I believe you knew my brother. Actually, I have some business to discuss with you. It's rather pressing." He motioned for Samuel to walk back across the parking lot with him.

"Your brother?" Samuel asked. "I don't think so. I just moved here. Unless your brother is from San Francisco?"

Ahmad clenched his jaw. "I believe the last time you saw him was in Alabama."

"Alabama? I don't think I've ever even been to Alabama."

Ahmad's dark eyes stabbed daggers at Samuel. "I believe you have."

"No, I don't think so."

The brunette woman spoke up. "Maybe you have the wrong guy."

Ahmad glanced at her, and his gaze barely flicked to her yoga pants. In Saudi Arabia, women could be arrested for wearing such tight clothing. The al-Sadr clan, however, preferred women to be stoned to death for not staying in line. "Please excuse us. I would like to speak to my associate in private."

Samuel caught a glimpse of the gun holstered inside Ahmad's tailored overcoat.

"I don't think he knows you," the brunette said.

Ahmad's lips thinned as he barely concealed a sneer. He turned back to Samuel. "I'm sure you'll remember my brother if we speak for just a moment. Please." He motioned again for Samuel to follow him.

"What was his name?" Samuel asked. "Your brother."

"You'll remember once I remind you."

Samuel drew his eyebrows together. "Uh, okay. Tell me about him. Why do you think I know him?"

Ahmad's tone hardened. "If you speak with me for *just a moment*, you'll remember. I'm certain."

The brunette spoke up. "I really think you have the wrong guy. You should leave and stop harassing this man."

Ahmad focused on her with those dark eyes that reminded Samuel of flint—sharp and flat, depthless. "You should remain silent while a man is talking."

The brunette rested her hands on her hips, and the blonde burst out with, "Excuse me?"

The brunette chimed in. "You should watch your mouth and show respect to women."

Ahmad seemed completely focused on the women. "Why should I show respect to a piece of property?"

Samuel stepped between him and the women and threw an elbow strike at Ahmad's face. Ahmad twisted back toward Samuel with a hook to the jaw. Samuel managed to deflect it. Then he reached in Ahmad's jacket for his gun.

Ahmad grabbed Samuel's arm with both hands. Samuel didn't let go of the gun, leaving his hand inside Ahmad's jacket.

"Tsk, tsk," Samuel said. "I have a feeling someone doesn't have a proper conceal-carry permit." He heard the women's feet shuffling behind him. He kept track of the sound so he could make sure to keep them behind him.

Ahmad sneered.

"I have my finger on the trigger. Shall we end this little dispute here and now, or would you like to live to fight another day?"

"I am not alone in this city," Ahmad said.

"Oh, I figured that. You never were able to handle things on your own."

Ahmad glared at him.

"You think I haven't done my homework on those who would kill me? Your family's had to bail you out more than once."

"You will die for what you did to my brother."

"Actually, I didn't do much of anything to your brother. He simply made a critical mistake." *Namely, getting in my ex-wife's way.*

Ahmad shifted.

"Uh-uh," Samuel warned.

Ahmad stopped and sneered at Samuel.

"Now, this is how it's going down," Samuel said. "You're going to provide me with a weapon, since I'm lacking one right now. Then you're going to lie down with your hands folded behind your back and your ankles crossed. You're going to let these nice ladies go without an insult, not even in your gross little mind. And then you're going to watch me walk away with your gun. But you can curse me under your breath if you want." Samuel smiled. "I'm nothing if not giving."

"I will do no such thing."

"It's either that or . . . splat. I'd really rather not do that in front of these nice ladies."

"You mean—"

Samuel pulled him closer by bending his right elbow and kneed Ahmad in the groin. Ahmad's grip on Samuel's arm weakened, and Samuel pulled out of his grasp, removing the gun from the holster. Then he used the butt of the weapon to strike Ahmad across the jaw with force.

Ahmad smacked against the pavement. The women gasped.

Samuel ejected the magazine to check the ammunition and popped it back into place. He racked the slide back to be sure a bullet was in the chamber.

Then he turned and faced the women. "My sincerest apologies. I made sure you were safe the whole time, you have my word."

"Who are you?" the brunette demanded.

Let's see how the truth works. "I'm CIA. This man is a member of a terrorist organization."

"Did you kill his brother?"

"My partner did, after he attacked her and the little girl we saved from him. I know you're freaked out right now. I'm sorry for that. But I need your help."

"Our help?" the blonde asked.

"I need you to call the police and tell them you think you found a terrorist."

"You or him?" The brunette nodded at Ahmad, who was motionless on the ground.

"Who does your gut tell you the terrorist is?"

The women paused, and they glanced at each other. The blonde pointed at Ahmad.

Samuel smiled. "And I really need a car."

"Are you serious?"

"Unfortunately, yes. And I don't have much time for you to decide. I'm sure someone else saw what just happened, or they'll look out the window any moment and see him lying on the ground. I need to get out of here." More al-Sadr members weren't far away. Ahmad liked to keep a contingent with him.

"If you're CIA, why don't you have a weapon of your own and a car?"

"I'm on the run. They're hunting me down. And, quite frankly, I'm not sure who I can trust. I'm on my own."

A pause.

The blonde reached into the small purse slung over her shoulder and took out keys. She removed a key fob and handed it to

Samuel. She pointed to the row of cars directly in front of the Chrysler 300. "It's over there. The black Lincoln MKC."

Samuel lowered his voice in true appreciation. "Thank you. Please call the police. Tell them two men had an altercation. You heard this man"—he pointed toward Ahmad—"say something about attacking an airport. That'll be enough for the authorities to take securing him seriously. Please don't give them a good description of me. Tell them you were too scared to get a good look. And please don't tell them I took your car or report it stolen."

"I do need it back."

"I'll leave it at Boston Common. Give me three hours."

"Three hours?"

"If I don't accomplish what I need to by then, I'm probably dead. If that happens, I sincerely apologize about the car."

"Are you serious?"

"Today, yes. But, normally, as infrequently as possible." He grinned.

A giggle escaped the brunette's lips, and she covered her mouth.

"Do you have all that?" Samuel asked.

The blonde said, "Call the police, we think he's a terrorist, didn't get a good look at you, don't say anything about my car."

"I can't explain how much I appreciate this." Samuel ran off toward the MKC.

Before he pulled out of the lot, he checked to be sure Ahmad was still down and that the women had moved farther away from him. The blonde was on her phone.

He turned right onto Needham Street. That's when he saw the other Mercedes—a big, boxy G-Class SUV. It turned out of the Men's Wearhouse lot and sped after him.

43

TRUDI

Boston, MA

"What's going on?" Eula asked. "Is Samuel okay?"

"For the moment. We should go. It's clear outside."

Eula and Dream followed Trudi. "What do you mean 'for the moment'?" Eula asked. "What happened?"

"Tell you in the car."

They walked quickly across the drive lane and to the car. She wanted to get out of there before the police showed up to investigate the disturbance Samuel had created. Within a few seconds, Trudi had pulled out of the lot and turned left, in the opposite direction of Samuel.

"What happened to Samuel?" Eula asked from the passenger seat. "Did he take down that man who was lying in the parking lot?"

"Yes."

Eula looked closely at Trudi. "There's something else."

"He took down Samir's brother, but another car raced after him when he left."

"Who's Samir?" Dream asked. "Is Samuel going to be okay?"

"Of course. He's incredibly skilled and well trained. This is what he does for a living." Trudi had to force herself to keep driving in the opposite direction of Samuel. *Samuel can handle himself, and I need to keep Dream and Eula safe.* "Eula, do you think you can figure out how to get to Old North Church?"

"Yeah, I think so." Eula picked up the atlas.

Trudi glanced in the rearview mirror. "Dream, do you think the artwork is somehow hidden in the church?"

"That's what I'm hoping, but I'm not really sure."

"Okay, let's look at the drawing and think it through." Trudi picked up her sketch of Dream's tattoos.

"We didn't draw the one on my hand," Dream said.

"Right. That one was an eagle, or at least some kind of bird, with outstretched wings."

"And it read, 'the dream within Dream,' right?"

"I think so. Do you still have your black light?"

"I think it's too bright for it to work."

"Of course it decides to be sunny today," Trudi said. Eula nudged Trudi and pointed, and Trudi took the on-ramp for I-95 North. "We'll just focus on the drawing first."

"Here, let me see." Eula took the drawing, and Dream carefully scooted forward in the back seat so he could see. He seemed to be moving better. Rest and food had done him well.

"Is there anything different about the poem?" Eula asked. "Anything off from the original? Even something really small?"

"No, it's right," Trudi said.

"What about *Hope* being capitalized?" Eula asked. "It's not the beginning of a line or a name."

"That's how it is in the original. Not sure why."

"I think what we need is in the clocks," Dream said. "Paddy was obsessed with clocks. He had me draw clocks before even starting on the forgeries."

"Okay," Eula said. "The clocks."

"How about the hands?" Trudi asked. "I drew them as carefully as possible. I couldn't see any kind of pattern when I sketched them."

"The first one looks like it's about 2:50. Then 3:10. Then about 1:08, I think. Then 4:00 on the nose." Eula turned to look at Dream. "Those times mean anything?"

Dream took a moment to think.

"Something to do with your schedule when you were with Paddy?" Eula suggested.

"We didn't keep a schedule. Sometimes we worked until three in the morning, and sometimes his inspiration would give out at three in the afternoon. It just depended."

"Say the times again," Trudi said.

"About 2:50, 3:10, 1:08-ish, and 4:00 exactly." Then Eula exclaimed, "Wait! Could it be an order, not a time?"

"That's what I'm thinking," Trudi said. "The hours are the order. One, two, three, four."

"So, there are four things we have to do," Eula said. "All at Old North Church?"

"It's really more of a small complex," Trudi said, "so maybe the artwork is hidden throughout. Maybe they split it up so if someone found one stash, they didn't have everything. Dream, do you think that's possible?"

"Maybe. But what about the minute hands?" Dream craned to see the drawing better.

"If the hour hands are the order," Eula said, "maybe the minute hands are telling us what exactly has to be in order. It's got to be related to the poem. Otherwise, why do all the work of tattooing that poem as well as the clocks?"

"To disguise what he was really doing," Dream said.

"Disguise from who?" Eula asked.

"From me and Southie."

"You don't think Southie knew Paddy gave you the map?" Trudi asked.

"No," Dream said. "He would've never let Paddy do it. If Southie didn't have the art, he'd rather no one have it."

"Even if he was dead?" Eula asked.

"Definitely."

"So, why'd Paddy give it to you?" Eula asked.

Trudi saw Dream shrug in the rearview mirror. "Maybe he thought he might eventually die or go to prison, and he didn't want the art lost forever."

"It sounds like he cared about the art itself," Trudi said.

Dream nodded.

"Did he care about poetry?" Trudi asked.

"He talked about art a lot more, but I think he liked the imagery of Edgar Allan Poe's work, and he knew I like it."

Eula raised her eyebrows. "He knew you would understand the imagery and the complexities. Not many people do."

Dream shrugged. "I guess so."

"He hid the clues inside the poem, knowing you could figure it out."

"I think you're right," Trudi said.

"So, if the clues are in the poem," Eula said, "and we trust that we're right about the hour hand being the order, then we should focus on the minute hands."

"Could it be the words the minute hand is pointing to?" Dream asked. "The hands are longer than I originally drew them. They're all the way to the edge of the clocks."

Trudi smiled. "That's one of the reasons he had you draw the clocks in the first place. He knew you, as an artist, would notice little details like that."

"And you're sure you got the hands exact?" Eula asked Trudi.

"I was as careful as I could be. I think it's right."

"Okay. The minute hand of the first clock is pointing to *avow*," Eula said. "What does that mean?"

"Where do you take vows in a church?" Dream asked.

"You think the art is hidden in the altar? Are any of the pieces small enough?"

"Not most of them, but there's the postage stamp–sized self-portrait drawing by Rembrandt or a finial that might fit."

"A finial? Is it solid gold or something?" Eula asked.

"It was bronze. It was taken off the top of a Napoleonic flag."

"One of the greatest art heists in history, and they bothered with the topper from a flag?"

"I bet they thought it was gold when they took it." Then Trudi said to Eula, "When do I need to exit?"

Eula picked up the map. "Take 90 East. It should be coming up soon."

"Okay. What's the next minute hand point to?"

"It looks like the word *roar*," Eula said.

Trudi pursed her lips.

"Not much roaring going on in a church, usually," Eula said. "I doubt they even let animals on the grounds."

They were quiet while they thought. Trudi exited I-95 and managed to figure out the convoluted ramp system to get onto I-90 East. She drove for several more miles.

"All right," Eula said. "I got nothing. Let's come back to that one." She looked at the drawing. "The next clock down points to . . . *golden*. Old North Church isn't one of those really ornate churches, is it?"

"I don't think so," Trudi said. "Early American architecture isn't known for being ornate."

"That's the clock with the hour hand pointed to 1:00," Dream said. "So, we have to figure it out pretty quick."

"Golden could mean anything," Eula said. "Unless . . . Could the minute hand really be pointing to *golden sand*, not just the word *golden*?"

"Maybe," Trudi said. "I know there are gardens there. Maybe it's something to do with that. When we arrive, let's start there. I'm guessing it'll be easier to start our search outside the church itself. We might raise less suspicion."

"It's a plan," Eula said. "The last minute hand points to *deep*. Thoughts?"

"Uh, do I need to exit soon?" Trudi asked. "I don't want to cross Boston Harbor, do I?"

"Take exit 24 toward I-93. It looks like it'll be on the left."

"You know," Trudi said, "I don't think most twentysomethings even know how to read maps."

"I used to help my dad navigate back in the day. Here, the exit's coming up."

Trudi took the exit.

"Keep left again to go north," Eula said. "Okay, now right."

Trudi did as told.

"Now, we go about a mile, it looks like, then take exit 23."

They exited, and Eula guided Trudi toward Salem Street.

Trudi found a parking lot and turned off the engine. "I hate to say this, but we should come up with a contingency plan."

"Contingency plan for what exactly?" Eula asked. "The people who are after Samuel aren't coming after you too, are they?"

"No. They blame Samuel completely."

Dream spoke up. "Contingency for if the people who are after me catch up with us."

"First," Trudi said, "if anything goes wrong and we're separated, we shouldn't come back to the car. We should all meet at Boston Common. We have to meet Samuel there anyway." *Samuel, you'd better take care of yourself and be there on time.*

Eula held up the atlas. "We should all memorize where that is related to our current location on the map." She pointed to where they were and then ran her finger along the easiest route to Boston Common.

"Got it," Trudi said.

"I understand," Dream said. "One more thing, though."

"Yeah?" Eula asked.

"Don't get into trouble for me. If they find me, let me go. I won't give either of you up."

Trudi turned in her seat so she could look at Dream properly. "We'll protect each other."

"No—"

"That's just how it is. We're all friends now. I would never forgive myself for not doing everything I could to help my friend, and I'm sure Eula feels the same."

Eula nodded. "There's no use in arguing. Just deal with it."

Dream didn't answer, but his expression softened.

"Okay," Trudi said, "let's go." She got out of the car, and so did Eula.

Dream carefully scooted to the left. Trudi opened his door and helped him stand from the car.

"You should probably keep your left hand in your pocket," Trudi said to Dream. "That many splints will draw attention."

Eula walked over to the driver's side of the car. "People might think we beat you." She winked at Dream.

Trudi asked Dream, "Want me to help hold your pocket open?"

Dream angled his left pocket away from her. "I can do it."

"Let me at least button your coat. It's freezing out here." She buttoned his coat, while wishing she had a heavier jacket herself.

Trudi said to both of them, "Try to pretend we're just your average tourists. Act excited and be friendly with each other."

Eula popped a friendly smile onto her face and slipped her left arm through Dream's right. "We'll walk slow, all right?" she said to him. "You just lean on me and use me for balance as much as you want. I'm stronger than I look."

They started walking. On Salem Street, they approached the church's steeple. The sidewalk turned to brick, and they came to the church's front doors, though they were blocked by a wrought-iron fence. They paused.

"A map," Trudi said, and she walked over to a basic map of the complex posted on the fence.

"Looks like they have several gardens," Eula said.

"Let's start with the Third Lantern Garden," Dream suggested.

They walked through the gate to their right and then walked around the left side of the building.

"Too bad we can't take a tour." Eula craned her neck to look in through the church doors as they passed.

At the side of the building, they came to a courtyard that was brick on all sides, including under their feet. To the left was a wall separating Washington Garden, and the Third Lantern Garden was just ahead. They headed through the wrought-iron gate and down the steps.

"I don't see any kind of sand," Eula said. "Gold or otherwise."

"Let's quickly browse through the other gardens." Trudi led the way back out and to the Washington Garden. They didn't find anything there either.

Then they walked around to the other side of the church to the Bigelow Courtyard, which was an expanse of brick pavers with eight trees running down the middle, providing shade. From there, they could see the other small garden areas. The Eighteenth Century Garden had more green than the others, but still no golden sand.

"Should we try the other clues first?" Trudi asked Dream.

"I think you're right that Paddy put them in order. He wouldn't have done that without good reason."

Eula walked out of the gated area and to the street. Trudi and Dream followed. Eula looked all around, up and down the street, and then she stopped and focused on the building to the right. "Is that part of the Old North Church complex?" she asked.

"Yeah," Trudi said. "That's the Clough House. There's a chocolate shop and a print shop."

"Is chocolate made with brown sugar?" Eula asked.

"I bet in the eighteenth century they used less refined sugar more often than we do now."

"Which would be browner, right?"

"Golden sand . . ." Dream said.

"You've got to be right," Trudi said. "Nothing else around here makes sense as golden sand." She headed toward the Clough House entrance.

Inside, they looked around, pretending to be tourists.

Eula whispered to Trudi, "We need to get into the kitchen."

"*One* of us needs to get into the kitchen. The other two can keep the workers busy with questions. Dream and I will stay out here and distract them. You slip into the kitchen. If you get caught, just smile that charming smile of yours, apologize, and say you got lost."

"You'd have to be pretty stupid to wind up lost in the kitchen. *Uh, I thought this was the bathroom with a big stove in the middle of the room.*"

"Being stupid has its perks."

Eula grinned. "More accurately, people thinking you're stupid has its perks." She meandered off.

Trudi walked up to an employee. "So, what was the process? Making chocolate back then?"

Dream found a different employee who looked like he was about to walk to the back, surely where the kitchen was. "So, Captain Jackson's Historic Chocolate Shop, huh? Who's Captain Jackson?"

Trudi had about run out of questions about the chocolate-making process when Eula finally emerged. She smiled at Trudi and Dream and walked out the door.

Trudi left a few seconds later, followed by Dream. He had a piece of chocolate in his hand.

Dream took a bite. "I think he was just trying to get me to shut up."

Trudi realized he'd stopped inspecting his food, which had to be a positive step for him.

The three of them got off the sidewalk and back into the Bigelow Courtyard, off to the side, away from other people.

"Did you find something?" Trudi asked Eula.

"I got desperate and stuffed my hand into a big bag of sugar." She kept rubbing her hand on her pant leg. "The bag looked like it'd been there for a while, sitting in the corner on a lower shelf, like maybe someone had decided that brand of sugar made subpar chocolate. I didn't see any other place where something might have been hidden."

"Was anything in there?" Trudi asked.

"Of course not. But when I pulled my hand out, the shelf shifted, and I heard a tinkling sound." Eula held out her other hand to show what was in it. "It was attached to the bottom of the shelf with a staple."

"That's what you found?" Dream asked.

44

SAMUEL

Boston, MA

The big, boxy Mercedes followed Samuel up Needham Street and past several stores. As he approached the light at Needham and Winchester, he switched lanes several times. The Mercedes stayed with him. *Yeah, they're definitely following me.*

He turned left onto Winchester. The Mercedes followed. Samuel got up to speed and then moved to the right lane.

Instead of going faster, he slowed down. Way down.

The Mercedes shot past him and then slammed on the brakes. The car behind it blared its horn.

Samuel considered turning, but he didn't know the area well enough to be sure he wouldn't hit a dead end. He continued driving at a snail's pace. Cars zoomed around him, and several honked. He smiled and waved as those cars flew by.

The Mercedes moved slowly along in the left lane. The cars that passed Samuel then switched lanes and passed the Mercedes. Every time the Mercedes slowed a bit more, obviously trying to get behind Samuel, Samuel put on the brakes. At one point, he actually stopped.

The Mercedes slowed down even more. A big Ford F-150 got in front of it to make a left turn and stopped.

Samuel punched the gas. The little MKC had a nice turbo engine. He blew by the Mercedes.

The Mercedes shifted forward to get around the Ford, but it didn't have enough room to cut the wheel, and all the people passing wouldn't let it over anyway.

Samuel drove a couple of miles, watching all the side streets and looking for a good place to turn. Before he could find a street to disappear down, he spotted the Mercedes in the rear-view mirror. *Great.*

He considered getting on Route 9 but decided to continue straight. A high-speed chase on a freeway was not conducive to staying off the radar.

He drove past a lot of houses but didn't risk a detour down one of the streets in case one of them ended in a cul-de-sac. Instead of hiding, he drove fast to try to put as much distance between him and the Mercedes as he could.

After driving by some kind of lake and over railroad tracks, he finally came to some more businesses. He happened to look down at the instrument panel and noticed the orange warning light. *Of course, I'm almost out of gas.*

He saw some parallel parking, turned, and swooped into a spot. The blonde lady would just have to figure out where her car was, because it wasn't making it to Boston Common. He got out and made traffic stop for him while he jogged toward some shops across the street. He walked up the sidewalk and looked at the cars. At this point, he wasn't above stealing if the opportunity presented itself.

Then he paused at an old Chevy pickup truck. On the back

end was a large American flag magnet, and under that was a sword standing upright with two crossing arrows behind it. On a banner under the sword was the phrase *De oppresso liber. Green Beret*, Samuel thought. *I'll take whatever good luck I can get.* The truck was parked just outside a Walgreens. Samuel headed inside.

He walked up to the counter and lay the key fob for the Lincoln MKC down. "Found this outside," he said to the clerk, a heavy-set woman with a big pink bow in her hair that reminded him of something Trudi would secretly think was fun. Hopefully, the clerk waited a little while for someone to come claim the fob before she called the police, because once the police were called, they would surely run the tags and call the car's owner.

Then he quickly walked away from the counter. The store had security cameras, but it wasn't as if a little Walgreens had facial recognition software that would alert the authorities to his presence. By the time Homeland Security realized he'd been here, his plan should—hopefully—be fully implemented, and no one would care about him anymore.

He watched out the windows as the boxy Mercedes approached. He'd parked with the back bumper of the MKC close to the next car to make the license plate difficult to see in passing. Surely, his entourage had taken note of the plate.

The Mercedes passed the parked Lincoln but then stopped. The car behind it honked. A man in the Mercedes's passenger seat hopped out and approached the Lincoln. He leaned down to get a look at the front license plate.

Samuel rolled his eyes and turned to walk farther into the store.

He passed the aisles for lotions, incontinence products, and nail care, and in the aisle for cold medicine, an older man took out a handkerchief and blew his nose just as Samuel walked by.

It sounded like he vacated enough mucus to clear out his entire skull. "Oh dear, pardon me, son."

"Feel better." Samuel turned the corner and squatted down in the next aisle by the baby aspirators. He could see the front door through a wide-angle security mirror. No one else was in the store but the cold-ridden man and the woman at the counter up front. The truck outside probably belonged to someone in a different store.

A couple of minutes later, two men walked in—one darker-skinned and middle-aged and the other lighter-skinned and much younger, likely an American recruit. Samuel knew al-Sadr had an American contingent, though very small. The group operated like a gang in a way and recruited the disenfranchised, made them feel like they had a family, and then sent them on suicide missions.

The two men separated and started through the store.

Samuel watched their paths, hoping to slip by them and back out the door, but the layout of the store made that option impossible. Then he thought maybe he could still avoid them.

The middle-aged man approached the other end of Samuel's aisle, and Samuel shifted silently to the endcap. Though Samuel hadn't gotten a terribly good look at him, he was pretty sure the man's name was Kismat, one of al-Sadr's top lieutenants. Once Kismat passed, Samuel squatted back in front of the baby aspirators.

But then Kismat turned back. The younger man came up from the other direction, caging Samuel in.

Samuel shifted from squatting to kneeling.

The younger man came up to Samuel first and stopped.

Samuel picked up one of the little rubber devices that looked like a short turkey baster. "Do you think this would work on an old man? I think it might be too small. Thoughts?"

The young man just looked at him.

"My grandfather has this monster cold," Samuel continued. "He can't seem to clear the congestion."

The young man said nothing.

"Cat got your tongue?" Samuel asked. "I know—it's a gross subject. Eh, he'll just have to hope the doc can give him something. Thanks, anyway." Samuel stood and turned in one motion, facing away from Kismat, and took a step around the young man. He was guessing this man had only seen a picture of him and might not realize who he was if Samuel threw him off. However, Kismat was not likely to make that mistake.

Samuel got around the young man and was about to turn the corner.

"Samuel Hill. We've been looking for you." It was Kismat's heavily accented voice. *Hill* sounded like *heel* when Kismat said it.

Samuel turned and grabbed the young man's shoulders from the back. He made it look like a brotherly, comforting gesture, but he dug his fingers into the man's clavicle notch and brachial plexus tie-in pressure points. The young man tightened.

Samuel murmured, "Don't want to draw attention, do we?" As Samuel got a good look at the other man, he confirmed it was definitely Kismat. His thick beard was longer than Ahmad's and had some gray streaking through it. His eyebrows were also thick and seemed to throw a shadow across his eyes. He wore a suit like Ahmad, but something about his posture made Samuel think he wasn't comfortable in it.

Kismat raised his eyebrows at the young man. "Philip, this is the man we were talking about. Do you remember?"

Philip nodded.

Kismat refocused on Samuel. "How have you been, Samuel?"

"Oh, you know, just running around getting things done."

"Errands can be a dreadful chore."

"Especially those others create for you."

Kismat took a step closer. "Worst kind of chores. One day, I'm minding my own business, handling my work, and the next, someone leaves a crater-sized hole in the organization I work for."

Samuel switched to Arabic, assuming Philip didn't understand it, or at least not well. "So, who's your friend here?" He pretended to rub Philip's shoulders but really dug his fingertips more deeply into the pressure points and shifted his hands closer to Philip's neck.

Kismat continued in Arabic. "Just an assistant."

"Pawn."

Kismat shrugged.

"So, what's the plan?" Samuel asked.

"I would kill you here, but Ahmad has reserved that right for himself. A blood war."

"And yet, I didn't kill his brother. I think something's gotten confused somewhere."

"I don't think that's likely. But you are welcome to ask Ahmad yourself. I'm happy to escort you to him."

Samuel smiled and dug his fingers into Philip's pressure points a bit more. Philip grimaced. "We have a saying here in America: crazy, not stupid."

"To defy al-Sadr is both crazy and stupid."

"So," Samuel said, still smiling, "where do we go from here? We both know I'm not going with you. I think it would be wiser for all involved to part ways."

Kismat sneered.

"Okay, one vote for not parting ways. Shall we have a seat in this aisle? Because we're not going anywhere together."

"I didn't say we expect you to go willingly."

"And how do you suppose you'll force me to do anything in

public like this? I doubt your status here in the US is terribly stable." Samuel wrinkled his nose. "You can't really afford to be making a big splash. Ahmad wouldn't be too happy. And then it would be bye-bye, Kismat."

Kismat took another casual step closer and drew something out of his jacket. "I can always tell Ahmad there was no other option." He showed Samuel a gun with a silencer, careful to keep it low so no one in neighboring aisles would see. "That would make this chore much more enjoyable." He rested his finger on the trigger.

Samuel held Philip in front of him.

"My assistant here will serve as additional silencing." Now just a couple of feet away, Kismat pushed the barrel of the gun up to Philip's gut. The gun was a 9mm, enough power to blast a bullet through Philip's soft, skinny stomach and into Samuel.

Someone slowly walked up behind Kismat. The older man with a head cold. Samuel wanted to tell him to back away, but he worried if he alerted Kismat to his presence, Kismat would act more drastically.

"Excuse me," the older man said with a thick, congested voice. "I need to see something on that shelf there." He pointed right next to Philip.

"Move on," Kismat muttered in English.

"Not when there are innocent civilians in this store."

In the second it took Samuel to realize the older man had spoken in perfect Arabic, he had grabbed the barrel of Kismat's gun and pushed it downward so that it was pointing at the floor. The older man slammed his knee into the side of Kismat's leg, and Samuel pushed Philip to the side, took the gun barrel, raked it to the side to pull Kismat's finger off the trigger, and then twisted and yanked it out of his grasp.

Kismat stumbled from the force of the older man's knee strike.

Samuel tucked the gun inside his jacket to keep it out of view, so hopefully, he might have a chance of the police not being called.

Philip stood to the side with wide eyes.

Samuel asked Philip quietly, "Are you armed?"

Philip stared at him.

"Answer me."

Philip reached behind his back.

Samuel shifted closer to conceal the weapon from view, took it, and tucked it inside his coat with Kismat's gun.

Philip opened his mouth but couldn't seem to form any words.

"He was about to use you as a silencer," the older man said with his thick, mucousy voice. "He was willing to sacrifice you."

"Do not listen to him," Kismat said.

"Use your own eyes," the old man said to Philip. "Don't be stupid."

The clerk with the pink bow started rushing toward them from the front of the store. "What's going on back there?"

"Go," the older man said to Samuel. "I'll handle this."

"Who are you?" Samuel asked.

"Former Green Beret and instructor."

Teaches me to make assumptions, Samuel thought. "You taught the troops in the Gulf War, didn't you?" That was why he could speak Arabic.

The older man smiled.

Kismat shifted, and the older man kneed him again. Kismat fell.

"Mr. Folsom?" the clerk said, still several aisles away. "Are you all right?"

The older man glanced back at the employee. "Got a bit of a situation, but I have it under control. This man was about to rob this young boy. Go call the police."

The clerk hesitated but then ran back toward the front of the store.

Samuel slipped Kismat's gun to Mr. Folsom so he could sell the story.

"Get going," Mr. Folsom said.

Samuel opened his mouth to ask why he was helping him get away.

"CIA, right?" Mr. Folsom asked.

Samuel raised his eyebrows.

Mr. Folsom just smiled, and then said, "Get."

Samuel walked back through the store, careful not to look too hurried and draw the attention of the employee. Just as he walked out the door, he heard the rumbly, wet sound of the old man blowing his nose. Samuel laughed under his breath. *Half dead with a nasty cold and probably sixty-five years under his belt. I hope I'm that awesome when I get to be that age.*

Samuel started down the street. He glanced around at the different stores and people, hoping to find some kind of inspiration. He needed a vehicle, but he couldn't steal one with so many people coming and going.

The door of a black Taurus he was passing opened, and a woman stood from the car.

"There you are, Samuel Hill," Tama Uribe said.

45

TRUDI

Boston, MA

"Are you sure that's what we were supposed to find?" Dream asked Eula.

"Finding a key stapled to a shelf directly under a bag of brown sugar is weird," Trudi said. "I think we have to assume it's something of interest."

"Okay," Dream said. "What do we do with it?"

"Go to the next place on the map," Trudi said. "I think you're right that *avow* is referring to the altar."

"That might be a tricky place to check out," Eula said. "I doubt they let tourists poke around the pulpit."

"I'll do it. You guys keep watch."

Eula followed. "The usual signal?"

"Yep."

They headed back through the Bigelow Courtyard toward the church. They walked around and went in the front of the church, through the vestibule, and into the main worship hall. Trudi had to force herself not to get distracted by all the history—the woodwork, the two-story curved ceiling, the original-looking hymnals, the box pews that were sectioned-off seating for each family.

At the front of the church was a raised pulpit and an altar blocked off by a low, white banister. Trudi walked at a casual pace and pretended to look around, but really she was watching the tour groups. She didn't see anyone who looked like an employee or security.

Without hesitation, she stepped over the low banister, as if she had every right to do so. Dream and Eula stayed by the first row of box pews. Above the altar was a painting of Jesus. *I promise I'm not stealing, or rather, I'm doing this for good reason. Please forgive me.* Trudi knelt down in front of the altar, a table covered in a long, intricate cloth. She lifted the fabric and let it fall down onto her head. It smelled a little musty.

The table was more than just a table—it was a cabinet with a locked door.

Coughing sounds, loud and obnoxious, interrupted Trudi's thoughts. Eula was talented at being obnoxious when she really wanted to be.

Trudi shoved the little gold key that Eula had found into the keyhole. The lock clicked, and the door opened. *Please be some part of the missing art, enough to win Dream his freedom.* Inside the cabinet was a small box.

"Are you all right?" came a voice from several feet behind her.

Dream said, "I think she's having a reaction to something."

Trudi grabbed the little box, closed the cabinet door, and let the fabric fall back into place.

"A reaction to what? Does she have any allergies?" It was a woman in an early American dress, complete with a bonnet.

"I don't know," Dream said.

Eula continued to cough dramatically. She rested her hands

on the woman's shoulders, as if she couldn't take it anymore and couldn't hold herself upright. She coughed in her face. The woman raised her chin and turned her head to the side.

Trudi stepped back over the railing and walked around the woman to Eula. She patted Eula on the back. "Are you all right? What's wrong?"

The woman stepped back from Eula with a disgusted look on her face.

Trudi rubbed Eula's back, and Eula's coughing started to quiet.

"Better?" Trudi asked.

Eula coughed one more time and nodded.

"Thank you so much," Trudi said to the woman. Then she turned back to Eula. "Come on, sweetie. I'll take care of you." She guided her away, back down the narrower aisle under the balcony. Dream followed, still moving slowly.

Back outside in front of the church, Eula asked, "What did you find?" Her voice was raspy.

"I have a feeling we aren't going to like it." Trudi opened the little box in her hand.

Dream's posture slackened, and Eula sighed.

Trudi took a little gold key out of the box.

"Okay," Trudi said. "What's the next clue?"

"The third one was *roar*," Dream said.

"What's loud in a church?" Eula asked.

"Other than obnoxious tourists who cough in your face?" Trudi said. "Nice touch, by the way."

Eula gave a curtsy. "We aim to please, m'lady."

"That was the signal?" Dream asked.

"More like a warning alarm and distraction all in one this time." Eula rubbed her throat.

"I'll get you some ice cream," Trudi said.

"To go with my birthday present." Eula looked around at the church and the other buildings in the area, offices to the left of the church and a gift shop to the right. "It doesn't have to be related to the original buildings or even the original purposes of the church, right? Maybe something in the gift shop? An annoyingly loud toy or something?"

"Maybe," Trudi said. Then she looked at Dream. "What do you think?"

Dream looked over at the gift shop. "I don't know. I think . . . Paddy would have wanted it to be something historic."

"But the candy shop wasn't original to the site, was it?" Eula asked.

"But it was still historic," Dream said. "Chocolate made the way it was in the 1700s."

Eula nodded. "Got it."

A tour group came through, and Trudi, Eula, and Dream shifted out of the way.

"How many stories is the steeple?" someone in the tour group asked. "It looks pretty tall. No wonder they used this as the place for the lantern signal."

"Actually," the tour guide said, "this is not the original steeple. It's been destroyed and rebuilt twice. In 1804 and 1954, first by snow and then by a hurricane."

"Can we go up there?"

"Not in today's tour, but I'll let you in on a secret. One of the bells has an inscription you wouldn't guess."

The crowd waited.

"It says, 'We are the first ring of bells cast for the British Empire in North America, AR 1744.'"

"The British Empire?" someone asked.

"It's now an American landmark," the guide said, "but remember this whole area was originally under British rule."

"The bells," Trudi said.

Both Eula and Dream raised their eyebrows at the same time. Trudi almost laughed.

She walked over to the tour group. "Why're there more than one bell?" she asked the tour guide.

"They're change-ringing bells. Each one has a different pitch."

Eula came up next to Trudi and asked the guide, "What're change-ringing bells? What's that sound like?"

"Have you ever watched the beginning of *The Hunchback of Notre Dame*?" the guide asked.

"Like the Disney movie from the nineties?"

"You were probably very little."

Eula suppressed a smile. "Wasn't born yet when the movie came out."

Trudi groaned. "Oh my goodness, I feel old."

Eula laughed. "Sorry, Boss." She turned back to the tour guide. "I remember the bells in the movie, though. It was a bunch of different bells, kind of a layered sound."

"And they're on a different kind of system—wheel mechanisms rather than rope and lever. Basically, instead of the bells and the sound they make being pointed down, they are pointed sideways when the bell actually tolls. It makes the sound travel farther."

Someone else asked a question about the vestibule, and the tour guide talked about it as he led the group into the church.

"That's the *roar*," Trudi said to Eula and Dream.

Eula looked up at the steeple high above them, then at the tour group entering the church. "Let's try to slide past them."

"I saw stairs in the corner," Dream said. "Inside the vestibule."

Trudi led the way into the church. The tour group was in the vestibule, but the tour guide was just inside the doors, just out of sight from the stairs. Trudi edged behind the tour group. Eula followed. A few steps up, Trudi looked back. Dream was still with the tour group. He appeared to be trapped between two large men. One of them must've stepped back into the way before Dream could slide past. He mouthed the word *go* to Trudi.

Trudi hesitated. It might not be wise to leave Dream alone, but the tour seemed to be focused on the guide—good opportunity to slip up the stairs unnoticed. Plus, Dream probably couldn't make it up the stairs right now, at least not quickly. Trudi turned and headed up. This area was definitely not built for the public. The rest of the church interior was painted bright white; these stairs were raw wood surrounded by raw brick walls.

"How much you wanna bet these stairs don't meet modern building code," Eula said.

"Probably not."

Finally, they made it to a room with ropes, partially covered in red-and-black-striped sleeves, swagging from one spot in the ceiling out in all directions.

"These must be how they ring the bells," Trudi said.

"What do you think," Eula said, "key hiding in here or up with the bells?"

"You take a look around here, and I'll keep going up and see what I find."

The passage up to the bells was even narrower, and the stairs were only that in a very loose sense of the word. Each tread was different from the last. She made it up to a small platform where she could see all the bells, most of which were positioned with the open end of the bell up and the base attached to wooden wheels. Trudi leaned carefully on the railing and stood on her toes to survey the area.

She assumed she was looking for another gold key. It couldn't be inside one of the upturned bells. The tour guide had said the bells turned all the way sideways when they were rung, so the key would fall out. Surely, Paddy would've accounted for that.

Okay, she thought, *whatever he did, he likely didn't have any better access than I do right now.* She guessed it would be out of sight but not all that difficult to reach, and he would have had to have been able to secure it in place pretty quickly and easily.

Maybe he taped it to a bell? No, it would've fallen off when the bells were rung. Then she thought maybe he'd taped it to the wood structure holding the bells. But tape wouldn't stick very well to wood, not well enough to be sure it would stick for a prolonged period of time, especially when the bells were rung and vibrated through the wood structure. No, Paddy had proven to be smarter than that.

She looked all around, even behind her at the brick wall.

Okay, the clue was roar. It had to be close to the bells themselves but probably not actually on a bell. She focused on the biggest bell, the one right in front of her and one of only a few with the open end down. It was hanging from metal straps attached to a thick piece of wood. She reached over and felt the far side of the wood support. Nothing but splinters. Then she knelt down, braced herself on the wood framing, precariously leaning over the opening for the bell, and felt the underside and back of the wood support. Nothing to the left of the bell. She pushed herself back, her weight fully on the platform, and shifted over to the right of the bell.

When she felt a small piece of metal, she smiled. It felt like a key, but it seemed to be secured by . . . It was a staple, one of those huge industrial ones that wasn't coming out easily. As she felt more, she realized the key was attached to the shackle of a tiny padlock, like you'd find on luggage, and the lock was secured to the wood with the staple. She had to unlock it to get the key off.

Paddy must have been taller than I am. She was barely reaching it, and now she had to use the key they'd found in the altar to open the tiny lock. She couldn't do it in this position. She pushed herself back onto the platform and reassessed.

All right, Tru-Bear, time for that black-belt balance of yours. Under the railing, she carefully crawled with her hands onto the side wood framing. She pushed herself from her knees to her feet but crouched under the railing, and she pushed herself forward until she could flip around and land her backside on the wood framing. More like half of one cheek.

She was holding the railing to help keep her balance, but she needed both hands to open the lock and take the key. With the ball of one foot on the platform for balance and the other foot dangling in the air, she leaned over the bell. She fished the key from the altar out of her pocket, held the lock in one hand, and inserted the key with the other. She had to grip everything just right or else when the lock opened, the new key would fall down between the bells. They'd never find it. She turned the key in the lock.

"Whoa." The lock popped open, and she almost dropped the new key. She managed to shove both keys into her pocket.

Now to get down from this thing without falling and dying.

Slowly, she scooted closer until she could reach the railing, then she threw her legs over and hopped down onto the platform.

She huffed in relief and then started carefully down the crazy steps.

Eula looked up from her search and grinned when Trudi held up the key—well, one of them.

Footsteps.

Trudi pocketed the key.

A middle-aged man in work pants walked up into the bell-ringer chamber. "Who are you? What're you doing up here?"

46

DREAM

Boston, MA

Go, I mouth to Trudi. The tour group and guide are distracted by questions about some kind of conspiracy theory related to Paul Revere and the Masons. We can't waste this opportunity.

She hesitates but then steps over the rope and slips up the stairs, closely followed by Eula.

A couple of people in the tour group continue to ask questions about the Masons and the Founding Fathers.

"I heard the Masons actually run the entire government. Our elections are just a hoax," a very large man next to me says.

The tour guide looks at him for a second, obviously at a loss for a response. "Uh, I've never seen or heard any indication of that."

A younger woman toward the front of the group turns around. "Actually, my dad's a Mason. They're just a bunch of old guys who eat dinner together and do charity work."

"No offense, but not everyone is allowed to know what's

really going on, and even if he does, he can't tell anyone, not even his family."

"But *you* do know what's going on?" the young woman asks.

"I have sources."

I look for a way to sneak off, but everyone is now staring at the conspiracy theorist next to me.

"What kinds of sources?" the young woman asks.

"Sources that are far out of your reach," the man responds.

"Got it," she says. "Sounds really reliable." She turns back around, and a few people in the group chuckle.

The tour guide resumes talking, a little louder and faster than he had been, surely trying to retake control of his tour. The group moves forward.

I linger back.

As the guide starts explaining the box pews, I wait until he's either distracted or turned away. The group walks farther along the aisle, but the tour guide remains facing the group, toward me. They get to the altar, and he finally turns to point something out. I turn toward the stairs and manage to get one leg over the rope, but I'm not sure if I can get the other one over.

"May I help you, sir?" Another man in a period suit turns the corner into the vestibule and walks up to me.

I try to think of something to tell him.

"The tour group is at the altar."

I just stand there with one leg over the rope.

"Please leave this area, sir. The steeple is not currently open to tours."

I feel myself slipping. I haven't felt this out-of-control feeling in days, even while they tortured me.

The man's voice is harder. "You need to come with me." He takes my arm.

"A fully grown oak tree expels seven tons of water through its leaves in a day."

"What?"

Some small part of my brain kind of detaches and starts to wonder why this little scene is causing me so much distress. Why could I handle torture and not this?

Because I focused so much on protecting Trudi and Samuel.

That's the key. If I concentrate on something really important, something much bigger than me, I bet I can maintain control. My immediate goal is to keep the staff and security away from Trudi and Eula.

I pull my leg back across the rope, and I think I do a pretty good job of hiding the pain I feel as I do it. "I heard you can tour the bell tower."

"Not today, sir. The bells are being inspected and any maintenance completed."

"Oh." I smile. "Okay, I understand. Can I walk around the sanctuary?"

The man's tone relaxes some. "Of course." He motions toward the pews with his hand. "Please."

I walk away. Inside a box pew, I look out the window, but really I watch the man peripherally. Eventually, he heads back through the sanctuary to a door to the left of the pulpit.

I head back over to the steeple entrance.

Quietly, and very slowly, I move up the stairs.

Then I hear Eula's voice, but there's a very different tone and cadence to her speech. "What are those red-and-black-striped things? Are they for protecting the bell ringers' hands? Who are the bell ringers? How do you become one? Could I become one? Or is that only for guys? Wait a second, wait a second—how many bells are there? There have to be a lot of bell ringers, right? How often are the bells rung? Will they be rung today? I'd really like to hear them. I mean, we came all this way. I really want to hear them. Can we stay up here while they're rung? Why aren't—"

"Hold on, sweetie." It was Trudi's voice. "I'm sorry. She's just really excited. I need to get her out of here before she gets way too agitated and I can't handle her anymore."

I hear footsteps on the wood above me. A few seconds later, Trudi appears, holding Eula's hand.

Trudi whispers, "There you are. Everything okay?"

I nod and turn back down the stairs. I manage to move a little faster on the way down.

Once back in the vestibule, I ask, "Did you find it?"

Trudi pulls another little gold key out of her pocket.

"Last clue," Eula says. "The last hand on the clocks points to the word *deep*. Do you think there's a crypt here?"

"Makes sense," Trudi says. "Now, let's see if we can keep getting around this place without having the cops called on us."

"I'll just act a little off-balance again," Eula says. "Man, that worked better than I thought."

"People are uncomfortable around the mentally handicapped or mentally ill," I say.

Eula grabs my good hand. I flinch. I'm not used to being touched, at least not so suddenly and with such ease. She smiles at me. "I'm not uncomfortable around anyone, not even completely normal, boring people."

"Gee, thanks," Trudi says.

"Who says you're normal?"

Trudi laughs. "Touché."

We walk into the sanctuary, well away from the tour group.

I point toward the door to the left of the pulpit. "I think we need to go through that door. There aren't any stairs going down anywhere we've looked, and that's the last place we haven't been inside the church. But I know at least one employee is back there."

Trudi leads the way down the left aisle. We move slowly, as if interested in inspecting each box pew. In the last one, we sit and wait for the tour group to be done and leave. I'm thankful to have an excuse to rest.

"They're taking forever," Eula grumbles.

Finally, the group seems to exhaust every possible question, and they start back down the main aisle. One at a time, they head up the stairs in the back corner, up to the second level with the organ on the back wall and pews flanking each side looking down at the church's open center.

Trudi, Eula, and I slip through the door to the left of the pulpit. A door to the left leads outside, and another door leads to a small bathroom. Eula tries the door to the right of the bathroom, peeks inside, then shakes her head. Trudi tries the door to their right, and I try the one just in front of me.

"Here," I say.

Trudi and Eula both follow me.

We go down the stairs until we're under the church. The walls are old, worn brick, and pipes bump us in the head—well, Trudi more than me. The floor looks to be modern concrete, smooth and clean.

"Do you have any idea where we should start?" Trudi asks me.

I shake my head and immediately regret it when pain throbs behind my eyes and in my temples. I'm having a hard time breathing from the cigarette burns inside my nose, but there's nothing I can do about that. I start walking.

The place has a weird smell. Kind of musty but something more. Like I can smell the remnants of death saturated into the walls after two hundred years.

Eventually, we come to an opening that leads to a tiny space with a curved brick ceiling. Exposed conduit runs to a bare bulb attached to the brick above. I imagine what this place felt like before electricity was run and every room was accessed by candlelight only.

On the back wall of the tiny room is a little shelf. There are two upside-down hurricane glasses for oil lamps and an oblong tapered hexagonal piece of wood, which I realize with horror is the top board for a baby's coffin.

Other pieces of wood lean up against the left wall. I take a chance and look behind them.

"Anything?" Eula asks.

I shift the wood to let some light shine behind it.

A box on the floor.

Trudi holds the wood for me while I scoot the box out. "It feels like there's more than a key in there."

"No way there's a Rembrandt inside," Trudi says. She hands the key to me. "I think this is the right one. They're all getting mixed together in my pocket."

I squat down and put the key into the lock on the box. It clicks open.

"What is it?" Eula cranes to try to see over my head.

I lift up the contents.

47

SAMUEL

Boston, MA

"Oh, hello," Samuel said to Agent Uribe. "I'm sorry, what was your name again?"

"Let's not be cute, shall we?"

Samuel grinned. "Can't help it."

"Get in the car," she said. "We need to chat."

"Not feeling chatty at the moment." He continued walking down the sidewalk.

She stayed by his side, and a young couple passed going the opposite direction. "I'm afraid I must insist."

Samuel heard a car door close behind them and looked back. A man was walking around from the back passenger side of Agent Uribe's Taurus to the sidewalk.

"You must be Chucky," Samuel said.

Chucky sneered.

Samuel continued forward. Agent Uribe stayed by his side, and Samuel heard Chucky's footsteps following behind them.

Agent Uribe's voice sounded forcibly casual. "Are you curious how we found you?"

"You figured I'd be back in Boston eventually. You think that's where your silly treasure is. And you hung out in the area where I'd stayed before. When you heard the robbery at the Walgreens on the police blotter, you headed this way."

"Very good."

"I have my moments."

"Now," Agent Uribe said, "let's use those skills for something useful for once."

Samuel smiled at her. "So you can steal the missing Gardner Museum artwork?"

"*Recover* the missing artwork," she corrected.

Samuel kept smiling and faced forward, still walking. They'd passed a luncheonette and a luggage place, and now they were passing a bank. *Let's get a bit farther away from all those cameras and security guards.*

"You can tell me where The Dream is now," she said.

"I would if I had any idea who that is. I think we covered that pretty clearly last time."

"Right, you're just a *tourist.*"

Chucky behind them snorted.

Samuel glanced back. "Why does no one believe I'm just a tourist? Detectives are allowed to take vacations, aren't we?"

Chucky stared at him with what was probably supposed to be an intimidating expression.

Samuel turned around and smacked him on the shoulder. "Loosen up, man."

Chucky sneered.

"Better be careful," Samuel said, "or your face'll get stuck that way." He turned back around and glanced at his surroundings. There was a small triangle-shaped parking lot across the street, and on the other side of that was another street with more tightly packed shops bordering it. He was looking for an exit, though he wasn't sure what exactly it would look like. Samuel focused on Uribe. "Let's do this. I'm a bit busy at the moment, but we can meet up a little later. Maybe we can go to that little diner again. They had great burgers."

"Busy with what exactly?" Uribe asked.

"Uh, I think I've been pretty clear. I'm a tourist, remember? Are you feeling all right?"

Uribe grabbed his arm and pulled him to a stop.

"Tsk, tsk," Samuel said. "You don't want to draw unwanted attention."

"I'm an FBI agent, Samuel. I don't need to worry about unwanted attention."

"That might be the case if you were on the up-and-up. But . . . I think we both know that's not quiiiite accurate."

Chucky moved closer, against Samuel's shoulder.

Samuel looked over at him. "May I help you with something?"

Chucky growled the words. "You can tell her what she wants to know."

Something clicked in Samuel's head. He knew the man's voice. All too well.

He tried to realign past events in his mind. They were all connected. He tried to see all the angles, but there were so many. He'd never considered anything like this. He'd thought maybe some connection to al-Sadr, but not this.

Samuel glanced around to make sure no shoppers were within earshot. "You're my handler. Charlie."

"Stop playing," Uribe said. "You're wearing on my last nerve. Perhaps I should simply bring you in and turn you over to Homeland Security."

"I don't think Charlie's going to let you do that," Samuel said. He looked at his handler. "Isn't that right?"

Charlie cocked an eyebrow.

"How long has this been going on?" Samuel asked.

Charlie didn't answer.

"You want me to give you information on Dream, right? Answer my questions, and I'll consider answering yours."

"What're you playing at?" Uribe demanded. "Charlie is ex-FBI. He's assisting me in finding the missing Gardner art."

Samuel continued to focus on Charlie. "I think that's the other way around."

Uribe shifted forward, trying to get in Samuel's face. "You deal with me. Leave him out of this."

"It's time to be quiet now, Tama," Charlie said, still focused on Samuel.

"What're you talking about? I've been letting you assist with this as a courtesy."

Charlie looked at Uribe. "Samuel already has a better concept of reality than you do." He turned back to Samuel. "I'm tired of risking my life for no pay."

"So, you want the art," Samuel said. "The question is, do you want the reward or do you want the art to sell on the black market?"

Charlie cocked his head. "At first, I really just wanted the reward."

"Until Tama here gave you the idea of selling it off piece by piece on the black market."

"Much higher returns. She has her moments of inspiration."

"What's going on?" Uribe growled at Charlie. "I trusted you."

Charlie smirked. "You trusted me about as much as I trusted you."

"He's right, isn't he?" Uribe said. "You plan on selling the art on the black market."

"And you're planning something different?" Charlie said.

"I plan on turning it in. Doing the right thing."

Charlie laughed. "That's why you've devoted all your resources. Your department pulled you off this case months ago. You've been using your leave time and your savings."

"I wanted the reward. I wouldn't sell the art—that's just as bad as stealing," Uribe said.

"You're an FBI agent. You can't get the reward. I saw the research on your phone."

"When did you look at my phone?"

"I'm trained in espionage, and I'm very good at it. Figuring out the pin for your phone wasn't exactly an arduous task."

She opened her mouth but said nothing.

"I slipped you information you couldn't get on your own," Charlie said. "How'd you think I was getting more information than you could? You turned a blind eye in order to get what you wanted."

"You're under arrest."

Charlie laughed. He was loud enough that a few people on the sidewalk looked over.

Samuel took a half step back, closer to the road.

"Under arrest for what?" Charlie asked.

"Obstruction of justice."

"You still have no idea who you're dealing with."

She lifted her chin. "I think that's the other way around."

A few people paused on the sidewalk. Samuel took another slow step, partially behind a middle-aged couple who'd stopped and were watching the argument.

Samuel slipped back onto the road. Then he crossed the street at a jog and headed through the parking lot.

"Hey!" Charlie yelled. "Stop!"

48

TRUDI

Boston, MA

“What is that?” Eula asked.

“It’s the Napoleonic finial,” Dream said.

“Nothing else?” Eula craned to see over Dream’s head.

“Empty,” Dream said.

“Seriously? That’s it?”

“Wait . . .” Trudi murmured.

They both looked at her.

Trudi asked, “Dream, do you have your black light?”

Dream handed the finial to Eula, still carefully using only his right hand, and fished the light out of his pocket.

“Can I see your hand?” Trudi asked Dream tentatively.

He held out his right hand.

“The other one,” Trudi said. She’d noticed how careful he’d been with it. Though he hadn’t complained once or even mentioned how much it hurt, she saw how he kept it well clear of anything around him and as immobilized as possible.

"You mean, you think it has something to do with my other tattoo?"

"Why else would Paddy make you go through all this just to get the one item of not much value?"

He stood and held up his left hand. Eula reached out to help him pull back some of the medical tape, but Dream said, "I have it." He picked at the edge of a piece of the tape and slowly pulled it back. Then he did the next one. Luckily, most of the tape was on his fingers, not his hand. He had to pull back only a few pieces. He handed the black light to Trudi.

"Here, keep your hand over in the corner where it's darker." Trudi shined the light on his skin.

"It looks just like the finial," Eula said. "But why?" Then she looked more closely at the piece of bronze in her hand. "Wait, the number is different."

Trudi shifted the light so she could see the square base under the eagle better. "It says '12.'"

Eula held up the finial. "This one says '1.'"

"Does that mean anything to you?" Trudi asked Dream. "Maybe something to do with time or dates?"

"They never let me know the date."

"Wow, that stinks," Eula said.

"How about time?" Trudi asked. "Paddy was obviously obsessed with clocks."

"Maybe you guys always did something between the hours of noon and one o'clock?" Eula asked.

"No, we didn't keep a schedule. We worked when Paddy felt like it and stopped when he didn't."

"There was another guy, right?" Trudi asked. "Did he keep a schedule? Anything relating to those numbers?"

"He was even worse than Paddy. At first, I tried to figure out his comings and goings so I could avoid getting beaten, but I eventually gave up."

Eula took Dream's good hand and squeezed.

"Okay, not time," Trudi said. "Anything else?"

"What's the rest of the tattoo say?" Eula asked. "Under the eagle and the number."

"'Dream within Dream,'" Dream said. "Like the poem."

"Actually," Trudi said, "it says 'the dream within Dream.'"

"Why is the first *d* lowercase and the second uppercase?" Eula asked.

Trudi pulled her eyebrows together. "Did Paddy call you Dream?"

"Yeah. What're you thinking it means?"

"Back in Atlanta," Trudi said, "you told me about what you most want. Remember?"

"I want people to forget me and leave me alone. I want all this to be over."

"He wants freedom," Eula said.

Trudi nodded. "And that jibes with Paddy's American history obsession. The fight for freedom."

"But how does that get us to the next step? I wish I had a phone. I'd Google-whip that in a second." Eula snapped her fingers. "Maybe I can talk someone into letting me borrow one."

Trudi clicked off the black light. "Maybe. We should get out of here anyway. Before someone finds us. I don't think they let tourists down here, at least not without a guide."

Dream gingerly pressed the medical tape back down onto his hand. His lips tightened, and he clenched his jaw.

Trudi led the way back through the crypt toward the stairs.

They managed to make it upstairs and outside the church without anyone questioning them, even with Dream hiding a bronze eagle under his coat. They headed around the back, through the gardens, and across the street to the Paul Revere Mall—a long stretch of brick pavers, trees, a fountain, and a statue of Paul Revere on a horse. Trudi figured they'd probably found everything Paddy had hidden in the church complex, and it was best to leave.

They came to a shadowed nook near the fountain and paused to figure out what to do next.

"Something to do with freedom in Boston, the birthplace of the American Revolution," Eula said. "Can we say needle and haystack?" She glanced around, surely looking for someone to sweet-talk into letting her borrow their phone for a few minutes.

"And the number twelve," Dream added.

"Right," Trudi said. She nudged Eula. "You head down that way toward the statue and I'll browse the fountain area."

"You're leaving me?" Dream asked.

"Just hang here for a minute," Trudi said.

"It's a lot easier to get someone to help a *helpless female* when she's alone," Eula said.

"You two are about as helpless as Samuel," Dream said.

"Ahh," Eula said. "You're so sweet." She grinned and walked away.

Trudi walked around the fountain and into the sunlight. A couple of young men with blaring headphones passed. Then a family consisting of a mom, dad, and two little girls stopped to take pictures of the girls in front of the fountain. Ideally, she was hoping to find a sweet old man alone. She felt a little bad playing the feminine card, but protecting Dream was worth it. She spotted a couple of young women on one of the benches and considered going the "sisters united" route. She walked in that direction and picked up on their conversation as she approached.

"The Old North Church," the woman on the left with short,

curly hair said. "See?" She pointed at something the other woman was holding, a brochure of some kind.

"Number thirteen. Do you want to keep doing them in order?"

"Yeah. I figure they put an order to them for a reason. Maybe just geographical."

"Excuse me," Trudi said.

They looked up.

"Is that a tour guide or something?"

The one with curly hair said, "Yeah. It's supposed to be all the best sites in Boston. The Freedom Trail. It's, like, literally built into the streets. Have you seen those lines of red bricks all over?"

Freedom—as in "the dream within Dream." "It's a major thing in Boston?" Trudi asked. "This Freedom Trail."

"Yeah. I bet at least half the tourists walking around Boston are following it."

"I'd bet more than that," the other woman said.

"Oh, that sounds awesome. I saw the Old North Church, but I'm not sure where to go next. I'm only here for the day, so I want to hit as much as possible."

"The next one's the Copp's Hill Burying Ground." The woman on the right showed her a picture in the brochure of a couple of headstones wearing vines like a wedding veil. Trudi wrinkled her nose. "Not into graves. They creep me out. The Old North Church is number thirteen? What's number twelve?"

"The Paul Revere House." The women with the brochure flipped back a page and held up a picture of a two-story, grayish house settled right up against the sidewalk.

"Oh, I like old architecture. Have you been already? Can you tell me how to get there?"

They gave her directions, and Trudi thanked them and walked

back to Dream, who was still standing in the corner of the little courtyard. She motioned to Eula, who jogged back over to them.

"The Paul Revere House," Trudi said. "It's number twelve on the Freedom Trail. From the look of the brochure, it's a pretty major sightseeing tour."

"Nice," Eula said.

Trudi added to Dream, "Didn't you say Paddy was a fan of Paul Revere's?"

"He named one of the squirrels Paul."

"Well, there ya have it," Eula said. "It's all about the squirrel. I'm starting to like this Paddy guy."

Trudi pointed toward the end of the mall, past Paul Revere's statue. "It's a few blocks."

They turned right down the sidewalk. Dream moved as fast as he could, but Trudi could see he was still in a lot of pain. She tried not to push him too hard.

Eventually, they walked up to the house from the brochure.

"I think we go in there." Eula pointed to an opening in a brick wall that looked to lead to a courtyard next to the house.

Trudi paid the five-dollar admission for each of them, and they walked into a tidy, brick-paver courtyard. It consisted of a couple of different levels and a few frosty planter beds. They walked up some steps and into what appeared to be the back door to the house. Inside, they found a huge brick fireplace, more like an 1800s version of an oven and cooktop. Period furnishings and décor filled the room, but luckily, no other people were within sight.

Eula looked at the brochure she'd picked up. "Obviously, this is the kitchen. This place has four stories, including basement and attic. How do we figure out where we need to go?"

"It won't be in the basement," Dream said. "He'd never risk harming it in the dampness of a basement."

"It's got to be awfully well hidden," Trudi said. "This place is probably really busy and cleaned often. It's not like he could've shoved it under a bed or something."

"The floor plan looks pretty simple," Eula said. "Not a lot of nooks and crannies."

They went into the next room and glanced around the main living space. Then they headed up the stairs. Eula was right, the place was simple: two rooms downstairs, two rooms upstairs. They took a good look around but didn't find any secret hiding places. Trudi started to worry Paddy had hidden the art too well.

Finally, they made it to the attic.

"It doesn't all look as old as I'd have thought," Dream said.

Eula was reading the brochure. "It says the house was restored in the early 1900s. It'd had a third story, which was removed during the restoration."

Trudi walked around. At the top of the stairs was a large, empty space above the main bedchamber below, which was above the living space below that. To the right was another space that sat above the second bedchamber and kitchen. There were no obvious places where a bunch of artwork could be hiding.

Then she tilted her head as she looked at the pitch of the ceiling, at where it met knee walls.

Eula walked up next to her. "You think it's behind there?" she asked.

"There might be enough space."

"It would fit," Dream said. "All the larger pieces were taken out of their frames, rolled up, and put in sealed tubes."

"Take a good look at the knee walls," Trudi said. "See if you can find a latch or just some kind of inconsistency."

They spread out and examined the walls.

Trudi got down on her knees so she could see better.

She heard footsteps on the creaky steps and stood. Before

she could say anything to Dream and Eula, a little boy and his dad came up the stairs.

"So, was this as boring as you thought?" the dad asked.

The boy shrugged but also looked around with interest.

Eula and Dream stood by the small window at the end of the larger space and chatted about the brochure. "Paul Revere lived here with his wife, five kids, and his mother," Eula said.

"How'd they all fit? There are only two bedrooms."

"At the time it was built, it was considered a fashionable home."

Trudi stayed over in the smaller area and pretended to examine the brick of the old chimney.

A few minutes later, the boy and dad went back down the steps.

Eula and Dream stopped mid-conversation, and they all resumed examining the knee walls. Eula started crawling around on the floor. Dream leaned but didn't look like he could bend over.

The sound of wood sliding across wood made Trudi turn and look over at Eula. She was pulling at something on the bottom edge of the wall. Trudi rushed over, got down on her knees, and helped.

There wasn't even a latch. Trudi didn't know how Eula had noticed the board. She must've dug her nails in to get ahold of it.

Dream stood between them and the stairs and kept an eye out. Trudi and Eula heaved the board. Eula put her foot on the wall for better leverage. The board creaked.

Then it gave way, and Eula fell back.

"Hopefully no one heard that," Eula said as she got back into a squatted position.

Trudi got down on her stomach and peered into the cavity.

"Here." Dream tossed over his black light.

Trudi shined it into the hole. It gave her just enough light.

"Well . . ." Eula prodded.

Trudi looked over at Eula, then back into the hole. She slid farther forward, now with her head and shoulders inside the cavity. She reached with her right hand, while trying to keep the light shining in the right place with her left.

"Pull me out," Trudi said.

49

SAMUEL

Boston, MA

"Stop!"

Samuel ramped up his jog to a run. He kept as low as he could while still running and zigzagged through the cars parked in the lot.

"You're under arrest!" This time, it was Uribe's voice. Samuel wasn't sure if she was trying to arrest him or Charlie.

While crossing the back end of a Chevy, Samuel managed to glance behind him. Charlie was still several yards away. Uribe had chosen a different direction to come at him. Instead of following behind him like Charlie, she was trying to flank him.

"Freeze!" Charlie yelled.

Samuel heard the metallic sound of a handgun being racked and ducked down behind a silver SUV. He dropped to his hands and knees and watched feet from under the car. There were some running feet of shoppers, and then Samuel spotted Charlie's brown boots. Treading slowly and cautiously. *Interesting.* He'd always imagined Charlie as a sneaker kind of guy. Then he looked over to the left and found Uribe's shoes—some kind of feminine-looking black boots that Trudi probably would have loved—moving more quickly.

"Sammy," Charlie called. "Come out, come out, wherever you are."

Let's just see what happens as Uribe moves closer, shall we?

"I just need a bit of information," Charlie continued. "Then I'll leave you alone."

Uribe called out, "I wouldn't trust that if I were you, Samuel."

Duh.

Uribe weaved around a car. As Samuel watched from under the SUV, he realized she was keeping in a crouch as she moved. *Wise.*

"Who do you think is more trustworthy, Samuel?" Charlie called. "Some FBI hack or your longtime handler and friend?"

Samuel glanced around. Plenty of people were all over the lot. Some had run away, but several were hiding behind cars. He could see plenty of UGG boots and tennis shoes and even a sparkly pair of pink shoes no larger than ones that would fit a five-year-old. He kept the gun he'd taken from Philip tucked in his waistband. Not worth the risk. But he didn't think he could talk his way out of this one either.

Finally, Samuel heard sirens approaching. The Walgreens employee had called the police after the incident, at the Green Beret's request. *It took them long enough to get here.* But Samuel couldn't risk getting caught by them either.

Uribe was getting closer, too close. Samuel risked moving from his spot, got off the ground, and darted from behind the silver SUV to a black Tahoe.

"Freeze!" Uribe yelled, and Samuel could hear her footsteps move faster.

A gunshot rang out.

Samuel looked through the tinted windows of the Tahoe and could barely see Uribe falling to the pavement.

Samuel ran across a drive lane and dove into a shoulder roll behind a minivan.

The little girl with sparkly pink shoes and her family were crouched down behind it. They clung more tightly to each other.

Samuel held his hands up in front of him and whispered, "No weapons. I just need to get out of here."

"That man is trying to arrest you," the middle-aged man in the group said.

"But that guy just shot that lady," a teen boy said.

"It's complicated," Samuel said. "No one is really who they appear to be. Including me. I just want to ask you one thing."

"Ask us something?" the man said. "I'm trying to protect my *family* here."

"And I won't put you in danger. I'm going to lead that man away. I just ask that you make sure the woman who was shot gets medical attention. That man is a good shot, so she may not have much time, if she's even still alive."

The middle-aged woman pulled the little girl closer and pressed her head to her chest.

"Stay down until I lead him away." Samuel stood and started running away from the family and Agent Uribe. He zagged around empty parked cars.

"Samuel, stop!"

Another gunshot rang out.

"I don't want to kill you, Samuel."

Samuel knew that was the truth—he couldn't tell him about Dream if he was dead.

The sirens grew louder, and Samuel saw flashing lights reflected in car windows as a police cruiser turned the corner. He slowed to a fast walk. He couldn't risk drawing police attention to himself.

Charlie's footsteps followed him, also at a walk.

Samuel glanced back. The police car was parked in front of the Walgreens, and Charlie was about fifteen feet behind him. Charlie smiled.

Samuel turned and kept walking quickly. At the corner of the parking lot, he turned left and crossed the road, now out of sight of the police cruiser. Then he turned left down an alley. It opened up to a small parking area behind the stores, obviously for employee parking.

"Ready to talk?" Charlie asked.

Samuel turned to face him. Charlie had put his gun away and was standing about ten feet back, blocking the path back to the road.

"How long have you been a traitor?" Samuel asked. How many years had he worked so closely with this man, trusting him with his life and not knowing he was capable of betraying that trust?

"Where's The Dream?"

"What do you plan on doing to him?"

"I won't hurt him. As long as he gives me what I want."

"You'll torture him for the information you want if you have to."

"No worse than you've done."

"I've hurt people," Samuel admitted. "Terrorists, bombers, recruiters. Never innocents."

"You're sure none of them were innocent?"

"I know Dream is innocent. He's a good man who just wants to live in peace."

"As soon as he tells me where the art is, he can have that."

"What if he doesn't know where it is? He's been traumatized. He doesn't remember chunks of his past, especially those couple of years he was held captive."

"Then I will gladly help him remember." Charlie slowly moved closer.

"I'm afraid I'm not able to permit that."

"I don't see how you have a choice." Charlie started to move his hand—

Samuel slid forward and landed a thrusting front kick to Charlie's right hip. Charlie fumbled, trying to stay on his feet and grab his gun. Samuel threw a hook across Charlie's chin.

Charlie stumbled sideways. Then he caught his balance and twisted back at Samuel with an upset punch to the stomach. Samuel had expected a punch to the face and didn't block in time. His fist dug into Samuel's gut, and Samuel coughed up air. Charlie followed up with a shot to Samuel's cheek. Samuel tried to catch his balance but fell to the pavement, landing on his back. Charlie drove his foot into Samuel's stomach.

"Where is he?" Charlie demanded.

"Why don't you find him yourself?" Samuel looked up at him. "Is that why you're just a handler rather than an agent?" Charlie had been an agent for years, a very good one according to some, but Samuel knew talking to him like this would push some major buttons.

Charlie's lip curled, and he reached down to grab Samuel. Samuel grabbed his hand, hooked his legs around Charlie's neck and chest, and brought him to the ground in an armlock.

He kept his leg pushed hard against Charlie's throat and pressed Charlie's elbow backward on his thigh.

Charlie used his other hand to try to push Samuel's legs off, but Samuel slammed his heel down on Charlie's ribs. Something snapped. Charlie kept struggling. Samuel pressed harder on his elbow, and Charlie writhed, surely trying to find a way to relieve the pressure.

Samuel kicked him again. Charlie cursed but continued struggling.

With both hands, Samuel yanked down on Charlie's arm.

His elbow snapped. It sounded like breaking an ear of corn off the stalk.

Samuel let go and jumped to his feet. With his good hand, Charlie tried reaching behind him, surely for his gun. Samuel kicked him in the ribs, then knelt on the ground and punched him in the face.

Finally, Charlie stopped struggling.

Samuel slapped his face to be sure he was completely out. Then he stood and ran back down the alley.

At the corner, he slowed to a walk and headed down the sidewalk. He made a couple of turns, and when he saw an older woman on the sidewalk headed toward him, he pretended to be a lost tourist and asked her for directions to Boston Common. It was a good seven to eight miles away.

He took Beacon Street for a few miles, trying not to stand out. Al-Sadr was surely still looking for him. He searched his pockets for his phone, but it must've fallen out. He muttered under his breath.

Finally, he found an MBTA station at Cleveland Circle. He had to wait a few minutes but managed to get on a tram. As he boarded, he thought he saw something out of the corner of his eye, but then he took a better look and there was nothing. *Stop being jumpy, Samuel.* He scanned the people on board, looking for someone friendly—not always an easy task. He spotted a woman holding a little boy in her lap. She had her dark hair pulled back in a ponytail and was talking with the boy.

"But LEGOs are your favorite, right?" she asked the boy.

"Yeah, I think so."

"Why do you think? Because you like to make things?"

The boy nodded.

Samuel asked, "Do you mind if I sit here?"

"Sure," the woman said.

Samuel sat.

"So, what's your favorite thing to make?" the woman asked the boy. "I see you make a lot of cars."

"I like robots too."

"That's right. I've seen you make plenty of those. I like making houses. How about I make houses for the robots and garages for the cars?"

The boy laughed. "Robots don't live in houses."

Samuel liked how she spoke *with* the boy, not *at* him. That's how Dalal always spoke with Atif. He fought back the sorrow he felt and the guilt for not protecting his little boy's mother. He reminded himself he had a plan for taking care of Atif, the best care he could imagine for any child—no more hiding and running from danger. He wanted his little boy to have a childhood like this boy, filled with LEGOs and robots and worries no bigger than the little girl who tries to kiss him in the sandbox.

Samuel said to the boy, "So, where do robots live if not in houses?"

The boy screwed up his face in deep thought.

"Did I stump you on that one?" Samuel asked.

"I know where they live. I'm just deciding if I should tell you."

Samuel grinned. Then he spoke more quietly. "I promise I won't tell."

The boy leaned closer and whispered, "Cybertron."

"I've heard of that place." Then Samuel sat straight. "Oh, man. I almost forgot to call my wife." He reached in his coat pocket, then his other pocket, then his jeans pocket. "My phone."

"Did you lose it?" the woman asked.

"I must've dropped it. Man, my wife is going to freak out on me."

"Here, use mine." The woman handed Samuel a cell phone.

"You are such a lifesaver." Samuel dialed and waited while the line rang. "Hey, it's me. . . . I lost my phone. I know, I know. . . . I need to stop at Boston Common and then I'm coming home. I'll see you there, right? . . . Great, thanks. See you." Samuel ended the call and handed the phone back to the woman. Hopefully she hadn't heard the male voice on the other end of the line.

50

DREAM

Boston, MA

"Pull me out," Trudi says.

Eula goes around to her feet and pulls.

Now out of the hole, Trudi rolls onto her back and holds up a leather-wrapped tube.

"That's it," I say. "That's the kind of tube they used."

"Holy cow!" Eula says. "We found it."

Trudi sits up and opens the tube. She barely touches the edges of the canvases, surely hesitant to disturb the art, scared of damaging it. "It looks like a few paintings are in here."

She lies back down, squirms deeper into the cavity, and retrieves another similar tube, and then a large, stiff envelope. The last thing she pulls out is a small crate.

"Okay," Trudi says. "Now, how are we going to get all this out?"

"We should leave it," I say. "We can call the police and tell them where it is."

"Do you think they'll believe us?" Trudi asks.

Eula adds, "The curators of this place aren't likely to let them start pulling the walls apart on some random, uncorroborated tip."

"Open the envelope," I say.

Trudi holds it open for me, and I pull out a small piece of plastic. I give it to Trudi. The plastic is clear and stiff and holds a tiny sketch of a man with a mustache and wearing a hat, no more than two inches by two inches.

"That's the proof," I say. "It's a Rembrandt self-portrait."

Trudi and Eula slide the art back into the cavity and push the board back into place.

Trudi hands the tiny Rembrandt out to me.

"You hold on to it," I say.

"You should. The reward is yours."

"I don't want the reward. I just want the art found so everyone stops coming after me."

"You can gain a lot more freedom with five million dollars."

I shake my head. "All that money. I'd still have something people want. I don't want it."

Trudi opens her mouth to argue.

Eula says, "We should get out of here. It's probably about time to meet Samuel."

I turn and head for the stairs. Trudi and Eula follow me.

We make our way back to the car.

As I sit in the back seat, I organize my thoughts, make my final decisions.

"You need to take the reward," Trudi says.

I don't answer.

A few minutes pass.

"You know I'm not a murderer, right?" I ask.

Trudi looks at me in the rearview mirror. "Where is that coming from?"

"Do you believe that?"

She pulls her eyebrows together. "Of course. Why are you asking me that?"

"It's just important to me that you know that." I look out the side window.

She doesn't push further, but I have the feeling she's plotting a way to make sure I take the reward. I'd meant it when I told her I didn't want it. If the art is found, no one has a reason to come after me anymore, and maybe Mr. Hayes will fade me like he promised . . .

With Eula's help, Trudi drives to Boston Common and manages to find a parking space in front of what appears to be a large apartment or condo building. We get out of the car and cross the street to the Boston Common visitor's center.

Eula looks around at the expanses of grass and trees. "This place is huge."

"And of course Samuel didn't specify where in all this he wants to meet." Trudi rolls her eyes.

In the visitor's center, we find a map. I have no idea where we should go, but Trudi says almost immediately, "This is it," and points to the Soldiers and Sailors Monument in the middle of the park.

We take wide asphalt walking paths behind the visitor's center and then turn left until we come to the monument. It's what looks like a granite tower, basically a Doric column, with a female bronze sculpture at the top and smaller sculptures and plaques on the pedestal. Around it is grass and a wide ring of concrete edged by concrete benches. There are no people around the monument itself, perhaps because the temperature has begun to drop even lower.

We look for Samuel.

"Why do you think he meant to meet us here?" Eula asks Trudi.

"Soldiers Monument. Trust me," Trudi says. "Spread out and keep watch for him. Make sure he doesn't miss us." Then she adds to me, "Try to stay hidden as much as you can. I doubt the Irish mob had a presence at the Old North Church or the Paul Revere House, but they might here."

We walk in different directions. I head to a path leading away from the memorial that has a lot of tree cover. The trees are well pruned with high canopies, but they're thick and make the area darker. I can see a building not far away next to what looks like a large pond.

Awkwardly with my right hand, I move the gun Samuel gave me from my left pocket to my right. I assume he took it from the guy in the ball cap back at the house in Atlanta, without Trudi noticing.

I wait.

I replay over and over again what I need to do.

"Dream."

I jump, and then I turn and see Samuel stepping out from behind a tree.

"How'd you get there?" I ask.

He opens his mouth to speak, but then his head snaps to the right. A man is approaching from the building.

Samuel curses. "Let me handle it, okay?" he says to me.

I nod and glance around, trying to find Eula and Trudi. I can't see either of them.

I turn back to the man approaching. I stare . . .

"Dream?" Samuel asks. "What's wrong?"

"Do you know him?" I ask Samuel.

"Not as well as I thought I did, but yes. I thought I'd lost him—that must have been him I saw when I got on the tram. I might need to handle it physically. Just let me deal with him." Then he adds, "What's wrong?"

The man was now within speaking distance. "Oh, I think Javier is having the same issue you had just a little while ago." He turns to me. "So, Dream, dream anything interesting lately?"

Samuel glances at me, then back to the man. The man I'd thought—hoped—I would never see again. He looks different. His short hair is now buzzed off, and he hasn't shaved his face in several days, but it's definitely him. I couldn't forget those dark eyes that'd always scared me a little, even when he'd tried to make them kind.

"Dream," Samuel says as he watches the man, "what's wrong?"

"I know him," I say. "That's Dr. Brone."

"Dr. Brone?"

"From the hospital. He was my doctor."

Samuel moves casually forward as he speaks to Dr. Brone. "Playing lots of roles, are we? Uribe's henchman, my handler, and Dream's doctor. How long have you been setting this up?"

"A while. You fell very nicely into the plan, by the way. Letting me talk you into going after the Gardner Museum art. Very helpful. Thanks."

"But not al-Sadr?"

"No, no. You did that all by yourself. I just used it to my advantage."

"You want the art?" I ask Dr. Brone. "You did all that to me, to Clara, all the others, just so you could get the art?"

"The money I can get from the art," he clarifies. "Once you give up the location, I'm gone. You'll never see me again."

"What about Samuel?"

"What about him?"

"You won't bother him once you have the art?"

"I couldn't care less about Samuel. Once I have the money, I'm gone. You have my word."

Samuel glances back at me. "You know what to do, Dream."

I take the gun from my pocket.

Dr. Brone laughs. "We both know you won't fire that thing." He draws a gun from his waistband and aims it at Samuel. "But I think you'll trust me when I say I don't have a problem firing a gun."

Samuel glances at me, nods slightly, and then pulls a gun from his pocket and fires at Dr. Brone.

I fire toward Samuel.

They both fall. I wipe the handle of my gun and throw it.

Almost immediately, there are sirens coming through the park, as if they were called in advance.

Flashing lights.

Two police officers run toward me from the building. "Freeze."

I put my hands up. "He tried to shoot us. Please call an ambulance."

Only a few seconds later, a police cruiser and an ambulance drive up the wide walking paths. The EMTs quickly load Samuel onto a gurney. They leave Dr. Brone. Perhaps they'll come back for him. I feel bad that I don't really care.

"Samuel!" It's Trudi's screaming voice.

She runs past the monument toward the ambulance.

I walk to the back of the ambulance where they're loading Samuel, and inside is a familiar face. He nods.

"Samuel!"

Someone closes the ambulance doors, and the vehicle drives around the monument toward a different path.

"Samuel!" Trudi runs past me and chases the ambulance. I've never seen anyone run with such exertion, every muscle being used to help her go faster.

Eula, running from a different direction, comes to a stop next to me. "Are you okay? What happened?"

I'm not sure what to say. This all happened so quickly. I knew what was going to happen, knew the consequences of it, but knowing and being prepared are more different than black and white.

Trudi gives up on chasing the ambulance and runs back to me. "What happened?" she demands.

"He's dead."

"What? What're you talking about? What happened?"

A police officer walks up to me. "You need to come with us, sir." One of them takes me by the arm, and I walk with them to a police cruiser.

"No," Trudi demands. "He has to tell me what happened!"

I sit in the back and look out the window at Trudi. She screams at me, but another police officer holds her back. "Let me go!" she yells. "What happened to Samuel?!"

Her face slowly crumples, and tears start streaming down her cheeks.

She backs up away from the officer.

Then she drops to her knees. I can hear her sobbing, even through the window. Eula kneels next to her and holds her as she falls apart.

"I'm sorry, Trudi," I murmur.

As the cruiser drives away, I pray I've done the right thing.

"Lord, help my poor soul."

ONE MONTH LATER

51
TRUDI

Atlanta, GA

Eula stood in Trudi's office doorway. Christmas music played in the background from Eula's computer: "O Holy Night." "I think you need to take more time before making such a big decision."

"It's done." Trudi taped up the last box of books. "Are you saying you don't like your birthday present?"

"Coffey & Hill Investigations isn't exactly what I had in mind." Then Eula added in a softer voice, "I think you need to take more time before making such a big decision. You need more time to grieve."

"It's been a month since . . ." She hadn't been able to say it. It was as if some part of her didn't believe Samuel was actually dead.

"There are no time limits on grieving."

"I just, I can't be here every day. And why should I try to make myself? I have five million dollars. Most people who have that kind of money stop working and go travel the world. Plus, we managed to get out of trouble with Homeland Security for escaping custody, so there's nothing holding me back." Trudi forced a little smile and passed Eula on her way out to the reception area. She put her box down on a chair.

Eula sighed. "Have you been able to learn anything about Dream?"

Trudi didn't let herself think too much about him. "Not much. I assume he's in protective custody. That's what he wanted—to disappear." She still didn't understand what'd happened, who had shot Samuel and why. At first, she'd assumed it'd been Chucky, but as she thought about it over and over, she realized Dream had held something back from her the whole time. She found herself not caring, though. Samuel was still gone no matter what.

But she also had moments when her mind refused to believe he was gone. She didn't let herself fixate on it—she couldn't afford to do that. The police had told her Samuel was gone, and when she arrived back in Atlanta, she even had Stepp verify it for her. Though Stepp had looked at her like she was losing it, he made a call up to Boston and got the same information they'd given Trudi.

Trudi walked back into her office. The space was now bare—no books on the shelves, no files on the desk. A big part of her would miss this place. But over the last few weeks, it'd become painfully apparent that there were just too many memories. She couldn't concentrate. Being there was stopping her from moving on. She had to leave.

She sat down in the chair one last time and picked up the day's copy of the *Atlanta-Journal Constitution*. *Safe.* A small smile tugged at the corner of her mouth. She liked to think *safe* also meant *happy*. She set the paper on the desk and replayed all the happy memories in this place. A lot of them were about Eula, but even more were about Samuel. Even in death, the man still wouldn't leave her alone. *The pig.*

She sighed.

Then she noticed something on the computer screen, the outside security camera feed.

Trudi walked back out to the reception area just as the door opened. She realized she still had the *Atlanta-Journal Constitution* in her hand and dropped it onto Eula's desk.

Darrent Hayes walked inside, holding the hand of a little boy.

Trudi stared at the boy. She knew exactly who he was. She'd seen his picture, and she saw Samuel in his features—the strong jaw and something both keen and kind in his eyes.

"What're you doing here?" Trudi demanded.

"Good afternoon," Darrent said. "I ask for just a few minutes. Then I'll leave, and you'll never see me again."

Trudi crossed her arms.

Darrent reached inside his jacket pocket. Trudi set her hand on her Tomcat, which was concealed under her shirt.

Darrent moved more slowly and took out a folded piece of paper. He handed it out to Trudi.

Trudi removed her hand from her Tomcat and took the note from him. She glanced at Eula to make sure she was paying attention and ready to react if Hayes did something stupid. Eula nodded.

Trudi unfolded the note. It looked like the same paper from the notebook Samuel had taken to carrying as a detective, and it was in Samuel's handwriting.

"He wrote it just a few days before," Darrent said.

Trudi read.

Dear Trudi,

I hope this finds you well. If you're reading this, however, I am not well. This serves as my will. I have only one thing in the world worth anything, and I beg that you take care of him.

I know this is a lot to ask. I know I hurt you and I wasn't what you deserved. I can never apologize enough. But please don't hold that against him. He's an amazing child—kind and happy and loving. I know you'll grow to love him very quickly. Atif Michael Hill is the son I should have had with you.

I have no right to ask anything of you, but I beg with all my heart.

Yours Forever, Samuel

Trudi looked down at the little boy, and he looked up at her.

"Are you Trudi?" he asked.

She nodded.

"My . . . my daddy said he wants you to take care of me. He said he wants me to be safe and have LEGOs and sandboxes." Then he added, "What're LEGOs?"

"Where's your mommy?"

Sadness washed over his face, and he looked at the ground.

"She died," Darrent said. "She died saving him from al-Sadr."

Her voice quieted as she spoke to Atif. "I'm so sorry, sweetie."

"My daddy is gone too."

"I know."

He looked up at Trudi with those sweet, dark eyes. "Will you take care of me?"

Trudi knelt down in front of him.

"Are you sure that's what you want? You don't want to go home?"

He shook his head.

Surely, he'd seen more than any child should see. All those memories were back home. She understood why he wanted to go away, because it was the same reason she wanted to leave this place—start new. But could she do that with Samuel's little boy, the little boy who was not hers? The little boy she'd often thought should have been hers. But could she take him, the fruit of Samuel's affair with another woman? The answer seemed obvious: of course not. But she kept looking at those sweet eyes watching her. He knew nothing of any of that. He simply knew his mommy and daddy were dead and wanted someone to take care of him, someone who could be his family.

"Come here, sweetie," she murmured.

He let go of Darrent's hand and moved closer. She pulled him into a hug, and he wrapped his little arms around her and squeezed as hard as he could.

52
EULA

Atlanta, GA

Eula sat at her desk in the reception area and watched Trudi hug the little boy. She lowered her gaze and wiped a tear from her eye.

Everything was changing. So quickly. Samuel dead. Trudi leaving and now taking on Samuel's child. And Eula was supposed to take over the agency. She'd often dreamed of doing something like this, of being like Trudi, but she didn't feel ready. Or maybe she didn't want it to happen the way it was happening.

She wiped her other eye and glanced at the paper Trudi had dropped onto her desk. It was folded open to the classifieds, and Eula happened to catch a one-word ad. Nothing more than one word.

Pig.

Mike Nappa is an entertainment journalist at FamilyFans.com, as well as a bestselling and award-winning author with more than one million books sold worldwide. When he was a kid, the stories of Edgar Allan Poe scared him silly. Today he owns everything Poe ever wrote. A former fiction acquisitions editor, Mike earned his MA in English literature and now writes full time.

Melissa Kosci is a fourth-degree black belt in and certified instructor of Songahm Taekwondo. In her day job as a commercial property manager, she secretly notes personal quirks and funny situations, ready to tweak them into colorful additions for her books. She and Corey, her husband of twenty years, live in Florida, where they do their best not to melt in the sun.